The Wellspring

T.J. Carroll

Cumberstone Press

To my mother, who taught her daughter to love books, and to my father,
who taught a bookworm how to hustle.

Thank you for everything.

CONTENTS

Chapter 1

It was the way Zayaa *looked* that made Dashi's control crack. Everything was flawless. Her clothing was unwrinkled. Her jewelry sparkled cheerfully. Her hair was a luscious black banner.

Dashi thought of her friends Altan and Baris, about how their flesh would have rotted away by now. About how their bodies, dumped in a pit with Karak City's other rubbish, would first have been stripped: clothes, boots, anything that could be sold. She knew what happened to the city's unclaimed dead.

Dashi lunged, her fist aimed at that perfect nose. Zayaa's eyes widened and she started to sidestep, but there was no need. Dashi's attack turned into an ungainly plummet, pouring her straight onto the floor. She barely had the strength to roll into it, coming up on all fours beside the small table and chair.

A weapon, she thought. *I need a weapon.* She reached for the chair leg, but Zayaa planted a boot between her shoulder blades, flattening her onto the floor.

"Ah, Dashi, you've always been so strong, so quick." The boot pressed harder. "Being weak as a newborn calf must be quite a comeuppance."

Boots tramped into the room.

"Shackles," Zayaa said. "The ones with teeth. She's weak today, but that won't always be the case. Ants are strong for their size." Zayaa ran a hand over Dashi's antennae, a legacy of the magical stitching she'd survived. Dashi jerked away from the touch, her cheek sliding over the cold floor.

Hands snatched Dashi's arms. There was a metallic click as cuffs closed around her wrists. The guards lifted her roughly into the chair, letting her cuffed hands fall into her lap. One of them pulled a second set of shackles from his belt. The metal spikes that lined the inside glinted, but Dashi paid little attention as they snapped around her ankles. All she could see was Zayaa: a waterfall of dark hair, gleaming teeth, hands that floated from one elegant gesture to the next. Until this moment, Dashi had believed that Zayaa's body lay in the pit beside Altan and Baris, three victims of the same attack.

"I *mourned* you," Dashi snarled. "How could you do that to us? How could you do that to *them*?"

The four of them—Dashi, Altan, Zayaa and Baris—had been together for years. They'd shared adventures and danger. Dashi found out much later that the other three had also shared the secret of living as spies in a foreign country. Altan and Zayaa had been more than friends; they'd talked of marrying one day.

If Zayaa was here, acting as the khan's consul, she was no miraculous survivor of the ambush that had killed Altan and Baris. She was its perpetrator.

"They were your *friends*." Dashi leaned forward, the movement more sloppy than aggressive. A guard pushed her shoulders back against the chair, preventing her from toppling. "They *loved* you and you...you...*Why*, Zayaa?"

Zayaa smiled coolly. "I wouldn't expect you to understand. You worshipped them too much to have clear eyes."

Dashi began to list sideways. This time, the guards picked her up, holding her elbows. Dashi hung between them.

"It looks like she'll pull through," Zayaa said, "so no more special treatment. Bring her to one of the cells."

Dashi's breaths sawed up and down her throat, ragged as an old blade. *I need to fight back. I need to do something.* Her muscles had failed completely, the anger that had sustained them burning off like a particularly ephemeral fuel. Even her neck was weak. Her head lolled as they carried her from the room, too heavy by far.

Only her hands retained any strength. Her fists stayed clenched, her fingernails trying to gouge a record of her anger into the meat of her palms. When she glanced down, however, she saw that the strange skin she'd grown—shiny like an ant's exoskeleton—wasn't even dented.

Chapter 2

The cell wasn't as filthy as the last one Dashi had inhabited. There were rats, of course, always in search of a morsel, but the waste bucket was emptied on a schedule and so far there were no fleas. Food and drink were doled out regularly. In terms of material comfort, incarceration in New Osb stood well above Karak City. But then, this wasn't *prison*; it was a holding cell. Holding for *what* remained to be seen.

Lying on the scratchy pallet where the guards had dropped her, Dashi raised one hand, examining her skin like it was a foreign object. Her knuckles glinted in the low light. Her palms were even stranger. Unlike the rest of her, they were dull, and covered in a scalloped pattern. When she pried at one of the scallops with her thumbnail, it rose slightly, revealing a bristly edge. She let her head flop back, overcome by disgust and exhaustion.

By late afternoon, Dashi had managed to pull herself into a sitting position and, on the following day, she stood again. By the fourth day, she was pacing along the wall, chains sliding incessantly against her wrists and ankles. Once, the chafe might have bothered her, but she barely noticed now. Perhaps it was her newly hardened skin. Or perhaps, having felt both magic and acid, arrow and sword, her calculus of pain had changed.

On the fifth day, she noticed the heady aroma of her breakfast drifting down the hallway long before the bowl was delivered. *I must be hungry,* she thought, rubbing at her scalp. Later that day, however, she predicted the arrival of the shepherd dog that sometimes accompanied the guards. What's more, she could *see* its scent invading the hall: a smear in the colors and textures of the world that grew thicker with each passing minute. Dashi rubbed her eyes. She looked back at the corridor. The smudge had progressed. A door opened somewhere out of sight and the distortion rushed forward, riding the current of shifting air. Reminded of the creeping taiga mist, she backed up, but the distortion floated aimlessly, uninterested in her. She watched it warily for ten long minutes until the dog itself arrived.

By the time the evening meal was served, she knew the scent of the guards themselves. Their trails lingered long after they were gone, a train for an invisible gown. With every pass they made, the smudge of scent grew wider and deeper. It mashed against the floor where their feet had touched, sticky and unyielding. *At least they bathe more often than Ejen's guards*, Dashi thought, rubbing once more at her scalp, which had developed an odd tingle at the base of her antennae. She stopped abruptly as realization crashed over her. It was her antennae, working in concert with her nose and eyes, which was responsible for this new sense. She yanked her hand back, repulsed.

She was still stewing on this development when a new scent reached over. *Human*, Dashi thought, interpreting it reluctantly. There was something that set this scent apart from that of the guards. *Younger, perhaps, or...female.* Dashi closed her eyes, concentrating, until the soft patter of footsteps reached her ears.

"Idree!" Dashi's voice came out as a croak.

"Dashi! You're...I'm glad to see you." Idree's eyes darted over Dashi's antennae, her skin, her eyes. If she was surprised at the changes in Dashi's appearance, she didn't show it. Then again, as the seamstress who wielded the golden needle, Idree had seen many dramatic transformations.

She'd stitched magic into each of the heralds who'd survived...and the ones who hadn't.

"Pacing, huh?" Idree asked. "That's probably a good sign. The last time I saw you, you couldn't get out of bed."

"I...don't remember much about that."

Dashi had seen the room of beds and chains where the stitched patients either recovered or died. It was a bleak affair and she wasn't sorry to find that her memories were mostly of Idree's face, hovering and full of encouragement. She remembered her dreams too. There'd been a particularly vivid one in which she'd kissed Sevlin, but also one of Altan and Baris, signaling her from across a tawny grassland. Another had been of Khagan Nuray, her expression set in disapproval as she castigated Dashi for some offense. Other than that, the time was a blank space in her mind.

"The heralds don't usually remember much of their first weeks," Idree said, "but I'm always with them until they're healthy enough to be moved."

"*Weeks?*"

"It's been four, minus a day."

Dashi stared.

"It can be disorienting," Idree said kindly. The words had a practiced ring to them. "You took longer than the others, but you...you were in really bad shape, Dashi." Her smile fell away as she glanced over her shoulder. "I don't have much time. I'm not supposed to be with the heralds after they're healed. They're worried—never mind. That's not what I came here to say."

They're worried you divide the heralds' loyalties, Dashi thought, remembering how she'd once seen the newly stitched patients staring hungrily after Idree. Her own attachment to Idree felt unchanged, as if the magic considered any new bond inferior to the existing ties of sisterhood.

"What happened?" Idree's hands were on the bars, one on each side of her face. "I overheard most of it from the guards: the Yassaris, your escape, the search of New Osb. At first, I thought you were running without a plan—"

Dashi snorted.

"Then they said you were in the taiga and I thought, 'If anyone can find a magical artifact in the middle of nowhere, it's Dashi.'" Idree paused for breath. "So...did you?"

The seamripper. Dashi looked away from those wide eyes. "It was—I think I was close, Idree. Really close."

When Dashi looked back all the hope had leached from her sister's expression. The seamripper was the only thing Dashi knew of with the potential to defeat the khan. According to Purek lore, it was the counterbalance to the golden needle. Sevlin and Dashi had thought it might be able to sever the magic stitched into each of the heralds, depriving the khan of his growing army of monsters. Since it could sever *that* magic, Dashi hoped it might also be able to break the golden needle's attachment to Idree, freeing her from the burden of being the seamstress.

"I had it in my hand, I think," Dashi said in a rush—anything so her sister would know that she hadn't failed without good reason. "I was at the end of a Purek maze and I found a wooden box. There was a cup inside and it looked like there was a false bottom and maybe a compartment big enough to hold a small artifact. I was working on opening it when—" Dashi stopped, her mind skipping away from the memory of burning leather, burning skin, burning muscle. "When the heralds captured me. I had to drop it so they couldn't get it."

"The seamripper is still in the taiga?" Idree blinked hard. "Are you certain? I heard the khan asking Zayaa about something...whatever it was, it sounded like they were close to finding it."

Dashi's mouth twisted doubtfully. "I dropped it from very high up. I had hoped that Sevlin might find it, but I saw the box shatter when it hit and Sevlin, he was..." Her voice faltered, as she remembered the way he'd sagged inside the Purek's trap, a spike through his leg. When she'd dropped the box, she thought she'd glimpsed him standing near the steamy pools, but the more she thought about it, the more hallucinatory that seemed.

Idree sucked in a breath. "*Sevlin* was with you? I thought he'd gone home with the other Tyvalarans."

"He doubled back and found me after I escaped the Yassaris. But he was badly injured the last time I saw him."

"If there was blood, the giant rats—" Idree chewed worriedly at her lip. "Do you think he made it back out?"

"We didn't have a problem with rats this time." *Giant shrikes that nearly impaled us and a huge toad that tried to eat me, yes. Rats, no.* "Sevlin—he might have..." Dashi swallowed. "I don't know, Idree. I don't know."

"Why did you leave him?" Idree's voice was barely audible.

Dashi couldn't tell if the question contained an accusation or if she only imagined it. Her feet started moving anyway, trying to dispel her emotions. "He told me to, Idree," she said, pacing away. "There wasn't much time and finding the seamripper was the most important thing. We agreed on that."

Sevlin's face, ashen with pain.

Cold bars between them as their lips met.

"I'm not asking you to stay, Dashi. I'm asking you to go."

What if she hadn't listened? What if she'd stayed to free Sevlin from the trap? Instead, he'd sacrificed himself for nothing. Not only had she failed to secure the seamripper, but she'd also gotten transformed into one of the khan's monsters. *You were dying from the Yassaris' poison,* her mind insisted. *Without the stitching, you wouldn't be here.* Dashi swiped a hand over her face, trying to wipe away the cascade of regrets.

Idree was silent for a moment, seeming to forget that her time was limited. "They will try to use the fact that Sevlin went with you," she said eventually. "Against Tyvalar, I mean."

"The khan?"

"And *her.*"

Dashi whirled around at the reminder. "Why didn't you tell me Zayaa was alive? It was like seeing a ghost." Except worse. A ghost could be mourned. A living, breathing Zayaa represented deceit so deep Dashi could barely comprehend it.

"When would I have done so?"

"The whole time I was trying to unlock your cuffs!"

"I...I don't really remember a lot about that," Idree said. "It's hard for me when I'm near my patients. When they're all together like that, they get so agitated, and my head...Everything gets foggy." She paused, thinking. "Telling you wouldn't have changed much in the end, would it? The Yassaris would still have chased you out. You would still have gone after the seamripper."

"I don't know. Maybe." Dashi considered. "Probably. But if I'd had a warning, I wouldn't have gaped like a stuck fish when I saw her standing there."

Idree smiled slightly.

"Anyway, no one knows Sevlin helped me. He wasn't nearby when I was captured. The herald who fought with Sevlin on the river is dead; *he* can't identify him." Dashi ignored the twist in Idree's expression at the mention of the fish herald's death. "*I* certainly won't volunteer it to the khan."

"You don't understand, Dashi." Idree's breath hitched. "The khan will *make* you tell."

"He can try," Dashi said, with the kind of bravado she hoped her sister would believe. She pressed the sharp edge of the cuff against her wrist and dragged it upward, showing Idree how it made no lasting mark. "I'm almost as tough as a taiga ant now."

"Even taiga ants can be hurt," Idree said, "and I wasn't talking about physical coercion anyway. I meant the magical kind. All the heralds are magically tethered to the khan—he forces me to do it—and he can use that tether to control you."

"What do you mean, *forces* you?"

"He threatens the person I've just stitched. I tried, once, to say no, and he...he took a heated sword and...and—"

"That wasn't your fault," Dashi said quickly, seeing the tears pooling in her sister's eyes.

"It was," Idree said. "I haven't made that mistake again."

"I'm tethered to him too?"

Idree nodded miserably.

"I can't feel it."

"He'll make it known to you at some point." Idree's voice was bitter. "That's what I came to warn you about. You're still young, in terms of being a herald, not even at your full ability. But, one day soon, he'll call you before him."

"And then what?"

"And then he'll make sure you know who your master is."

Dashi made a choking noise.

"He does it with all the heralds," Idree said, misinterpreting the sound as disbelief. "With you, it will be worse. Zayaa will be there for it, I'm certain. She has plans for you. They'll be looking for any trace of independence, of insubordination, any excuse for the khan to exert his power. Don't give them one, or it will only be worse." Idree reached through the bars to grab Dashi's wrist. "Save your ferocity. Save your fight. I know that's difficult, but you have to pretend. You have to keep your head down."

Dashi's wrist hung limp in her sister's hand. "Save it for *what*, Idree? It's not like there's help coming."

"Save it so you can stay *alive*, Dashi. Stay alive, no matter what."

"Alright." Dashi took a deep breath. *Stay alive, no matter what.* "Alright," she said again, as much for herself as for Idree. "You'll stay alive. I'll stay alive. I'll figure out a way to steal the needle and then we can escape and find another place like Ejen."

Idree frowned. "I don't think it will be that easy. Before, I'd never wielded the needle. Now it's...it's part of me. Both Zayaa and the khan will—"

Dashi stiffened, her antennae swiveling toward the empty corridor. Somewhere down the hall, a door had opened, pushing a tide of air and scent before it.

"Four people and a dog," Dashi said. "It's the next guard shift."

"I have to go." Idree squeezed Dashi's wrist once. "Save your fight, Dashi."

Chapter 3

When the guards led Dashi into the great hall a few days later, the khan was slouched on his throne. Even from across the hall, the difference in his appearance was striking. His cheekbones jutted through pale, crepey skin. Veins bulged darkly at his temples and nostrils. In only a few weeks, he'd aged decades. Dashi's mind flew to Ese, her erstwhile enemy, and to the vial of poisonous Adder's Dust he'd worn around his neck. Although Dashi had stolen a portion of it to sicken the khan's servants, Ese still had some left over. Perhaps the khan's deterioration was Ese's work.

Scents swirled in front of Dashi, smudging the air in ever-expanding whorls. Her antennae whipped maniacally under the onslaught of stimuli. Embarrassed, she willed them to stillness, but it took effort, like trying to stop herself from blinking. As soon as her concentration wavered, they sprang back into motion.

The usual contingent of people stood around the dais: guards and servants, nobles and advisors, a cloud of bodies that followed the khan wherever he went. As Idree had predicted, Zayaa was there too. She glanced up and smiled in greeting. *Like we're still old friends.* Her purple deel perfectly matched the ancestors-damned amethyst that hung around her neck.

Dashi's gaze skipped away, her eyes traveling a well-worn groove to find her sister. Idree's face was a rictus of anxiety, immobile except for her eyes, which pinged between Dashi, the khan and Zayaa. The other heralds who'd been at the Founding Day feast—an owl, a moth and a stag— stood near Idree. The fish-man had been replaced by a sable, whose mostly human face was covered in beautiful dark fur.

Dashi shuddered at the sight, then shuddered again thinking how many people had died from the stitching in order to make them. *Us*, her mind whispered. *You're a herald now, too.* She wondered if the other heralds saw her antennae and thought 'monster.' *She* did when she looked at their fur and wings.

The khan rose. Despite his pallor, he was steady on his feet.

"My newest herald," he said. "You've finally come into the fold."

There was a murmur of recognition from the assembled audience.

"Yes," the khan said, gesturing grandly at Dashi, "this is the fugitive who escaped not only my esteemed palace guard but also the famously long arm of the Yassaris."

Low murmurs on one side of the room drew Dashi's gaze: the Yassaris. She recognized a few. Not from her almost-execution—their faces had been covered by yellow hoods then—but from around New Osb. An older man stood at the front of the delegation, his head tipped back so that he watched her over his meticulously trimmed beard. Behind him, stood the curly-haired Yassari woman who'd tried to take Dashi into custody at Sevlin's room. Her eyes darted to Dashi's, then away again. The rest of the Yassaris stared straight ahead, giving no indication that they heard the khan's taunt.

"There's no need for chains," the khan said, not taking his eyes off Dashi.

Both the guards and her shackles vanished with an almost magical speed, leaving Dashi alone in the center of the hall. She kept her hands at her sides, determined not to fidget.

"Come," the khan said, pointing to the ground in front of him like he was commanding a dog.

Dashi's feet jerked forward, eager to obey.

"Kneel."

Her legs bent, so that she was staring up at him from the bottom of the dais.

She pretended not to see Zayaa and Idree from the corner of her eye. It was bad enough that her body was operating without her consent, but to know that she was doing it in front of people who knew her? *That* would be unbearable. Dashi smoothed her expression over, trying to hide her horror. *Don't show that it bothers you,* she ordered herself. *Just like Idree said: save your fight.*

"You said she had a penchant for—" The khan glanced at Zayaa. "What was it she enjoyed when you knew her, Consul?"

"Acrobatics, Most High," Zayaa said placidly. "Showing off."

"People are watching now," the khan said to Dashi. "Perform for them."

Dashi rocketed to her feet before she knew what was happening. She executed a neat backflip, landing exactly where she'd started.

"Again." The khan smiled slowly. "Until I tell you to stop."

Over and over, her legs responded. Her muscles began to burn. Her breath sped faster. She could feel humiliation shining on her face along with her sweat. The audience tittered and murmured. Only the Yassaris stared stoically ahead. Dashi continued flipping, until her legs grew uncoordinated and her stamina, only tenuously recovered, began to falter.

I'm going to fall, she thought as she flipped across the great hall, her landings becoming increasingly unsteady. *I'm going to perform until my muscles fail and I can't even stop myself.* Trying to give her legs a break, she turned onto her hands and began walking upside down.

"Freeze."

Her hands stumbled to a halt. She stayed there, blood pounding in her head, while gravity warred with her muscles.

"Enough," the khan said just before her arms gave out.

Dashi staggered to her feet, wobbly and out of breath. Her eyes darted to her sister. Idree's face had gone even starker than before. Her lips pressed together, cheeks puffed as she held in her cry.

"Now you see the power of the tether I hold." The khan's words echoed in the hall. To Dashi's roaring ears, it sounded like there were many khans speaking at once. "I have complete control, in whatever way I choose."

Dashi swallowed, her dry tongue sticking to the roof of her mouth.

"Now," the khan steepled his fingers expectantly, "tell me about your bid to free the seamstress. Do not lie."

"I pretended to be a servant." The words tumbled from Dashi's lips exactly as she'd thought them. "I picked the locks and then found Idree, but I didn't have enough time to free her before the guards came."

"Use a fitting title when you speak to me."

Yes, Most Pompous Ass. There are so many titles that fit you. The thought was instantaneous and it burst from her mouth nearly as fast.

"Yes, Most P—" Dashi slammed her mouth shut, eyes bulging with effort.

She glanced at Idree. Her sister's expression was half terror, half pleading. The silence stretched out, every eye in the room boring into Dashi's skin. The khan's command hung over her, a lash about to fall. The urge to speak built, but if she opened her mouth what would come out?

Her panicked thoughts clung desperately to one realization: she had managed to stop herself mid-blunder. She must retain *some* control over her speech. Words depended not only on the physical body—the mouth, lips and tongue—but also on the mind, and the khan had no control inside her head. *Order your thoughts,* she told herself. *Save your fight.* Dashi pushed her real response to the back of her mind, trying to concentrate only on the khan's immediate command.

"Yes, Most High." Her tone sounded almost respectful.

The khan's eyes narrowed. "*If* you'd freed the seamstress," he asked, his tone conveying heavy doubt, "where would you have gone?"

"Maybe the taiga. Maybe Thracedon," Dashi said, trying to reply quickly so that the khan wouldn't realize how hard she was working to frame her answer. "I hadn't really decided, Most High."

"As I told you, Most High," Zayaa murmured, barely audible, "the girl does not have much faculty for planning."

The khan considered this. "Then who put you up to this? Who did you work with?"

"No one, Most High. I went to Idree on my own." This was true. She'd tried to cut Sevlin out at every step and, while Ese *had* provided the Adder's Dust to poison the guards, it was only because she'd stolen it from him.

"My heralds," the khan said, gesturing to the moth and the owl, "saw someone with you on the boat. Who?"

Dashi swallowed. Idree had warned her against defiance, but what choice did she have? Betray Sevlin, after she'd already abandoned him in the taiga? The one thing about which he'd been adamant was that no one could know he was involved. He'd done his best to mask his actions, hiding his face in the race for the golden needle and, most recently, acting the part of arrogant nobility and improvising a tryst with Dashi when they'd been caught together. If the khan declared war on Tyvalar because of Sevlin's involvement, thousands would die. She couldn't—*wouldn't*—let that happen in Sevlin's name.

The urge to speak was strong, like the need for oxygen. Dashi swallowed, pressing her tongue against the roof of her mouth. Her jaw ached to open. Idree's words came back to her. *He'll make sure you know who your master is.*

The khan pushed himself out of his throne and stepped down from his dais.

"Who was with you on the boat?" he asked again, so close that Dashi could hear the moist slide of his tongue. His scent washed over her, cloying and sickly.

Sevlin. Sevlin. Sevlin. She could feel the word bubbling up from inside. Her tongue was starting to form the syllables, even though her mouth remained shut. Her jaw trembled violently, her mouth cracking open little by little, and, in the way that a tiny hole can make the whole dam weak, a sound began to emerge.

"Ssss." *Think of something else,* she ordered herself, trying to corral her mind. Perversely, the harder she tried *not* to think of Sevlin, the clearer his image became.

"Who?" The khan leaned closer.

"Sss." *No,* she thought, but the word kept forming. A line of sweat trickled down her forehead, stinging the corner of one eye. *Fight it,* she thought. *Fight him.* Dimly, she was aware that this was the exact opposite of what Idree had advised. As she stared into the khan's dark eyes, however, she found that she couldn't turn away from the struggle. It was no longer about protecting Sevlin or preventing war but had morphed into a battle over her dignity, a fight for some essential part of herself.

From the corner of her eye, Dashi saw something shimmer: a thin filament of light, stretching from the khan's chest to her own. Her concentration flickered involuntarily.

"*Ssseee.*" Another sound slipped out, another clue for the khan and Zayaa to mull. In fact, she thought, even that initial sound might have given it away. As a prince, Sevlin was known to both of them, as was his association with Dashi, since both the guards and the Yassaris had found them together on different occasions.

Why, then, was the khan still staring at her so intently? Why was she still fighting?

Say a name. Any name. Even if he knows it's a lie, you won't have said what he wants you to say. That will be something. Sener, she tried to say. *Sybetta.* There were hundreds of names that began with S, but her tongue refused to perform the trick of lying. Her whole body began to tremble. The khan smiled, mean and satisfied. She was going to fail and they both knew it.

Dashi's control shattered suddenly, though not in the way she'd expected. Sevlin's name turned into a scream and then she was lunging at the khan, fists raised. His guards were too far away. Her hands would be around his throat. She would—

The khan caught her before she could touch him. Not with his hands but with the shimmering thread of light Dashi had seen from the corner of her vision. It slammed into her chest, glaring brightly, strong enough to hold her immobilized, her toes barely brushing the floor. She had a moment to realize that the khan didn't look the way she'd expected. Despite his sickly pallor, he didn't look frightened by the possibility of assault. In fact, he looked...*delighted.*

Pain burst in Dashi's chest and she was thrown violently to the floor, her head and elbow cracking against the stone. She blinked upward in time to see the khan wave his guards back. Zayaa watched from the dais, her mouth stretched in a beatific smile.

"Like the horses in my stables and the dogs in my kennels, you are mine," the khan said in a quiet voice. "A beast domesticated for my use, and the most basic lesson of domestication is that, if a beast snaps at its master, it must be broken."

Pain shot through Dashi, lighting up the filament that connected her to the khan. Her limbs jerked outward, seizing, as one convulsion cascaded into another. Her hands clawed at her chest, ripping at the fabric, scrabbling over the hardened ant skin beneath, but there was no way to undo the pain or tear out the tether. It was every bit as bad as the stitching, blotting out all thoughts, all senses, until the only thing left was a deep despair that it would never be over.

It ended suddenly, leaving Dashi panting, facedown on the floor. Her senses stuttered, intermittent as a flickering candle. The air smelled burnt, like lightning, and then like nothing at all. Her vision went dark, then resolved into too-bright colors, painful and alive: a pane of stained glass, crimson; the white flash of teeth as one of the Yassaris smiled; a shock of purple when Zayaa leaned forward to whisper something to the khan.

The khan's silk slippers stopped next to Dashi's head. She wondered if he would kick her in the face but couldn't make herself move.

"Get up, Ant."

Moving jerkily, Dashi heaved herself onto her elbows and then onto all fours. Her arms quaked, unable to straighten. Her bottom jaw clacked against her top teeth. The urge to obey her master was relentless and, despite her weakness, she pushed to her feet, swaying dangerously.

The khan's eyes glittered as he surveyed her. "Seamstress, come here."

Idree took a hesitant step in their direction, two guards peeling off from the rest to flank her.

"*No.*" The word was gasped, barely making it from Dashi's lips, but the khan was close enough to hear.

"Be quiet." His eyes stayed on Dashi's face as he motioned Idree closer.

Dashi swallowed. Idree had warned her that resistance would be punished, but Dashi had done it anyway. Now, whatever the khan was about to do, Idree would have to watch. Dashi tried to open her mouth to beg. No sound emerged. The khan had commanded her to silence.

Idree stopped next to the khan, facing Dashi. Her face was deathly pale, a sharp contrast to her eyes, which gaped like two black holes punched into stretched fabric.

The khan held out his hand. "Take this."

Dashi's hand closed obediently around the handle of the knife. It was slim-bladed and encrusted with pearls, a weapon for show, not blood. Light glinted off the edge, long ago sharpened and never used. Dashi felt her gorge rise.

Idree was staring at Dashi, dark eyes begging, but she stayed silent. *What can she say*, Dashi thought. *The khan will command and I'll obey.* Whatever he had planned, at least it wouldn't be a mortal wound, Dashi thought, searching desperately for the bright side of whatever was about to happen. *Pain can be handled,* she reassured herself. *He must want me alive or he wouldn't have had me stitched.*

Idree's eyes squeezed shut. Dashi's throat worked, wanting to utter her sister's name, to beg Idree's forgiveness for what she was about to see, but her chest felt as if it was encased in iron bands.

"Hold her," the khan said.

Dashi braced herself, but the guards reached for Idree instead, pinning her between them.

Her sister's eyes flew open. Dashi could feel the shock mirrored on her own face. This couldn't be what the khan intended. He needed Idree. *She* was the seamstress. *She* was important. She—

"She doesn't need ten fingers to do her job," the khan said to Dashi. "Small finger on the left hand. Remove it."

Chapter 4

Dashi tried to scream, but there was only silence. She tried to stop her body, but it kept moving: one hand bracing against Idree's, forcibly extending the delicate fingers when Idree instinctively tried to curl them under. Using her other hand, Dashi swiped downward, hard, with the pearl-encrusted knife.

For a fraction of a moment, everything froze. No sound reached Dashi's ears, though the area around the dais was stuffed with onlookers. Idree's mouth hung open, soundless with surprise. The stump of the damaged finger glared up at Dashi, white and wet and smooth: a clean cut, refusing to relinquish her gaze. Dashi's own fingers, beautifully intact, clenched around the ornate knife, ready in case the khan needed to use them again.

Then the tableau roared back to life. The severed finger flopped to the floor. It bounced once, ruined nerves spasming. Idree screamed. There was a roar of sound from the other heralds, deafening and primal. Dashi's hair whipped into her face, fanned by the owl's wings. Blood seeped from Idree's wound, slowly at first, before resolving into a steady flow that spattered the floor.

"Silence," roared the khan. The heralds' voices instantly choked off. The khan turned to the Yassaris. "As you see, she is no longer the person who stole from you, nor is she capable of independent will. She is as far beneath my boot as the rest. Does that satisfy you, Convoymaster?"

Instead of answering, the older Yassari man half-turned, motioning to a man standing behind the other Yassaris. As the second man made his way forward, Dashi caught a strange scent. It was tinged pink and tan, like that of the guard's dog, but it reminded Dashi of musk and decaying leaf litter, and she was sure she hadn't encountered it since becoming a herald. Then the man stepped into the middle of the hall and Dashi saw the beast that stalked at his side.

The Yassari thiefmark.

It was just as sleek and horrible as Dashi remembered, a nightmare comprised of bunching muscles and gleaming fur and a muzzle as sharp as an ax. Its movements were slow and the leash around its neck hung slack, but Dashi stiffened immediately. She'd seen its aggression at close range.

She must've looked as if she was about to bolt because the khan said sharply, "Hold still." Dashi did.

The hollow rasp of the thiefmark's breathing grew louder as it approached, even blotting out the panicked pants coming from Idree. Its claws tap-tapped against the marble floor. When he was arm-length from Dashi, the Yassari handler tapped a quick staccato, three-fingered, on the beast's shoulder. It stretched out its neck and, with a quick, wet swipe, drew its nose over the tough skin on the back of Dashi's hand. The thiefmark exhaled in a long rattle, then looked away from her, apparently disinterested.

"You see, Convoymaster?" the khan blurted, his impatience obvious. "Your beast agrees."

The convoymaster took a step forward, examining Dashi down the long line of his nose. "It appears so," he said, "yet I must tell you, respectfully, that you are both mistaken." There was a collective intake of breath—no one told the khan he'd make a mistake—but the Yassari leader continued speaking, unperturbed. "She is still a thief. I know it and you know it, even if her recent change has fooled the thiefmark. I cannot grant a pardon. Her debt was not paid in gold and now it must be paid in red. Yassari justice—indeed, its honor—demands it."

"Unacceptable." A ropey vein along the khan's temple trembled.

The thiefmark's handler rejoined the other Yassaris, closing ranks to face the khan. The curly-haired Yassari woman glanced down at Idree's severed finger, then looked away quickly, her expression turning remote as she raised her face to her leader.

"I cannot grant a pardon," the convoymaster continued, "but I *can* grant a postponement, at least until the terms of our deal are completed."

The khan's eyes flicked to Zayaa's. "Agreed," he said to the convoymaster. "You may take her into custody as soon as my objective is secured."

"I will make the necessary changes to the contract." The convoymaster bowed shallowly and walked out of the great hall, the other Yassaris filing out behind him. The curly-haired woman didn't look at Idree again.

Everyone else began to leave too.

The khan dismissed the other heralds with a flick of his fingers. "Go. Practice whatever skills might prove useful to me."

Finally, only Zayaa and Idree, held tight between two soldiers, were left.

The khan turned to Dashi. "Now—"

Zayaa cleared her throat. "Forgive me, Most High, but the seamstress..." She trailed off delicately. "We wouldn't want her to get an infection."

At the khan's nod, Idree's guards suddenly became solicitous. The soldier on the left conjured bandages seemingly out of thin air and used them to bind her finger. The other soldier who, moments ago had pinned Idree's arms like she was a criminal, now patted her shoulder awkwardly.

Idree swayed once, her eyes closed. Two more soldiers arrived in the hall. One man, much younger than the rest and with a thick, mop-like head of hair, touched Idree's shoulder surreptitiously and murmured something to her. She opened her eyes and gave him a tremulous smile. Wound bandaged, Idree turned toward the door, her head high and her bottom lip tucked stubbornly between her teeth.

Idree, Dashi begged silently. *Look at me. Show me you're alright.*

Idree, in a credible impression of the stone-faced Yassaris, stared straight ahead. The slam of the door echoed in the rafters, rattling the panes of stained glass.

"You may speak and move, Ant," the khan said into the silence. "Do you understand the price of defiance?"

Dashi's voice croaked back to life. "Yes, Most High." She couldn't take her eyes off the door, couldn't stop seeing Idree's finger or her silent surprise as Dashi sliced right through it.

"Your sister need only retain her ability to stitch. Her toes, the fingers of her left hand, her ears, none of that matters to me. Do you understand?"

"Yes, Most High."

"Good. My consul has some questions for you. Answer them truthfully."

"Yes, Most High."

"Look at me, Dashi," Zayaa said.

The command lacked the force of magic behind it, but Dashi obeyed, dragging her eyes away from the door.

"Good girl." Zayaa's smile said she knew exactly how condescending she sounded. "Who was with you in the taiga?"

Dashi swallowed. "Prince Sevlin of Tyvalar."

Zayaa and the khan exchanged a glance. Neither looked surprised. They'd suspected Sevlin's involvement all along. Idree had lost a finger for nothing. *Save your ferocity. Save your fight. If only I'd listened.*

"Where is Sevlin now?" Zayaa asked.

"I don't know."

"Tell me—us—about the last time you saw him."

"He was..." Dashi cleared her throat. "Bleeding. Quite badly. He'd been stabbed through the leg by a spike and was caught in a Purek trap." She was speaking to Zayaa, she realized, knowing that her former friend would understand the dangerous nature of the ruins. Dashi dropped her eyes. *Don't look for understanding there just because she's used to clambering among old stones.* "He was trying to pry the trap apart when I left him, but I'm not sure if he was able to."

"Why did the two of you go into the taiga in the first place?"

"After the Yassaris realized I was not a servant and alerted the guards, I left to search for the Purek seamripper. Prince Sevlin followed me."

Zayaa leaned forward, eagerness written in every line of her body. "And what did you find?"

"I—" *I found nothing.* The lie came into her head easily enough, but forcing it out of her mouth was impossible.

"Everything," Zayaa said coolly. "Or should Idree be called back?"

Dashi told them everything, her words rushing shamefully over one another, debasing themselves in their effort to spare Idree. Her sister's blood had not been cleaned up yet; she wondered if that was for her benefit. The closest splatters were congealing like scabs, going dark and brittle at the edges. Her recounting was greeted with a silence that stretched so long that, eventually, Dashi looked up from the blood.

Zayaa had moved in front of the throne, her eyes distant and her mouth vaguely dissatisfied. The khan was watching her.

"Go over the part about the cup again," he ordered Dashi, a dangerous timbre to his voice, "in as much detail as you can remember."

"At the end of the maze there was an acid lake with an island in the center," Dashi said. "That's where I found the box with the cup inside. The box was made of thick wood, with handles on each end and a padded interior. The cup was silver, plain except for a silver braid around the bottom, but the base was thick. I thought there might have been something else—a clue, a secret compartment in either the box or the cup base—but I didn't have time to check."

"A thick base? Silver braid?" the khan asked. Though the question was intended for Dashi, it was Zayaa on whom his gaze rested.

"Yes, Most High," Dashi said.

"It means nothing. She has always been slow at the academic side of this," Zayaa said, smooth-voiced. "She could fetch the Purek artifacts well enough, but I rarely depended on her for much else."

"And yet she sounds certain about what she found," the khan said, "while *my consul* appears to have been studying the wrong artifact." He wiped his forehead, removing the curtain of sweat hanging there.

Zayaa opened her mouth, but he held up a hand, his attention swinging back to Dashi. "I have a different cup in my possession. One that was retrieved from the spot where you say you dropped the box, but it has words etched on it and no base at all. Where did it come from?"

"I do not—" Dashi stopped, picturing Sevlin standing in a crumbling Purek home.

The slide of shadows over the scarred side of his face.

A flash of silver as he tossed the cup at her without warning.

The glint of amusement in his eyes when she caught it anyway.

"I had another Purek cup," Dashi said, "one that I picked up in a ruined building along the way. I had lost my pack so I took it with me to drink from. It was also silver, with a Purek saying on it. '*Be ruthless as waves and magnanimous as rain.*" She remembered the words exactly because they'd so closely parallelled what Khagan Nuray had told her in the taiga mist. "That cup was hanging from my sash, along with the Purek box and the cup from the maze. When I cut my sash, everything fell together."

"Consul?" The khan fairly spat the word.

"You are right to be disappointed that we did not find the seamripper, Most High." Zayaa bowed her head, hiding the bitter frown that was threatening. "However, this changes nothing. We can still succeed."

"If it changes nothing, then why did we waste so much time on it?" The khan's breathing had grown labored, Dashi noticed, his chest rising and falling in excited bursts. "You've searched the taiga how many times now?"

The knowledge that the heralds had been unable to locate the artifact she'd dropped provoked no sense of satisfaction in Dashi. It was not a victory. Victory would have been holding the seamripper in her hands and obliterating the khan's growing army of heralds. Victory would have been freeing Idree instead of hacking off one of her fingers.

Zayaa raised her head, her expression now placid. "Three, Most High, and I did so to prevent the seamripper from falling into the hands of our enemy. As long as no one else holds the seamripper, *especially* not the Tyvalarans, it is unimportant."

"You sound very certain of that. And yet, I've heard you say time and again that Prince Sevlin is not to be underestimated, that he is the real power behind the Tyvalaran throne, that it is he who has been thwarting me for years." The khan pointed an accusing finger at Dashi. "*She* says she last saw the prince in a trap, but the owl and the moth reported that he was roaming free."

Dashi's heart rate picked up. Maybe the figure she'd glimpsed from above *hadn't* been a hallucination.

"Roaming free, yes, but badly injured, with a giant taiga beast bearing down on him. When the owl circled back there was no sign of him or the beast. If he'd managed to kill the animal, its body would have been there. Since it was not, it must have consumed him and gone on its way. Even if Prince Sevlin somehow survived the encounter, his leg had been impaled and an acid tide was flooding everything. It is unlikely that he got out of the maze, let alone made it out of the taiga. You have spies in every border town, Most High. No one has seen him reenter Tyvalar. No one has seen him in the Tyvalaran capital either."

Dashi's hope evaporated. She'd known there were giant bats in the maze and she'd left Sevlin behind, bloody and unguarded. Zayaa was right; he'd probably escaped from the cage only to be ripped to pieces by an animal.

"As to the artifact," Zayaa continued, "you commanded the moth and the owl to search to the best of their abilities. If the real Purek cup or the wooden box were visible, they would have brought them back. Since they did not, the artifacts were probably destroyed by the acid." She finished in a firm voice. "An unrecoverable seamripper is no threat to our plans."

The khan didn't appear to register her words. He'd slumped back into his throne, his forehead shiny with sweat. There was a faint yellow hue to his skin.

Zayaa hurried to his side, suddenly solicitous. "Are you feeling ill again, Most High?"

He nodded once, eyelids fluttering.

Zayaa tugged a cord that hung behind the throne. "I've called your personal servants, Most High." She turned to Dashi, the bright expression on her face at odds with her worried tone. "Before you retire, however, I think it would be wise to give your newest herald her standing commands."

The khan forced his eyes open to glare at Dashi. "You will not raise your hand to me, my consul, or anyone or anything that is mine unless I order it." His voice was gravelly with either pain or fatigue, but the words flowed easily, well-practiced from the heralds who had come before her. "You will not attempt to free yourself or anyone else. You will protect my life with yours." He paused, breath rattling like the thiefmark's. "And you will aid my consul in locating the Wellspring and bringing me to it."

Chapter 5

Dashi was taken back to her cell. She slumped against the wall, too hungry and too despondent to do anything else. She was always hungry, it seemed. No sooner had she wolfed down one meal than her stomach started clamoring for another.

She dreamed of food that night, a huge banquet like the one she'd served the khan's guests for Founding Day: racks of lamb and roasted stag haunches, platters of potatoes and fried dumplings filled with cabbage and mare's milk curds. Instead of sitting at a table to eat, however, she was lying on a cold marble floor, so hungry that it hurt. She reached for a piece of byaslag, but the cheese crumbled into nothing before she could get it to her mouth. Zayaa's tinkling laugh filled the room and, from her position on the floor, Dashi saw the khan's slippered feet approach.

"Like the horses in my stables and the dogs in my kennels, you are mine, Ant," the khan whispered. "I always make sure my beasts have the very best to eat."

He lowered a silver platter in front of Dashi's face. On it lay Idree's finger, still as plump and bloodied as the moment it was severed.

"This is the price of defiance."

Dashi curled up and retched until her stomach screamed, not with hunger but with the effort of emptying itself.

"This is the price of weakness." The voice was different this time, brusque and disappointed.

Dashi looked up. The khan's slippers had been replaced by a pair of ornate sandals, the straps winking with gems. Khagan Nuray bent down, glaring at Dashi like she was a thick student. "You ran from the battle, but the war has found you anyway."

Dashi startled awake. The cool silence of her cell was almost comforting after her nightmare. Her stomach was knotted and tight. A faint scent tugged at the edge of her awareness. There was no one near her, but there had been. Her fingers brushed a small, damp mound, scattering it across the floor.

Sand, she thought, then changed her mind. The pieces weren't small enough. Some were soft. She piled the fragments into her palm and walked to the barred opening of her cell, where the light was best.

Crumbs. The food scraps had been piled in the middle of the floor. Surely she would have noticed them if they'd been there before? Dashi started to brush them away, then paused, considering the assorted scraps. Most of the crumbs were from bread, but there was also a sliver of onion and a shriveled segment of berry. She hadn't eaten berries.

A barrage of confusing scents surrounded her, but Dashi had little experience interpreting them. Part of her wanted to flinch away from trying, to pretend she was a normal person again, but the idea of a visitor entering her cell while she slept was enough to make her push aside her aversion.

It was a curious experience, sorting through scents, a combination of smelling, tasting and seeing all at once. The air held textures and patterns she'd never noticed before: signal flags, announcing information about the people who moved through a space. She recalled the scents of the guards, that stew of soap and food, ale and animal, perspiration and emotion. She thought of the guard's dog and the thiefmark: the slight animalistic tinge to their scent imprint, the way their fur seemed to tickle against her antennae.

The scent in her cell was nothing like that. It was simultaneously weaker but more pervasive. It was, Dashi thought, like someone—or something—with a weak scent had paced her cell hundreds of times, adding layers with each pass. Outside her cell, the air stirred and a new scent came to her: someone who'd been in the great hall.

A minute later, the curly-haired Yassari woman appeared. "The consul has summoned you to the planning room," she said stiffly, opening the cell door.

Dashi's mind instinctively formulated a plan—strike the woman in the face, grab the keys, *run*—but her body refused to obey. The Yassari woman started down the hall, showing no unease at turning her back on Dashi. *Why should she,* Dashi thought as she followed, fuming at her own impotence.

"Are the Yassaris acting as servants now?" she asked.

The woman ignored her.

They'd nearly reached the lift box that would take them to the khan's floor when Dashi realized that the Yassari woman was completely silent. It wasn't just that she wasn't speaking. It was that her feet made no sound against the ground. Her clothes never rustled. *Yassari engineering,* Dashi marveled, watching as the woman's garment flapped soundlessly. Silent garments and footwear would be a useful thing to have, but she knew now that the price of stealing from the Yassaris was not worth the prize.

"I will answer your question if you answer one of mine," the Yassari woman said, startling Dashi. She unlocked the lift box and stepped inside.

Dashi glanced down at the platform beneath the lift box. She and Sevlin had hidden there, shoulder to shoulder, side to side. She briefly contemplated refusing to follow the woman—the khan's commands didn't compel her to—but the image of Idree's finger on a silver platter was still fresh in her mind.

She stepped inside. The Yassari woman pulled the lever, sending the lift box creaking upward.

"What's your question?" Dashi asked.

"Did you really give the golden needle to the khan?"

"Yes, I was hoping to be rewarded with a comfy cell and some antennae. Look how well it worked out for me."

The woman's gaze darted to Dashi's head.

"*No,*" Dashi said when it became clear the Yassari woman wasn't going to speak. "I found the golden needle in a temple in the taiga, but I didn't give it to the khan."

"You knew what the needle could do?"

"Not in all its specific glory," Dashi gestured to her antennae, "but in general terms, yes. I knew what it was and I knew I didn't want that—" Dashi shut her mouth on what she'd been about to call the khan. "I hid it. It was stolen."

"It's a shame when someone takes liberties with your property."

"A lecture on property rights *and* an escort to the consul? The ancestors must smile on me today."

"A simple observation."

The woman's lantern swayed with the lift box, splaying light over her face before yanking it away again. She was younger than Dashi had thought, in her twenties instead of her thirties. What kind of person voluntarily came to New Osb to help the khan?

"The consul does not trust the guards or the servants," the woman said. "That is why she sent me to bring you. She said they make the best-placed spies: nobodies, who manage to have access to everything. Taken for granted, yet still granted the power to stick a knife in your back." She paused. "Those were her words, you understand, not mine."

Zayaa would know all about sticking knives in backs, Dashi thought bitterly. "So she sends a mercenary who sells to the highest bidder? That's a precarious kind of trust."

"We Yassaris adhere to a strict policy of neutrality; it is written into the Treaty of Yassumova. We do not take sides in political strife. We do not weigh right and wrong. We do not judge civil discourse or its lack. In return, we have the right to move in and between the continental countries without harassment, theft, or hindrance and we have the right to punish violators." She looked sideways at Dashi. "It was my understanding that this arrangement is well known."

"Well rumored, maybe." Dashi shrugged. "Isn't running errands for the consul a bit different than neutrality? Or is there extra money in it if you make yourself indispensable enough?"

"The Convoymaster appointed me to act as the consul's liaison." The woman's chin rose. "It is an honor."

The lift box drifted to a stop and Dashi reached for the door without waiting for the woman. "The last people who worked with the consul are dead," she said. "*That* arrangement may not be as well known as your treaty, but it should be."

Dashi stepped out, her feet sinking into the thick carpet. She'd been here before, though not since becoming a herald, and her antennae twitched restlessly, automatically cataloging their new environment. There were rooms for dressing, sleeping, official business, guests, mistresses, and—Dashi's attention snagged—a dedicated room for the seamstress.

She didn't need to be told where to go. Zayaa's trail was strong, crossing to and from a doorway on the left. Her antennae gave a quick flinch, trying to remind her that nothing good came from this scent. *Like I don't know that already*, she grumbled, stepping inside.

The room looked like she remembered. A few pieces of ancient art-work provided splashes of color, but the room functioned mainly as a place to store and study Purek scrolls. Shelf after shelf of them lined the walls. Small scribe-style desks were scattered throughout the room. A larger table at the center showcased a map of the entire continent. Clusters of colored pins sprouted across its surface. Military forces, Dashi thought, noting how many were concentrated along the Tyvalar-Karakal border.

Zayaa leaned over one of the small desks, her hair falling forward to reveal a spiderweb of scars on the back of her neck. An unfurled scroll lay before her, the weights on each corner staking the ancient parchment open for examination. It put Dashi in mind of something she'd once seen with Sevlin: a skeleton splayed over an altar, arching in eternal agony.

"What do you want, Zayaa?" Dashi asked. Beside her, the Yassari woman stiffened.

Zayaa straightened, one finger tapping the pointer she'd been using to keep her place. "No formal title?"

"The khan didn't say anything about being respectful, but I'll use a title if you'd prefer. I've thought of a few."

"And to think I convinced him that your defiance was cured."

Dashi crossed her arms, trying not to picture Idree's finger. "I didn't ask you to speak up for me. I hope you're not about to feed me some line about past friendship or, ancestors protect me, *loyalty*."

Zayaa's lips flattened. "You see through me well enough. A pity you never could with Altan and Baris. What blinded you: your terror of being alone or the fact that you were half in love with both of them?"

Realizing she'd walked into a conflict that was years in the making, the Yassari woman took a step toward the door.

"*I* was in love?" Dashi sputtered. "You were actually *with* Altan! He thought the two of you would marry! And Baris—"

"Baris and Altan were both fools. No stronger or more clever than any other man." Dashi opened her mouth to argue, but Zayaa cut her off. "I didn't call you here to listen to your dewy-eyed recollections."

"No, I'm here because the khan wants one more Purek artifact for his collection."

"The Wellspring isn't an artifact," Zayaa corrected smugly. "It's a place. One you will help us locate before you're given over to the Yassaris."

She shifted a pile of scrolls, revealing a flash of silver: the Purek cup that Sevlin had given Dashi.

"Useless thing." Zayaa shoved the cup onto a tray of half-eaten food.

"Am I supposed to tow the khan through the taiga as I go?" Dashi asked, remembering that the khan had commanded her to bring him there. "Why does he want to go anyway?"

"Why don't you do what you're best at, Dashi: fetch things that are hard to get. Leave the big picture to someone who's suited to it."

Dashi's fists tightened. "Fetch *what*? You said the Wellspring was a place."

Zayaa smiled grimly. "We need more information. That's what you'll be acquiring."

"Scrolls?"

"Yes, but not from a ruin, from the Tyvalarans. I'll give you the schematics of the palace later today—and the khan will repeat all of this to make it binding. That way, you can't run away."

The Yassari woman pursed her lips at the mention of theft but didn't say anything.

"The Tyvalarans have a trove of scrolls, most of which I've already seen," Zayaa continued. "I need anything mentioning the Wellspring that came after Altan and Baris."

Dashi wasn't sure what emotion she'd expected from Zayaa. Embarrassment? Nostalgia? *Something.* Instead, her tone was businesslike, devoid of feeling.

"Sounds straightforward enough," Dashi said brightly. "At what point should I betray everyone who loved me?"

"If only Altan and Baris were here to pat you on the head and tell you how fearless and strong you are." Zayaa's mouth slipped easily into a snarl. "You'd already be halfway to Tyvalar by now."

The urge to smash Zayaa's face gripped Dashi, making her chest rise and fall unevenly. She could imagine Zayaa's look of fear, could feel the blood wetting her fist as she broke that perfect nose.

"You will not raise your hand to me, my consul, or anyone or anything that is mine," the khan's voice said in her mind. Dashi's fists didn't move.

Zayaa unfurled a scroll. "Your antennae move a lot when you're agitated."

Dashi could feel them zigzagging through the air. The room was filled with an astringent scent that screamed aggression in some primal language Dashi was only beginning to understand. *I'm doing that,* she thought, torn between surprise and disgust. *I'm putting out that scent.* Vaguely, she recalled a similar scent when the khan had commanded her to hurt Idree, though she'd forgotten it until this moment. The thought, while distressing in its own way, distracted her, returning a measure of calm.

"Just tell me what I'm supposed to do," she said, more than ready to be away from Zayaa.

Zayaa raised an eyebrow. "So obliging." She pointed at a cluttered desk. "Study this."

Dashi sat down heavily and began reading through translations in Zayaa's neat handwriting.

"The Wellspring is the fount, the very heart of the world. From its loins ventured the seamripper and it was this stream that Hamujakah stepped into, reemerging as the first seamstress."

Dashi paused, noting the name of the first seamstress, which she'd never seen before. Another page of translation included a similar description, with the added admonition: *"To return a gift of the earth here, at the very core of nature, is to unbind it, leaving the power unrestrained."*

A single scroll, the only original Purek item on the table, depicted a craggy tree, with what looked to be a mouth in the trunk. There was a list of khagans and the years of their respective reigns. While this didn't seem pertinent, the khan had commanded Dashi to help Zayaa, and Zayaa had commanded her to study everything on the table, so Dashi's eyes roved over that too, noting Khagan Nuray's name in the most recent position.

Across the room, Zayaa was speaking to the Yassari woman. "I know the khan has primarily spoken of procuring Yassari weaponry, Tuya, but I'd also like to commission silent clothes like the ones you're wearing. In dark colors, please."

"I will bring it up with the convoymaster," Tuya said, polite but elusive. She hurried from the room, silent as when she'd entered.

Zayaa crossed back to Dashi's desk, waiting for her to finish. The remaining translations were similar to the first: everything underscored how important the Wellspring was to the Pureks, but there were no specifics on where it was located or why, exactly, one would want to go there.

"The older scrolls," Zayaa said, "the ones Altan smuggled into Tyvalar, will be in their archives, but anything Sevlin found more recently will be in his tower. It will be heavily guarded, of course, even if no one has seen him in weeks."

"Scrolls that *Sevlin* found," Dashi repeated. "When?"

"When you and Idree were in hiding. I've arrived at more than one ruin to find it already picked over." Zayaa glanced at Dashi's face and gave a tinkling laugh. "Always blinded by your infatuations, Dashi. Sevlin is a hunter who tracks many animals; didn't you know?"

But Sevlin can't even read Purek—Dashi stopped, remembering how she'd glimpsed his lips moving when they'd explored a ruin. If he *could* read Purek, why would he hide it? *I didn't tell him where I got the Adder's Dust. Maybe it's not so surprising that he didn't trust me either,* she thought, but her fingers started drumming against her leg.

Dashi gestured at a map on Zayaa's desk. "*Another* map of the taiga?"

Unlike the maps that she'd seen for the golden needle and the seamripper, which had been riddled with swaths of blank space, this one was very detailed. Rock formations were noted. Rivers were named. Precise distances were meted out, though the measurement system was a Purek one.

"Wait..." Dashi sucked in a breath. "An *original*?" In all the time she'd searched the Purek ruins, she had never seen an original map this complete.

Zayaa nodded, her eyes on the map. For a moment, their enmity faded, eclipsed by shared awe.

"It's designed to be disassembled and stored separately, a failsafe to protect the location of the Wellspring." Zayaa pointed to the seams running through the map. The edges were carefully shaped, not torn, and minute handwritten notations indicated exactly where each piece would line up with the next.

"Four sections, hidden in sculpture bases, behind paintings and beneath murals. I have three pieces. Sevlin has the missing one."

Dashi thought of Sevlin making trips to Purek ruins, searching for pieces of a map she hadn't known existed. He'd never mentioned anything when they'd been searching for the seamripper.

She leaned forward, bracing her hands on the table to avoid touching the fragile map. She recognized the line of the taiga immediately, as well as the library where she and her friends had sometimes sheltered. It was one of the first places Altan had taken her. To the east of it, a river plunged out of the taiga with frigid abandon. They'd all jumped into it once, made desperate by the heavy summer air. From there, slightly to the north, was another ruin. It had partially collapsed when Dashi was inside and the others had spent a day removing debris so she could worm her way out.

She didn't say any of that aloud, but she could feel Zayaa watching her. The churn of their shared memories—a river of a different kind—stretched between them, with Zayaa, now a stranger, standing on the opposite shore.

"Enter the taiga here." Dashi's finger hovered over a notation at the edge of the taiga. The map laid out markers at regular intervals to track their passage: rivers, rocks, geological features. It should be easy to follow, Dashi thought, tracing the route along a ridge and over a river to a cleft canyon, where the trail appeared to end.

"The gate?" she asked, translating the characters. "It looks more like a dead end."

"*Gateway*," Zayaa corrected. "Sevlin's piece shows the final leg of the journey." She tapped her pointer against a handful of unfamiliar Purek characters. "Memorize these. Wellspring. Fount. Heart of Life. In addition to the map section, bring back anything pertinent to the Wellspring's origin, its uses, or its characteristics."

Dashi was silent, picturing herself breaking into Sevlin's rooms, stealing something he'd obviously deemed valuable.

"I'm showing you this now so that, as you sort through Sevlin's trove, you can more easily determine what will be valuable to me," Zayaa said.

"To the khan, you mean."

Zayaa inclined her head, eyes sharp. "Exactly."

"What's so important about this place that *the khan* wants to go see it?"

"It's a sacred Purek site. No one has laid eyes on it for centuries. Isn't that reason enough?"

For Dashi, it was. For the Zayaa who'd pretended to be her friend, it would have been too. But for *this* Zayaa? For the khan? She doubted that curiosity figured into their plans.

The door opened and Tuya reentered.

"The Convoymaster has...stipulations regarding your request," she said, giving a deferential half bow.

"And?" Zayaa walked over, angling the conversation away from Dashi.

Dashi heard words like "silent" and "proprietary," followed by a sharp exclamation of, "It is more complicated than simply tagging along," from Zayaa. Their disagreement eventually dwindled, giving way to a negotiation on price.

Glancing at Zayaa, Dashi stepped closer to the adjacent desk, where another scroll had snagged her attention. It gleamed up at her, fresh and unstained. Her eyes moved from the imbroglio of Purek characters to the bright illustrations.

The first picture showed the aftermath of a destroyed village: two children cowering as a winged monster—presumably a herald—hovered over their smoldering home. The children were teenagers in the next picture, walking along a river through the taiga. The final illustration showed the young man, rigid with shock, watching as the girl, bathed in purple light, stood with her arms stretched up in exultation. The illustrations were a variation of the seamripper origin myth that she and Sevlin had seen painted on the walls of ruins.

"*He kept watch until midnight,*" Dashi translated, "*when the seamripper...ventured forth from the land's heart.*"

I was so close to finding it, she thought. She skipped through the text, picking out the pieces that translated readily: *"pain," "balance," "half-torn."* She paused on that last word. Its inflection meant it referred to both a person and an animal. A few lines later, she understood: *"bastards of magic...not allowed to die, nor free to live...neither animal, nor human...but torn between all these things."*

Heralds. It was talking about *her.*

"Like oxen, they are led—" No, *led* wasn't the right word. *Controlled.* *"Controlled by both whip and rein."*

The whip obviously referred to the pain the khan wielded against them. Reins must mean the tether itself.

"Two ways to sever the reins," she read silently, her heart beating faster.

Using one finger, she edged the scroll open further and saw an additional illustration. It showed a man stretched out, unconscious. Discarded in the grass beside his head were two ram's horns. Standing over him was a shrouded figure. One outstretched hand grasped the glowing tether, now broken in two, that extended from the man's chest.

"First, the seamripper...must have the half-torn in hand—"

Zayaa appeared suddenly, rolling the scroll up and tucking it possessively under one arm. "The seamripper is unimportant now. That door closed when you dropped the maze's artifacts into an acid flood."

Dashi gestured at the scroll. "This ink is too bright and I've never seen parchment that pristine. It's a copy?"

"Sevlin has had the original for years. The copy that Altan sold to the khan's former consul contained intentional errors. Fortunately, I was able to correct them."

It wasn't the first time Zayaa had dispensed with Sevlin's title. Dashi wondered how well they knew each other, though she would never give Zayaa the satisfaction of asking outright.

Zayaa pointed to Dashi's desk. "Have you familiarized yourself with what's here? I don't want you to return with duplicates of what I already have."

Dashi nodded. "After I sift through Sevlin's scrolls and gather the ones pertinent to the Wellspring, then what?

"Then you and your companions will return to New Osb."

"Companions?" Remembering the snippet of conversation she'd overheard, Dashi glanced at the door. "The Yassari woman wanted to come too?"

"No. The Yassaris will be joining the expedition to locate the Wellspring, not to steal Sevlin's scrolls."

"Why would they join that?" Dashi asked, going suddenly cold.

"Not for you. Well," Zayaa paused, lips pursing. "Executing you at the earliest opportunity might be an additional benefit, but it's not their main reason. They want to study the mechanics of Purek traps. For the journey to Tyvalar, your companions will be the other heralds." Zayaa paused with mock delicacy. "I believe you've already met the moth? Beautiful wings. Excellent at capture-and-return assignments."

"I assumed the tether meant I wouldn't need keepers," Dashi said, probing carefully. She'd hoped the khan's control diminished with distance.

"The other heralds will be there to help you get inside." Zayaa smiled. "Don't trouble yourself with the tether. We've already tested it on the others. It's strong enough to ensure anyone's cooperation, even yours."

Chapter 6

The morning they were due to ride out of New Osb, Zayaa summoned the heralds to the planning room. Dashi had been moved from her cell to a small room on the second floor, which had formerly been earmarked for visiting regional officials. She'd kept apart from the other heralds, but their rooms were all around hers—a veritable wing of monsters—so, when the summons came, they all went up together. Glancing back, Dashi saw that the entire servant's staircase was covered, wall to wall, with their distinct scent trail: the colorless smudge of humans in some places, and the pink-tan eddies of animals in others.

The stag, who'd bounded up the stairs first, waited until they'd all gathered around the door before knocking, his antlered head bowed politely. The owl didn't make eye contact, but the moth woman caught Dashi's gaze and flashed her dainty, needle teeth: a greeting and warning in equal measure. The sable was covered in shiny fur, dark on his throat, cheeks and hands, but fading to chestnut around his eyes and mouth. His ears—what Dashi could see of them through the fur—were still human. His jaw was elongated, ending in a black smudge of a nose and a spray of whiskers. He turned his sharp face toward Dashi and offered her a nod as he wriggled his nose, taking in her scent.

"Come in," came Zayaa's voice.

They fell into single file, soldiers parading before a commander. She was silent, assessing, and then she unrolled a map of northwestern

Karakal and eastern Tyvalar. Known troop locations were marked in red and blue along the border. The proposed route to Rucharla, the Tyvalaran capital, was delineated in black thread, which wound over the river and into the heart of the country like a spreading necrosis.

"Through the near-taiga?" Dashi asked. "Due west would be much shorter."

"If you go northwest instead, you cross the border in the Kurlar region," Zayaa said, her finger tracing a path. "There's less chance you'll be spotted and you'll reach the capital city almost as quickly as if you'd taken a more direct route." Zayaa glanced up, waiting for their nods. "The khan won't bind you to this exact route, just to his objectives. That way you can maintain some flexibility if it's needed."

"Isn't the Kurlar region supposed to be heavily armed?" the stag asked. It was the first time Dashi had heard him speak and his voice was soft. "There was a battle there." He glanced around at the other heralds, seeking consensus.

The sable and Dashi both nodded. Dashi couldn't recall the details, but it was enough to make her dubious about the map's sparsely marked troop locations.

"It wasn't a battle, per se. A group of Kurlarians made a bid for independence. It was years ago and it failed," Zayaa said flatly. "The Tyvalarans aren't worried about secessionists right now; they're worried about the khan invading. However, Karakal could never launch a full-scale assault through the Kurlar region because of the depth and speed of the river there, so the Tyvalarans won't waste resources guarding it. The soldiers stationed there will be a skeleton force."

Dashi glanced at the pale blue line of the river dividing the two countries. "How are *we* going to cross?"

"Simple." Zayaa straightened as the door opened. "You'll fly."

It was Tuya, holding an armful of black cloth. "Everything is here," she said to Zayaa.

"Is there anything they need to know before using it?" Zayaa asked.

Tuya gave the heralds a dispassionate glance. "You each have a set of Unheard clothing. It will not rustle or swish, and it will absorb small involuntary noises, such as heavy breathing. It will *not* hide loud noises. If you speak, if you bump into something, if you fall, you will still be heard."

"No footwear? I've heard the Yassaris make fine boots," Dashi said, her voice casual.

"Crafting boots is time-consuming." Tuya's eyes narrowed. "A single boot takes six months and requires—"

"Enough," Zayaa said sharply. "The khan will be here any minute and I don't want to waste time watching you be punished for being antagonistic." She looked pointedly at Dashi. "Your provisions have been assembled and your mounts have been selected. Everyone has memorized the Purek characters for the Wellspring. Dashi, you're the only one who can read more Purek than that, so you're responsible for vetting anything that's found."

She placed a slight emphasis on the word *responsible*, which Dashi assumed meant that she would be the one blamed if she returned with anything Zayaa considered worthless.

"Are there any other questions?" Zayaa asked.

Dashi was distracted from answering by the sudden incursion of the khan's scent, smudging the air where it seeped over the threshold. Unlike the other scents she'd encountered, his had a rotten, almost oily taste to it that made her want to shake it loose from her antennae and spit it out of her mouth.

When the khan appeared, he wasn't dressed in his normal finery but wore a dressing gown of green silk with small golden wolves embroidered down the sleeves. He looked just as sickly as before. The heralds bowed their heads.

"You look well, Most High," Zayaa said when the khan released them from their obeisance.

His response was inaudible to Dashi but she saw the flash of Zayaa's radiant smile.

The khan turned to the heralds, his expression severe. "Moth, Owl, Sable, Ant, Stag, I am commanding you to go to Tyvalar." He looked at Dashi. "Ant."

Dashi's jaw clenched. "Yes, Most High?"

"You will return with any scrolls that will aid my search for the Purek Wellspring." He turned to the others. "Owl, Moth, Stag and Sable, the four of you will assist Ant in any way you can. My consul has given you each a detailed plan; you will follow that unless forced to improvise."

"Yes, Most High," they intoned.

The khan's eyes moved between them, lingering on Dashi once more. "You will pursue this goal with your full ability and return to me directly. You will aid one another when you can, but your health and that of your companions is of secondary importance to your objective. You will not speak of this to anyone outside of this room. You will not sabotage this effort, nor will you be captured. You will not provide aid to the Tyvalarans. You will move as quickly and as unobtrusively as possible to avoid interference and capture."

Dashi imagined the words settling around her, invisible snares pinning her in place. The orders were specific enough that she could not see much room for circumvention. Already her muscles felt taut, primed to march to Tyvalar.

"Complete your final preparations and leave within the hour." The khan's voice rang with an authority that Dashi felt deep in her bones. Her legs began moving. One step, then another, the sound fading beneath the footsteps of the other heralds, each of them swept along on a tide not of their own making.

Dashi thought of Sevlin as she'd last seen him: trapped and bloodied, her pitifully small knife cradled in his palm. This was how she pictured him most often, though she knew from Zayaa that he had managed to extricate himself. He had probably risked his life finding the final piece of the Wellspring map and now, after leaving him behind in the maze, she was going to his home to steal it. In her mind's eye, Sevlin's expression turned accusatory.

Her legs kept moving: down the last set of stairs, across the courtyard, and out to the stables. Two strings of mounts waited there and every one of them was stiff-legged with fear, their eyes rolling and white-rimmed. Dashi stopped a few steps away, watching a familiar gray horse with stubby legs and a blocky head. He thrashed against the rope, trying to flee the strange scent of the heralds. He wore the saddle that Altan had given her years ago. A sword and her unstrung bow were strapped to one side.

"I don't miss having to travel like that," the moth drawled from behind Dashi. The owl clacked her beak in agreement. The noise sent a fresh wave of panic rippling through the horses.

"Well, the sable and I aren't as fast as the stag and we can't fly," Dashi snapped. "We can't ride either if you keep crowding the horses."

Dashi waited until they left the stableyard before approaching. The sable hung back, as nervous about the horses as they were about him.

"They're scared because they can't tell what we are," Dashi told him in an undertone. "Go slowly and speak softly. They'll acclimate."

"Why don't you show me how it's done," he muttered, his doubt obvious beneath his sarcasm. "I'll take bets on how many times they kick you."

Dashi took a step toward her string of horses. They shied immediately, the hindquarters of one bumping into the flanks of another.

"Hey, old man."

One of Spit's ears swiveled in her direction, but his neck stayed high, straining against the rope. He snorted indignantly, sending small clouds into the frigid morning.

"It doesn't feel right to be tied here when you could be racing over the steppe, huh? I understand how that feels. What do you say we go do that now? It's been too long." She kept up the flow of words, edging closer with each softly spoken promise of adventure.

When she reached him, Spit was still wide-eyed, but he'd turned his head toward her and his body was no longer twitching with tension. He stretched out his nose, whuffed softly at her palm, and shuddered.

"It's a big change for me too, old man." She ran her other hand down his neck and over his withers, gathering up the scent of horse like it was a warm blanket. "Guess we have to get used to it though."

The other horses in the string had quieted too, though none was as calm as Spit. She went to each of them in turn, speaking softly and letting them smell her. To her right, the sable was doing the same, though with less impressive results. *He smells like a predator*, Dashi thought, going over to help him.

The sun was cresting the horizon by the time the sable convinced a horse to let him mount. He was slightly built and wiry—a body type well-suited to horsemanship—but he sat stiff in the saddle, his inexperience obvious.

"Relax your legs," Dashi told him. "Keep your grip firm but move *with* your mare, not in opposition to her."

"Oh yes, easy," he snapped.

Dashi shrugged. It would come to him eventually; he couldn't hold himself that tightly for days on end. She turned Spit toward the gate, glancing up suddenly at the scent of someone hovering outside of the stableyard. Her eyes searched the stand of fruit trees that lined one side of the palace grounds until she found Ese, barely visible among the trunks.

She led her string of horses to the watering trough adjacent to the trees.

"This is the second time my horse has found his way to me at your hands," she said, careful to look at Spit instead of the trees.

"Thank your old friend for that, not me." Ese's voice slithered out from the trees.

"Zayaa?" Her happiness, both at finding Spit and at the thought of someone—even Ese—acting as her ally, shifted to wariness.

"I'm not the only one who knows how much you value the nag, nor how much he increases your chance of success."

Dashi shook her head. "I don't think having Spit will help me succeed this time." She opened her mouth but found that she could tell Ese no more than that. "What we're doing…I won't even be on horseback for the hard part."

"I don't know then," Ese said, a shrug in his voice, "but the consul strikes me as someone who always has a reason."

"Why didn't you tell me Zayaa was alive?" It was the same accusation she'd leveled at Idree.

"You forget, little Dashi, that I didn't know you and your friends in life. I learned of them the same way I learned of you: by asking questions and making inferences. The new consul was beautiful, which was how your friend Zayaa was always described, but so are many women. *You* assumed she was dead because you saw the bodies of your two other friends. *I* assumed she was dead because you did. She goes by 'Consul' now. I didn't hear her real name until after you'd scampered out of New Osb."

It was a lot of words for Ese, who never liked to give out more information than he got, and his answer appeased Dashi. Not because of the explanation, but because of the tone. *Defensive,* she thought. *He's embarrassed he didn't know. That makes two of us.*

"Why are your antennae moving like that?" he asked.

"I wondered if you'd have the same scent as the khan," she said. "From handling the Adder's Dust."

He peered through the tree branches enough to give her a withering look. "Don't be stupid. I wouldn't have handled it directly against my skin when I poisoned him. Anyway, I'm out; someone stole half of mine."

Dashi studied him, wondering if he was telling the truth. He would have heard by now that the khan could compel her to tell him anything and that she'd been commanded to protect him. The less information she had about the Adder's Dust, the better.

"What does it smell like?" he asked.

"Oily. Foul. Like something going bad."

"That's how it kills at high enough concentrations: organ failure," Ese said, sounding cheerful.

"Well," she said, carefully, "whatever is ailing the khan, I hope it continues." She pulled Spit's muzzle from the water and left without another word.

"*Finally,*" the moth spat, as Dashi and the sable rode to the gate. "I was about go dormant from all this cold and waiting." A small pack was clipped over her chest, its straps perfectly positioned so as not to obstruct her wings.

"And I would have been devastated," Dashi said, but the moth was already in the air.

The owl woman had eschewed the cloak that normally concealed her torso, instead donning a multi-pocketed vest that would not interfere with her wide, brown wings. With some ungainly hopping, she launched herself into the sky. The stag bounded forward, his legs moving with springlike precision. His wide rack of antlers was so ostentatious that Dashi had never noticed the lower half of his body. She saw now that his joints bent at inhuman angles and that he wore no boots under his close-fit pants. Black cloven hooves clicked smartly against the cobble-stones

Spit shied violently at the burst of activity from the heralds, but Dashi held him in check, murmuring encouragement. Both sets of gates swung open to reveal the steppe, sparkling under a layer of heavy frost. Above them, the moth banked in the chilly air, her wings glowing in the reflected sunrise.

Despite everything, a deep peace settled in Dashi's chest, if only for that moment. A horse and open space: these were the things she was meant for. Wings would have been superfluous.

"Together again, old man," she murmured, gently rubbing a circle on Spit's withers.

She gave New Osb one last look over her shoulder, wondering if Idree was watching somewhere. Instead, she saw Zayaa standing at one of the balconies, her gaze steady on Dashi. Even from a distance, she was radiantly beautiful, the rising sun limning her face and hair in gold.

Dashi nudged Spit into a canter and took off for Tyvalar.

Chapter 7

Dashi shrugged deeper into her furs, trying to provide a smaller target for the cold. Though they'd stopped between two hills, the wind of the near-taiga found its way to them nonetheless. It ruffled the fur that covered the sable's cheekbones, swaying it like steppe grass. Dashi eyed her saddlebag but made no move to retrieve her fur-lined hat. She'd tried to wear it the first day, but it was claustrophobic against her antennae. For now, she'd take the cold.

The moth was silent and staring, firelight dancing in her oversized eyes. Farther from the glow, the owl paced, her head turning at a sickening angle with each pass as she kept them all in sight. Behind her, the horses shifted, nostrils quivering as they tasted the wind. Dashi matched the direction of Spit's gaze, but the wind was wrong and she could scent nothing.

"A wager on which log topples into the fire first," the sable said. He pointed to the lean-to of logs, trembling under the flames.

"There's nothing to wager *with*," the stag murmured.

"I know," he sighed. "I can see why no one comes to the northlands." He pushed his hands closer to the fire. Despite the fur covering his face and arms, he still wore the winter clothes from his saddlebags. "It's a cursed thing, having to travel so far in winter."

"Some of us have had to travel farther than this for the khan," the moth said.

"There's time for that yet," the sable said gloomily. "We all heard him; he's after something else."

The owl made a distressed noise, her pace quickening.

"I don't like the sound of that wilderness," the sable continued. "Do you think we'll all have to go?"

"My guess is yes," Dashi said. Mention of the taiga made her muscles tense. Her anxiety was tempered only by the thought that Idree would be safely in New Osb. She couldn't see the khan risking his precious seamstress.

"Oh," the sable said, then brightened. "A larger party means safer travels though. What could stand against foes like us?"

"There are worse monsters than us in the taiga," Dashi said. "Giant rats and frogs."

The sable cocked his head, pink tongue darting between pointed teeth. "How large?"

"Too large for you to eat."

He wrinkled his nose, disbelieving. "I wouldn't bet against me. I can pack away a lot since I was changed."

The stag nodded, his antlers dipping dangerously close to the sable's face. "Crates of vegetables. Entire loaves of bread."

"No venison?" the sable asked. One side of his elongated face bunched, his version of a smirk.

The stag gave him a level look but didn't answer.

"I'm always hungry too, but maybe it's just the season," Dashi offered. "Animals eat a lot to counter the cold."

"I never saw any monsters in the taiga," the moth said. "Lots of fat fish but no monsters."

Dashi glanced at her over the fire. "You weren't *in* the taiga though. You were above it."

The moth's lip curled. "Obviously."

"So you don't have a good idea of what's in those trees." Dashi jutted her chin toward the sable. "*He'll* be on horseback if he goes, not in the air."

"And you're going out of your way to help him, are you?" The moth woman sniffed, rose gracefully to her feet, and disappeared into the darkness.

At this sudden animosity, the owl halted and tucked her chin into her feathers, visibly bracing for a blow.

"She's always been touchy," the sable said to Dashi. "As long as I've known her anyway."

"You are a few weeks, um, older than me?" Dashi asked.

"I was stitched a few weeks before you, yeah, but I've known Solongo for longer than that. We were in the prisoner camp since spring. Same work shift and everything."

Dashi started, glancing involuntarily at the stag.

"I was there too," he said, "on the same shift as..." The fire lit up his wide eyes, making them look haunted and sad. "As the fish."

"You too?" Dashi asked the owl.

She gave a meep of alarm and shrank further.

"She and her sister were with Solongo and me," the sable said. "Solongo was the first to be stitched. Imagine waking up after it was over and knowing there was no one else like you in the whole world, that no one else had survived and, for all you knew, maybe never would. You could ask—" He glanced behind him, but the owl had vanished into the night. "Oh, never mind. She's flown away too. Anyway, I know Solongo has a kid somewhere, but I sure have a hard time imagining her taking care of anyone else. Seems to resent everyone around her." He gave a little laugh. "Heh, it's a good thing *she's* not the one with the sharp beak. We'd all be missing fingers." His shoulders twitched, a movement that wasn't quite a shrug. "I get a little touchy too, but only when people crowd me. Comes from being packed in there for too long."

"How'd you end up in there?" Dashi asked.

"Fell on the wrong side of the wrong people. Isn't that the downfall of all tricksters and cons?" His right hand moved to the luxurious fur around his neck, meticulously grooming it.

"Shagai?" Dashi asked, remembering the way dice games pervaded the dirt circle, the poorest section of Karak City. Every corner looked the same: people crammed into a desperate knot, necks craning, mouths begging a favor from the ancestors, waiting for the bone dice to change their fate.

"Dice, cards, betting, whatever might make money that day. But one day I emptied the purse of the strongman's younger brother—" He glanced up, an earnest expression on his furred face. "I wouldn't have done it if I'd recognized him, you understand. He'd shot up in the last six months, barely looked like the same fellow. I tried to return the money, but as I'd taken it in a, er, somewhat public and humiliating way, he was very angry. Next thing I know, prefects are dragging me out of my woman's bed and through the street. Then it was five months chiseling stone. We worked in shifts, never a full night's sleep, never a day of rest, never enough to eat. I thought the prefects in Karak City were a corrupt, malicious bunch, but the guards in the prisoner camp were..." He made a slicing motion, fingers winking in the firelight, sharp-tipped and black. "I'm glad I got out before winter."

Dashi thought of Karak City's prison, where she'd spent a few months. The experience had been anything but pleasant and yet Ese, who'd once been in charge of the prison, had told her he'd cracked down on the guards' depravity. She wondered if the worst offenders had simply left to run New Osb's prisoner camps.

"I got behind on my taxes," the stag said, barely audible over the crackling fire. "The prefects were threatening to throw me out onto the street—me and my mother. She lived with me. Could no longer work because of her hands. I paid them off once, but the next time they came around they demanded more. I couldn't afford to pay them, not with what I'd already sent in for the taxes. So I," he swallowed, "I took a little from the merchant I worked for. He'd always been fair with me and I was going to pay it back."

The sable rolled his eyes.

"I was," the stag insisted.

"Oh, I believe you," the sable said.

"But when the merchant found out, he wouldn't listen..." The stag's ponderous head bowed. "I was sent to New Osb straightaway."

Dashi knew better than to ask what had happened to his mother.

"What was your name before you became—" Dashi caught herself before she said 'monsters.' She motioned vaguely at their group.

"Sable fits just fine for me." His hand rose and fell nonchalantly. "Don't see much use for names anymore. The khan, the consul, the guards, they all call us by our animal name."

"Most of us do the same now," said the stag.

"Solongo is the only one who still likes to be called by her old name. Well, and you," he amended. "I heard the consul calling you Dashi."

"She and I...knew each other." Dashi picked up a stick and jabbed at the pine needles covering the ground, raking up a small pile. "Before."

Sable gave a sharp-toothed grin. "Some bad blood there. I could smell it even if I wasn't part animal."

The stag snorted a laugh.

"She betrayed some friends of mine," Dashi said, though that seemed too pale a description for what had occurred, as if Zayaa had merely cheated at a game or gossiped to the wrong person, instead of masterminding murder and treason and theft. "I never thought I'd see her again, and I certainly don't like her being in charge of me."

"No one does," said the sable, "but you have to make the best of it."

"Make the best of it? We're little better than puppets. The khan can…" Dashi trailed off, her mind supplying a horrifying array of possibilities. *He can make me hurt Idree. He can make me kill innocent people. He can make me kill* myself. "He can do anything he wants."

"Why does every head bow when the khan comes into a room? Why does everyone call him 'Most High?' Because he's *always* been able to do what he wants, with everyone, not just the heralds." Again Sable's shoulders gave a quick shiver, too fast and fluid to be called a shrug. "The way I look at it is that, now, I get something out of it." Sable grinned. "You should see me climb. I don't think I'd be too shabby in a fight either, and I wouldn't even need my knives." He wiggled his sharp-tipped fingers playfully, but when he spoke again, his voice held a serious note. "And I won't die in the dirt circle. That's something."

"You're just going to *accept* this? Give up your old life? You said you had someone back in Karak City. What about her?" Dashi pushed a small pile of pine needles toward the fire like an offering. They began to pop and crackle as soon as the heat touched them, long before the flames ever did.

"It's not so much a question of accepting as it is about adapting, isn't it? And she wasn't *mine* mine, just when her husband was away. She was warm enough. Nothing to fret over though."

Dashi shook her head, baffled. Even if she spent her whole life as a herald—and just the thought of it was enough to make her want to stab something—she could never see herself accepting it with Sable's equanimity. "But you have no power over your own life. And the khan…the khan is doing terrible things." She saw Idree's finger hit the floor.

"I've had word from my mother," the stag said. "Or rather, about her. As long as the khan is pleased with me, she won't be put out on the street."

"I'm sorry about the seamstress," Sable said, his eyes sharp. "If I had been free to stop that, I would have. We all feel...very strongly about her." Across the fire, the stag nodded in agreement. "But the khan has been doing terrible things long before all this." He gestured to his fur-covered face and Dashi's antennae. "Did it trouble you then?"

"No. I was happy to keep my head down and let the khan and his nobles play their games."

"Seems like the happiest course to set now too."

"And let the khan turn me over to the Yassaris to be executed when he's done?"

"Ah, that is some rotten luck there." Sable's whiskers twitched sagely.

It's easy to sound wise and unemotional when it's not you on the line, Dashi thought. "What about Idree?" she pressed. "What if she's cut up, bit by bit?"

"Well, don't anger the khan further and the cutting will be reduced." Settling onto his bedroll, Sable curled into a ball, his head pillowed on his paws. "That's what I meant by making the best of it. Other than that, there's not much else you can do about your sister's lot, is there? Or yours, for that matter."

"*No.*"

Sable closed his eyes and sighed contentedly, unaware that her response hadn't been directed at his question but at...*everything*. No, she wasn't going to make the best of it. No, she wouldn't be content with a life where she was murdered by the Yassaris and Idree was a prisoner. No, she wouldn't accept that there was nothing she could do.

The stick she'd been using to herd the pine needles caught fire. Dashi held it up, watching it burn. *I will find a way to free us, or I will die trying,* she promised herself.

They'd reached the river boundary with Tyvalar when Dashi scented it: something upwind, something...strange. She wheeled Spit in a tight circle, her eyes searching the land. The old scar along her side, a legacy of the khan's race, throbbed without warning, and she had to work to keep the tension out of her hands and legs, lest she spook Spit. To one side, the near-taiga mounded up like the folds in a blanket, while on the other it melted away to join the river. The owl and the moth waited at the water's edge, conserving their energy for the herculean task of flying Dashi, Stag, Sable and a half dozen horses across the river. She could see Tyvalar on the other side, but the morning fog and the silvery winter sky combined to make it look distant and surreal.

Nothing stirred. *A good time to cross,* Dashi thought. If there were Tyvalaran soldiers, they would be tired now, lulled into complacency by the silence and the soporific half-light.

Still, she could sense it. *Them,* she corrected herself, though she couldn't put into words how she knew. There were several of them, and they were wary. Dashi chewed her lip, probing this sudden conclusion. Yes, wary was the correct description; it was her own certainty that surprised her. She could recognize the people around her by scent alone; she was even starting to make sense of older scent patterns, the path someone had trod hours, or even days before. But inferring emotions? That was new.

"Ant!" Sable's voice was a hiss, trying not to echo over the river. Dashi flinched at the intrusion into her concentration. "What are you doing? Dashi!"

She waved a hand over her shoulder, reassuring Sable. She let Spit pick his way back over the saddle of land they'd just crossed, laying her reins against his neck once or twice to angle him to the north. The scrub trees were thick here, jostling for access to a small stream.

That way. Closer. Her antennae jerked left and right, absorbing tendrils of pink and tan, earthy and alive.

In the shadow of one of the hills, she saw them: oblong heads and segmented bodies. Antennae, identical to hers, only longer, danced gracefully in the air. The ants were cloaked in shadows, and Dashi couldn't tell if they were the large coppery ants that had once patched her wounds, or if they were of the darker species she'd seen while she searched for the seamripper. The wariness rolling off of them had increased tenfold since she'd come into sight. Spit pawed nervously at the thin crust of snow.

Dashi knew the taiga's giants sometimes ventured out of the dark forest during the lean winter months, but she had a vague notion that ants were dormant then. She frowned. Coming out of the taiga was one thing; coming *here*—where she happened to be—was something else entirely. The notion that she'd drawn them somehow, pulled them from their cozy tunnels and out into the cold air, flitted through her mind. Her gaze traveled toward the taiga, an ominous smudge in the distance. They couldn't possibly have scented her across such a distance, could they? *You were traveling much closer to the taiga a few days ago*, her mind countered. Could they have been following her since then?

Dashi turned Spit back toward the river, keeping the ants in her peripheral vision. What would she do if they started to follow? They remained where they were, however, tucked into the shadows amongst the barren trees.

"What was that about?" Solongo asked when Dashi was within range. A horse-sized canvas sling lay on the ground between her and the owl. Sable, Stag and the horses were gone.

"I thought something was following us," Dashi said.

"And?"

"I don't think there's a threat."

The moth blew out a breath. "We could have used your help calming the horses. Stag went ahead to scout so Sable is with them now." Her tone conveyed doubt in his ability with the horses. The owl croaked once, ruffling her feathers in agreement.

"It's the smell of predator," Dashi said.

"Well, he's all they've got right now." Her features sagged with exhaustion. "You first or the nag?"

"Him." Dashi slid from Spit's back, coaxing him forward with one hand tapping his rump. He planted his front hooves stubbornly, ears pinned against his skull as he surveyed the other heralds.

The moth tossed Dashi a length of cloth. "For his eyes."

"Thanks." Dashi tied the blindfold over Spit's eyes, snugging the ends into the bridle so that nothing flapped near his ears. She ran her hand over his muzzle, reassuring him of her presence. It had only been a few days ago that he'd found her scent strange, even threatening. Now, he whuffed softly against her palm, his ears gradually relaxing.

"C'mon, old man," she murmured. "Just a couple of steps."

When she tugged him forward, Spit followed, stepping into the sling. She held his head against her while Solongo secured the sling with a network of straps that reminded Dashi of the talon-like contraption the heralds had once used to capture her. She remembered Sevlin's leg stretched out next to hers in the moment before she was snatched up: a point of warmth in the cool darkness.

Spit squealed when his hooves left the ground. Dashi dug her fists into her thighs and watched. His legs thrashed uselessly against the air, trying to find purchase. The other horses had already gone across, she reminded herself, presumably without mishap.

"It's okay, old man," she muttered. "It will be over in a few minutes."

Maybe Spit heard her, or maybe the terror of swinging through the air sapped his fight, but he suddenly stopped moving, his legs hanging limply from the sling. The heralds pummeled the air with their wings, struggling to rise. With a sinking feeling, Dashi thought of how exhausted Solongo had looked. On cue, they dipped, Spit's hooves skimming the water. Dashi held her breath. After a long moment, the two heralds managed to lug Spit upward, finally landing on the opposite shore. Minutes later, the two heralds rose into the air again, recrossing the river in a fraction of the time.

"Ready for your turn?" Solongo touched down, giving Dashi a toothy grin. She flopped the canvas sling onto the ground between herself and the owl. "Didn't seem like you enjoyed our previous flights very much."

Dashi stepped into the sling, ignoring the straps and fisting the material in her hands instead. The idea of voluntarily tying herself up was more than she could bear.

"No, but I did enjoy making you return to New Osb empty-handed."

All amusement fell from the moth's face. She leaped into the air without warning. The owl gave a startled squawk and took two running steps to catch up. Dashi swung precariously between them, but she leaned forward, determined not to cry out as the river fell away at an unnatural angle.

She glanced once over her shoulder. The giant ants were on the move, heading back toward the taiga. She couldn't help but notice that it was only now, as she took to the air and crossed a river, that they'd decided to return to their lair.

Chapter 8

They stayed beside the river, under the cover of the trees, for the remainder of the day. Both the moth and the owl were too exhausted from the river crossing to fly farther without rest and, now that they were in Tyvalar, it was best to travel at night anyway. The five of them took turns dozing and keeping watch, barely speaking except when necessary.

Dashi was tense at first, waiting for the tether to react to this delay—the khan had directed them to travel quickly after all. She felt no compulsion to move, however, or at least not beyond her normal restlessness. Since the khan had also charged them with being "unobtrusive," she concluded that the tether must somehow be able to weigh their intentions, distinguishing between a delay in the name of prudence and one born of procrastination.

At dusk, they began readying the horses. Although Solongo had several times referred dismissively to the owl's lack of hands, Dashi had since learned that wasn't strictly true. The owl *had* fingers; they just weren't good for much. Her digits were jointed normally, but they were a fraction of the length they should be, sharp-tipped and buried halfway up her wings. After watching her wrestle with her bedroll, the stag graciously offered to roll it for her if she would keep watch. She perched atop a tree, scanning the landscape, while the rest of them packed up camp.

The bedrolls Zayaa had provided were specially made for cold weather: thick fur on the inside and waxed canvas on the outside, vastly superior to the thin fabric one Dashi had used on her last venture. Her mind wandered to how she and Sevlin had shared it, taking turns sleeping and keeping watch. The bedroll had still been warm from his body when she'd climbed in. Spit stamped in annoyance as Dashi yanked too hard on the girth.

"Sorry, old man," she muttered, patting his neck.

He flicked an ear in her direction, not even deigning a backward glance.

"Still mad about the flying?" She dug into her pocket for the crust of bread she'd saved. When she held it out, Spit sniffed once, then wolfed it down in a single gulp. "Not mad enough to turn down food though, huh?"

They would have one night of travel, another day of hiding and resting, and then they'd be through the Kurlar region and at the doorstep of Tyvalar's capital, Rucharla. *Tomorrow night*, Dashi thought, *I will be stealing from Sevlin*. She checked the leads for the packhorses and pulled herself into the saddle. There was a rustle of branches from above, followed by the sound of a beating drum, rapid and muffled, as the owl launched herself into the air. The horses barely shied this time.

The stag looked at Dashi and Sable. "I have to run ahead."

"Have to or want to?" Dashi asked.

"Both. It's the same, isn't it?" He angled his face away from her, pointing into the oncoming breeze, and Dashi had the sense he was ashamed. His nostrils flared, cataloging the same scents that she was. "To plod along, out in the open like that..." His dark liquid eyes flicked back toward her. "It's insufferable. I know that I used to be fine with a relaxed pace, back before I was stitched. I know that I'm thinking like a prey animal. But I can't ignore it. It's too uncomfortable." A shudder ran through him.

"Ah, go on then," Sable said, keeping a wary eye on his horse as he took the stirrup in one hand. "If I could run on my own two feet instead of riding this beast, I would." His horse stared back at him, ears laid flat. "And they call *us* monsters..."

A fingernail moon kept pace as they rode, but its weak light illuminated very little. Dashi let Spit have his head. He kept a sedate pace, at times slowing almost to a stop to pick his way over washed-out portions of the road.

The appearance of a low mossy wall and the scent of cattle made Dashi think that at least a few people lived nearby, but they saw no one awake. *No wonder the khan wants this land,* she thought, scanning her surroundings. *It looks like it produces food without even trying.* Despite the season, tall grass poked through the snow. The homes were fat and round, like clustered beehives, and even the roofs of far-flung outbuildings appeared to be snug and in good repair. Everything was made from rounded fieldstone, of a type Dashi had never seen. It held a white-green sheen in the moonlight and, combined with the muffled rhythm of hoofbeats and the hiss of wind through the grass, made the night seamless and dreamlike. If not for the moon, Dashi couldn't have tracked the hours.

To pass the time, she let the surrounding scents wash over her, testing herself to see if she could parse one from the other. She caught the scent of horses and far-flung cattle and the occasional whiff of the moth and the owl when the wind was right. Nearby, Sable was an intricate twist of fur and heat and hormones. There were less familiar scents too: one that was light and smelled of grass, and another that was deeper and muskier. *Field mice,* she thought, unsure how she knew, *and the stoat that's hunting them.* The thought of being hunted reminded her of the giant taiga ants.

"Do you have any affinity with other sables?" she asked, maneuvring Spit so that he was abreast of Sable's mount. "The normal, non-herald kind, I mean."

Sable cocked his head, his eyes glinting with moonlight. "I don't think I've come across any sables since I was stitched, but my sense of smell is very acute. I assume I'd be able to smell a sable as well as I could anything else."

Dashi nodded, though that wasn't what she'd meant. Maybe it was different for Solongo. Like Dashi, she had antennae. Plus, she'd been a herald longer and might have a fuller understanding of what those changes entailed.

"Nervous?" Sable asked.

"About going to Rucharla? A little, I suppose." Nervous didn't exactly describe her emotions, but it seemed wiser not to verbalize how she felt about Sevlin.

"I'm worried I'll end up with an arrow in me if I'm spotted." He gestured at his fur-covered face. "It's not like I can blend in with a crowd if everything falls apart."

"None of us could for long. The khan's tether wouldn't allow it, and no one speaks Tyvalaran."

"I do." He shrugged, anticipating Dashi's question. "Gamblers aren't picky about their company, and I had a partner who was half-Tyvalaran and half-Thracedonian. We bilked so much money from the merchants. I used to be able to fit in with whoever I was playing with, but now..." There was a plaintive note in his voice. "Abilities aside, it must be comforting to know you're one of the less conspicuous heralds."

"We're all changed past the point of blending in, Sable. Do you think no one would notice my antennae or my solid black eyes?" She glanced at him. "Besides, I thought you liked the change?"

"I said it has its benefits. Doesn't mean there are no downsides." His shoulders gave a restless twitch. "Irrelevant, either way. Want odds on our success or failure?"

"I'm not in the mood to bet," she said, remembering who their target was.

"A frank assessment then, not a bet. From the way the consul talked, you have experience with this sort of thing. Although," his eyes turned toward her, dark and measuring, "I think I would've heard of you if you were as prolific a thief as she said. Thieves are gamblers at heart, after all. Our paths must have crossed. "

"I lived in the leather circle, not the dirt, and I wasn't the type of thief you're thinking of."

"*Type?*" Sable snorted. "Let's not play at respectability. The only type of thief is the one who takes things that don't belong to her."

Dashi tilted her head, conceding.

"Still, what do you think our chances are?" he persisted.

Dashi thought of the detailed layout of the palace that Zayaa had given them and the inhuman abilities of her companions. She thought of Sevlin, missing and likely dead, unable to defend his home.

Her mouth twisted, already bitter before she answered. "I think the khan will be very pleased with us."

Daybreak found them hunkered in a wooded tract close to Rucharla. Solongo slept. Sable played an unfamiliar dice game against himself. Owl had the first watch. Dashi knew she should try to sleep. If she had been about to brave a Purek temple, she would have, and without any trouble. When she curled up in her bedroll, however, sleep eluded her entirely. Instead, she spent the day staring up at a patch of sky, imagining a scenario in which she'd found the seamripper, rescued Sevlin and freed her sister.

By the time night fell again, her eyes were gritty with fatigue. She got up, forcing herself to eat. The moth and the owl took off, flying toward Rucharla on different tangents to surveil as much ground as possible.

"Here it is," Sable said, giddy.

He pulled out a bundle of black clothing and shook it open with a snap—or what *should* have been a snap. It took Dashi a moment to realize that no sound had emanated.

"Silent as a specter," he pronounced with satisfaction. "I should have worn this the whole way."

"There was no one to sneak past."

"Who cares?"

Dashi smiled, thinking of the Yassari boots she'd stolen and how excited she and Idree had been to examine them. "Why didn't you?"

"Consul's instructions. The soundless part decreases with use." He drew his face back from the clothing suddenly, whiskers twitching. "There's something on this. Something...strange."

"Of course there is. It's Yassari."

Shadows moved over them: the moth and the owl, descending fast.

"A squadron guards each bridge into the city," Solongo said brusquely, "but they have few long-range weapons. If we fly high, they won't see us."

Sable stood up. He had knives strapped all over his body. He slipped the Yassari clothing over his head, belting it loosely so that he could reach inside it for his weapons. "I'm ready when you are."

The stag nodded. "Ancestors guide you." He would stay behind to make sure no one discovered the horses.

"You can fly with me," Solongo said. Instead of clothing, she and the owl had been given a plain length of the Yassari cloth, which they could pin as needed to accommodate their wings.

"Like a baby," Sable said primly, "not a sack of turnips. I was dizzy for a week last time."

Solongo grinned nastily and scooped him into her arms, lifting him easily. "We'll meet you on top," she said, launching herself into the air.

The owl flapped her wings, testing the makeshift garment, then bent to buckle enormous spikes to the toe and heel of each boot. When she was finished, she turned her head all the way around until her globular eyes were fixed on Dashi. Since the owl couldn't hold Dashi and fly at the same time, Dashi would ride in a sling attached to the owl's waist by a thick leather belt.

"I guess this is better than you wrapping your legs around me," Dashi said, eying the sling dubiously. "Is it easier if I run or stand still?"

The owl nodded to the east, where the trees ended and the land sloped downward. Dashi took off across the open space, the owl quick behind her. The beat of wings was loud in Dashi's ears, and she had to fight to keep from looking over her shoulder as some part of her mind screamed that she was being hunted. Suddenly, the owl was above her, rising higher and higher, until the straps of the sling were taut and Dashi was pulled from her feet. She careened wildly beneath the owl for a few moments, before the movement settled into something more predictable. *Dip and rise. Dip and rise.*

Fields passed swiftly below, giving way to rows of neatly thatched structures and a gently curving road, all dipped in silvery moonlight. The buildings swelled and multiplied, flavoring the air with the woodsmoke of countless fires. The Tyvalaran palace appeared out of the night, made from light-colored stone and lit with a thousand torches. It had been constructed on an island at the center of a placid lake. A swath of trees had been left standing around the lake and paths cut through them, winding to various parts of the city. The shores of the lake were empty at this time of night, but Dashi could imagine people gathering to admire their queen's home or to enjoy fair weather.

All of the bridges that led to the island were raised for the night. As they neared the palace itself, Dashi saw that a high stone wall had been built around the island's periphery. The top prickled with guards, still and wary in the moonlight. They looked like ants from her vantage point, and Dashi was struck by the absurdity that *she* would compare someone else to an ant. A dog barked angrily as they passed overhead. In their dark Yassari clothes, silent despite the whipping wind, the heralds were invisible.

The palace was a mass of turrets and towers in a variety of widths, heights and styles, as if they'd been constructed by a child playing out the principles of architecture. It was the tallest tower, rising straight and plain from the center of the jumble, that was their destination.

Dashi had been shocked when Zayaa pointed it out on the blueprints. *Sevlin lives* there? "Shouldn't that be the queen's?" she'd managed.

"If you asked, they would say that everything is the queen's," Zayaa had said, "even those who don't wish to be. She spends her time in the lower towers so the people can spot her eating breakfast on the balcony." Zayaa tapped the tall center tower. "Sevlin likes to keep his eye on everything at once."

There was a flash of pearly wings from below as Solongo landed on the tower roof. The owl shifted into a downward glide, the tower looming larger in Dashi's wind-blurred eyes with each passing moment. Its outer wall was embedded with windows, which wound upward, marking the ascension of the spiraling staircase on the inside.

"All the guards are outside at the base of the tower," Zayaa had explained, her fingernail denting the carefully labeled schematic. "There are doors on the staircase, set at regular intervals, triple-locked in either direction. Each of the doors is attached to a concealed cable, which goes all the way to the guardroom and rings a bell when a door is opened. If all the bells are not rung in quick succession—because, for instance, someone has to pause to pick the locks—the guards will swarm."

"Even *you* can't pick them fast enough, Zayaa?" Dashi had asked with a raised eyebrow.

Zayaa's lips flattened. "If I can't do it, you can't either. This is not a viable entrance or exit."

The top of the tower was also ringed with windows, but these were shuttered against the night and, presumably, Sevlin's extended absence. *No balconies for* his *breakfast,* Dashi noted, though the view would undoubtedly be spectacular when the shutters were open. The tower's conical roof was covered in slate shingles.

"It won't be easily shredded, like thatch," Zayaa had warned, "but it should be well within your capabilities."

The owl's wings flared just above the tower roof, pulling them up. It was so close that Dashi could see the texture of the stones and the way Sable's fur flattened in the wind. She pressed her lips together, bracing for the impact of landing, but a minute adjustment from the owl had them touching down on the slate with barely a bump.

Dashi was used to precarious perches, but Sevlin's tower was in an entirely different category. The cone of the roof was steep, with nothing but slick slate to which they could cling. The moth crouched, her wings flexing to counteract each blast of wind. Sable was prostrate, his mouth set in a frozen snarl.

The owl unbelted her half of the sling and tossed it to Dashi, who kept low, bracing one hand against the roof as she unfastened the straps that held her in place. She rose slightly, balancing on one leg so she could step out of her harness, when a gust of wind caught the canvas sling like a sail, tipping her sideways. Dashi heard Sable's exclamation of alarm, but all she could see was the edge of the roof, looming rapidly as her fingers scrabbled for purchase on the slate.

Chapter 9

The edge of the roof careened toward Dashi as she bounced over the slate shingles. She caught an upside-down glimpse of the guards below, oblivious to the body that was about to come crashing down on them.

Then her body jerked to a stop, her fingertips somehow gaining purchase on the slate. The sudden change in momentum wrenched her shoulder and she bit back a cry of pain. Dashi hung there for a moment, her feet dangling over open space as the wind beat at her silent Yassari clothing. She reached her left hand up, searching for a handhold. There was nothing but slick slate, yet somehow she managed to grasp it. She pulled herself back onto the roof, flopping gracelessly on her belly and taking great heaving breaths.

There were no discernible handholds beneath her fingers. Instead, her fingers and palms had sealed to the surface of the slate. Cautiously, she pulled at her left hand, twisting and rotating it with increasing force until it finally shook loose. She stared. The scalloped pattern she'd noticed on her palms, which had been flat before, was now raised, standing on end like a frightened cat. A thatch of hooked bristles covered the end of each scale.

"Ancestors above," she breathed, but for once she felt only gratitude for her transformation.

She crawled back to the top of the conical roof, using her hands to anchor her against the wind. The other heralds watched, their eyes wide.

Sable cocked his head, eying her from his prone position. "What do you put our odds at now?"

"Certainly no *worse* than before," Dashi said, giving him a weak grin.

"Let's go," said the moth, brusque as always. "Each minute wasted is one in which we could be spotted."

"Easy for you to hurry," Sable said. "You have wings if you get blown off this roof. Although, after last time, I guess you'd rather not be the one who survives to tell the khan we failed."

The moth shot him an ugly look, her teeth snapping.

The owl secured a rope around the point of the conical roof, and Dashi and Sable held onto it, steadying themselves. Dashi reached into her bag and pulled out a thin metal bar. As Zayaa had predicted, breaking in was well within Dashi's ability. Muscles slid beneath the gleaming skin of her arms. She was stronger than she'd been even a few days ago. With the metal bar to aid her, the slate shingles flew off like fish scales. Sable snatched each one from the air as it popped up, stacking them to one side so that nothing would fall and alert the guards.

Once the exposed area was big enough to admit a person—even a person with moth wings—Dashi grasped two of the supporting rafters, punching her feet through the insulating thatch beneath the shingles. She tumbled into the room below, dust and thatch raining down on her. There was no need to cover her tracks. The point was to take Sevlin's cache of information about the Wellspring, not hide the fact that it had been stolen in the first place.

Sable slipped through after her, cursing when the owl, who followed close behind, nearly impaled him with one of her boot spikes. The moth was last, maneuvering disdainfully through the opening to avoid scratching the diaphanous expanse of her wings. Although the room had a full circle of windows, the shutters were bolted tight. Dashi lit the lantern she'd brought, turning slowly to take in her surroundings. No artwork warmed the walls. The floor had only a single, threadbare rug to clothe it. A layer of dust covered everything, further evidence that no one had been here in weeks. The rest of the room was jammed with desks and tables and shelves, all overflowing with stacked scrolls, books, papers, astronomical charts, writing instruments, and a bead frame for keeping track of sums. The sole comfortable-looking piece of furniture—a stuffed chair perched in front of a small cold fireplace—had been patched too many times to count.

Dashi felt her eyebrows rise. She'd expected Sevlin to be, well, *neater*. As she glanced through the closest pile of papers, scrutinizing the inked illustrations, she realized the problem. Sevlin was stockpiling information on *everything*: agricultural yields, not just for Tyvalar, but for Karakal and Thracedon as well; census results, both current and decades old; Thracedonian political analyses; weather predictions and astronomical events for the coming year and for years past. There was a book about seasonal storms on the Yassar islands and a volume on the evolution of animal husbandry. A book of folklore was open to a passage about the wilewing, a fantastical bird Sevlin had once told her about, which impersonated people and wreaked havoc on all who trusted it.

It was not that Sevlin was messy, per se; his tower room was simply too small to contain all the information he'd hoarded. It was all meticulously organized and cross-referenced according to subject and date and, in some cases, author. There were books written in Karakalese, Thracedonian, Yassari and Tyvalaran. *Sevlin is a hunter who tracks many animals,* Zayaa had said. Dashi was only just now realizing *how* many.

She blew out a breath, thinking. Any information about the Wellspring would be old—in scrolls, not in books or loose sheets of paper. *Unless of course, it's already been copied and translated and the originals have been put elsewhere.* Dashi frowned. The missing section of the Purek Wellspring map should be recognizable enough, but she was also charged with finding any *other* information Sevlin had collected on the Wellspring. Since she knew precisely zero words in Tyvalaran, deciphering anything Sevlin had already translated would be impossible.

"Sable," Dashi said over her shoulder. "Do you read Tyvalaran or just speak it?"

"Both."

"Good. See if you can find anything that references the Wellspring in this stack."

He sighed, uncurling himself from the threadbare chair. "Alright."

"Solongo, Owl, you can help me." Grabbing supplies from one of Sevlin's many desks, Dashi quickly sketched out a few Purek symbols. "Remember: these are the words we're looking for: Wellspring. Fount. Heart of Life. I don't know if Zayaa explained, but they all have the same root character," Dashi pointed to a few dark lines of ink, "in case you're having trouble remembering. Call out if you find something."

They set to work, Dashi selecting the largest pile of scrolls for herself. She sifted as quickly as she could, mindful of the passing minutes. A headache formed at her temples, the result of squinting at faded writing in poor light. Her fingers paused over one scroll, attracted by its familiarity. It was the seamripper's origin story again. *How many times have I come across some variation of this,* she wondered. Zayaa's scroll had been a copy. This was the original. Dashi unfurled it, her fingers moving deftly to the spot she'd been reading when Zayaa snapped it shut.

"Bastards of magic, not free to die nor free to live, neither animal nor human but half torn between all four things. Like oxen, they are controlled by both whip and rein, with but two ways to sever the reins. For the first, the seamripper must have the half-torn in hand."

The illustration stole her breath, just as it had the first time she'd seen it: the unconscious man with his detached horns and the bright line of the tether, now cut into two pieces. She tried out the next line, frowning at the clunky linguistic style of the Pureks. "*By attending...attention...no, with focus...the seamripper can...*" There was something here, she thought, something she needed to see. The thought was more instinct than logic, but as soon as her mind articulated it, Dashi found her hands picking up a different scroll.

Her jaw clenched in frustration. She'd been commanded to execute Zayaa's instructions and Zayaa had told her specifically not to bother with anything about the seamripper.

Dashi opened the next scroll, placing it beside the one about the seamripper. Her gaze automatically scanned it for anything related to the Wellspring, carrying out the letter of the khan's commands while, from the corner of her eye, she tried to read about the seamripper.

"*The seamripper can...dig?*"

It was slow going since she had to hold two different translations in her mind at once, but eventually, she came up with the next sentence. "*With focus, the seamripper can root out all of the magic or only some.*" Dashi's fingers tapped the desk in thought.

"I think I found something," Sable said, handing her a paper full of incomprehensible scribbles. "It mentions 'ancient magic' several times, anyway."

Dashi waved a hand toward her pack without looking up.

"This is gibberish," the moth grumbled, pushing a scroll aside. "I've found nothing."

"*The second way,*" Dashi read, "*...is by the...master's....death.*" Her heartbeat quickened. The khan's death? Now here was an approach to freedom she could back wholeheartedly, if she ignored the inconvenient detail that, as his herald, she could not harm him.

Trying to squash her frustration at her faltering pace, Dashi discarded one scroll as having nothing to do with the Wellspring and opened another, again placing it next to the seamripper scroll so she could continue her double translation.

"If a...cart driver? Wagon driver?"

Another scroll was cast aside, deemed irrelevant to the Wellspring. Dashi moved on to the next.

"If a cart driver dies, the oxen will run off, the whip cast aside and the reins left to trail. So too with the half-torn."

Dashi nudged the seamripper scroll open further, only to stop in dismay. The scroll moved on to the subject of the golden needle, the different seamstresses and their backgrounds. It might have been interesting under other circumstances, but at the moment, it wasn't worth the effort of translating. She flipped through more scrolls, searching for references to the Wellspring while she mulled what she'd just learned.

There were two ways to undo the magic sewn into the heralds. The first way, the seamripper, was no longer a possibility. The second solution, the khan's death, was both eloquently simple and logistically difficult. As a herald, Dashi herself could not harm him and she didn't know many others who possessed both the motivation and the ability. The best choice would have been Sevlin because he was good at planning and from a rival country, but he wasn't here. Ese was the other obvious candidate since he'd already made an attempt on the khan's life with the Adder's Dust, but he couldn't get close to the khan without being recognized.

Idree was often in close proximity to the khan, but Dashi shied away from the thought of involving her sister in her machinations. She couldn't live with the thought of Idree being punished if the khan survived.

Zayaa? Dashi felt herself start to recoil, but she forced herself to chew over the possibility as she flipped through scrolls. *No*, she decided after only a few minutes. Zayaa could never be trusted.

Eventually, Dashi had glanced at every scroll in her pile. Though they were all Purek in origin and she found several more mentions of the seamripper and the golden needle, nothing pertained to the Wellspring. The owl and the moth hadn't found anything either, even after Dashi double-checked their work. They began turning over the room: shaking books to make sure no loose papers were hidden between the pages, emptying desk drawers and flipping them over to make sure nothing was secured to the underside. The other three heralds went after the room with relish, motivated by the khan's orders, but Dashi watched the destruction of Sevlin's property with a sick feeling.

After seeing the sheer volume of information Sevlin had collected, Dashi felt certain that Zayaa's hunch was correct: Sevlin most likely had the missing section of the Wellspring map. But where? She paced the width of the room, swerving to avoid the dilapidated chair. Under the compulsion of the khan's tether, Dashi's focus had narrowed, as if she'd glimpsed the gleam of treasure beneath a closed door. It was how she felt when she hunted. It was how she felt in the Purek ruins.

She stopped in front of the old chair, idly tracing the numerous patches on the back. The stitches were neat but large, certainly not the work of a professional. Sevlin had done it himself, Dashi thought with a wry smile. *No wonder he didn't confess to reading Purek or tell me he'd explored ruins while I was in Thracedon. He doesn't even trust anyone to repair his furniture.*

On a whim, she flipped the chair over, but she found only cobwebs and a rip that Sevlin had missed. *Where else...?* Her gaze lit on the fireplace. It was small, nowhere near the size it would need to be to warm the entire room. And, she thought, remembering her approach to the tower with sudden clarity, there had been no outlet for smoke. She began prodding the bricks, treating the fireplace exactly as she would a Purek ruin. *Hopefully, Sevlin hasn't set any traps,* she thought, only half joking.

One of the large hearth bricks shifted under her touch and Dashi sucked in a breath. She eased it upward.

Over her shoulder, Sable whooped. "You called it!"

Like the other heralds, Dashi feared the possibility of their mission's failure—and the certainty of the khan's punishment. But as her shaking fingers pulled the trove of scrolls and papers from their recessed compartment, she realized that she dreaded success almost as much. *I've done it,* she thought, and felt her shoulders sag. *I've found Sevlin's most prized possession and I'm going to take it from him.*

Chapter 10

Despite her misgivings, Dashi's hands eagerly cradled the scrolls. She knew the moment her fingers touched them that they were originals. There were four in total and she unrolled each one, scanning to make sure it wasn't anything already in Zayaa's possession. Beneath the scrolls was a flattened piece of parchment: the final section of the Wellspring map.

In the dim light, the characters were incomprehensibly tiny, but Dashi recognized the dead-end canyon that Zayaa had described as a gateway. Marks on two sides of the parchment showed where the map section should be juxtaposed with Zayaa's. Once the pieces were aligned, slightly overlapping, there would be no dead end, only the facade of an elaborate building decorated in gold paint.

Dashi wet her lips, wondering what it would look like in person. Beside the building was a passageway, narrow but extremely long, which led through the canyon wall to a valley on the other side. *The Gateway, indeed.* There was a lake in the valley but no markings to show where the Wellspring was located. However, a key in the lower corner listed a detailed set of instructions. Even without translating, Dashi could tell that the instructions were incomplete. The rest would be listed on one of Zayaa's adjoining map sections. It was a genius way to protect the Wellspring's location.

The remaining papers pertained to Tyvalaran affairs, not Purek ones. There were no illustrations to help her understand the content, but she picked Queen Lyazzat's name out of the jumble of Tyvalaran words. She had no doubt Zayaa and the khan would want to see them; they must be important if Sevlin had kept them hidden in his tower.

Too bad my orders were to bring back information about the Wellspring, Dashi thought with a grim smile. She slid the bricks back into place, concealing the Tyvalaran papers just as Sevlin had.

"This is everything?" the moth asked.

Dashi nodded.

"Good. Let's go."

Sable groaned, clearly not relishing the return flight. Dashi cast a regretful glance at the hole she'd made in the roof. She hoped it would be discovered soon, before a winter storm flooded the tower and ruined Sevlin's things.

Suddenly, the owl held up a wing, flagging their attention.

"What?" the moth asked.

"I hear it too," Sable said. "Guards."

The owl croaked in alarm.

"How could they know we're here?" The moth eyed Dashi accusingly. "The windows are shuttered. We flew in the dead of night. We have *these*." Her fingers plucked at the Yassari clothing.

"We need to leave," Dashi said, hurriedly placing the scrolls in the lightweight box she carried inside her pack, made specially to protect them. Within moments, she heard it too: the tramp of feet; voices, pitched low so as not to be overheard. She laid the Wellspring map carefully on top of the scrolls, fastened the lid, and returned the box to her pack.

The owl kicked over Sevlin's moth-eaten chair, hopping onto the side so that she could swing into the rafters. Above her, the night sky beckoned through the jagged hole. She levered herself upward, the reduced mobility of her wings making the movement awkward and slow.

The thunder of boots was loud enough for everyone to hear now.

"Hurry up," the moth hissed, her glance diving between the door and the struggling owl.

"You next," Dashi said to the moth, sizing up the breadth of the other herald's wings. Though the moth carried a sword, her wings would only be a hindrance in a conventional fight, especially in a room of this size. Better to get her and the owl outside first. Without them, Dashi and Sable weren't going anywhere anyway.

"Be ready to fly as soon as we come out," she added.

The moth nodded curtly and started pulling herself up. The footsteps were close now. Dashi slid her bow free from the side of her pack, stringing it as she pivoted toward the door.

"Sable, get ready!"

The door to the tower room flew open, slamming the wall so hard that the wood splintered. Dashi already had an arrow in the air. It hit the shield of the first guard, bouncing off harmlessly. She adjusted her second shot, sending it just below the shield's edge. The woman fell to the side, clutching her leg. On the other side of the room, Sable popped up from behind a table. His wrist flicked, so slight and fast that Dashi didn't recognize the motion as deadly until she saw a knife slot perfectly between the ribs of a second guard. She let another arrow fly, striking a third guard in the clavicle.

It wasn't enough. The Tyvalaran forces poured into the small tower room, shields raised to protect themselves from the onslaught.

"Stop your attack," one of them yelled, and Dashi was surprised to hear that the command was given in mangled Karakalese, as if they already knew who the intruders were. "You will not be hurt!"

She would have laughed at *that* if she'd had time between shots. *Aim and fire. Aim and fire.* The rhythm felt as natural as breathing. But she wasn't fighting for herself this time, she was fighting on behalf of the man who held her sister prisoner, on behalf of the woman who'd killed her best friends. She was fighting to escape Tyvalar with stolen scrolls.

Dashi drew another arrow and let it fly, watching it embed in the throat of a too-slow guard, unleashing a fountain of blood. He crashed into a window, the sound of tinkling glass lost beneath the din of the fight. "You *never miss. If you hit him, it's because you meant to.*" The words were from a dream she'd had months ago, but Baris' voice sounded clear and close. It felt like an indictment, not a compliment. She wanted to leave.

Dashi glanced up at the roof. The moth was pulling her legs through the hole.

"Sable," she yelled, backing up. "Time to go!"

The moth screamed and Dashi turned to see a raft of bright blood sliding down her calf. Sable, meanwhile, had gotten pushed against a wall. He drew his sword, leveraging his speed and agility to make up for a lack of skill. Two guards rushed at his exposed side. Dashi sent an arrow punching through one broad back, then the other. The sound of their bodies hitting the floor was just as inaudible as the breaking window had been.

"Sable!" Dashi drew her short sword and, with her other hand, tucked the bow into a loop on the side of her pack. "Now!"

The guards were nearly on top of her, with more reinforcements flooding in behind them. She and Sable had a minute, maybe two, before they were overwhelmed. Already a guard had gotten behind Dashi, scrambling up through the hole and onto the roof, with another on his heels. A shrill cry split the din before fading away as someone fell from the top of the tower.

She caught a glimpse of Sable's dark fur before a guard stepped in front of her, his sword meeting hers in a clash of metal. She parried a strike, then another, before finally gaining an opening to plunge her knife into his side. He fell back, alive but badly wounded.

The Wellspring map in her pack felt heavy somehow, freighted with the khan's desire. The urge to leave pulsed in her head. *Sable.* Dashi darted a glance in his direction, glimpsing his pinwheeling arms as he fought with blades and nails and teeth. A guard fell, victim of Sable's darting hands, only to be replaced by another. She was close enough now to hear the noises coming from the center of the melee: a horrible spitting and growling, the sound of a wild animal fighting for its life.

Dashi raised her sword, intending to join the fray. The guards surrounding Sable had their backs to her; she could knock a few out of the fight before they realized she was upon them. Even as she thought it, she knew it was a losing battle. More guards were on the way. She was only one against many.

The khan's command swam through her, an invisible current dragging at her body. *"You will aid one another when you can, but your health and that of your companions is of secondary importance to your objective."* Her sword arm lowered. *I can't just leave him,* she thought, but she turned from Sable anyway.

A guard moved between Dashi and her exit.

"Keep her here," someone shouted from the other side of the room.

Dashi darted left, but the man was there, sword raised, blocking her. He didn't attack, but it was clear he wasn't going to let her leave either.

"As quickly as possible," the khan had said. *"Avoid capture."*

She fell back a step. The guard lowered this sword. He held out his free hand, palm up, inviting her to do the same.

Dashi lunged sideways without pausing. He tried to pull his blade up to block, but she spun behind him, reversing her sword into his thigh.

His leg collapsed beneath him, blood immediately drenching his pant leg. An arterial wound, Dashi knew. Without really wanting to, her gaze moved to his face. His eyes were wide, his lips parted in surprise.

The khan made me do this, Dashi wanted to protest, but there was no one to listen. Although she'd killed before, it had never been like this, never with such wild abandon. She felt sick, even as her feet moved unperturbedly toward the flipped chair, bounding onto its side and, from there, into the rafters. She heard Sable call her name and she didn't even pause.

Dashi drew a ragged breath, reeling even as she climbed. Her body had been changed and now she suspected she was losing some other, deeper part of herself as well. What was a person but their choices and experiences and actions? Her choices were made *for* her now and her actions were striped in blood. Her experiences were fast becoming painful and guilt-ridden. What did that make her?

A hand grabbed her boot, nearly yanking her out of the rafters. She kicked savagely, but the hand hung on, twisting her off balance. She turned the fall into a flip, landing on her feet, ready to strike. Dashi's mouth fell open as she took in the man standing before her.

It was Sevlin. He was staring at the Tyvalaran blood coating her sword.

Chapter 11

For a heartbeat, Dashi was frozen. Blood slid down her blade to the crossguard and then onto the floor. The noise of the room fell away.

He's alive. Her eyes raked over him, taking in everything from his face, one side twisted with scar tissue, to his long legs, which bore no sign of injury. For someone who'd had a near-death experience in the taiga and then an undoubtedly arduous journey home, Sevlin bore remarkably few signs of wear. Her antennae darted back and forth, tasting his scent. Memorizing it.

Sevlin's gaze flicked to Dashi's head, then back to her face. She knew he saw a monster, an extension of the khan. She'd thought the same thing herself many times since her stitching, but now, imagining herself through Sevlin's eyes, she felt a sudden, hot rush of shame.

"Sevlin, I—"

She leaned toward him and Sevlin tensed. Reality came roaring back. Her sword moved with a mind of its own, slicing at an angle toward Sevlin's side. His blade was ready, catching hers in a crash of metal before it could do any damage. For a moment they strained against each other, swords locked, faces so close that Dashi could see the stubble covering his jaw. She lunged for the chair, intent on escaping back to the rafters, but Sevlin was there, blocking her. His eyes cut to the pack on her back and Dashi saw a flicker of fury.

"How are you *here*?" she blurted.

"I came to stop you."

She opened her mouth to rephrase her question, to ask how he'd gotten out of the taiga and the Purek maze, but Sevlin shook his head. "My turn. How are you, Dashi?" His voice was warm, despite the anger she'd glimpsed.

Behind him, she could see the guard she'd mortally wounded. Another guard was trying unsuccessfully to staunch the bleeding.

"Awful," she said.

She lunged, her sword sweeping upward with savage speed, trying to slip past Sevlin's guard and into the muscle of his shoulder. He deflected her blow, then expertly transitioned into an attempt to disarm her. She shifted, warding him off. She could feel the compulsion of the khan's commands, urging her to flee with the Wellspring map, but Sevlin was herding her away from the hole in the roof. Several more guards had climbed into the rafters in the meantime, intent on pursuing the owl and the moth.

"Why are *you* here?" he asked, bringing his sword around for a disarming strike. Dashi recognized the move and threw herself backward, out of range.

She shook her head in answer. The khan's commands prevented her from even addressing the subject.

"Not to kill me in my sleep, I hope." His tone was light, but Dashi knew better. His lips were a tight line, slightly pulled down on the scarred side.

"I thought you were already dead, Sevlin," she said. Her sword met his, scraping steel against steel. "Your leg and the taiga bat and the acid...and I left you." To Dashi's horror, she heard anguish leak into her voice. Sevlin blinked. Her sword cut toward him. He parried just in time.

"Zayaa said you were missing," she said. "I kept thinking that you'd—maybe if I'd—" The clamor of their swords cut her off and she let the sentence dangle.

"I told you to leave me. I wouldn't have blamed you."

"*I* would have!"

Humor touched his face—a twitch at one side of his mouth, a crinkle along the edges of his eyes. But then Dashi's blade slashed toward his head. He ducked and she struck the wall behind him with such force that it lodged there. She pulled it clean, swiveling in time to see Sevlin pop back to his feet, his amusement gone.

"And now you would kill me if the khan asked."

Dashi didn't answer. She would have dropped her eyes if she'd been in control of her body. Instead, she moved toward him again, executing a complicated series that she'd once practiced with Baris until she thought her arm would fall off. Now, however, the khan's commands pushed her through the strain. Sevlin was always there, ready to block her each time she thought—feared—she'd found an opening.

"The seam—" she began, then discovered that the words had seized inside her. *Do not aid the Tyvalarans in any way,* the khan had said. She'd been about to tell him that she'd dropped the Purek box and cup. To beg him to go back and find it.

"It's not something you need to worry about," he said gently, misunderstanding her.

She swallowed. "I'm glad you made it, Sevlin."

She watched as he deflected her next attack with swift precision, the muscles of his shoulders bunching then lengthening beneath his deel. It reminded her of the first time she'd fought him—the first time she'd met him. She'd had the same feeling then as she did now: that he could finish the fight at any moment but was choosing not to. He was testing her, she realized, waiting until she was so tired that he could disarm and capture her easily.

It pays to be underestimated, Baris said sagely in her ear. *When he thinks he has you, go in for the kill.*

No, she thought, appalled at the remembered advice, even as her body started to carry it out. She had a sudden image of Sevlin, falling to his knees like the guard she'd attacked minutes ago. *Not like that. Not by my hand.* Her arms began to slow, subtly, as if the fight had begun to sap her endurance. She fell back, deliberately retreating into a corner, though she always kept her exit in sight.

Sevlin loomed over her, his scent curling around her in an alluring wave. *Don't trust this*, she wanted to tell him. *Don't trust me.* She parted her lips, pretending to struggle for breath, and watched Sevlin's eyes flick to her mouth. Her sword slowed further. Instead of pressing his advantage, however, Sevlin checked his swing, clipping her blade instead of diving beneath it.

He doesn't want to hurt me. The thought pierced her worse than any blow Sevlin might launch. *Attack me*, she tried to scream. *Don't you know I'm trying to kill* you? Her feet tripped over themselves, a study in clumsy fatigue.

There was a flash of dark fur at the corner of her vision: Sable, in a spitting fury, making a desperate bid for escape as the Tyvalarans pressed forward, piling onto him. Sevlin's eyes flicked sideways, drawn by the shouts of his men, and Dashi's traitorous body reacted. She surged against the wall at her back, using it as a springboard to launch herself at him. Her muscles, far more resilient than she was pretending, swung at his unprotected head.

Her blade met empty air. She moved through the swing, spinning away. He was behind her now. Her back brushed against the solidness of his chest. She feigned reversing her sword to the right, then drove left, palming a knife and plunging it toward Sevlin's ribs. Somehow, he shifted away just in time, the phantom touch along her back gone. The knife struck the wall, showering dust onto her hand.

Despite the relief flooding her, Dashi kept moving. She was too far from the hole in the roof to make her exit. Instead, she bounded onto a tabletop, sheathing her sword as she did so. Jumping straight up from there, she caught a joist and swung herself up. Sevlin's hand swiped uselessly in her wake. She skipped through the rafters, jumping from beam to beam, stomping on the hand of a guard who was trying to climb up. Finally, she reached the hole. Unlike the owl and the moth, she had no wings to maneuver. Dashi thrust up with her arms, shimmied her hips through, and pulled herself onto the roof in one breath.

The scent of fresh blood and winter air hit her as she stepped onto the slate. The moth was struggling with three Tyvalarans, who'd thrown a net over her as they grappled. Blood streamed from the gash in her leg and there was a ragged hole in one of her pearly wings. A few feathers clung to the slate, evidence of the owl's involvement, though she was nowhere in sight.

Dashi started toward the moth's assailants, drawing her sword. The owl streaked into sight, hitting one of the guards in the back with her spiked boots. He slid past Dashi, screaming as he picked up momentum, then disappeared over the edge of the roof. From behind her came Sevlin's voice, cursing vehemently.

Dashi whirled, her sword raised. "Go back inside, Sevlin."

Her tone was threatening. *Go back inside so we don't hurt you.* If he tried to stop them from leaving with the scrolls, she had no doubt that's what would happen. The khan's commands demanded it. She shifted closer to the moth, not taking her eyes off Sevlin. Behind him, another guard climbed onto the roof, then another. A rope, hastily looped around their waists, trailed back inside the tower room, acting as an anchor.

The guard standing behind Sevlin spoke in a low voice. "Prince Sevlin, you shouldn't be out here."

Sevlin ignored him, his eyes on Dashi. "I can help you," he said. He held out a hand, beseeching her to stay, but Dashi saw him shift his feet, preparing to launch himself at her.

In her mind, Dashi took his hand, holding it carefully, the same way he'd cradled her knife when they'd parted in the Purek maze. She would apologize for failing to find the seamripper and for ransacking his tower. She would ask how he'd escaped the maze. She would tell him how much she—

Dashi dove toward the moth, just as the owl burst out of the darkness again, her spiked boots aimed at the guards' heads. At the same moment, the moth surged upward, yanking her wings free of the net. Dashi's arms locked around Solongo's waist and then they were falling from the tower roof. Sevlin shouted, involuntary and formless, but Dashi's focus was on the sky, spinning above, and the ground, speeding toward her. Her stomach lurched as the moment dragged out, time stretching and contorting. She was falling for a split second; she was falling forever. Then the moth fanned her wings, catching the air with a whip-like crack, and they sailed upward.

They were close to the ground. The lake lapped gently. The light from the palace spilled over them, making the moth's wings blaze.

"Now!" someone shouted. Arrows sliced the air nearby.

Solongo gasped as one hit her shoulder. Her wings stuttered and for a sickening moment, they dipped back toward the ground. She kept flying, pulling them incrementally upward, but the rhythmic beat of her wings was broken.

Dashi knew the guards would be scrambling for fresh arrows. She knew she and the Solongo were still in range. Glancing back, she saw Sevlin's lean figure gesturing wildly at his guards. No curtain of arrows came. Instead, bows were lowered and the Tyvalarans began to retreat through the hole that Dashi had put into their roof.

The black waters of the lake were nearly behind them when the screams began: long, undulating wails, an animal caught in its death throes. It took Dashi several minutes to recognize the voice, far as it was from human speech.

Sable.

Chapter 12

The moth made it out of Rucharla before she tumbled to the ground. Dashi bounced over the frozen furrows, hitting her shoulder and hip before she finally rolled to her feet. The moth lay where she'd fallen, moonlight catching on her quaking wings.

She peered up at Dashi, ashen with pain. "What happened to Sable?"

"The Tyvalarans captured him. He's not coming unless we go back to get him," Dashi said. *'Your own health and that of your companions is of secondary importance.'*

Solongo rallied enough to give Dashi an accusing glare. "You were right beside him."

"Yes, well, I don't get to choose my actions, do I?" Dashi turned a quarter circle, squinting at the landscape. The moth lay next to a hedge that divided a fallow field. The deep shadow of the hedge might shield them from a passing glance, but it wouldn't be enough to hide them if someone was really searching.

And someone would be.

Sevlin would try to recover the scrolls before they reached the border. *She* certainly would, if their positions were reversed. The thought made Dashi want to find the nearest road and sit down to wait for him. Somehow she could still taste the particular scent of him, a tune hovering at the edge of her thoughts. The khan's orders on capture were clear, however. The urge to move was a hot coal, inching closer to her skin until she was practically hopping with the impulse. She waved at the night sky, trying to catch the owl's attention.

"I can see her heading away from us," Solongo said.

"If anyone should be able to find us in the dark, shouldn't it be her?"

"Too frightened. She should have been remade as a mouse, not an owl."

"Isn't she bound by the tether to help us?"

"Like you helped Sable?" Solongo sneered and closed her eyes.

"*We* have the scrolls."

The tramp of boots echoed from somewhere in the direction of the city. The tether sent a sizzle of pain up Dashi's spine. She stiffened, antennae rigid. The moth hissed.

"She won't have seen us drop off because we were behind her. Her eyes are in the front of her head, and when she's focused on something—prey in sight, escape from a threat—she gets tunnel vision. She'll circle back when she realizes what happened, but until then she won't be much help."

"Well, get up then. I know you feel the tether telling you to move. The horses aren't far. You can ride Sable's mount once we get there."

The moth's sneer deepened, but she opened her eyes. "I'd sooner be captured."

"I'd sooner you were too, but that's another one of those things I don't get to choose." She looked at Solongo and knew they were lying. They'd both felt the painful prod from the tether, and they'd both heard Sable's screams; Dashi wouldn't wish that on anyone.

She held out a hand and, when the moth clasped it, she pulled the other herald to her feet. "Right now, I still think we can both escape. Let's go before that changes and I have to leave *you* behind too."

They hobbled frantically in the direction of the horses, Dashi bearing most of Solongo's weight as they ducked through hedges and scurried across fields.

"Ancestors above," Dashi grumbled. "You may look like you're all delicate bones and wings, but you don't feel like it."

"And I thought an ant," Solongo panted, "would be able to lift me without breaking a sweat."

"Apparently not." Dashi helped the other herald across a ditch.

On the other side, Solongo sagged against a fence. "I just need to rest—"

"Get up," Dashi snapped. Already she could feel the urge to leave Solongo building in her body. "You have a child to stay alive for. No one wants their mother bleeding to death in a foreign country."

Solongo gave a bitter laugh. "There is no question," she said, wiping her forehead with a bloodied hand, "that my child would be better off if that arrow had hit my heart."

The stag had smelled Solongo's blood and fear a long way off. He was waiting for them at the edge of the trees, holding the saddled horses. Both the horses and the stag stood stiff-legged, eyes rolling, as they reacted to the anxiety that hung in the air. He could barely stand still as he helped Dashi hoist Solongo into a saddle. As soon as she picked up the reins, he bounded away.

The owl swooped down on them as they neared the river.

"Took you long enough," Dashi shouted up at her. The horses were flagging from the run, and the sun had risen hours ago, both of which increased their chance of capture.

The owl ignored Dashi, her round, lamp-like eyes turning toward Solongo. It was hard to tell, between the feathers and the beak, but Dashi thought she saw concern on the owl's face.

Solongo *did* look bad, Dashi thought, eying the other herald's waxy complexion. How much was due to fatigue and how much to blood loss, she didn't know. *Not just blood*, she corrected herself. There was something else flowing out of the wound Dashi had bandaged, and it was too pale to be called blood. Dashi didn't know how much the moth had lost—or how much she could stand to lose—but, inhuman anatomy aside, it was usually best when the liquid stayed on the *inside*.

At the river's edge, Dashi selected Spit and a placid sorrel for the moth, blindfolded both, and led them toward the owl. She would be ferrying Dashi, the stag and the two mounts on her own. The packhorses and most of their provisions for the return trip would be left behind. The moth leaned against a tree trunk, her arms wrapped around her stomach. She'd insisted that she could fly herself across, but Dashi did not feel confident. *Even Sable wouldn't want to wager on that*, she thought grimly.

"Are you sure you can do this?" Dashi asked the owl. Better to see Spit left behind altogether than accidentally dropped in the middle of a freezing river because the owl had overestimated her strength.

The owl snapped once and stretched her wings in what Dashi supposed was a show of confidence. Spit threw his head back, nostrils quivering. Suppressing her unease, Dashi positioned him over the sling harness, hooking it around him. He turned his head toward her, ears twitching nervously. She ran a reassuring hand over his neck.

"Believe me, old man, it's better to be first this time."

Both ends of the sling were fastened around the owl's waist. Though Spit balked under his blindfold, Dashi tugged him into a reluctant trot—anything to give them some momentum—while the owl ran beside them. Dashi peeled off to one side as the owl took to the air, Spit swinging and snorting beneath her. His hooves hovered just above the river, and Dashi watched their progress, lips pressed together and fists digging into her thighs, until they'd made it to the other side.

The owl's second trip was even more precarious. The sorrel's hooves never lost contact with the water. Then it was Solongo's turn. She nearly plunged into the river, righting herself only at the last moment.

By the time they were all safely inside Karakal, the owl and the moth were nearly collapsing from exhaustion. Dashi pushed them forward anyway. If it had been anyone else in pursuit, a national boundary would have conveyed some sort of protection, but with Sevlin, she couldn't be sure. Thus, the tether compelled her to move.

They stopped only when the sun began to sink behind the hills of the near-taiga. The air turned frigid with its departure. They huddled in a semi-circle, chewing instead of talking. They had enough food for half a dozen men; the four heralds could easily demolish twice as much.

Cold settled on Dashi in a mantle. Hunger gnawed from within. She turned her hands over in her lap, wishing they held more food. Perhaps it was the absence of Sable's chatter, but the night was more ominous than it had been on the way to Rucharla. Deep pockets of shadow bracketed the hills, impenetrable to the naked eye but fertile ground for the imagination. *There's nothing nearby; you'd scent it.* The bony fingers of scrub trees reached toward the moon. More than once, Dashi thought she saw a silvery finger of taiga mist questing over the land, but whenever she turned her head she found only a path of moonlight. The mist won't come here, she assured herself; the taiga is two hours away.

Unease continued to roil her. She always felt this way near the taiga, like she'd stepped into the strike circle of a steppe adder. The other heralds seemed to second her feelings. The owl picked at her feathers, smoothing, ruffling, then smoothing again, the nervous gesture of some-one too tired to move but too restless to sleep. Solongo was a statue across from Dashi. Her face, profiled in the stream of moonlight, was hard.

"He'w dddoasthh uthh," the owl said, her beak clattering nervously after each word.

Dashi jumped. "I didn't think you could speak," she blurted.

The owl's head bobbed once.

"You just don't like to?"

Another nod.

"Why will the khan punish us?" She couldn't tell whether the owl had said "he'll toast us," or "he'll roast us," but either way the implication wasn't good.

"Thwaaabwew."

Dashi stared, uncomprehending.

The stag spoke, his voice a hoarse whisper from the shadows. "Because of Sable."

"*Sable*? Because we're coming back without him?"

The owl's feathered head bobbed.

"The *khan* was the one who told us to leave one another if it meant getting the scrolls to safety. We did what we were commanded to do."

"It won't matter," Solongo said bleakly, stirring for the first time since they'd stopped. "It didn't matter when we lost Fish either. Maybe Sable is the lucky one after all."

Dashi shuddered, remembering the sound of his screams. Would the pain keep up for as long as he was captured, or would the tether eventually calm down?

"How did the Tyvalarans know we were there?" The moth asked. "The tower windows were shuttered."

"I don't know," Dashi said. "The man I was fighting—Prince Sevlin—said he came because he knew we were there. If someone had spotted us flying we'd have heard the alarm being raised."

The owl ruffled her feathers.

"They had nets," Solongo said. "Like they were expecting to capture someone."

A trap. Trust Sevlin to be one step ahead, Dashi thought, though for the life of her, she couldn't figure out how he'd gotten back from the taiga—and in apparent health—with enough time to organize an ambush. *Zayaa won't be happy he's alive,* she thought, but the thought of Sevlin, alive and safely out of the taiga, warmed Dashi's chest and spread to her limbs, slow and sweet as honey.

Solongo cast Dashi a suspicious look. "Don't look so pleased. Getting ambushed won't be an excuse."

A day of travel and a night with no sleep had made Dashi nearly as tired as the winged heralds. She fell asleep as soon as her eyes closed, though she was awakened several times by the complaints of her empty stomach. Hours later, the first rays of dawn slid beneath her eyelids, chasing away her dreams of food. Dashi lay in her bedroll for a few minutes, dreading that first step out into the cold. Her stomach was prodding her incessantly, however, so she forced her eyes open and rolled over.

Snow coated the ground and dusted the waxed exterior of her bedroll. Next to her cheek, however, a small patch of color remained: a pyramid of crumbs. *Just like in my cell.* Dashi gave the pile a cautious poke. This offering was different from the previous one, full of tiny seeds, shriveled berries, and insect corpses. *What in the name of the ancestors...?*

Her antennae were better at solving the puzzle than her brain was. They danced through the air, finding a twist on a scent she already knew. *Taiga ants.* How could that be? There were no footprints. Dashi frowned, not understanding until she bent to study the unmarred covering of snow. In the perfect, clear light of morning, she could just make out lines of minuscule tracks crossing between her bedroll and a stand of trees. Not giant ants but tiny ones, roused from dormancy to bring her food from their meager winter stores.

They reached New Osb two days later. The people of the prison camp labored steadily on the outer wall, their arms bare in the freezing air. Dashi noticed Solongo, still on horseback, watching them but carefully, from the corner of her eye. A boy with an unruly head of curls and wind-plastered clothes looked up, pausing in his labor to shade his eyes. The old man next to him did the same, then another prisoner and another, each staring silently until the monstrous heralds had passed.

A cage hung over the inner gate. In it was a putrid set of bones: Jochi, the khan's brother. Dashi darted a glance at Solongo, wondering if the other herald felt any guilt at being the one to put him there, but she stared straight ahead.

In the great hall, the khan was slumped on his throne, even yellower than before but, unfortunately, still very much alive. There was no audience this time, save Zayaa and the normal contingent of guards. *At least Idree isn't here*, Dashi thought, tension sloughing off her shoulders.

Dashi took off the pack and placed it at the foot of the dais, backing away with her head bowed. Zayaa leaned forward, rigid with excitement. The khan ignored the pack. His eyes were on the heralds. Without warning, pain whipped through Dashi, burning up her spine and shooting into her limbs. She crashed to the floor, writhing onto her side. Beside her, the owl was making a horrible croaking sound. Her taloned fingers scratched uselessly against the marble.

The pain stopped as abruptly as it had started.

"On your feet," the khan said.

Dashi lurched into a standing position. Her breath came in painful gasps. Her legs wouldn't straighten fully. The moth and the stag stood on either side of her, wide-legged, braced for a blow. The owl crawled behind them.

"Pwwpwwpp," she panted, pulling herself to her feet. Her beak was vibrating so much that her words were even less discernible than usual.

"Silence," the khan roared. The owl's beak snapped shut. "Someone who can actually *speak*: tell me why only four of you have returned."

Solongo dipped her head. "We were ambushed, Most High. The Tyvalaran prince and his guards knew—"

Zayaa ripped her attention away from the pack. "Prince Sevlin is *alive?*"

Dashi nodded.

"He and his men stormed the tower, Most High," the moth said to the khan. "Sable was captured."

"I said not to be captured." The khan's tone was dangerous. "I hope his tether burned him alive before they killed him."

Burned alive by the tether? Killed? Dashi kept her face still, thinking of Sable's screams. Beside her, the stag jerked with surprise.

"Yes." The khan smiled. "The sable is dead. I can feel the absence of his tether." He looked at Zayaa. "You promised me the heralds would be an invincible fighting force, but two have been killed already. Tell me, Consul, how does that factor into your plans?" He flicked his fingers and all four heralds crumpled to the floor, gyrating with pain.

Through her own strident gasps, Dashi could hear Zayaa's voice, the cadence rising and falling rhythmically.

Without warning, Dashi's pain stopped, leaving her gasping in its aftermath. The owl, the moth and the stag were still being punished, though their cries had turned to whimpers.

"Having a second pair of eyes, no matter how amateurish, makes the process go much faster," Zayaa was saying. "So the ant must be spared for now."

The khan made a dissatisfied grunt, but Zayaa responded in a tone both placating and confident. "Our plan is still viable, Most High. The heralds are vital to conquering the continent, yes, but they will be playthings compared to the power you will soon wield. We will find the Wellspring."

"When?" the khan demanded in a low voice.

"If we have the final piece of the Wellspring map, we can leave within the week," Zayaa said. "Now, shall we look at what your heralds have brought us, Most High?"

The khan must have given his permission because Dashi heard her pack being opened.

"Yes," Zayaa breathed. "The missing piece of the map."

"Good," the khan said, but he sounded sullen.

"Armies take time to grow," Zayaa soothed, nearly inaudible over the keening sound coming from the stag. "Your heralds are few in number, but they won't always be."

"The ant is no stronger than a normal person. The moth is too slow at flying to be of any use in a fight, and the owl is fast but can't hold a sword or bow while she's in the air."

"Then we will make you more heralds."

The khan made a sound of annoyance. "Get up, Ant."

Dashi crawled to her feet, standing between the crumpled, twitching heralds like their vanquisher. A bitter scent perfumed the air. *Fear*, she thought, and realized that she must be emitting it as well as reading it. Solongo's spine arched. Her head cracked against the floor in a sickening rhythm. Was this how they'd been punished the first time they'd failed to bring Dashi back from the taiga?

Zayaa stared at the scroll in her lap, her forehead creased in thought. "Look at this, Most High."

The khan gave it a cursory glance, before turning his attention back to the heralds.

"This is everything you discovered?" Zayaa asked Dashi.

Focus on the exact question. Dashi forced her mind away from the other things she'd learned on the journey: that the khan's death would break the tethers as surely as the seamripper would; that ants sometimes brought her food when she was hungry; that Sevlin had other secret documents, which she'd purposely left behind.

"I brought anything that might pertain to the Wellspring," she said. Then, worried that her answer sounded too brief, she added, "The tower is well-protected."

"Yes, Prince Sevlin would not want these to fall into our hands," Zayaa murmured.

But they have, because of me.

Zayaa replaced the documents in their protective box and stood, cradling the whole thing in her arms. "If you would excuse me, Most High, I wish to examine these further."

The khan nodded, not bothering to rise.

Zayaa took a step, then stopped. "I beg you to remember what happened last time, Most High." She tilted her head at the other heralds. "We must have them in good condition if we are to leave on time."

Dashi tensed, certain that the khan would react violently to being admonished. To her surprise, he merely slumped further on his throne. "I will heed your advice, Consul. Only a few more minutes."

"And the ant, Most High?"

"You may have her." He looked at Dashi. "You will follow the consul's instructions and aid in her preparations to the best of your ability."

The moth, the stag and the owl lay on the floor, writhing in foul-smelling puddles. Dashi turned obediently, stepping over them to do the khan's bidding once more.

Chapter 13

In the planning room, Zayaa went directly to the center table to lay out the final piece of the Wellspring map. She leaned over to study it, her amethyst pendant swinging forward to dangle over the tabletop. Her hand came up, toying with it absently.

Dashi couldn't take her eyes off the pendant. It winked with light each time it moved. She knew it was unwise to provoke Zayaa, but the khan's treatment of the heralds had left her upset and combative. It was not a frame of mind for resisting temptation.

"Why do you even wear that?" she asked.

Zayaa glanced up to see what Dashi was talking about, then gave a negligent shrug. "Why shouldn't I? It's stunning, and it's mine."

"Because you *killed* the people who gave it to you?" Dashi vividly remembered how Altan and Baris had come to her separately. Each man had been struck by the beauty of a pendant he'd seen in a Purek ruin. Each man wanted Dashi to retrieve it so he could give it to Zayaa.

Zayaa smiled cheerily and handed Dashi one of Sevlin's scrolls. She pointed to a small reading table. "Translate. I'll look over it. If there are any uncertainties about tense, note them. It could be important."

Zayaa's refusal to engage made Dashi even angrier, something she hadn't known was possible. She was gentle with the scroll, however, unfurling it and pinning it open with the mismatched set of weights assembled on the table: two heavy silver baubles; an odd finial made of purple glass; a rough chunk of milky green stone, threaded through with turquoise. As her fingers brushed the rock Dashi yelped, jerking her hand back.

"What *is* that?" She leveled a glare at Zayaa.

"Lechitite." Zayaa picked up one of the scroll weights she'd been using and walked over to swap it out with the milky green rock. She tossed it in the air once, assessing its weight. "It reacts to magic." She glanced at Dashi. "Badly."

The burning, electric feeling still prickled her fingertips. "I've seen that stone before. In Purek temples. And some of the buildings in the Kurlar region were made of it."

Zayaa's eyes snapped to her face. "It occurs naturally in that part of Tyvalar," she said, sounding somewhat cautious. When Dashi didn't reply, she added in a more relaxed tone, "As for the Pureks, they used it because the veins of magic tend to wander. When they built a temple around one, they would first dig a pit and line it with lechitite to keep the vein in place."

"So that it didn't drift into another part of the temple and burn people."

Zayaa nodded.

"What happens when an entire vein touches it?" The brief contact with her skin had felt like it might start a fire.

"My understanding is that the vein withdraws as soon as contact is made. The reaction is entirely on the magic's end; the lechitite isn't corroded or melted. People who aren't touched by magic can handle it just fine. There was a certain era when it was popular in Purek jewelry making. Not for heralds, of course." Zayaa's voice turned thoughtful as she wandered back to her table. "Now that I think about it, keeping a chunk of this around isn't a bad idea. A useful deterrent."

Dashi propped her elbows on her desk, settling in for the slog of translating. At first, it seemed that the scroll she'd been assigned had nothing to do with the Wellspring. It was a biography of sorts, describing the life of a particular seamstress with mind-numbing detail. Dashi's jaw cracked in a yawn. Finally, at age forty, after hundreds of successful stitchings, the seamstress' life became interesting. She'd participated in a religious rite at the Wellspring. Having just completed a stitching, she was wearing the golden needle around her neck. As she bent to deliver her offerings, the chain holding the golden needle somehow broke and the needle fell into the Wellspring.

"The Wellspring swallowed the golden needle and Nature's balance was shifted," Dashi translated with care. *"Without the needle as a valve, the magic erupted. Sparks danced from her fingertips. The priest next to her cried out in fear and his heart was turned to stone. Terror-stricken at this Unbalance, the other priests beheaded"*—here, Dashi sat up straight—*"the seamstress, hoping to restart the cycle. Eventually, the needle reemerged from the Wellspring and graced them by choosing a new wielder."* After that, the high priests made sure that the golden needle was never carried into the cavern of the Wellspring again.

The sun was slanting through the window by the time Dashi finished checking her translation. She'd written down half a dozen variations of the more complicated sections because she was unsure which was correct, but diction didn't change the overall tale. She leaned back in her chair, torn between horror at the idea of a seamstress being beheaded, and elation at the thought of Idree having power of her own, however brief. Her gaze shifted involuntarily to Zayaa as she imagined Idree shooting magic from her fingertips.

"If the translation is finished, bring it here," Zayaa said, not looking up.

Dashi rose, taking the scroll and her translation with her. Zayaa handed her another, smaller scroll in exchange.

"Now translate this one."

Dashi returned to her table and opened the scroll. It was short and plain, with none of the illustrations and decorated initials that usually adorned Purek scrolls. As she started translating, she noticed other differences as well. It was recorded in first person, like a journal entry, instead of the dry third person that Purek scribes typically used. There was no scribe mark at the beginning of the scroll or, when she paused to check, at the end, which meant that the scroll was technically unofficial.

The first half of the scroll took the better part of two hours to translate. It was a description of a battle, fought against a bellicose country to the north of the Purek empire. Dashi paused, double-checking this translation. Current geography showed nothing north of the taiga; she'd never heard of anything on the other side. She fell back into the translation, absorbed by the descriptions of battle axes and blood. The scroll's author was a fierce fighter, who thoroughly enjoyed describing every battle conquest.

A servant arrived bearing food just as Dashi reached a stopping point in her work. When she tried to get up, however, she found that her legs wouldn't obey. She considered ignoring the food—the idea of asking Zayaa's permission to eat was enough to turn her appetite—but when her stomach growled loudly, Dashi pictured ants parading through the room to bring her crumbs. She cleared her throat.

"Can I...?"

"You may eat." Zayaa gave her a lazy smile. "Not over the scrolls."

Obviously, Dashi thought, but she said nothing, afraid her permission would be revoked. After she'd eaten, she washed her hands in a basin of soapy water that had been provided for that purpose, drying them thoroughly with a clean cloth to avoid harming the scrolls.

Back at her desk, the first thing she noticed was that the latter half of the scroll shifted in tone: not victorious but frantic. *"They have taken him,"* Dashi translated, copying the words in careful Karakalese. *"Unloved whoresons, each one. While I was beating back an incursion of savages, the people of my own motherland conspired against me. They hold him captive—I know not where—and sent two messengers with a list of demands, including the right to have future heralds tethered to them, and the anointing of a new khagan, to whom I must pledge submission. I will never submit again, even for my son."*

There was no telling when the scroll had been written. The Pureks were constantly taking land and losing it, then going to war to take it again, so the battle scenes were hardly definitive. Even the kidnapping wasn't a watershed event; these types of political machinations were common in Purek history. It was all part of nature's balance, they believed, to disrupt established power. The author was clearly a person of importance, based on the kidnappers' demands. The fighting described at the beginning of the scroll, combined with the absence of a scribe mark, made Dashi think the author was a general, rather than a high priest or a khagan. The latter two groups usually kept an official scribe in their entourage.

"I hung the head of the first messenger from a chain, threaded through his eye sockets. Then I pierced the second messenger with a spear, all the way through, just below the shoulder so that he didn't bleed out, and hung the chain from the spear's shaft, so that he had no choice but to bear the first messenger's head back to his co-conspirators."

Dashi's eyebrows rose. *Definitely a general.* She thought of Ese who, while not a general, had once been high up in the Karak military. He seemed capable of a similar level of ruthlessness.

"The priests preach the Path of Balance, but it has brought me only suffering. There were those who said I acted asymmetrically when I killed the

bastard who came before me. Yet it has resulted in unparalleled happiness for myself and prosperity for the empire. I have no choice but to break from the Path again and hope that they are wrong a second time. I will not submit. I will not let someone use my son against me, to inflict suffering on him the way that it was inflicted upon me."

The scroll ended abruptly without detailing the author's plan. Dashi's fingers drummed out a rhythm on the table. It wasn't just the journal-style writing that was strange, she thought. Even the words themselves looked different: smudged and crossed out in places, as if the author had been in too much of a hurry to fix the mistakes. Another one of Sevlin's scrolls had been the same, she remembered, though she couldn't recall if it had also been unsigned.

Zayaa looked up, eyes sharp. "What did you find?"

"I guess I'd call it a heroic epic," Dashi said, "but an unfinished one. It never mentioned the Wellspring."

"Battle stories." Zayaa waved a hand and went back to her work. "There's rarely anything useful in those. That's why we always assigned them to you for translation."

"You could have told me the truth." The words came before she could stop them. The thought had plagued her ever since she'd found out her friends were Tyvalaran spies.

"Oh, Dashi," Zayaa crowed, propping her chin in one hand with every appearance of delight. "I'll bet that's what really gets to you, isn't it? The way you followed Altan around like a lost calf and begged for Baris' attention." Zayaa made her voice rougher and more childlike, an imitation of a young Dashi. "*'Oh Baris, spar with me. Notice me, please.'* You were so besotted with Baris and Altan, but they never even told you who they were."

Dashi could feel her hands trembling. She crossed her arms so Zayaa wouldn't see. *Rage*, she told herself. *That's all you're allowed to feel in front of Zayaa. Not sorrow. Not betrayal. Only rage.*

"I was young when I met Altan." Dashi forced the words to come out slowly. Calmly. "Back then, he didn't tell me because he was trying to protect me. No one with a conscience would put a child in the middle of espionage—"

"He *did* put you in the middle, you fool! Altan suspected he was close to being discovered and did he call you off? *No.* He kept you in danger because he had a goal to accomplish and *he needed you to do it*. Altan with a *conscience*!" Zayaa threw back her head and laughed, the sound so at odds with the tone of their conversation that Dashi flinched. Zayaa leaned forward, her dark eyes shining maliciously. "You have no idea what Altan and Baris were capable of."

"No matter what it was, you did much worse," Dashi said, and by some miracle, her voice stayed even. She picked up her quill and stared blindly down at the scroll, determined not to give Zayaa the reaction she so clearly wanted. No matter what Zayaa said about Altan and Baris, Dashi had known them. They were not cruel men.

Zayaa got up and walked to the large table, leaning over to study the map of the continent. She appeared so engrossed that, for a minute, Dashi could almost believe that the subject had been let go. But this was Zayaa. She never let anything go, just paused while she reassessed her next strike.

On cue, the khan shuffled through the door, leaning heavily on a cane. Dashi had never seen him use it in public.

Zayaa looked up, the bitter expression melting from her face in favor of a buttery smile. "Good evening, Most High. I hope you slept well."

"I told the Yassaris we will go forward with the agreement," the khan said, not bothering to return the pleasantries. "I have ways to get the full amount."

More people might be thrown into jail and their property auctioned, Dashi thought darkly, but the khan and the Yassaris would have their deal, no matter the cost.

"Excellent, Most High," Zayaa cooed. "I'll have Tuya finalize everything."

The khan nodded, his gaze falling on the scrolls Zayaa had been pouring over. "You better have found something."

"I have, indeed," Zayaa said in a bright voice. "Let me find—" She raised her head with the air of someone who'd just remembered something. "While I'm searching, I wonder if you might help me with something, Most High? Ancient Purek is a very complicated language and needless blather distracts me when I'm translating. It would be helpful if your herald stayed silent unless spoken to."

Dashi's head jerked up, just as the khan's red-rimmed eyes swerved in her direction.

"She wasn't punished fully because you needed her," the khan said. "If she's not working, then I don't need to stay her punishment any longer."

"I do still need her, Most High," Zayaa said quickly. "Her work is satisfactory, it is only that her tongue needs stilled. There's also the issue of protecting our plans...She shouldn't be able to tell anyone about what she's been translating."

"Very well." To Dashi, he said, "When you are in this room, you are forbidden to speak unless you're asked a direct question. When you're out of this room, you're forbidden any form of communication about the Wellspring or what you've learned here, unless it is to answer a question from me or my consul. Do you understand?"

"Yes, Most High," Dashi said.

Smiling, Zayaa held up Dashi's translation. "Here we are, Most High, listen to this."

The khan moved toward the fireplace while Zayaa trailed after, reading aloud. She must have sensed his impatience because she skipped over the seamstress' early life and went straight to the most relevant part.

"The Wellspring swallowed the golden needle and Nature's balance was shifted. Without the needle as a valve, the magic flowed into the priest standing next to the seamstress and sparks danced from his fingertips."

Dashi's lips parted in surprise, but the khan's commands kept her silent. That's not what the scroll had said at all; the magic manifested in the *seamstress*, not a bystander. Unless her translation had been wrong and this was one of the corrections Zayaa had made? Dashi held the notion for only a moment before discarding it. She hadn't seen Zayaa make many corrections, for one thing. Secondly, she had checked that particular section repeatedly. She was certain she had accurately captured the overall events in the Purek story.

Zayaa was angled toward the khan, her dark hair forming a gleaming curtain that hid their faces. Dashi leaned forward, straining to hear what was being said.

"...not, Most High?...standing closest to the seamstress when it's dropped...power would be limitless."

"As you say, Consul." The khan rose, a satisfied expression on his sallow face. "As you say."

The two of them left the planning room, still in quiet conversation, but a moment later Zayaa was back, a smirk fixed upon her flawless face. "Now that you can't dwell on the past—out loud at least—I think we'll get along much better."

It was a clear attempt to bait her, but Dashi was too stunned to react. She stared at the scroll in front of her without seeing it, her mind wrestling with the implications of what she'd just learned. Why would Zayaa lure the khan to the Wellspring with the promise of magic, when everything Dashi had read suggested that, if the golden needle was dropped into the Wellspring, the magic would go to Idree instead? The khan would realize he'd been duped—at the Wellspring, if not before—and then he would have Zayaa punished. No, Dashi corrected herself, he would have Zayaa *killed*.

And good riddance, she thought cooly, except she had a feeling that it wouldn't come to that. There was something else at stake here, something Dashi couldn't see. Something Zayaa was already working toward. *She's prevented me from telling anyone about this, and she did it before I even knew anything was afoot,* Dashi thought grimly. *Silencing me had nothing to do with our conversation about Altan and Baris. It's to prevent me from saying anything that might give up her plans.*

Dashi shook her head. In a contest of wiles between the khan and Zayaa, she would put her money on Zayaa every time. She just hoped she could keep Idree clear of the mess.

That's when it hit her. *Idree*. The khan believed that if Idree dropped the golden needle into the Wellspring, he would gain power. Regardless of what was driving Zayaa's lies and obfuscations, Idree wouldn't be staying in the safety of New Osb. Her sister would be going back into the taiga too.

Chapter 14

The ants brought more crumbs to Dashi overnight. She swept them out of sight when she awoke. It felt primitive, to be seen wallowing in the discards of other people's meals. *Every scrap of dignity counts at this point,* she thought grimly, remembering how she'd had to ask Zayaa's permission to stop translating so she could eat. Now that the khan had commanded her to be silent in the planning room, she wouldn't even be able to do that. She bolted her breakfast while she waited to be summoned, thinking about how Zayaa had outmaneuvered her.

Her summons, when it came, was a surprise. "You are to accompany me to the practice yard for instruction," Tuya announced in a formal voice.

Dashi didn't move. "What subject could you possibly be instructing? How to assassinate people with carnivorous plants?"

Tuya's lips thinned. "The *justiseed* is hematophagous, not carnivorous, and it should not be spoken of lightly. The dispensation of justice is the sacred duty of all citizens of the United Yassari Merchantry."

Dashi didn't bother to hide her disgust. *Duty. Ancestors protect me.* She pushed away from the wall she'd been leaning against and followed Tuya.

"Does it go after any blood or only human?"

No answer.

"Do the thieves turn into trees?"

This earned a scoff from Tuya. "It's not a children's story. Nothing can turn someone into something—" With a flustered glance at Dashi's antennae, Tuya broke off. "The seed germinates in the presence of blood. Any blood."

"It does a lot more than germinate."

"It continues consuming blood until it reaches a state of maturity. As it grows, it releases a neurotoxin to prevent its host from escaping so that the remainder of the blood and tissue can be absorbed more slowly."

"So it uses your blood to grow fast at first and then it slows down and takes its time digesting you?"

"Not *me*," Tuya said primly. "I am not a thief."

"Blessed ancestors, you Yassaris are a sick lot. How did you even *think* of that?"

"We didn't invent it. It grows naturally in Yassar."

"One of you thought to use it against other people."

"It is no more and no less than a thief deserves," Tuya said, but there was a note of reserve in her voice that made Dashi glance at her.

"You didn't like it," Dashi guessed, feeling unaccountably smug.

No answer.

"You'd never seen it done before? I figured it'd be a common thing in Yassar: groves of trees instead of prisons."

"Yassaris do not steal, so no." Tuya slid her an assessing glance as they stepped into the courtyard. "The khan's consul does not trust you."

Dashi shrugged. "It's mutual."

"How long have you known each other?"

"Years. Long before she was the consul."

"You were close?"

"I'd rather not talk about it."

Tuya hesitated, then said, "I have a cousin in Yassar. She and her lover did everything together: always laughing, always whispering, always touching. But when the relationship ended...I've never seen two people fight like that. She would have set herself on fire if it meant burning him too." She glanced at Dashi. "You two remind me of that."

"If you're asking if I was her lover too, the answer is no," Dashi said dryly.

"The commonality is the disintegration of trust and affection," Tuya said, "not necessarily the nature of your relationship."

"That—"

Dashi broke off, her antennae twitching. Moments later, Zayaa and the Yassari convoymaster rounded the corner.

"Ah, Tuya, I see you're about to hold class," Zayaa said gaily. "Where are your other pupils?"

Tuya dipped her head. "Two soldiers were recommended for their archery skills. They are waiting in the arena."

"Very good. The khan will be watching from his balcony and hopes to see a successful demonstration today."

Although Zayaa was speaking to Tuya, Dashi knew the words were meant for her: *succeed, or else.*

"Tuya is well-practiced with our invention," the convoymaster said to Zayaa. He placed a slight emphasis on the word '*our.*' Tuya's head turned. "Both archers will be in good hands with her as an instructor."

"There will be three archers," Tuya said, indicating Dashi. "The ant is also renowned for her skill with a bow. I am certain that her talent will honor *our* invention."

The convoymaster's mouth pulled tight above his fastidiously trimmed beard, but he said nothing.

"What was that about?" Dashi asked, as soon as Zayaa and the convoymaster had gone.

"The convoymaster dislikes that you escaped justice. He especially dislikes the idea of you handling more Yassari inventions."

"He should be feeling confident, not petty. He's already got it worked out how he's going to get me in the end," Dashi said. "But I meant why were you baiting him?"

"Baiting him?" Tuya's mouth was set in a hard line.

"Oh, come on. All that *'our'* invention stuff. What was that?"

Tuya didn't answer at first. "All Yassari children want to be inventors," she said finally. "They daydream about making innovations that will save lives, bring joy or ease to someone's life, and earn glory for Yassar. From the time they can walk, they learn the principles of design, the sciences of movement, air, water, earth and fire. To be chosen for an inventor position is a fortuitous thing." She glanced at Dashi to see if she was following. "It is the greatest honor in the Merchantry."

"Are you saying all this to impress me?"

"What? No!"

"I was certain the next thing out of your mouth would be, "And I'm an inventor." Dashi adopted a lofty tone.

"I...well, I...am."

"So what's the problem with the convoymaster then? He's not appropriately dazzled by your presence?"

Tuya frowned. "Stop doing that. I am attempting to answer your question. The convoymaster spearheaded the secondary research on how one of my primary inventions could be used. I hold a...different opinion on the matter."

"You can't overrule him?"

"The Merchantry Council takes control of each finalized discovery and decides which will be most useful. These are given to senior inventors for a secondary investigation into their applications. The Merchantry Council decides which secondary applications are pursued, not the original inventor."

"It's *your* invention."

Tuya shook her head. "It might be listed beside my name, but it's already been assumed by the collective."

"That," Dashi said, as she walked through the gate into the practice arena, "sounds like sanctioned theft."

The arena behind the stables had been used for training horses the last time Dashi had been there, back when she'd still been entirely human and was pretending to be a servant. Now it was a practice yard for the heralds. Their scent trails, each in a distinct animal-human hybrid of color and smell, tracked back and forth across the space. The moth hovered gracefully in midair, leveling a small crossbow at a target below her. The owl stood on a high platform parallel to a line of straw-filled, vaguely human-shaped targets. Without warning, she plunged from the platform, raking the dummies with her spiked boots. Straw drifted from the split canvas, covering the muddied snow. The stag was nowhere to be seen, but Dashi noticed another row of dummies, the kind usually used in sword practice. She wondered if they were for him.

Two soldiers stood next to a small handcart at one end of the yard, managing to look exceedingly uncomfortable without even moving. Snow sifted from the gray sky, whitening their hair and the shoulders of their uniforms. Their scents reached out to her. Dashi recognized the younger of the two as the soldier who'd quietly touched Idree's shoulder after her finger had been severed. They didn't shrink away from Dashi as she neared, but she saw the twitch in their shoulders that said they wanted to.

Tuya strode past them with a brisk nod, stopping next to the handcart. Using a key on a cord around her neck, she unlocked the handcart and extracted something black and diamond-shaped. She held it up, balancing it between her thumb and forefinger.

"This is a pyro-tip," Tuya announced. "As you can see, it is quite light. Light enough to be attached to an arrow shaft." She tapped the elongated black object gently. "It does increase air resistance, however, which can diminish the arrow's range and make it tricky to aim, especially if there is wind. However, it has other advantages to offset that."

Pyro-tip. Dashi dug her fist against her thigh and thought of the black-smith she'd visited all those months ago, back when she was desperate to remove the pyrothrite belt strapped around her waist. "Just a flash of fire and a big hole where the boulder had been," he'd said, describing what the pyrothrite could do.

"Pyrothrite," Tuya said, "is a highly reactive, highly explosive substance. The pyro-tips are hollow and will crumple on impact. This brings the saltpeter and pyrothrite into contact, causing an explosion." She flicked a finger and one side of the diamond popped open, revealing a checkerboard design of white and black triangles.

Dashi's mouth went dry.

Tuya returned the black diamond to the handcart, nestling it carefully inside. On the other side of the yard, Zayaa and the khan emerged onto a balcony. The gray-bearded convoymaster was there too.

All my enemies gathered before me and a pyrothrite arrow within arm's length, Dashi thought bitterly, *and no way to use it.*

Tuya picked up another diamond-shaped object, this one a dull gray. "This is a sample tip. It contains a single nodule of pyrothrite."

She fit the gray diamond onto the end of a crossbow bolt, her movements confident and casual. Even so, Dashi took an uneasy step back. It *was* pyrothrite, after all.

Tuya motioned to one of the soldier's crossbows. "May I?" He handed over the weapon and Tuya raised it, sighting carefully. "Observe." The bolt released with a *swish* and Dashi knew instinctively that the shot was true.

Boom.

There was a brief impression of fire and a billow of black smoke. A wave of percussion rattled along Dashi's skin and up her antennae. The shrubs around the arena shook themselves, sending snow cascading to the ground.

On the balcony, Zayaa began clapping. The smoke drifted higher, revealing a pile of splinters where the target had stood.

"How much pyrothrite is in a real one?" the older soldier asked, his eyes on the black smudge in the snow.

Tuya returned his crossbow. "That is proprietary information."

"They're designed to crumple with impact, you said," said the soldier who knew Idree. "Isn't it dangerous to transport them over long distances?"

"A Yassari expert will assist in the storage and use of the pyro-tips until the termination of our deal with Karakal." Tuya reached into the handcart, handing Dashi and the soldiers each a tray of the diamond-shaped tips, though these were white, not gray or black.

"These are filled with sand to approximate the weight of the real thing. Get used to handling them," Tuya said. She opened a drawer in the cart and produced a quiver and a recurve bow: Dashi's own, which she'd had to surrender at the armory after she returned from Tyvalar. "The consul said you'd be more comfortable using this."

"I am, yes." Dashi picked up one of her arrows and fitted the arrowhead into the slot at the back of the white diamond. She balanced it experimentally on her forefinger, noting the added weight and width.

She overcompensated on her first shot, sending the arrow long. Her second shot fell short. Tuya held out a third arrow, already prepared with the fake pyro-tip, and Dashi bristled, sure that the other woman was about to give her advice on shooting. Tuya stayed silent, however, allowing Dashi to get a feel for the strange arrowheads on her own.

"Why would the consul want these along?" Dashi asked. The khan's commands wouldn't allow her to mention the Wellspring expedition specifically, but Tuya seemed to know what she meant.

Tuya hesitated. "That's not something the consul briefed me on."

"But you know," Dashi said. She accepted another arrow. This time her shot hit the target, albeit at the outside edge.

"The consul did mention that there will be...obstacles along the way."

Purek traps. Sevlin's map section had depicted a building in the seemingly dead-end canyon. Naturally, it would be loaded with deadly surprises.

"Her first choice is for you to breach them," Tuya murmured, watching Dashi fit another arrow, "but if for some reason you cannot..."

You mean if I die trying, Dashi thought. "If I cannot, then the pyro-tips might clear the way."

Tuya inclined her head in agreement. "There is something I do not understand."

"Oh?" Dashi launched another arrow. This one hit the target dead center.

"Why not use the pyro-tips to clear the obstacles from the beginning?"

"The type of places we're going...there's a cascading sort of design." Dashi felt around for the right words, striving for a general answer that wouldn't be limited by the khan's commands. "You figure out one puzzle and it gives you a clue to the next or unlocks a door somewhere else. Using force isn't usually the best way. Sometimes it makes getting through more difficult. Or deadly."

"That sounds fascinating," Tuya said, and sounded like she meant it.

Dashi nodded at the handcart, where the black and gray pyro-tips were nestled in a straw-lined box, a clutch of deadly eggs. "Who is the Yassari expert assigned to mind the nest when it's traveling?"

"Me."

Dashi glanced up in surprise. Despite what Tuya had said about being an inventor, her tasks in New Osb had mostly revolved around carrying messages and rewriting contracts. Dashi had assumed that Tuya's position as liaison to the consul was administrative.

"The pyro-tip arrows aren't sealed," Tuya explained. "It was attempted, but the process made them too heavy. As a consequence, the pyrothrite inside has to be...coddled a bit, to ensure optimal performance."

"Coddled? Like temperature or humidity?" Dashi asked, still thinking of a hen turning her nest.

"That is proprietary information," Tuya said, but she smirked when Dashi rolled her eyes.

"What happens if they aren't coddled?"

"They can become unstable."

Dashi turned to stare, aghast.

"No one else is as adept at managing the pyrothrite as I am," Tuya said calmly. "The success of the expedition is in good hands."

"I am flooded with relief."

Tuya smirked again.

"You must have worked hard to be considered the best at handling pyrothrite," Dashi offered grudgingly. Tuya wasn't much older than she was.

"Yes." Tuya closed the handcart with an air of finality, stirring the curls next to her face. "I also invented it."

After the pyro-tip demonstration, Dashi wanted to go check Spit over before the journey. Because the khan had ordered her to help Zayaa, however, she first had to ask permission. Zayaa pursed her perfect lips and pretended to weigh the matter. It was excruciating, but there was little that Dashi could do except stand there, fingernails digging into her palms.

I should be able to visit my horse without begging it as an ancestors-damned favor, Dashi thought, storming back through the courtyard. She frowned as she caught the scent of the Yassari convoymaster. He was standing to one side, inspecting the sacks and saddlebags being assembled for the journey to find the Wellspring. With everything else that had happened, she'd forgotten the Yassaris would be going into the taiga too. To study the mechanics of Purek traps, Zayaa had said. *As if they need any pointers on being dangerous. As if this journey could get any worse.*

Seeing Dashi, the convoymaster started toward her. In some strange configuration of timing, they were alone in the normally busy courtyard. Dashi's stride stuttered. She had no desire to speak to him, but Idree's punishment rode heavily in her mind now, and she was wary of offending anyone too high in rank.

He stopped a few paces away. "Do not think," he said, his eyes fixed over her left shoulder, "that you are somehow irreplaceable since you were selected to use Yassari goods. The khan will still honor our agreement. You will be remanded to Yassari custody when this is all over. You have not escaped our justice."

"I...didn't think that," Dashi replied truthfully.

"I've met plenty of would-be thieves." The convoymaster sniffed. "They *always* think they can avoid the consequences."

He tugged his collar down, revealing a cord that encircled his neck and disappeared beneath his clothes. He didn't need to tell her what hung from it. *Justiseed.* Dashi's lips parted, suddenly dry. The convoymaster nodded, apparently satisfied, then turned and strode away. Dashi whirled in the opposite direction, not slowing until Spit was in sight.

"Hey, old man," she whispered.

Spit whickered a greeting, ambling in her direction. His winter coat had grown in, a thick layer of white-gray that turned him puffy and soft. *Like a winter spirit,* Altan whispered laughingly in her memory. Spit stretched his neck over the rail to lip at the front of her deel.

"I don't know how I'm going to get us out of here," she whispered.

Her hands were shaking. She couldn't stop thinking of the *justiseed* in the pouch around the convoymaster's neck. She couldn't stop remembering the plant, crouching greedily over her pooled blood, and the horrible, alien feeling of its tendrils writhing beneath her skin.

Dashi twisted her fingers into Spit's mane, trying to draw comfort from the warm, familiar feeling of him. She laid her forehead against his cheek.

"Moping?" a mocking voice asked from beside her. "I didn't know ants were capable of that."

Dashi didn't turn. Ese's scent had announced his presence before his voice had. She studied him from the corner of her eye: sharp cheekbones, crooked nose, untidy beard, glinting spectacles over bloodshot eyes. It was hard to believe he was the same man who'd once circled her like a caged cat, tossing out nuggets of information the way some people toss seeds for the birds.

"I can't be as ugly as this nag you insist on riding," he said, noticing her stare. "Has his head gotten *larger*?"

Dashi scratched Spit's chin. "Don't listen to him, old man. He's jealous because your whiskers are neater."

Ese ducked through the fence. "Why are you here, little Dashi?" He bent to shovel some manure into a bucket, near enough that she could hear him but far enough that they did not appear to be talking. "Don't you have a journey to prepare for? Two days, isn't it?"

"You know about that?"

"Everyone knows about that. The servants have been working for days, preparing. They don't know *where* exactly—and I assume the khan has taken pains to prevent you from blabbing." Ese slanted her a look. "I was hoping he'd be too weak to go. I'd like to know that I've denied him *something* he wants, since he gets to live when Jochi doesn't." He leaned on his pitchfork, glaring into the distance at the thought of how the khan had killed his own brother: Jochi, the man Ese had loved.

"You can't...?" Dashi asked.

"I already told you; I gave him the last dose."

Dashi tried to stifle her intake of breath.

Ese cast her a knowing look. "Don't get too excited. That was days ago. Does he look dead to you?"

She took a step back, reeling. She'd hoped that Ese had been lying before, when he said he'd run out of Adder's Dust. *He didn't run out,* her mind supplied, recalling Ese's anger when he'd discovered that she'd used some of his stashed poison to incapacitate the khan's servants. *This is* your *fault.*

"'*The most bitter medicine is regret. It lingers and scars, impossible to forget,*'" Ese said, quoting the old Karak song. He didn't sound smug, however; he sounded tired. He turned back to the manure, filling the silence with the rhythmic scrape of pitchfork tines against the rim of the bucket.

"The Yassaris seem like they'll do anything for the right amount of gold," Dashi said cautiously, aware of the tether. She doubted she would be able to go much further in plotting.

"How much gold do you think I have left, little Dashi?" Ese snorted. "Anyway, I didn't get it from the Yassaris."

Spit stretched out his neck, butting her chest to remind her to keep scratching. Dashi bowed her head, pressing her forehead against his warm one. *What if I'm never free of the tether? What if I'm the khan's puppet for the rest of my life?*

"How have you been able to go on?" she asked Ese quietly. There must be something, she thought, some target to aim for. The thought of years—*decades*—stretching in front of her without hope for improvement was too desolate to contemplate.

"Ah, *now* you're moping."

Dashi pulled a piece of dried fruit from her pocket and gave it to Spit. It was foolish to expect empathy from the man who'd once strapped her with pyrothrite. Spit was a far better companion.

"You don't want to take advice from me," Ese said after a beat. "Jochi is dead and Temur still breathes."

"You wouldn't still be here if you didn't have a plan."

"Maybe I need the wages." He shot her a mirthless smile. "Rebuilding an estate isn't cheap."

"You don't care that the estate was burned."

"No. Not anymore." Ese picked up the bucket, now full of manure, and lifted it over the fence. He placed his hands on the rail, turning to regard Dashi through his flashing spectacles. "I won't leave without Jochi. Every night I fall asleep knowing that the khan's soldiers are a stone's throw away. All it would take is one word from you—or someone recognizing me—and I'll be shoved into a cage next to Jochi's bones. Then he would never escape." His voice dipped as he looked away. "Every morning I wake up and no one has come for me."

"It wouldn't be of my own volition," Dashi said, "if I told him about you. He would have to force me."

Ese swung himself over the fence, his shoulder brushing hers as he passed. "I know," he said, "but that wouldn't make any difference."

Chapter 15

Two days later, Dashi found herself watching a snaking line of horses and sledges in disbelief. It seemed like all of New Osb had turned out for the expedition into the taiga: not just soldiers to protect the khan but advisors and servants as well. Animals too, she thought, silently tallying the horses, oxen, hunting birds and yaks. The Yassaris brought their own sledges, lumpy and mysterious beneath layers of yellow canvas. Already the expedition had stopped twice, once for a lamed yak, and once for a lamed soldier, whose foot had been run over by a sledge.

Dashi had stared when Zayaa first told her how many people would be joining them. "*One hundred?*"

"We will be a large party," Zayaa said calmly.

"*Twenty* is a large party. One hundred is a small town."

"The khan believes that a group of this size will deter the taiga beasts." They'd locked eyes for a long moment, for once in perfect accord.

Now, the northern wind had died out, making the air seem comparatively warm, and the mood almost festive. Though the soldiers rode straight-backed and heavily armed, there was a laxness about their features that said they weren't expecting any threats. They swapped jokes and stories, their eyes focused on their audience instead of flicking over the near-taiga the way Dashi's did. Only Tuya echoed her tension, albeit for different reasons. She rode on the Yassari sledge that carried the pyro-tipped arrows, rechecking the harness and cargo at every stop, fussing like a new mother.

Zayaa and the khan rode in the middle of the procession. Idree, seated stoically astride a black mare, followed. Dashi had not seen her sister since the Great Hall. The sight of Idree's face was a balm on her soul, as was the number of soldiers buffering her on all sides. If Idree had to go into the taiga, at least she was in the safest possible position.

The khan's exhaustion was plain in the slump of his head. His hand bumped against his leg, moving in time with his horse's gait instead of with a life of its own. Still, when Zayaa called a halt to debate some point about their route with the captain who accompanied them, the khan leaned forward to give orders with great vociferousness. *Not nearly as close to death as I'd like,* Dashi thought bitterly.

Dashi sidled up to Zayaa before they started moving again. "There are too many," she hissed. "The line is so long that we'll get separated in the trees. Ancestors above, I just heard a group of soldiers *singing*, Zayaa. They're marching to their deaths, and they think it's a festival."

Zayaa took a long draft from her waterskin. "This is not how I would have planned it, no. I was pleased he agreed to the Mori horses. I was sure he'd override me and say they were too ugly."

Dashi glanced to the north, where the dark ridge loomed larger as the day wore on. "Well, he's wrong about this. A large herd of deer attracts *more* wolves, not less. It's not too late to send some back."

Zayaa shrugged, fatalistic. "That is the khan's decision, not mine. If his people die, they die. It's nothing to me."

Dashi thought of her fellow guards in Ejen. There had been a few brutes among them, as there are in any occupation, but most had just wanted to ensure their family's next meal. Surely some of those who wore Karakal's colors were the same: more or less decent, only here because it paid better than the alternatives.

"Dying people will attract animals," she said. "They will slow us down."

"Then I will step over them and walk faster. I am here for the Wellspring, not to play nursemaid."

Dashi watched the other woman walk away. Zayaa had said '*I.*' Not '*we.*' Not '*the khan.*' Dashi still didn't know what Zayaa wanted from the Wellspring, but it was sure to be something for herself.

The wind returned in the afternoon, thundering out of the taiga with outstretched fingers, intent on leaching warmth from everything in its path. The hills grew steeper, and the yaks grew fatigued, straining against the heavy sledges. Their stops increased in frequency, and Dashi tucked her mittened fingers under her arms at each one, conserving heat. Her antennae twitched, trying to sort through the scents that crowded around her. Their group left such a trail that the air around them looked oily, so thick was it with scent smudges. With some surprise, she caught a familiar scent threaded through the rest. She followed it, meandering as though she was merely stretching her legs.

"Ese," she hissed when she found him tending a team of yaks. "What are you doing here?"

He glanced up, but the reflection from his glasses obscured his eyes. "You recognized me?" His hood was pulled low over his forehead and a fur wrap covered the bottom half of his face. Even his coat was several sizes too large, obscuring the lithe way he moved.

"I wouldn't have except for these." Dashi tapped the top of her head. "You must have been at the end of the line all day if I just now found you out."

"The very last person," Ese confirmed, "aside from the rear guard of soldiers."

As far from the khan as he could get, in other words. His being here was still an incredible risk, fraught with the potential for recognition.

There were no shadowy stables where he could retreat from scrutiny. Dashi narrowed her eyes but knew better than to ask what he was planning. He'd never trust her with his plans.

"They've expanded your responsibilities," she said instead. "A few days ago you were only managing horse manure. Now, you've graduated to yak."

"A promotion, they called it. I played the fool and acted excited." Ese made a shooing motion with one hand. "Go, little Dashi. You are too recognizable to speak with for long."

By evening the next day, they were approaching the ruined Purek library. Dashi recognized the curvature of the hills and the line of stone squares, low and uneven, that tracked over the land. Periodically, the stag would bound into view, always way ahead of them. He never seemed to want to stay with the larger group and, anytime he was called in to report, his body was rigid with tension. *He knows he's safer far away from this assemblage of prey*, Dashi thought.

For her part, Dashi had positioned herself as close as possible to her sister. As they neared the library, Idree slowed her mare, causing the soldiers around her to slow too. When she was nearly abreast of Dashi, Idree cut her reins hard to the right, forcing her horse between the soldiers' mounts in a flurry of equine protests. Dashi hid her smile, recognizing the stubborn set of Idree's eyebrows. With a few hand signals and shared looks, the contingent of soldiers readjusted themselves to include both sisters at their center.

Idree rode well now, erect in the saddle instead of hunched fearfully over the animal's neck. Dashi's eyes lingered on her sister's hands. She wore mittens against the cold, but Dashi could see the slight indentation on the far side, where Idree's little finger no longer filled out the material.

"How's the horse?" Dashi asked, settling on a neutral topic of conversation, something the soldiers wouldn't feel duty-bound to report.

"She's no Bat." Idree glanced over. "I never did get to ask if you left her in Ejen."

"I brought her. I'm not sure where she ended up, but I did see a piebald hauling stone in the prisoner camp."

Her sister turned, aghast. "Bat's *there*? That place is horrible! Some of the heralds have told me things..." She shook her head. Her eyes moved to Spit. "I miss...riding her."

Dashi swallowed, soaking up Idree's unspoken words: *I miss everything familiar.* "Bat is better off there than here." At least in New Osb, Bat wouldn't be attacked by giant taiga beasts.

"I suppose so," Idree said. She lowered her voice. "I haven't heard much about where we're going."

"I can't talk about it," Dashi said. Seeing Idree's accusatory look, she added, "I was commanded, Idree. I really can't."

"The veins of magic are supposed to be thicker where we're going," Idree said. "I know that much. The khan is hoping the survival rate for the stitching improves. I think that's why I had to come too."

"Does it work that way?"

"No idea." Idree shrugged. "Can I ask you something?"

"You can ask, but I probably won't be able to answer."

"Why are your antennae always moving? Do they tell the temperature, like a snake's tongue?"

Dashi glanced at the soldiers around them, feeling self-conscious. Idree's expression was so open, her curiosity so genuine, that Dashi found herself answering, tentatively at first because of the soldiers but more confidently as she began to focus solely on her sister. Still talking lightly, they emerged into the level valley where the library and its adjacent ruins lay, peeking up through the patchy snow like the bones of some mythical beast. The ridge of the taiga, wearing its perpetual mantle of dark trees, loomed in the background. Although they should have been near enough to see between the trunks, the remaining daylight bent away from the forest, rendering its interior impenetrable to the naked eye: an unopened box, dark and secret.

"Remember the last time we were here?" Idree looked at the ruined library with a fond smile.

Dashi understood the sentiment. It had been fewer than two years since the race to find the golden needle, but already those memories were shrouded in the bittersweetness of the distant past, the relic of a less complicated time.

"I remember. We got into an argument about where our *companion* was from and you—" Dashi sucked in a breath, her eyes fixed on the far side of the library, which had just become visible. The back of the domed roof sagged, its cracked ribs sticking out at odd angles.

Someone called an order to dismount. Dozens of boots hit the ground, accompanied by not-quite-suppressed sighs of relief. Dashi went through the motions of setting up camp, but her mind wasn't on it. As soon as she could, she started for the library. The soldiers halted Idree before she could follow, but Dashi kept walking.

She knew there were scroll cabinets beneath the fallen portion of the dome, but the big tapestries were a little farther away. *They might have survived*, she told herself, almost running now. Altan had loved them: the magnificent colors; the detail wrought into each figure; the way the scene changed subtly depending on where you stood. If they'd been spared she could roll them up and move them to one of the side chambers, safeguarding them until...*until when?* She almost slapped her head at the absurdity of her thoughts. She wouldn't be back to protect tapestries, or anything else, not unless the khan commanded it.

A familiar scent draped over the front steps. The rock cairn that held the door closed—carefully rebuilt by Dashi the last time she'd exited the library—had been pushed aside. She shouldered her way through the door, ignoring its squeal of protest. There were no windows, and Dashi didn't have a lantern, but it didn't matter. Sunlight stabbed into the murky depths of the library, illuminating the dust motes dancing through the air. To one side lay the familiar slump of white bones: the skeleton Altan had nicknamed years ago so Dashi wouldn't be frightened.

Dashi nodded in greeting. "Karli."

"She's holding up well, under the circumstances." Zayaa stood in front of the enormous tapestry on the far wall—Altan's favorite—her head tilted back.

"I'm surprised to find you here," Dashi said, picking her way through the detritus covering the floor.

"This place has too many memories to avoid."

Dashi glanced up at Zayaa's tone, but it was the tapestry, partially bathed in sunlight, that caught her eye. Sunlight wasn't good for the ancient fibers, but as long as it had escaped water damage it could—

Dashi's gait slowed as she neared the tapestry, close enough to take in its distorted images. Khagan Nuray's picture was distended, the fibers that made up her face swollen with moisture. Instead of hawkish and strong, her features were monstrous, barely human. The colors of her ceremonial robe, once a bright array of blue and purple, had morphed into soggy shades of brown. The bright gold strands that made up the straps of her sandals and the signet ring on her left pinky finger were blackened with mold.

It was ruined. Utterly. Dashi stood there for a long moment, her breath rattling up and down her throat. *Dead*, it said. *Everything here is dead, dead, dead.* Which was complete foolishness, she knew. The library had been full of death, both human and cultural, long before she'd first visited.

"It was inevitable," Zayaa said in a hushed voice.

She sounded...moved, Dashi thought with surprise. "It was such a grand building," Dashi said. "Part of me thought it would be here forever."

"Even the unassailable fall eventually," Zayaa said. "It's a good reminder, every time I feel like giving up."

Dashi looked at the patch of sky visible through the hole in the roof, then back at Zayaa standing before the tapestry that Altan had loved so much. She reached for her anger, but the destruction of the library had gutted the flame.

"We did all the same things and knew all the same people," she said, shaking her head, "but it's like we lived in two completely different worlds. How can you look back at all the good times we had here—and everywhere else, too—and react so...coldly? Was—" She hesitated before opening herself up to Zayaa. "Was *any* of it real?"

"Cold, is it?" Zayaa made a derisive sound in her throat. "I was born along the border of Tyvalar. Just like Baris and Altan, which is why we all spoke such fluent Karakalese. But I was from the Kurlar region, where people dared to talk of independence. You probably passed through the land my family used to own on your way to steal from Sevlin." She gave a chilly laugh. "I remember sitting on my father's lap while my older brothers talked about how Kurlar could achieve independence. They laughed every time I tried to pronounce the word."

She spoke slowly, her face turned toward the tapestry. "When I was twelve things began to change around our estate. There was a subtle charge in the air. It was in every hushed conversation between my parents and in the way my brothers practiced their swordsmanship in the yard. It was in the large shipments that would suddenly come through my family's land in the middle of the night, requiring my father to get up at all hours. Anticipation. Excitement. Nerves. I recognize it now, but at the time it just seemed like everyone was keeping secrets from me. No one with a conscience would put a child in the middle of espionage, right Dashi?" Zayaa smiled bitterly. "No one with a conscience would involve a child in rebellion either. So they didn't. They swirled around me, whispering and planning, thinking I was none the wiser. But I knew *something* was happening.

"Things reached a head a few years later, though at the time I did not understand why. My two oldest brothers had left to serve in the Queen's Guard, and for months the two brothers who remained at home had sulked about not being old enough to go. I remember the morning that everything changed because they were almost giddy, picking me up and passing me between them like I was a baby, ignoring my demands to be set down. By the next morning—" Zayaa turned abruptly and Dashi sucked in a breath at her expression. It was a mire of grief and nostalgia, two things she'd never associated with Zayaa. "By the next morning Altan and Baris had killed all four of my brothers and my parents as well."

Dashi blinked.

Zayaa held up a hand. "You're about to argue that it couldn't have been them, or that it was self-defense, so let me stop you. They burned my family's house down with us still inside. I peered through the flames and saw the oil cans in their hands. I never forgot their faces."

"That—" Dashi started, but Zayaa spoke over her.

"We had a hidden room in our house in case of border skirmishes. We'd all crammed inside it for the night because my mother was nervous. She'd wanted to leave the house entirely, to go stay with some cousins.

At first, I couldn't understand it. There had been no talk of border raids—my brothers wouldn't have been in such a great mood if that were the case—but then I overheard my parents talking and I realized the true source of my mother's concern. That day, far away in the capital city, my two oldest brothers had made a bid for Kurlar's independence. No one had heard the outcome yet. My mother was worried that it would fail. My father tried to calm her down, telling her that we had allies from Karakal standing ready and that the Tyvalaran spymaster—the old one, not Sevlin—was secretly on our side, so what could go wrong? But my mother insisted we'd be safer if we didn't sleep in our own beds. The hidden room was tiny. One set of bunks for my brothers and one for my parents. I was the smallest, so I slept on the floor beneath my mother's bunk.

"I awoke in the middle of the night to an inferno. Beads of sweat were rolling down my face, and I could see orange through the cracks in the walls. Even on the floor, the smoke was so hot it felt like it would scald my lungs. I scrambled up and went to my parents' bunks, then my brothers', but they wouldn't budge. I tried to open the door to the secret room, but it was stuck. I called for help as best I could—I was choking on the smoke—but no one came. Not the servants. Not the Karakalese forces my father had snuck over the border. Not the Tyvalaran spymaster who'd plotted against the old queen and recruited my brothers for the Guard. No one came for me."

Zayaa's voice was flat, like she'd prodded the memory for so long that she'd become numb to it, but Dashi had a bruising grip on the edge of the scroll cabinet. She'd gone to her own past as Zayaa spoke, to the fire that had nearly consumed her and Idree. Her mother's shrill screams echoed in her head, fading in and out.

Zayaa snorted. "Poor little fire orphan. Was that difficult for you to hear? Altan was always so concerned with *you*, with your *trauma*. All your fighting, all your recklessness, could be traced back to that, according to him." Her voice dropped low, imitating the cadence of Altan's, full of exaggerated sympathy. "'*It's not her fault. She's been through so much, you know.*' But he never cared about trauma when he was inflicting it, and he never tried to delve deeper into how I got the scars on my back."

Dashi let out a slow breath. She'd forgotten about that. Zayaa—effortlessly beautiful, wickedly intelligent, exuding confidence in all ways—had always been self-conscious about her scars. She only swam fully clothed and wouldn't change in front of anyone, even Dashi. Even so, Dashi had glimpsed the old wounds over the years, stretched like a web over Zayaa's shoulders and upper arms, creeping up the back of her neck. *She doesn't like to talk about them*, Altan had advised when Dashi asked once. *I don't pry. Neither should you.*

"How did you get out?" Dashi asked.

Zayaa looked away, her right hand rubbing the back of her left arm. "A beam fell. It crushed half of the room, but it left a hole just big enough for me to squeeze through. The back of my shirt caught on fire and so did my hair, but I got out alive. I could see Altan and Baris through the caved-in walls as I crawled, standing at the edge of the yard with their oil cans. By the time I got outside, they were gone."

"Whoever you saw must have been a fair distance away—"

Zayaa snorted. "They might have been wearing the uniform of the Queen's Guard then, but I know who I saw, Dashi: Baris, as wide and solid as a stone wall even at that age; Altan with his golden hair shining in the light of the flames. The thing I remember most is that they weren't even watching the fire. Baris was chattering away as if he hadn't just condemned a family to death. Altan was toying with that ancestors-cursed sun pendant he always wore. I didn't know until later that his mother had given it to him, that he had the nerve to be thinking of his mother, moments after he'd taken mine." Zayaa's lips twisted. "If it wasn't for that pendant, I might have been charmed by him, but every time I saw it, every time he touched it, every time I heard him talk about how wonderful his parents were, I hated him a little more. That pendant was long gone by the time I tossed their bodies in the cesspits. I hope the khan's men pawned it for drinking money."

Dashi swallowed, thinking of the stylized sun pendant she kept in the secret compartment of her saddle. "And me?" she croaked. "Was I supposed to survive the ambush?"

Zayaa's mouth twitched into a smile. "I argued against you being sent ahead to scout, if you'll recall. You were supposed to be with Altan and Baris." She shrugged. "But Negan's men didn't want to search in the storm, and I didn't care enough about you one way or the other to make them."

Dashi leaned against the wall. She could feel her throat working. "They were good men," she said finally.

"You only say that because Altan and Baris fell all over themselves to help you and your sister, sad-eyed little orphans that you were. As if being nice to one parentless child made up for taking the parents of another."

Dashi tried again. "I'm sure they must have—"

"Made a mistake? *Accidentally* poured oil all over my family's home?" Zayaa was suddenly shouting. "Even now you refuse to see them clearly, Dashi. You, who are supposed to be so blunt and quick-mouthed, suddenly grow abashed and full of excuses when faced with the truth that *you didn't know them at all*. Altan and Baris were murderers."

Zayaa lifted her amethyst pendant so that it swung from her fingers, a flashing purple star. "I came in here for the same reason I keep this pendant: to remind myself what I've accomplished so far, and to remember what still needs to be done."

"You're Consul of Karakal," Dashi cried. "You have power and prestige and that ancestors-damned necklace while Altan and Baris rot in the cess pits. You've already done enough!"

"No," Zayaa said. She swept past Dashi and out of the crumbling library. "I haven't."

The hair rose on the back of Dashi's neck as she watched Zayaa kick the cairn stones down the steps. *Breath of the ancestors,* Baris whispered, but she didn't need anyone to tell her that Zayaa was still plotting vengeance. She had only to think about Zayaa's story and the upheaval that would have followed the assassination and attempted coup. Altan and Baris would have been junior soldiers at the time, possibly only cadets. They would not have gone to the Kurlar region to burn a house unless they'd been ordered, and Dashi was fairly certain who would've issued such an order.

Someone who had nearly died fighting off the coup and who'd dedicated his life to shepherding the new queen after the old one was assassinated.

Someone who was still so paranoid that he wouldn't even let an upholsterer patch his chair.

Sevlin.

Chapter 16

When Dashi awoke the next morning the first thing she saw was the dark line of the taiga. The trees crouched on the ridge, not yet overhanging the ruined library but leaning forward as if they might like to. A restive mist wove through their tops, casting a silvery pall over the evergreen needles wherever it touched. Dashi watched, motionless, as a white finger slowly unfolded from the top of a spruce and crooked toward the southwest, pointing them back the way they'd come.

She sat up, dislodging the dusting of snow that had collected overnight. The day was already markedly colder than the previous one. Even after she was up and moving, her toes and fingers held a chill. She retrieved an extra pair of gloves from her saddlebag and put them on, pulling her mittens over top for added warmth.

"Is it always this bleak?" Ese was bent over, checking the hooves of a horse, but Dashi could make out the edge of his salt-and-pepper beard beneath the curve of the animal's belly.

"Technically we haven't even entered the taiga," she said. "New Osb doesn't seem half bad now, does it?"

"Have you ever been there in the winter?"

"When I was little, my father told me a story about a Mori man who ventured too close to the taiga's doorstep and was caught by a winter storm. He killed a bear and climbed into the still-warm carcass to keep from freezing to death. Wolves came and ate the bear's body and the man's too. So, no," Dashi said, "I've never gone into the taiga in the winter. I'd never really been there *at all* before you forced me into the khan's race. There are plenty of ruins that straddle the boundary between taiga and near-taiga. Altan always kept our explorations there."

Ese grunted. "That story sounds like it was made up to frighten children."

"Maybe. It worked."

"I couldn't have lasted much longer in that place," Ese said, and she knew he was speaking of New Osb now. "I wouldn't have made it until spring." He straightened, reaching for the next horse, and Dashi saw the tremble in his hands. There were no bottles in the taiga.

"How will this be any better?" she asked. "*He's* still here."

"I like the odds." Ese looked meaningfully at the encroaching taiga. "Lots of hungry animals. Maybe I'll watch him get eaten by wolves, like in your story. In any case," he offered a wry smile, "the cold will be a good distraction for me." He pulled his hood down further, adjusting his furs so that everything was covered but his spectacles and the intense, red-rimmed eyes behind them.

Dashi swung onto Spit's back, flinching as the chill of the leather seeped through her clothes. The soldiers were already mounted too, but they had to wait long minutes, the horses stamping and blowing in the cold, while the khan finished a leisurely breakfast. Zayaa smiled placidly, but Dashi knew her former friend well enough to spot her anger at the delay. Eventually, the khan pushed to his feet and, somewhat unsteadily, made his way to his horse. Despite his apparent weakness, he managed to mount on the first try. The line of travelers lurched into motion behind him.

During the race for the golden needle, Dashi had entered the taiga near the ruined library, keeping to a dry riverbed that allowed for relatively easy travel. This time, they veered east, following the Wellspring map to a place where the slope of the taiga gentled, enticing them inside. The owl and the moth landed in front of the khan, reporting a clearing with ruins just inside the borders of the taiga. They'd seen no animals, giant or otherwise.

Even so, Dashi stiffened as Spit slipped between the dark trunks and stepped into the taiga. Without the summer orchestra of birds and insects, it was eerily silent. Even the horses' hooves made no sound, muffled as they were by the cushion of powdery snow. As the last soldier passed beneath the canopy of trees, the taiga exhaled: a slow, deliberate gust that made the branches creak and scrape overhead. Horses shied, spraying fans of snow. A yak bellowed, sounding its distress.

Dashi maneuvered Spit as close to Idree as she could, wanting to be near if danger arose. *When, not if.* She searched the gaps between the black trunks, her gaze moving from left to right, then jerking left again when a branch trembled. It was only the wind, however, and she slid her arrow back into her quiver, feeling foolish.

For the next six hours, the teams of yaks and oxen battled against the land. At times, the terrain was so difficult that the sledges were forced to backtrack and take a more circuitous route. This caused the line of travelers to stretch, eventually breaking into smaller groups that were blocked from view by the screen of trees. Dashi's only solace was that the khan insisted that his precious seamstress ride next to him. Since he'd commanded Dashi and the stag to stay close to protect him, it meant that Idree was always in her sight.

Finally, just before dusk, they reached the clearing that the other heralds had scouted. It was a long narrow scar in the forest, where the footings of ancient buildings poked up through the frozen ground. The stones were so dark in places that they tricked the eye, appearing as gaping holes. A single building remained intact, a gray cube at the edge of the clearing.

"Ant," the khan called, almost as soon as Dashi had dismounted. "Come here."

Dashi's body jerked into motion. The khan was standing with the Yassari convoymaster and a sour-faced Zayaa. The cold had turned his cheeks ruddy, lending an appearance of robustness that had been missing for days.

"The consul has mentioned how useful you are at navigating ruins," the khan said.

"We already have the map. We don't need—" Zayaa began but stopped at his quelling look.

"My Yassari guests would like to examine that building," he said to Dashi. "Give them a tour and answer their questions."

Dashi's eyes met Zayaa's. *A tour. Like it's one of his gardens.* "Yes, Most High," she said.

"And Ant." The khan fixed her with a hard glare. "If you let them get injured in there, someone will pay."

"Yes, Most High."

"Be careful," Zayaa muttered, handing Dashi a leather wallet of lock picks.

Yes, 'be careful' so I'm alive and well when she needs me to tackle future obstacles.

The Yassaris fell in behind her, Tuya included. Each of them carried a wax tablet and a stylus, ready to take notes like good little pupils. Twin ribbons of paving stones stretched out from the ruins, one road running north/south, while the other traveled east/west. According to the Wellspring map, they would follow the northern road to the not-a-dead-end canyon, the Gateway. Then they would turn northeast. Dashi squinted at the horizon, calculating. So far, they'd been roughly paralleling the route she'd taken during the race for the golden needle, though that had been at least three hours to the west.

Dashi stopped in front of the building they would be exploring, taking in the Purek's perfect mathematical proportions. It had been snowing steadily, but the ground was nearly bare; even the wind was determined to scour away all trespassers. Ruins were typically devoid of life, and not just in the obvious sense that people no longer lived in them. Plants left them alone too. It was most obvious here, with the trees ringing the clearing, but it was true even in the near-taiga, where vines and grasses refused to colonize the Purek's stones. Speculating about the magical cataclysm that ended the Purek empire had been a pastime among Dashi and her friends, and she had the sudden urge to turn to Altan. It was followed by a sharp throb of sorrow.

"The first thing you need to know," Dashi said, facing the Yassaris, "is that the Pureks put traps on anything of value. This doesn't appear to have been an important settlement, but you can never be too careful." She found herself looking at Tuya as she spoke, probably because hers was the most familiar face. The wind had blown Tuya's curls askew. She brushed them back with an impatient hand, her eyes fixed rapturously on the building.

"Was there anything you particularly wanted me to show you?" Dashi asked.

"The timing devices on the traps," Tuya answered immediately. "How is it that they still work? How could they be applied to—"

"That's enough." The convoymaster's voice was sharp. "Our research is not an open discussion."

Tuya's mouth snapped shut.

"Proceed," he said, staring at the front door instead of Dashi.

Swallowing her irritation, she stepped into the vestibule that sheltered the front door. Because it was protected from the elements, the door was in good shape, its hinges strong and its lock intact. Dashi pulled out the lock picks, trying to ignore the sound of the Yassaris breathing at her back. The lock clicked open. She gave the door a push, hesitating on the threshold. There were no windows. By the light from the doorway, Dashi could see that the building was empty, except for a few stone benches, one of which supported a lounging skeleton.

She pointed to a slight indentation in the floor tile. "Here's a pressure plate." Scanning the walls she found the place where the weapon would exit. "Over there, see? It's a small hole, which means it's probably an arrow, but I've seen poison-tipped darts before."

The Yassaris edged closer.

"Can you...?" A dark-haired Yassari man motioned at the floor.

"Sure." Dashi shooed them backward, then went out and got a large rock. She lobbed it onto the pressure plate. An arrow flew from the wall, the shaft snapping when it hit the tile.

"Now we can excavate it safely?" the man asked, still managing not to look directly at Dashi.

Borrowing a lantern, Dashi checked the rest of the building for traps. It was small, so it didn't take long, and she found only one other pressure plate. When she triggered it, the back wall of the building slid sideways, revealing a small recessed room. The Yassaris murmured in excitement.

"There's nothing in there," Dashi told them, but they neither looked at her nor acknowledged her words. Instead, they divided themselves into three groups. One group examined the place where the wall had shifted, while the other two began dismantling the floor around each of the pressure plates. Dashi slouched against the wall, unsure what to do now that she'd given the Yassaris their 'tour.' Eventually, she drifted into the hidden room, trailing her fingers along the marble walls, careful to avoid the milky-green stones in the decorative inlay.

"What was this room?" a voice asked from behind her. Tuya's scent curled over Dashi's shoulder.

"The building was a government one, so...maybe a secure place to store tithes before they were sent off to the khagan?"

Tuya glanced around dubiously. "How can you be sure it's a government building?"

"No windows and the walls are double-thick. Probably why it's the only building left standing." Her mouth curved up. "There's also a sign by the door."

Tuya looked behind them.

"See the symbols in the tile?"

"I thought that was just part of the design."

Dashi shook her head.

"How did you learn all this?"

"Remember how I told you that Zayaa killed the last people she worked with? Before they died, they taught me about this." Zayaa had too, of course, but Dashi didn't want to give her any credit.

"They were good friends?"

Dashi nodded, throat constricting.

"And the consul was too."

Another nod, warily this time.

"She's doing a good thing though," Tuya offered. "Finding a place where people can be healed by the magic."

Dashi opened her mouth, but no sound came out. *When you're out of this room, you're forbidden to speak about the Wellspring, unless it is to answer a question from myself or my consul.*

Misinterpreting Dashi's expression, Tuya continued. "She explained everything to the convoymaster. He thought I would want to know because my father is very sick. He will not last much longer, but maybe..."

The Wellspring as a place of healing. This must be the story Zayaa had sold to the Yassaris. To the khan, she'd sold a different one: the Wellspring would give him the power of the seamstress. Each sales pitch was crafted for its audience, and both were made possible because no one could read Purek and contradict her lies.

"I'm sorry to hear about your father," Dashi said finally. "I was surprised you want to learn more about timing devices," she said, feeling her way to a different topic. "From what I've seen, you Yassaris are well-accomplished in that field."

"What do you mean?"

"The timing devices on the pyrothrite belts."

"Belts?"

"Belt, then. I assumed you'd made many, but maybe mine was the only one. Lucky, right?" Her grin was wry.

Tuya shook her head, her gaze searching Dashi's face.

Dashi rolled her eyes. "I know 'research is not an open discussion,' but I'm not going to run to the convoymaster and report you. If he has his way, I'll be dead soon anyway and then I *can't* tell anyone."

"No, it's not that," Tuya said. "I just...have no idea what you're talking about."

Dashi described the pyrothrite belt with its timing device and tamper-proof lock and told Tuya how it was used to force her to find the golden needle. She was vague about who'd strapped the belt to her, leaving Ese out of it.

Tuya's forehead furrowed. "But...you said you didn't give the golden needle to the khan. So how did you get the belt unlocked?"

Dashi thought of V, the name she'd given to the giant taiga ant that had tended her wounds and chewed the belt off in exchange for her saving its life. "You wouldn't believe me if I told you."

"The arrows are bad enough," Tuya said softly. "I wonder if the Merchantry Council knows about this."

"The belts? Why wouldn't they?"

Tuya's mouth stretched into a displeased line, but she didn't answer.

"I bet your convoymaster knows. He seems to notice most things." Dashi glanced at the main room, where the Yassaris were ripping up the floor. The snap of the tile sounded like cracking bones. "Except for me. He won't look at me."

"It is bad luck to look at someone condemned to the death you will have." Tuya frowned. "Not 'bad luck,' exactly. Unclean? Soiling? Like if we've had too many direct interactions with you, the justiseed will sense it and jump from your body to ours."

"You mean '*contagious*,'" Dashi murmured. When she was sure her voice was steady, she added, "You don't appear too concerned."

"Sometimes I forget." At the reminder, Tuya's eyes darted away. "Anyway, it's nonsensical. The justiseed does not work in that way, sniffing out a guilty party like the thiefmark. It is most attracted to whatever blood it first encounters and—" She broke off when she looked back at Dashi. "And you probably don't want to talk about that."

"No," Dashi admitted, but Tuya was already backing away, giving Dashi an awkward little bow on her way out.

In the main room, the Yassaris were passing something between them, chittering like a flock of birds. Dashi caught the glint of bronze and something else that was black and dull. Holes gaped in the floor and the wall, a cadaver with the ribs cracked open and the organs removed. Whatever it was, the Yassaris packed it into a leather satchel, gathered their wax tablets, and bustled toward the door. Dashi started to follow, but Solongo and the owl appeared in the doorway, stepping around the Yassaris as they flowed outside. Dashi raised her hand in greeting, dropping it when she saw their expressions.

"Have you recovered from your punishment?" Solongo asked, sauntering forward. Her tone was bristly and resentful, not commiserative. Her wing had healed from the fight in Rucharla, but scar tissue wrinkled the previously flawless expanse.

Dashi cast the two heralds a wary glance. The owl's feathers puffed. Her beak clattered.

"Oh, I forget," Solongo continued. "*Your* punishment was reading old scrolls."

"That's what the khan commanded me to do," Dashi said.

"Didn't he also order you not to let Sable be captured? And yet *we* were the ones rolling in pools of our piss, not you."

At Solongo's words, the owl puffed up further. Dashi didn't know whether it meant she was uncomfortable or feeling aggressive, like a dog with its fur standing on end.

"The khan's command was for *none* of us to get captured," Dashi said. "It wasn't just directed at me. And Sable's capture wasn't my fault."

"You were the one inside the tower with him."

"We were specifically commanded to leave each other if it meant bringing the scrolls back safely."

"Sable's dead now."

"I heard what the khan said, but the blame lies with the Tyvalarans who fought him. Or with the khan for ordering Sable there in the first place."

"You should have been slow-roasted on the floor along with us," the moth hissed, her wide eyes turning to slits.

"My torture wouldn't reduce your pain or the amount of time you were on the floor."

"It would have made it fair."

Dashi made an exasperated noise. "*None* of this is fair, Solongo. I had to cut my sister's finger off."

"Don't talk to me about sacrifices. I had to whip my own son! That was because of you too, because you escaped when I was ordered to bring you back to New Osb."

"And you think I should have, *what*? Let you grab me off the river without fighting back? Given myself up so that I could take part in this sorry existence sooner?"

"Yes!" Solongo's hand balled into a fist.

The owl jerked back from the brewing confrontation, cowering against the wall.

"Don't touch—" Dashi started, but it was too late.

The owl squealed in pain, falling forward onto her knees.

Immediately, Solongo forgot about Dashi, bending over the trembling owl. "What? What is it?"

"Thhhwwww wawww—" The owl tried.

"The wall," Dashi said. She pointed to the decorative inlay, outlined in pale green lechitite. "That stone, specifically. It repels magic so when we touch it—" She snapped her fingers to imitate the zap of pain.

Solongo pulled the owl away from the wall and into a sitting position. "Are you alright?"

The owl nodded and got to her feet.

"Come on," Solongo said. "The khan will be looking for us. It's time we got back into the air to scout."

"It's not me you're angry at," Dashi said to their backs. "*I'm* not the one who made you whip your child."

Solongo let out a breath, her shoulders slumping. "But you're the only one I can yell at."

"I know," Dashi said quietly as she watched them walk outside.

With no new orders from the khan, Dashi prowled the piles of Purek stones. She was restless after the confrontation with Solongo. In the camp, a group of soldiers threw dice, laughing and jostling like they would in the barracks. The stag rested against a tree trunk. The crisscrossing shadows made it impossible to tell which lines were antlers and which were not. The khan discussed something with Zayaa and the two advisors who'd accompanied him. Only Idree looked tense, her gaze nervously sweeping the trees as she huddled next to a fire.

Always fretting, Dashi thought, torn between fondness and exasperation. In the taiga, at least, Idree had good reason to worry. Unexpectedly, Dashi was hit with a yearning for Sevlin. If she had to be in this dark place again, she wanted it to be with him. It wasn't just that she associated the taiga with him, although after two trips together, she certainly did. It was also his quiet competence, the sense that he could best anything that was thrown at him. It was watching him handle a sword. It was the way he approached her, levelly, as an equal. He didn't pick fights, but he didn't shy away from them either, always confronting her when he thought she was wrong. *If he were here right now, I'd tell him that I'm never wrong,* she thought, picturing how his lips would twist derisively.

She glanced back at Idree, still sitting alone. A soldier—Dashi recognized him as the young archer from the practice arena—walked over and handed her a cup, steam curling from the surface. He gave her a good-natured pat on the head before returning to his comrades. To everyone around her, Idree was the seamstress, a possession that shouldn't be misplaced. *Sevlin* would have noticed Idree's discomfort. He would have not only handed her something warm to drink, but then stayed to keep her company. Made a joke at Dashi's expense, perhaps, or lobbed a casual question that would make Idree light up like the sun. Although Dashi had often accused Sevlin of only caring for Tyvalar, she knew it wasn't true. Sevlin cared about Idree, and not only because she was the seamstress. He'd been kind to her long before that, when she was only an annoying tagalong in the race to find the golden needle.

Dashi's mind drifted to the way his lips felt when they'd said goodbye in the Purek maze, and the subtle play of emotions over his face when he'd seen her in Rucharla. She caught herself quickly. There was little point in allowing herself to get lost in daydreams. If she could not free herself and Idree from the khan, she would likely never see him again. *Or worse,* she thought, *I* will *see him again: when I'm sent to murder him in his sleep.*

That thought returned her inexorably to the conversation she'd had with Zayaa in the ruined library. Dashi had laid awake for hours, picturing Baris and Altan torching Zayaa's childhood home. She couldn't reconcile their actions with the men she'd known, nor could she justify what Zayaa had done. She hadn't just killed Altan and Baris. She had *obliterated* them: trashing their rooms, selling their belongings, dumping their bodies, and then working to aid the very man they were dedicated to stopping.

The idea of Zayaa bent on more vengeance, this time with Sevlin in her sights, filled Dashi with dread. *She's wrong. She must be.* The idea of Sevlin giving the order to burn down a house full of people was unimaginable. *Then again, I can't imagine Altan and Baris carrying it out, yet Zayaa swears they did.*

Chapter 17

In the morning, they followed the Purek road out of the clearing. Around midday, Dashi picked up a scent that made her hair stand on end. It was a muskier, more pungent version of rat, which she'd grown accustomed to in New Osb. The visual smudge it left was oilier too, but when she followed it between the trees, it disappeared. Though she kept a wary eye on the dark forest all day—and warned the stag to do the same—she neither smelled nor saw it again.

The festive atmosphere had dissipated. Now, the soldiers grumbled as they slid from their horses to make camp. Sturdy travel lanterns were pulled from packs, tiny beacons that stared futilely into the advancing night. The wind, sensing vulnerability, picked up, whipping snow from the ground in great stinging gusts. As the darkness closed in, so did the taiga mist, creeping closer through the treetops, its dense, white tendrils absorbing lantern light wherever it touched.

Dashi slid to the ground, feeling stiff from the ride and the cold. Spit also looked ready to drop. She took off her outer mittens so she could unsaddle him, but when she went to stuff them into her pocket, she realized Zayaa's lock picks were already taking up the space.

Zayaa was nearby, talking to the Yassari convoymaster. He pointedly looked away when Dashi approached. She held out the lock picks to Zayaa. "Here. I forgot to give these back to you yesterday."

Zayaa waved a careless hand. "So put them back. Righthand saddle-bag, front pocket."

Zayaa's horse stood with a lowered head, waiting for someone to come tend to it. "She knows how to take care of a horse," Dashi informed the mare, along with a commiserating pat. "She's just too important now."

Back when they'd ridden together, Zayaa had used a plain, comfortable saddle. It was already twenty years old when Altan bought it and was so sturdily made it would've easily lasted another twenty. The one she used as consul was positively frilly, with designs stitched into every available expanse of leather. The girth had been dyed a flamboyant shade of red. Dashi located the correct saddlebag, but as she slid the lock picks inside, she heard a dry crackle. Unthinkingly, she pulled out a twisted shred of parchment covered in dark, graceful script. It was written in Karakalese, but she could tell by the wording that it had been translated from Purek. Zayaa must have done the translation; Dashi didn't recognize it.

"*They have brutalized,*" she started to read. Footsteps crunched through the snow, and she immediately stuffed the parchment into her pocket, worried about being caught snooping. One of the khan's advisors passed as she hurried away. She half expected the tether to stop her, but the khan had not given her any commands about taking property; she made it back to Spit without trouble. Before Dashi could examine what she'd taken, however, Solongo alighted next to her.

"I know you're supposed to be the expert," the other herald said. "How much does it usually snow here?"

Dashi studied Solongo's expression, unsure whether the moth was genuinely curious or if the question was meant as a peace offering. "I have no idea," she said, unbuckling the girth. Spit let out a gusty sigh of relief, like an old lady taking off uncomfortable shoes.

"I was daydreaming about the khan freezing to death in a snow drift overnight."

A peace offering, then. Dashi played along. "Did you know," she asked in a barely audible voice, "that if the khan dies our tethers are set free? I read that in one of the old Purek scrolls." Satisfaction surged through her; the khan may have forbidden her to speak of anything she'd learned in his planning room, but *that* tidbit had been gleaned in Sevlin's towers.

Solongo's wings flicked dismissively. "Too bad we can't harm him."

"And are forced to protect him from those who can," she agreed.

Dashi's attention jerked to the horses. They quivered at the end of their leads, their eyes white-rimmed. Beside her, Spit turned a quarter-circle, his hindquarters bumping Dashi back two steps.

She stuck out a hand, absently smoothing his flank. "Easy, old man. I sense it too." Her hand reached for her bow. "Get into the air," she told Solongo. "Something's coming."

The moth launched herself upward, her wings stirring Spit's mane. He didn't even flick an ear in her direction.

Dashi's gaze slid to Idree. Her sister rummaged through a saddlebag, unaware of the danger. The khan stood nearby, waiting impatiently as a servant tried to kindle a fire with damp wood. They'd made camp where the Purek road dipped into a ravine, with the hope that the high sides might offer relief from the driving wind. The sledges had been positioned to the north as a further windbreak. They would, Dashi now realized, also hinder movement.

The scent of the horses' fear was almost overwhelming. Dashi started moving toward Idree. She dodged a hill of saddles piled unceremoniously on the ground, her legs churning with panic. The soldiers standing closest to the khan saw her rapid approach and flew to their feet, weapons bared like teeth but at the wrong enemy. They stared with distrust as Dashi skidded to a halt in front of Idree.

"Dashi?" Idree flew to her feet. One hand let go of the blanket that had been clutched around her shoulders and it fell partway to the ground, trailing like a child's nightshirt.

"There's something nearby. I—" She broke off as another wave of sour musk flooded her senses. "Go to the khan. That's where the soldiers will make their stand."

Idree nodded, worry furrowing her forehead, but as she stepped away dark shapes burst from the ground at the forest's edge. Dashi had a fleeting glimpse of humped backs and sharp faces sliding down the slope. She saw honey-colored incisors the length of a man's hand. *Underground,* she thought, with a burst of clarity. *They have underground burrows, connected by tunnels.* No wonder the scent had disappeared before.

"Bears!" someone yelled, incorrectly.

"Rats!" Idree screamed.

Dashi elbowed Idree out of the way and sent an arrow into an oncoming mass of fur. The arrow plunged into a furred flank, but the taiga rat didn't break stride. It darted to the left, avoiding her second arrow entirely, but her third shot sank home in its throat. The rat stumbled and fell, plowing snow with its forward momentum. Another rat leaped over its body, racing down the slope toward them.

The soldiers formed a tight circle around the khan, weapons facing outward. Zayaa, Tuya, the Yassari convoymaster, and both of the khan's advisors were also inside the protected sphere. Idree, however, was not. She ran a few steps toward the khan's men, realized she wasn't going to make it, and dove toward a pile of saddles, worming her way beneath them. A rat came close to her hiding place but veered sideways instead, catching a servant and slinging him to the ground. The khan's soldiers shot as it turned. The rat fell sideways onto the servant, crossbow bolts jutting from its ribs.

Turning, Dashi saw that the rest of the camp was in disarray: legs churned, arms flailed, jaws snapped. She counted no less than twelve taiga rats. Three more lay dead on the ground. The rats seemed to enjoy the chase, lashing out at whatever humans—or animals—came into reach, wounding as much prey as they could on the first pass. The primal snarls of rats, the shrill terror of horses, and the shouts of pain and exhortation combined to create a din that was weighty, almost physical.

Another rat approached Idree's hiding place, its nose quivering as it caught her scent beneath the leather. Dashi grabbed for an arrow, weighing the hazards of shooting it so close to Idree in case it fell onto the saddles. Perhaps she should try to draw it away?

The khan's voice, thready against the roar of battle, brought her up sharp. "Heralds, to me! Protect me!"

Idree, Dashi's mind protested, but her legs moved away from her sister.

The khan huddled inside the circle of soldiers. Tuya crouched beside Zayaa, who had swiped a burning stick from the nascent fire. She held it aloft, spine rigid, waving it threateningly whenever one of the rats came too close. A dead rat lay nearby. Two more circled warily, but the soldiers had stopped shooting. They'd run out of bolts, Dashi realized as she closed the distance.

One of the rats turned to look at her, its dagger incisors bared. It wasn't much, just a momentary shift of its head, but Dashi was ready. Her arrow plunked into its eye socket. The other rat darted forward, grabbing a soldier by the ankle and whipping him onto his back. The man screamed as he was dragged away.

The stag shot past Dashi. For one stretched-out moment, he hung in midair, his long legs curled beneath him. Then, sword flashing, he descended, cutting a red swath into the back of the rat. The rat released the soldier's leg and turned, snarling, but the stag sprang out of reach.

A second later, he materialized from the darkness, his legs springing and straightening effortlessly. He moved like water, so fast and smooth that the rat barely had time to react. The grate of steel against bone split the air, and the rat slumped heavily to the ground. The stag paused, his majestic head raised, then bounded off into the darkness. When Dashi glanced at the knot of people he'd been defending, she saw the same look of awe reflected on each face.

In the lull, two soldiers dashed toward the nearest sledge, grabbing for bandages and crossbow bolts. With the khan no longer in immediate danger, Dashi felt the hold of his command slacken. It was still there—she couldn't stray far, in case he needed her protection—but she could jog to the pile of saddles where Idree lay, a fawn hidden in high grass.

"Idree?"

Her sister's response was immediate, though muffled. "Are you hurt? What's happening?"

"No—"

A terrified scream punctured the air. Dashi turned to see more rats pouring from the ground at the far side of the camp, driving a morass of horses, yaks and humans before them. *To me! Protect me!* The khan's command reverberated through Dashi. She took off.

The khan's soldiers hustled him toward the sledges, hoping to make their next stand within easy reach of extra crossbow bolts. Zayaa had exchanged her flaming log for a sword, her grip firm and sure. Seeking a good vantage point, Dashi leaped onto a sledge, her eyes on the coursing rats. She estimated their number at three dozen now. The rats that had attacked during the race for the golden needle hadn't been nearly so numerous.

She reached for an arrow and then froze, staring at the yellow oilcloth beneath her feet. She was standing on top of a Yassari sledge.

"It's fine," a voice said.

Dashi glanced up to see Tuya, firelight bouncing off her dark curls.

"The pyro-tips are packed securely," Tuya said. "They can support your weight."

"It's not my weight I'm worried about," Dashi muttered as she nocked an arrow, trying to ignore the crackling fire which, only moments ago, she'd found comforting.

Dashi shot again and again, pausing only to steal glances at Idree's hiding place. The moth and the owl appeared periodically out of the night sky, but this fight wasn't like the one in Tyvalar, where they'd been able to push their opponents from a rooftop. When the moth dipped close to the ground, sword in hand, the rats reared up and nearly caught her leg. The owl used her spiked boots to injure a rat here and there, but she was nothing compared to the stag. He was a hornet weaving in and out of the carnage, delivering sting after sting without altering his calm expression.

A yak, still harnessed to a sledge, careened toward the trees. The sledge tipped over, spilling salt and meal and dried meat into the snow: precious supplies, gone in an instant. Two horses thundered past, lead ropes flapping as they disappeared into the trees. *We can't last much longer,* Dashi thought, glancing at her dwindling supply of arrows. She drew her sword.

The rats began to crowd around them, jostling two and three deep. A pointed head lunged, yellow incisors sinking into a shoulder and uprooting a soldier in the blink of an eye. Another rat leaped onto the sledges, craning its neck, serpent-like, toward the khan. Dashi charged, slashing horizontally across its side and then dodging away. The rat twisted backward, almost rolling over in its effort to reach her, but Dashi sank her blade into the soft space between its shoulder blades.

Dashi tried to move back to the khan, but teeth pierced her sleeve, dragging her off the line of sledges. She managed to rip loose as she fell, but she landed without her usual grace, face splattered with mucky snow, teeth rattled by the impact. Her sword thudded to the ground. She rolled away from the rat, the world spinning in a sickening kaleidoscope of shadows and pinpoints of lantern light. Only the Yassari's sledge was stable; the yellow oilcloth was a refuge Dashi had to reach. Her bow still lay on top, beckoning from where she'd dropped it.

"Tuya!" Dashi screamed as she dodged the rat again. A second rat moved in on her other side. "My bow!" She didn't dare turn her head to see if Tuya had heard her. "*Tuya!*"

Her bow arced through her peripheral vision and Dashi's hand shot out to snag it. The closest rat gathered itself to leap, a harsh, slightly sibilant growl forming in its throat. Dashi matched its movement, feinting one way and then flipping in the opposite direction. She landed in front of the yellow sledge, her bow and her last arrow gathered in one hand while she drew a knife with the other.

"No! You're too close!"

Someone was screaming frantically, but the words made no sense. Dashi's blade tore through the oilcloth. Her fingernails pried at the rough cases beneath, swiping at clouds of soft cushioning. From the corner of her eye, Dashi saw a taiga rat burst over the adjacent sledge and grab one of the khan's advisors. Tuya dove into the open, picking up a discarded sword and windmilling it erratically. Zayaa was more disciplined, her weapon held in a proper defensive position as she fended off a rat.

Dashi's fingers found one of the diamond shapes and fit it to her remaining arrow, glad now for the practice in New Osb. She drew the bow, arms tensing as her brain suddenly connected Tuya's words to what she was about to do. She *was* too close. They were all too close. If she fired the pyro-tip here, the percussion would knock them all out, maybe even kill them. A snarling rat leaped at her, and Dashi went down on one knee, leaning sideways as she fired: not at the rat that was about to kill her but at another rat, savaging the body of a Yassari man at the far edge of the trees.

The rat hit Dashi as the arrow released, knocking her onto her back. Her mouth worked soundlessly, her lungs unable to fill beneath its immense weight. Its incisors matched the length of her face from hairline to chin. Dashi got a hand up and shoved the rat's face sideways before it could rip into her. Beneath the curve of its neck, she glimpsed Tuya, charging toward her with a sword in hand. The rat's snout quivered, deadlocked against Dashi's hands. Its incisors brushed her throat. A string of saliva fell onto her cheek and slid slowly toward her ear.

Screaming, Tuya launched herself at the rat, her sword moving in a wild, shaky arc.

Then the world ripped apart at the seams.

Chapter 18

Tuya brought the sword down just as the ground shook with the blast. The rat—and Dashi—rattled along with it, as light and inconsequential as pebbles. Tuya sprawled onto Dashi's stomach, legs thrashing. Her sword dug into the ground next to Dashi's cheek.

Dashi rolled over, throwing Tuya off as the world tilted. Tuya's mouth was moving, but her words were eclipsed by the steady roar in Dashi's ears. *To me! Protect me!* Despite the painful heaving of her lungs, the tether forced Dashi to her feet. She dragged Tuya's sword toward her. The weight of it almost upset her balance, but she caught herself on the Yassari sledge. The yellow oilcloth gaped along the wound she'd made.

The rats fled, whisking between tree trunks and down into the earth in an exact reversal of how they'd emerged, only this time dragging bodies with them. They took great pains to avoid a darkened section of the forest and, in the low light, it took Dashi a moment to realize what she was seeing. It was a crater, spreading outward from the spot at which she'd aimed.

The khan's fire had been kicked apart in the chaos, but even by its dying embers, she could see that bodies were everywhere: human, yak, ox, horse and rat, though the latter were comparably few. Dashi stumbled to the khan, compelled to check on his safety. He leaned against a sledge looking dazed. There was a long cut on his forehead and blood stained the collar of his furs, but he was otherwise unharmed. Soldiers lay in front of the sledges. Dashi couldn't tell if they were dead or only stunned by the explosion.

Idree. She started to her sister's hiding place, dizziness making her lurch sideways when she tried to run.

The pile of saddles that had sheltered Idree was scattered over the snow. Dashi picked one up, her fingers trembling as she traced the long gash in the leather. She tried to pick up Idree's scent, but the percussion from the blast had a strange blanketing effect on her antennae and she could get nothing. She began searching the ground, moving slowly in the bad light, until she spotted a crumpled figure lying in the snow. She lurched toward it, breath caught in her throat, the scored saddle clutched to her chest like a talisman.

The person had been mangled, making it difficult to tell what size they'd been when whole. Dashi's feet crunched to a stop. She reached out a shaking hand to flip the body. The face had been torn away. The rat had gone straight for the soft abdominal cavity, ripping it open to feast on intestines. Dashi turned her head, steadying her breathing before she continued. Gingerly, she lifted a flap of fabric a little higher up. The chest, still mostly intact, was muscled and indisputably male. Dashi dropped the cloth, her pent-up breath tumbling out. *It's not her*, she reassured herself, but her hands wouldn't stop shaking.

"Dashi?"

Dashi spun around.

A slight figure emerged from the trees, sliding in the mess of snow and mud and blood. Still stumbling with dizziness, Dashi skidded into Idree, crushing her in a tight hug.

Idree chuckled weakly. "Did you make that explosion?"

Dashi nodded into her hair. "Pyrothrite."

"Huh. Guess it can be used for good after all." Idree stepped back. "Are you hurt?"

"My head is ringing like a bell but nothing serious."

"*You* get the blame for that, not the rats," Idree pointed out, "but it was good timing. Two rats were closing in on me when everything blew up."

Dashi blinked, trying not to think about how easily she could've hit the section of forest where Idree had been.

"The pile of saddles got knocked over and Solongo pulled me out. She saved several of us like that," Idree added with some pride. "I bet that changes the soldiers' view of the heralds."

A moan from the darkness caused them both to jump. Dashi walked forward cautiously, nearly stepping on the man before she saw him. He'd been partially dismembered: one leg gone just above the knee; a stump where his arm should be; his stomach torn open like a package, its glistening contents undulating gently with each breath. So much blood had poured from his body that it had melted the snow, and now he lay in pools of red-tinged water, shivering with shock and the cold.

Idree knelt beside him, both of her hands chafing his remaining one as if that could keep him warm. "Give me something to tie off his leg."

"Idree..." It was like the race all over again. They'd stumbled upon a dying racer and Idree had insisted he could be saved.

When Dashi didn't move, Idree scrambled for a piece of his deel, tearing it into strips. Dashi pictured Sevlin, slitting the throat of the racer's mangled horse, letting it bleed out while he spoke softly. She squatted beside the soldier, drawing her knife surreptitiously. He opened his eyes, staring up at her dully, and she recognized the young archer from the pyro-tip practice, the same one who'd been kind to Idree.

"No!" Idree's voice cracked as she caught sight of Dashi's knife.

"Idree," Dashi tried. "His wounds..." She gestured helplessly at the open abdominal cavity. "Why prolong his suffering?"

"I can save him."

"With what? You don't have the needle and there's no vein—"

"There is! Close by. I can feel it. If you carried him, I could lead us."

Dashi shook her head, picturing them stepping into a dark forest filled with giant rats. "We can't wander—"

"We'll stay on the Purek road the whole time. It's *right there*. Okhron has been kind to me and I—*please*, Dashi."

"The khan won't let you have the needle." She hadn't meant it as an agreement, but Idree took it as such.

"Thank you!" She clasped Dashi's arm. "Stay with Okhron?" Idree dashed off without another word.

Dashi squinted after her, wondering how Idree intended to prise the needle from the khan. He guarded it jealously, wearing it on a chain around his neck, and Dashi couldn't see him relaxing those strictures just because Idree asked nicely.

She squatted next to the dying soldier, studying his face. He was handsome, in a bookish sort of way, which was an unusual look for a soldier. If there was something exceptional to warrant Idree's desperation, Dashi couldn't see it, but she knew her sister wouldn't need much of a reason. Idree would try to save almost anyone.

"The khan wants to speak to you," Idree said, appearing out of the darkness.

Dashi stared. The khan was actually entertaining this notion?

"Quickly." There was a touch of impatience in Idree's voice. "So we can find the vein."

Dashi hurried to where she'd last seen the khan, looking up only when she crossed Ese's scent. She glimpsed him in a circle of skittish horses, four lead ropes sprouting from each fist. *Spit!* With a stab of guilt, Dashi looked for her own horse, not finding him until she'd reached the khan. Spit stood between a pair of sledges, so close to the khan that it looked like they were in conversation. His eyes and ears were trained warily on the trees.

"Clever old man," Dashi murmured, scratching his neck as she passed. "You found the safest place, didn't you?"

The khan hadn't moved since the last time she'd last seen him, his pallor testifying to his state of shock. It was Zayaa who was issuing orders: telling the surviving soldiers to collect bodies and pile them a short distance away; directing others to build the fires up and remake the camp.

Dashi bowed her head respectfully. "You asked to see me, Most High?"

His eyes drifted blankly up to hers. A trickle of blood slid from his left nostril, winding toward his upper lip.

"The seamstress said..." Dashi prompted.

Some focus came into his gaze, but he did not wipe away the blood. "The seamstress is stitching Okhron. Protect her and protect *this*," he pulled a golden chain from beneath his furs and held it out for Dashi to take, "and return them both to me."

Dumbfounded at his acquiescence to Idree's plan, Dashi held out her hand and took the small statuette. Khagan Nuray's face blazed up at her.

She felt the angry buzzing through the gold: the golden needle, agitating to be returned to the seamstress.

"Return it to me," the khan repeated, his voice fading to a whisper. "No matter what. No one else."

"Yes, Most High."

He sagged back as she left. On impulse, she stopped at the still-gaping Yassari sledge and fumbled a pyro-tip into her free hand. Tuya was nowhere to be seen.

Idree looked up as she approached, giving a satisfied nod when Dashi patted the chain around her neck. Idree had bound Okhron's abdomen and wrapped him in a bedroll while Dashi was gone.

"Hurry," she said. She grunted as she lifted what was left of Okhron's legs, trying to help Dashi maneuver him across her shoulders. It was the only way to carry him; even divested of some of his limbs, Okhron was heavy.

"Who is he?" Dashi asked, grunting as she stood under his weight. "The khan knew him by name."

"His father is a noble in Karak City. He has two older brothers—not much chance of being made heir—so he became a soldier instead. A younger sister too." Idree stopped to grab a lantern, then hurried along the Purek road, leading Dashi away from the camp.

"And you know this...?"

"He told me. Neither of us wanted to be in New Osb."

Hearing the fondness in Idree's voice, Dashi bit back a retort. She hoped her sister hadn't fooled herself into believing that she had a real rapport with this soldier. No matter what, he was still the khan's man.

"He said I reminded him of his sister," Idree said, glancing at Dashi's expression. "I know he might just be saying that, but for weeks he was the only one who had a kind word to say to me."

Dashi waited for someone to tell them to stop—Zayaa, perhaps, or a sentry—but the effort to tend wounded and reset camp was all-encompassing, and they stepped through the line of sledges without any trouble. Dashi tried to keep her gait as smooth as possible out of deference for Okhron's wounds, but if the occasional jolt bothered him, he didn't show it. His head flopped over her shoulder, his unconsciousness deep and consuming. *Not a promising sign.*

"Okhron's father is very wealthy," Idree continued. "A lot of holdings and a lot of influence."

"Well, that explains why the khan doesn't consider his son expendable." She wondered what kind of influence the khan would be able to wield over the family once Okhron was magically tethered to him.

Her sister's hand turned up in the equivalent of a shrug. "I made some other good arguments too."

Dashi smiled slightly. "Such as?"

"The khan is worried about letting the needle leave his sight. I pointed out that I could feel a vein close by, right on the road practically, and that the needle is probably safer with you than with him, especially with so many wounded..." Idree shook her head. "Anyway, once the stitching begins, I doubt anything would come near us."

Dashi grunted in agreement.

"I also pointed out that a new herald would make the khan even better protected than he is now."

"If he survives." Dashi's boot skidded on ice, and she staggered, nearly going down under Okhron's weight. "I'm still surprised he agreed to it."

"Well, I'm not sure if he would have, normally, despite my excellent reasoning. But I'm fairly certain he got hit on the head when the pyrothrite blew up. Luckily, Zayaa was too busy ordering people around to interfere."

The lantern bobbed cheekily in the darkness. Dashi gave a bark of laughter.

"Slow down," Idree said, her voice dropping to a whisper. Snow crunched beneath her feet, the only sound besides her voice. "There *is* a vein along here. I wasn't being manipulative about that part."

They hadn't gone far. The camp was still visible, its fires burning brighter with each passing minute as the soldiers worked to build them up.

"I don't want to think about what the khan will do if he changes his mind after his mind clears."

"Cut off another finger, probably."

Dashi inhaled sharply.

"Am I not allowed to be flippant about it?"

"No." Dashi crunched to a stop. "You're not."

"*You* didn't do it, Dashi. The khan did. You were just the tool he used."

Dashi was silent. "I don't think," she said, finally, "that if our situations were reversed, that logic would make *you* feel better."

"Maybe not at first, but I expect you'd prevail in telling me not to be stupid."

Dashi snorted softly.

"My finger doesn't hurt much anymore. You should know that. A little ache is all."

Which meant, Dashi thought, that the opposite had once been true. The thought of Idree in pain made her stomach knot. Idree's screams still sounded in her head whenever she thought of that day.

"I didn't know you could tell where magic veins are," Dashi said, wishing to speak of anything else.

In the circle of lantern light, Idree's head bobbed once. "I said 'feel' before, but it's more like hearing. Like people whispering, but I can't quite catch the words."

Dashi glanced involuntarily at the treetops, remembering the way it had felt—and sounded—when the taiga mist closed in on her. The trees were free of mist, but when she looked over her shoulder, a white bank was closing over the road behind them. Whether it was regular fog or taiga mist, Dashi couldn't tell. Of the camp, she could now see only bustling silhouettes, strangely distended through the white knit. Even the sounds coming from the others had died, which only heightened her nerves.

Okhron stirred, his chest heaving a great gurgling breath.

Idree looked up sharply. "Was that—Is he—?"

"Still alive, but I don't think it'll be long."

Idree began to jog. "It's not far."

Dashi squinted dubiously into the dark. Her clearest memory of her own stitching was of virulent purple light that had infused every cell of her being. "Why can't we see it?"

"It's just below the surface."

"I'm not digging, Idree." Idree opened her mouth, but Dashi rushed on, anticipating her sister's stubbornness. "The ground is frozen solid and I don't have a shovel. I can't look out for threats if I'm clawing at the dirt with my hands. And," she nodded backward at Okhron, "I don't think we have that long anyway."

Idree took several more steps, then stopped. "Here, I think."

When Dashi drew abreast of her, she saw that her sister's eyes were closed. Idree's hand drifted up, her fingers open and waiting. Dashi half slid, half dumped Okhron from her shoulders, settling him heavily against her legs. Then, she pulled the chain over her head. The golden needle exploded into motion, banging around inside its prison so vociferously that the chain fishtailed through the air, nearly causing Dashi to drop it. She managed to place it in Idree's upturned palm, watching as it stilled. No more spinning. No more bouncing. It was home.

Idree's mouth began to move. Though Dashi stared at her sister's lips, she could not discern the words. If it had been anyone besides her sister, Dashi would have assumed another language was being spoken. But this was Idree; the only other language she spoke was Thracedonian, which Dashi also knew and should have been able to decipher. The shiver that had been hovering over Dashi finally crested, making the hair stand on end along her neck and arms.

Eyes still closed, Idree dumped the needle into her palm, then dropped to her knees and pressed her forehead into the snow. The air vibrated, a deep thrum of satisfaction that multiplied in intensity with each passing second, coming from the encircling trees, from the ground beneath Dashi's feet, from the air that invaded her lungs. In front of Idree, something shifted beneath the snow, rippling the blanket of white like a fish swimming just below the water's surface.

There was a sudden explosion of light and Dashi shut her eyes, taking an involuntary step backward. It, too, came from everywhere at once, so that even when she turned her head, it pierced her eyelids, painful in its brightness. Dashi gritted her teeth, gripping Okhron's shoulders to keep him from sliding sideways. After a few moments, the light dimmed. Dashi lifted her head. A ribbon of violet light waved jauntily in front of Idree.

"You'll need to hold him," Idree said. Her voice was husky and melodic: a stranger's.

Dashi leaned Okhron over, letting him sink in the snow because there was no place else to put him. Her hands were on his arms, trying to do what Idree asked while simultaneously leaning away from the convulsing purple vein. Okhron never moved. If it wasn't for his pulse, feather-light beneath her fingers, Dashi would have thought him dead. Her own heart pounded erratically, making her lightheaded. *Take a breath*, she told herself. *It's not you who's being stitched.*

Memories of her own stitching came flooding back, although she'd had trouble recalling the ordeal before this. She could see Idree's face hovering above her, reassuring her in the moments before she was stitched. She remembered the agony of her destroyed feet, melted into an unrecognizable pulp by the Purek's acidic lake. She'd thought the pain of that injury was unbearable until Idree drew the needle through her skin. Then she'd known true pain.

Both her memories and her hold on Okhron were broken when Idree touched the needle against his skin. All at once, he charged back from the brink of death, jackknifing upward with a quickness and vitality that startled Dashi so much that she lost her grip on him completely. He looked around wildly, not recognizing either of them. Then his eyes rolled back and he collapsed into the snow, his breaths ragged.

Idree pulled the needle back. "Could you hold him?" she asked sharply, sounding more like herself.

She waited until Dashi pulled Okhron into her lap, wrapping both her arms and legs around him, before trying again. This time, Dashi saw the moment when Idree shifted into a stranger. A cloud passed over her normally observant expression, transforming it into something unfocused and sleepy. Her hands moved gracefully, dipping the needle into the wavering purple light. Although nothing visible trailed from the needle, magic crackled in the air, prickly against Dashi's skin.

Okhron bucked against Dashi's chest as the golden needle dove into his skin, his scream slashing through the quiet. His legs moved against hers as, even at the brink of death, his body found one final reserve with which to flee the pain. The needle rose and fell inexorably in Idree's hand as she worked her way up Okhron's arm and into his shoulder, then stepped over his body so that she could continue down the other side. She planted stitches along his torso and along his legs, before returning to his chest to concentrate on the skin above his heart and then above his abdomen, mending the torn flaps of skin so that his intestines were once again covered. This brought a fresh bout of screams from Okhron.

Dashi's face was slick with sweat as she relived every newly-remembered agony of her own stitching. How was he still alive, she wondered. How was he still awake? But something about the stitching prevented the patient from slipping into blissful unconsciousness. She remembered that bitterness all too clearly.

Idree moved to Okhron's head, sewing the magic into his scalp and face, ears, nose and mouth. Finally, in a movement that made Dashi turn away and clamp her jaw shut, Idree plunged the needle into his eyes.

Okhron tried to bolt upright, but Dashi held him fast, silently begging Idree to finish.

Okhron fell silent, slumping against Dashi. She ran a hand over her face, watching her sister. Idree's hands moved mechanically, rolling the needle over and over in the purple light. She made a final shooing motion and the vein crackled, deflating immediately. It was still aboveground but only barely, its stream sullen and sluggish compared to the bright dance it had performed only minutes ago. Without its light, the taiga became even darker, encroaching on either side of the road.

When Idree looked up, she was herself again, her dark eyes alert and sympathetic. "I'm not very aware of the passage of time when I stitch, but that seemed like a long one."

Barely suppressing the urge to flinch away from Idree, Dashi gave a noncommittal grunt. It wasn't just that her sister's voice had turned into a stranger's. It was that she hadn't been moved by Okhron's suffering, hadn't even *noticed* it. Dashi knew she wasn't being entirely fair. After all, some detachment was necessary with battle wounds, even for mundane healers. You couldn't blubber over every patient. In the past, she'd criticized Idree for being *too* emotional. But seeing Idree with that blank, uncaring expression had badly shaken Dashi, and she didn't want to hurt Idree's feelings by revealing how much.

Idree started to hand Dashi the needle, then caught herself. "Sorry." She fished the statuette from her pocket and deposited the needle inside, spinning Khagan Nuray's head on straight. "I always forget that it burns other people."

Dashi hung the chain around her neck, happy to give her trembling hands something to do. "We should get back," she said, her voice low to hide the well of emotion.

Dashi crouched in the snow. With Idree lifting Okhron's lower half and Dashi's hands beneath his armpits, they managed to heave Okhron across Dashi's shoulders a second time. Exhausted from the effort of holding him during the stitching, Dashi stumbled beneath his weight as she started back. Idree fell into step beside her, her arms wrapped around herself for warmth. The ethereal menace she'd possessed only a few minutes ago had vanished. She looked cold and small now, a child wandering in a great dark forest.

"You're very quiet," Idree said. "Was it awful?"

Dashi hesitated. "I'm just not sure if he's going to make it," she said, settling on a strategy of deflection.

"I couldn't let Okhron die without trying. He's my friend. That's what I like about being the seamstress: I have the chance to save people. Not just strangers but people I care about. Like you."

Dashi's steps stuttered, as looking ahead, she realized that the camp was still hidden behind a wall of white. Some primal, long-suppressed instinct compelled her to look behind her—a sense of movement, perhaps, or maybe of being watched. The night and the taiga blended into one, a lightless void at their backs.

Idree glanced at Dashi's antennae. "Did you sense something?"

"I'd like to get back to the camp, is all." Dashi turned, her breath coming hard as she looked at the trees on either side of the road: streamers of silvery white festooned the tops of the trees, white fingers that slithered toward the ground.

"That mist," Idree said slowly. "It sounds funny. Like the vein of magic but with more voices."

Dashi swallowed. "Do you remember the last time? When we were with Sevlin?"

"Kind of. It's hazy though, like an old dream. There were...people. They told me I would be great one day, that I would hold the magic of the land in my hands. They said that exact phrase, 'the magic of the land.'

I thought it sounded old-fashioned, like one of the stories Altan used to tell."

Dashi's head whipped in her sister's direction. "And you never thought to mention that?"

"I thought it was a dream."

"Even when it turned out to be true?"

Idree shrugged. "By the time I might have realized it was important, I didn't have a lot of time to talk with you about old dreams or…whatever that was."

Dashi turned back to the mist, startled to see that it had advanced significantly during her brief interlude with Idree. Now it was creeping toward the edge of the road, roiling and expanding as if something pushed it from the other side. Dashi chanced a look over her shoulder, only to see a screen of solid white there too.

"I don't think it was a dream," Dashi said. "I think it was a message. From the spirit world. From the ancestors."

"What did *you* see in the mist last time?" Idree shot her a suspicious look.

"One of the Purek khagans."

"But if the mist is really a…a vehicle for the ancestors, shouldn't that mean that we see only our own lineage?"

Dashi shrugged. "What do I know? Maybe that is our lineage. Or maybe spirits can visit whoever they want, not just their descendants."

"What did the khagan say?"

Dashi slid her a sideways glance. "She told me to protect the seamstress. And hinted that I would need to sacrifice myself to do it."

Idree was silent, and Dashi knew she was remembering the standoff with the khan's former consul, Negan. Dashi had purposely triggered a Purek trap in order to free Idree from his clutches, nearly dying in the process.

Idree sidled closer, her arm brushing Dashi's as the mist surged forward, halving the distance. "You would have done that anyway. You didn't need a dead khagan to tell you."

Dashi gave her a small smile. "I saw mother and father too."

"I wonder...a man came up to me. I don't remember what father looked like though."

The mist was blocking the road now, sliding across the ground at waist height, then chest height, then towering above them, hiding the warm glow of the camp. They were close enough to the camp that they should have been able to call for help, but Dashi knew the mist would swallow the sound before it got anywhere.

"Help me get him down before the mist gets here," Dashi said, struggling to slide Okhron from her shoulders. Working together, they settled him onto the cold ground. Dashi grimaced. If blood loss and the trauma of the stitching didn't kill him, the cold soon would.

"Assuming you're right," Idree said, "the mist is coming toward us because...?"

"The ancestors have something they want to tell us?"

"That's what I thought you'd say." Her sister swallowed nervously. "I'm scared."

"Me too."

The mist swallowed Okhron's outstretched legs, reaching out for Dashi's feet.

"Set the lantern down," was the last thing she told Idree. "Before you drop it."

Chapter 19

Moisture was the first thing Dashi noticed. The mist was clammy against her face, wet hands feeling over her exposed skin. She took a deep breath, steadying herself before she turned to Idree.

Idree was gone.

Dashi stretched a hand into the white, searching. "Idree?"

No one answered.

It's just like last time, Dashi assured herself, *which means Idree is fine.* She didn't call again, instead straining her ears for the voices her sister had mentioned. They came to her gradually, alternately fading and gaining strength, as if the wind that carried them was continually shifting directions. The words were indiscernible, the speakers just out of earshot, but the cadence of the voices was unmistakably mid-conversation.

The mist was a featureless blanket around her, white and smothering. Still, Dashi knew *they* were there, biding their time perhaps, or still traveling across whatever great distance they had to cross. The back of her neck prickled. *Breath of the ancestors.* Baris' name for that feeling of foreboding had never seemed so apt. Dashi felt a slightly hysterical giggle rise in her throat.

The susurrus around her crested, transforming into a single, definable word.

"Dasssshi."

She stared at the wall of white, forcing her breathing to remain calm.

"Dassssshi."

"You've forced your way into my dreams for months." She was surprised at how calm she sounded. "No point in being shy now."

The voices fell silent. It was like entering a crowded room and having everyone turn to stare, their conversation forgotten. Dashi felt a stab of alarm. Had she spoken too cavalierly? She bit her lip, unsure how to strike a conciliatory note with inanimate mist.

"I apologize," she said, finally. "My impatience sometimes gets the better of me. I welcome whatever, er, messages you have."

After a long pause, the voices resumed. Dashi exhaled shakily.

"I would not advise offending the ancestors," said a voice.

Dashi jumped. A shadowy figure came toward her, the movements eerie and stilted. Although the shroud of mist was enough to obscure her face, Dashi recognized the voice.

"Khagan Nuray."

"You have been changed, little one." There was a pause as Nuray examined her. "Yet you seek my counsel in the taiga once again."

"What I'm seeking is a way out of this." Dashi gestured to her antennae. "If you have any counsel on the subject, I'm primed to hear it."

"The question you ask is the wrong one."

Dashi waited, keeping a tight rein on her mouth. The mist swirled around Khagan Nuray, obscuring her rock-hewn features in layers of gauzy white. Only her eyes cut through the swathing, dark and aggressive.

Dashi shifted beneath that gaze. "Fine, will you tell me what the right question is then?"

Khagan Nuray floated closer, her face gaining clarity as she closed the distance: first, the sharp nose, then the prominent cheekbones and jaw. Her features were too rawboned to be called beautiful, but they bespoke a strength of will that was alluring, daring the viewer to look away. The mist pillowed thickly around Nuray's knees. Dashi glanced down, wondering if it hid her feet, or if that part of her was unformed.

"If a powerful ruler gave you a gift, would you throw it back in her face?" Nuray asked.

"I guess it depends on the gift." At a hard look from Khagan Nuray, Dashi amended, "Probably not, though."

"Why?"

"Because it would be offensive and I wouldn't want to offend someone who has the power to hurt me."

Khagan Nuray nodded once, satisfied.

"Is that...it?" Dashi asked. She could feel the mist beginning to drag at her, a bone-tiredness that was both unnatural and impossible to resist.

"What do you know of my reign?" Khagan Nuray shifted closer, the mist between them thinning enough for Dashi to see colors. Her hair was black as pitch and the tone of her skin was identical to Dashi's own. She wore a green robe, each sleeve embroidered with purple thread to show a pair of stags locked in battle. Her accoutrements were gold: an elaborate headdress, stacks of bracelets and armbands. Gold flashed from the signet ring on her littlest finger.

"Mostly the artwork," Dashi said. "You're called Nuray the Generous and Nuray the Just." *No, that wasn't quite right.* Dashi ran a hand over her face, trying to marshal her words. "Except you once told me you didn't like those titles, that it wasn't all that peaceful. There was a rebellion and, um..." She remembered Nuray lecturing her on legacies the last time they had met in the mist, but the particulars eluded her. "Which part of your reign did you want to talk about?"

Khagan Nuray made a dismissive gesture with one hand. "The beginning was rebellion. The middle was peace. The end was death."

"Isn't that the pattern for most lives?" Dashi could feel her words slurring.

"Nature is content in its balance, in the pull of one season against another, in the never-ending circle of predator and prey, birth and death. But I was not born content; there was always something more to be gained." Her voice was bitter. Behind her, other figures began to appear. Whitish-gray in the mist, they slid over the ground, the movement unnaturally smooth.

"Even in death, I cannot rest. I prowl the edge of the present but am caught in the past, unable to intervene."

Dashi nodded, her head moving with a little too much momentum. "Wait, intervene...in what?"

Khagan Nuray's dark eyes seemed to snap, boring into Dashi like twin augers. "Do not offend a powerful gift-giver. The price is death."

"Right." Dashi's eyes fluttered closed. Her thoughts scattered, as though the mist's white fingers were reaching inside her head.

"You are too narrowly focused." Khagan Nuray stabbed Dashi's chest with a finger. "Like I was. *Selfish.* This is not about your friends and your enemies. It is much bigger than that. It is about balance. It is about life and death. For everyone."

Dashi batted the hand away with her own mittened one, some still-alert part of her brain noting that, for a spirit, Khagan Nuray felt surprisingly substantial. "I don't like when you do that," she said crossly. "Are you telling me this because you know what will happen to me, or are you only guessing?"

"The dead see clearly what the living do not."

"So that's a...yes?" A yawn cracked Dashi's jaw wide. Her eyelids were growing heavier by the second.

Khagan Nuray looked away, her expression regretful. "My words are guarded by necessity. Action is the purview of the living. The dead can only watch."

"You're…not…," Dashi sat down hard in the snow, no longer feeling the cold, "…much help then."

Khagan Nuray glared down at her. The expression of disappointment she wore was familiar, which made it vaguely comforting. From the corner of her eye, Dashi saw more figures in the mist. They crowded close together, bending over as if they'd just stumbled upon something precious. When she turned her head, however, all she could see was the dark shape of Okhron's boots, the soles pointed toward her face.

Chapter 20

Lantern light pierced Dashi's shuttered eyelids. She groaned and slung her arm over her face, sluicing snow against her neck. With a gasp, she lurched upright.

Every one of the lantern's dented metal shutters was closed, muffling its light, but the fires from the camp were clearly visible once more. Black tree trunks, outlined against the snow in sharp relief, stretched along the road like the bars of a cage. Dashi squinted at the lantern, confused. She knew Idree had opened it before—*Idree!*

Dashi sprang to her feet, head spinning from the quick movement. Her heart beat irregularly, all but eclipsing Khagan Nuray's words. Okhron lay nearby, but the snow on the Purek road was unmarked and clean, with no sign of the steps they'd taken to get there. What if she couldn't find Idree? What if—

She stopped, noticing the small, shadowy figure at the same time that her antennae registered Idree's scent. Her sister sat in the snow, arms hugging her knees.

Dashi let out a breath. "What are you doing?" she asked, approaching cautiously.

Idree blinked up at her. "Shivering and waiting for you. They said you might be a while, but I didn't want to go back to the camp and leave you here."

There was no need to ask to whom Idree referred. Dashi glanced around. The mist had returned to the trees, but she knew the movement for what it was: not a retreat, merely a posting of sentries.

"What else did they say?" Dashi asked.

Idree's shrug was noncommittal. "Just talked about the honor of being seamstress, of the lives I could save."

Dashi barely kept in her harumph of disagreement. *The* honor *of being chosen, indeed*. To her, the golden needle was the source of all their problems.

"Anyone you recognized?" she asked instead.

"Only Mother, but she was less interested in the needle and more interested in just...looking at me. She looked good, Dashi, not...not like she had. She told me she loved me."

Dashi felt a twist of envy. The only person the mist had shown *her* was the frustratingly vague Khagan Nuray.

"Who did *you* see?" Idree asked.

Dashi made a face. "A Purek khagan."

"The same one as before?"

Dashi nodded.

"What's important about her? Other than the fact that she may or may not be our ancestor?"

"Khagan Nuray. She was the last khagan before the cataclysm. She was very worked up about balance and nature and—" Dashi frowned in thought. "Maybe she's not an ancestor if she hasn't visited you."

"Maybe she has. I might not have realized she was, you know, important."

"Oh, she'd have told you. She's pushy. And perpetually disappointed in me."

"Perhaps I'm better off without the visit," Idree said dryly. "She doesn't sound very nice."

"Nice is not a word I'd use for her, but I get the feeling she wouldn't want to be described like that anyway. Do you think—"

"Okhron!" Idree jumped to her feet. "How is he?"

"Same as before, I guess," Dashi said, but Idree was already striding toward her patient.

She sank to her knees beside him, running her hands over his neck, the stump of his arm, and his abdomen. His eyes fluttered open.

"Help..." His voice was barely audible, but the sound of it made Idree hiss in a breath, drawing back like she'd been burnt. His eyes rolled, closing instantly.

"He...spoke." Idree's voice was hushed.

"Mmhmm."

"I've never seen someone recover so quickly."

"This is recovered?" Dashi wondered what she had been like after her own stitching.

Idree pulled up Okhron's tattered pant leg. A strange sheath had formed over the wound there, tinged violet but still transparent enough to see the raw flesh beneath. It glowed faintly.

"It's a start," Idree said. "Grievous wounds need to heal before the transformation can begin, but it usually takes days for the layer of magic to become this thick. Some never do get it."

"I see."

"And to be conscious and speaking. I've *never* had someone do that so soon after the stitching."

"Maybe it was..." She trailed off, unwilling to put words to something so strange. *Maybe it was the mist...the spirits who'd hovered over him.* The idea sounded preposterous on its face, yet time had a way of moving irregularly within those creeping, white confines. She vividly recalled her first experience with the mist and the horror of waking up to find that the pyrothrite belt she'd worn had registered the passage of several *days.*

A thoughtful "hmm," was Idree's only response.

"So you think he'll make it?"

The awe drained from Idree's voice, leaving behind flat factuality. "Too soon to say. It's a promising sign, but I've lost plenty even after this point."

"And his tether?"

"What about it?"

"The khan wasn't nearby when he was stitched, so will Okhron be free?"

"Oh. No. I can give him the tether when I get back to camp. That's what I usually do. He doesn't want to stand around and wait for me to finish stitching."

Dashi glanced down at the statuette, nestled against her chest. "Can you...attach it to yourself instead? Or—"

"No." Idree's voice was firm. "If the khan isn't given the tether immediately afterward, he will kill the person I stitched, before they've had a chance to recover. I can't...I won't be responsible for that again." Idree plucked at her sleeve, her voice low. "I don't think the magic is supposed to be used like this. When I stitch, it feels warm and...peaceful."

Dashi's eyebrows shot up. *Peaceful* was not how she would describe what had just taken place.

"It feels like it should be a blessing," Idree continued, oblivious, "a saved life, not a life sentence. The tether is supposed to be a safeguard, I think, not a vehicle for more abuse. Like if someone was," she paused, casting about for an example, "a bully before being stitched, the tether could be used to rein in their excess. But if I was stitching someone who was a good person, maybe I could just attach the tether back to them. Then they wouldn't have to be under anyone's control."

Dashi was quiet, digesting this. She thought of Sable's cheerful acceptance of his physical changes. What would it be like to be a herald *without* being tethered to someone else?

"Does it hurt when the khan takes the tether?" Dashi asked finally.

"Doesn't appear to."

She sighed. "There is no justice in this world."

Idree smiled faintly and glanced at the camp. "Let's get Okhron beside the fire."

Once more, Dashi knelt in the snow while they maneuvered Okhron awkwardly across her shoulders. He was still limp and unconscious but less pale, Dashi thought. His head lolled against her shoulder and she glanced sideways at him, studying his long lashes and the cheeks that retained a trace of babyish fat. *His ears.* They were slightly pointed now and covered in nascent gray fur. Once, not long ago, she would have called the change monstrous, but in that moment, she felt only compassion. She wondered if he would live long enough to become a herald. She wondered if he would be forced to hurt someone he loved.

The moon had finally shredded the heavy clouds, bringing the threat of snow to an end. As they reached the line of sledges that marked the outskirts of the camp, the stag stepped out of the shadows. His gaze went from Idree to Dashi, before resting on Okhron.

"Is he...?"

"Too soon to tell," Idree said softly, "but I'll do my best."

He nodded, a mournful glint in his liquid eyes. If history was any guide, there would be more, Dashi thought as she trudged on. That's how the Pureks had done it. According to Sevlin, it had been considered an honor. Dashi almost snorted aloud. There was that word again—*honor*—just like the spirits in the mist had told Idree. How could something be an honor when it was forced upon you?

Zayaa's voice, tight with anger, was the first sound to reach Dashi over the crackling of the khan's huge fire.

"—let the seamstress and the golden needle disappear!"

Disappear? She knew the mist had blocked them from sight, but had it blocked out Okhron's screams as well?

"They are mine to command, *Consul*," the khan snapped. He sounded more alert than he had when he'd given Dashi the needle.

"Indeed, Most High. And if we lose them both? How do you propose we access the Wellspring then?"

"We will not lose them both. I commanded the ant to return the needle at all costs, even if that means leaving the seamstress."

Zayaa pinched the bridge of her nose. "One without the other does no good."

"Then you will find another way."

"There *is* no other way. There is an ancient order to these things that—" Zayaa broke off, visibly trying to calm her rising voice. "I did not invent this, Most High, and I cannot circumvent it. The principles of magic are part of nature itself and they must be followed if we are to achieve the desired results."

"We need more heralds. An *army* of them, which is what I was promised." He gave Zayaa a pointed look. "If the seamstress can deliver another herald, we'll be that much safer."

"It will take weeks before—"

"No," Idree said, shocking Dashi by striding into the middle of the conversation. She motioned for Dashi to set Okhron close to the fire, then knelt beside him, pointing to his furred ears and to the purplish sheath that covered his worst wounds. "He has already begun the transformation process, not even an hour after the stitching was completed."

Dashi's hands went to her neck, pulling off the chain. The khan leaned forward hungrily, accepting the golden needle before turning a triumphant gaze on Zayaa. If she noticed, she didn't show it. Her eyes were narrowed on Idree

"Why is it so accelerated?" Zayaa demanded. "Did you stitch him any differently?"

"I only know one way to stitch."

"There must be some reason he's so different than the rest," Zayaa pressed. "You're the seamstress. You have no theories?"

"None," Idree said smoothly.

"There's no telling if he'll be more likely to survive," Zayaa said to the khan. "A transformation has begun, yes, but that ultimately means nothing."

"No one can see the future," Idree interjected again, a slight edge to her voice, "but I think we can all agree that the khan was very wise to order a stitching here."

"Yes," Zayaa said. Her voice had turned silky, dangerous. "Very wise."

The khan considered Idree thoughtfully, then barked an order over his shoulder. "Bring me ten of the most grievously injured soldiers." He turned back to Idree. "You will stitch them too. Tonight, from the same vein. But first, Okhron's tether."

Dashi flinched, both at the khan's command and at the thought of watching him take control of another person, but he motioned her away before she could see anything. "Tell the moth that both of you will be standing watch over the seamstress while she stitches. The stag and the owl will be on watch at the camp."

Ten more stitchings. Dashi stole a glance at her sister's blanched face. Could Idree stand that many? Could *Dashi* stand that many? Then there was the matter of trying to replicate Okhron's rapid transformation. Dashi was fairly certain it had to do with the taiga mist, not the vein. What would happen when the khan realized the subsequent stitchings had yielded far less miraculous results?

Zayaa gave the order to break camp before dawn. Idree's final stitching had ended only an hour before, and Dashi stumbled through the process of readying Spit. Ese's scent drifted to her, mixed with that of the animals he was tending. The lower half of his face was covered with a woolen scarf. One lens of his spectacles had cracked and his eyes were almost as bleary as hers. Dashi glanced uneasily at their thinned ranks. It would be more difficult for Ese to blend in now.

"You put up a fight last night," Ese said, lifting a saddle.

"Not much choice. How did you fair without a sword?" Servants weren't supposed to carry weapons.

"I found an abandoned one quickly enough."

"And bragged about it afterward like a good soldier?" She'd tussled with Ese once, but she'd never seen him *really* fight. She could tell he was good though; it was written in every movement.

He shot her a reproachful look. "Was it you who fired the pyrothrite?"

Dashi nodded. The wash of blood had frozen overnight and the first rays of sunshine made the red ice sparkle. She plucked a frozen droplet from her furs and held it up, a red pearl shining in her mittened palm.

"Violent stuff, that."

"I still have dreams of strapping it to you one day." Dashi picked up her saddle, inspecting the girth and stirrup straps for damage.

"You'll have to get in line, little Dashi. There are many people who'd like to send me to my ancestors early."

"That seems more likely now that there are fewer servants and soldiers for you to hide behind."

Ese's shoulder rose, a study in nonchalance. "From the way the soldiers are telling it, the most likely punishment would be stitching, not death. The khan is looking for any excuse."

"You'd hate serving him even more than I do."

"I'd sooner kill myself than be one of his monsters." He eyed Dashi's antennae over the gentle dip of an equine back. "No offense."

She waved his words away, too tired to take any.

"They say one of the soldiers who was stitched is already changing," Ese said.

"It went...better than it normally does, apparently." Dashi tried not to think about Okhron's screams. Or about the screams from any of the others.

"The khan and the consul argued about it."

Dashi's eyebrows rose. "I thought you tried to stay away from the khan."

"Little Dashi, are you concerned for my safety?"

"Just wondering how smart you are."

"Very smart." Ese winked. "Soldiers gossip more than old women. I let them do all the information gathering for me." He ran a hand down the horse's leg, stopping at the fetlock to lift the hoof. "The consul is in a great hurry. She thinks your sister's patients will only slow us down."

"Of course they will. But we'd be slow anyway. There are so many wounded."

"I expect those who can ride, will."

She registered his phrasing. "And those who can't?"

"Your sister's patients are the lucky ones. The khan won't abandon them as long as there's a chance they can serve him as heralds."

"But the others—most of them would recover with a little time and rest."

Ese gave her a shrewd look. "By now you should know to expect nothing less from Temur." He stuck a mittened finger beneath his spectacles to rub one red-rimmed eye. "How far today, do you think?"

Dashi thought back to the Wellspring map. She wondered if the khan's commands would let her speak, but the answer flowed from her mouth without impingement. Logistics, it seemed, were fair game for discussion as long as she steered clear of the Wellspring itself.

"We'll reach a river later today," she said. "There will probably be a way to cross since it's off this main road, but it will take some time to secure all the animals and supplies on the other side. My guess is we won't get much farther than the opposite shore by tonight."

"A bridge will be slick this time of year," Ese said, eying the sledges.

"And there's a high likelihood of traps. I have no idea how long it will take me to clear it."

"So you'll be busy while the rest of us stand on the shore waiting," he said softly. His words sounded like a complaint but there was a gleam in his eyes.

"My apologies. Maybe you should take up dice so you're not bored."

Ese looked over her shoulder. When he spoke she could hear the smile in his voice. "Don't worry about me, little Dashi. I'll find something to do."

As she led Spit away, she rubbed her eyes. It was going to be a long day. Even Spit was tired. His head drooped and he butted her pocket with his nose, asking for a treat to get him through the day.

"I'd give you something if I had it, old man," she said, gently pushing his muzzle away. "Unfortunately, I—"

The crinkle of parchment cut her off: the shred she'd found in Zayaa's saddlebag when she'd gone to return the lock picks. Between the rats and the stitching, she'd forgotten all about it. Ducking around Spit so that he was between her and the rest of the camp, Dashi leaned into his warmth and pulled out the parchment. Smoothing it against Spit's side, she stared down at Zayaa's elegant script.

\#

"They have brutalized my son and, though he is safe now, the knowledge that he will always be targeted because of me has only hardened my resolve. Tomorrow, on the most Balanced of days, I lay my troubles at the source and reject what was forced on me."

\#

From the way it had torn, Dashi could see that it was the end of the translation, yet Zayaa had copied no scribe mark. Dashi thought back to the Purek document she'd translated, the one about the vicious Purek general who'd hung the head of the first unlucky messenger on a spear protruding from the shoulder of the second messenger. She'd largely forgotten about it—it hadn't seemed pertinent to finding the Wellspring—but there were definite similarities between that translation and this one. First and most obviously, there was no scribe mark on either. The author certainly *sounded* self-important, but the upper echelons of Purek society always employed scribes. It was almost unheard of for someone important to write in their own hand.

Secondly, the tone of Dashi's previous translation mirrored this one, more like an angry journal entry than an official account of empire happenings. This was personal, about the author's son being mistreated. Dashi closed her eyes, trying to recall the words she had translated, seemingly ages ago. There had been a son in that one too, she remembered. The author's son had been kidnapped. In exchange for his safe return, the perpetrators demanded that future heralds be tethered to them and that the author pledge loyalty to a new khagan. Dashi frowned, suddenly noticing the discrepancy between the author not using a scribe, something a commoner would do, and the kidnappers' demands, which could only have been directed at someone with power.

"'I lay my troubles at the source and reject what was forced on me,'" she read again. She felt more certain than ever that this translation and the one she'd made were originally written by the same person. Was the author about to lead a campaign of retaliation against her son's kidnappers? Doing so on 'the most Balanced of days'—for the Pureks, that meant the summer or winter solstice—would certainly be considered auspicious. Still, she could feel her attention waning. Who cared? She'd hoped to find a clue to Zayaa's plans, but this translation had probably found its way into the saddlebag by accident, lost among more relevant information about the Wellspring—

Dashi froze midway through the act of stuffing the parchment back into her pocket. In her mind, she could hear the echo of Zayaa's voice: "Memorize these. Wellspring. Fount. Heart of Life." She'd shown Dashi a list of different characters that could be used to mean the Wellspring. Her eyes swooped back to the parchment. *"I lay my troubles at the source."* The word 'source' had been translated with the same inflections as the other synonyms for Wellspring that Dashi had memorized. Maybe this *was* about the Wellspring.

Dashi rubbed the cantle of her saddle, thinking of Altan's pendant hidden inside. Back in the library, Zayaa had said her ultimate goal was avenging her family's death. Presumably, this was directed at Sevlin, though Dashi still couldn't bring herself to think that he'd ordered Zayaa's family to be burned alive. But what did that have to do with the Wellspring and why would Zayaa have lied to the khan about it? By any logic, she shouldn't have needed to. The khan would have been every bit as eager to harm Sevlin, the prince of a rival nation, as Zayaa was.

Yet Zayaa had deliberately mistranslated one of the Purek scrolls so that the khan thought dropping the golden needle into the Wellspring would make the magic go to the nearest bystander: *him.* It didn't even make sense. The magic had preferences for certain people, both in terms of who was selected as the seamstress and who survived the stitching. The unlikeliness of the magic suddenly jumping to someone based on the happenstance of physical proximity was nonsensical, though she doubted the khan realized it.

The actual lore had said the magic would stream into Idree directly if the needle was put into the Wellspring. What did that get Zayaa? It wouldn't hurt Sevlin, who was safe in Tyvalar. It wouldn't give Zayaa any more power. And Idree...would she lose the ability to stitch magic? Or would her abilities be somehow *enhanced* when the needle was in the Wellspring? Dashi shook her head. If it were merely a matter of making more or better heralds, Zayaa wouldn't have needed to lie to the khan. Nor would she have taken steps to bar Dashi from speaking about it. Even now, the khan's command not to communicate information about the Wellspring unless asked directly prevented Dashi from bringing any attention to Zayaa's deception.

Dashi shoved the parchment back into her pocket and swiftly mounted Spit, her movements jerky with frustration. She was missing a piece of the picture, she knew: a piece that Zayaa was deliberately concealing.

Chapter 21

The dead, both human and animal, were stacked neatly in the center of the road and burned. Almost half their number had been killed by the rats. Half the Yassaris too, though Dashi considered that to be less of a loss. With fewer mouths to feed and a shortage of uninjured animals, scores of sledges were abandoned.

As Ese had predicted, those who were badly injured but unstitched were left behind. There was a pretense of it being temporary. The sledges were encircled protectively and Zayaa made a show of all the food that was being left for them. "Until we come back through on the return trip," she kept repeating with a bright, false smile. But the rat attack was still fresh in everyone's mind and the general mood was bleak, proof that no one had entirely swallowed what she was selling.

"We are lucky to be alive," Tuya said when the much-reduced train of sledges stopped to rest midday. She was perched on top of one of the Yassari sledges, trying to tighten the yellow oilcloth with additional rope. The Yassaris had consolidated their sledges too, dropping from four to two. "I don't think the consul will pursue breach of contract."

Dashi glanced up. "What breach?"

"We agreed on transport. The pyro-tips were supposed to arrive safely at the place where the consul plans to use them."

"And where is that?" Dashi asked, casually probing for how much Tuya knew.

"There is a canyon that needs to be demolished," Tuya said. "As I understand it, the pyro-tips are for when—that is, *if*— we need to get through one of its walls."

"You don't sound too confident in my abilities," Dashi said dryly.

"The consul told the convoymaster it will be difficult. I'm not sure she thinks you can do it." Tuya cocked her head. "Are *you* confident?"

"Anything Purek has a mechanism for opening. There is always a way through; you just have to find it."

"That is the approach I take to inventing as well. Every problem has a solution; you need only the patience to uncover it." She looked at Dashi thoughtfully. "I hope you succeed. Then I can examine the Purek mechanisms underlying the gate." There was a trace of giddiness in her voice.

"It's hard for me to want to succeed at something that helps Zayaa, but to blast something that old seems..."

"Wasteful."

"Wanton," Dashi agreed. She picked up a yellow flap, pulling it taut so Tuya could tie it down. "I see you've decided to carry a weapon now." The Yassaris, she'd noticed, didn't usually carry visible weapons, but Tuya had strapped a sword to the driver's seat of the sledge.

"It seemed prudent in this locale."

"You nearly sliced my face off last night."

Tuya's gaze stayed on the knot she was tying, but she sniffed disdainfully. "I have never laid claim to swordsmanship."

"It's not an admired skill among the Yassari?"

"Of course not. Only those without brains would waste their time on physical pursuits."

Dashi almost smiled, imagining what her friend Baris would have said to that. He'd been a proponent of all physical endeavors, always teasing Altan and Zayaa for being so academic.

"But everyone says Yassari blades are the best," Dashi protested. "To create such fine weapons you must first be able to wield one, surely?"

"That is research. Yassari blacksmiths are trained so that they're familiar with the products they're creating. And even that practice was probably frowned upon by the elders when it first began."

"Only a few of you know how to use a sword?" Dashi asked, incredulous. "How do you hope to defend yourselves?"

"We managed just fine in the last war." Tuya picked up another length of rope. "Brawn will always lose out to brains."

"Why settle for one when you can have both?"

Another prim sniff. "I don't delude myself that I have an aptitude for fighting—it would be a waste of time to even try—but my other skills are more than enough to compensate."

"The invention of pyrothrite, you mean?"

"It saved us from the rats."

"As much as I hate to admit it, I think that's *all* that saved us last night."

Tuya slid her a glance, suspecting sarcasm. Seeing that Dashi was serious, she gave a single, formal nod. "You performed well yourself."

Dashi snorted. "Are we exchanging compliments now?"

"It seemed polite."

They worked in silence for a few minutes, not quite companionable but not antagonistic either. "Why pick up a sword to try to defend me from the rat in the first place?" Dashi asked finally. "You think I'm a thief."

"You *are* a thief." Tuya slid to the ground, stepping back to admire her handiwork.

"Not that long ago you tried to murder me," Dashi pressed.

Tuya's eyes strayed to Dashi's arm, once marked by the Yassari's malevolent plant. "That was an execution, not murder."

"Excuse me if I don't see much of a difference."

"You committed a crime beforehand, for one. Secondly, it was sanctioned by your khan and allowable under the treaty."

Dashi flipped her hand dismissively. "You're very defensive for someone who already admitted to not liking it."

"It was a lawful action," Tuya insisted. "The problem with you is that, in your opinion, you're not culpable for anything."

"Don't mistake culpability with an apology. I'm absolutely guilty of stealing from a Yassari caravan, but I won't apologize for trying to punish the kind of people who could put pyrothrite into a belt, knowing it would be strapped to a living person." Suddenly annoyed, she jabbed a finger in Tuya's direction. "The problem with *you* is that you believe whatever the other Yassaris believe. You follow Zayaa around, you curry favor with your convoymaster, but you don't care about right or wrong, or about what happens to anyone else."

"I wouldn't expect a thief to understand honor or the sublimity of invention." Tuya stalked off across the snow, saying over her shoulder. "Next time I'll let the rat have you."

It occurred to Dashi later, after they'd started traveling again, that she and Sevlin had once had a similar argument, not long after they'd met. He'd accused her of only acting for her own benefit, whereas he acted with the whole of Tyvalar in mind. It was strange to find herself on the opposite side of the argument, especially since she wasn't sure when the flip had occurred. She imagined Sevlin would've laughed if he could have heard her lecturing Tuya on right and wrong.

Her own words kept ringing in her head, sometimes joined by Khagan Nuray's gravelly voice: "*You are too narrowly focused. Like I was. Selfish. This is not about your friends and enemies. It is much bigger than that. It is about balance. It is about life and death. For everyone.*" Dashi shut her eyes for a moment, letting the sway of Spit's gait assuage her annoyance as she tried to remember what else Nuray had said. What was it that she was supposedly being selfish about? Being a herald? Zayaa's revenge?

The weather changed an hour later, ending Dashi's ability to concentrate on anything but the cold. It was an immediate switch, a door closing, shutting them off from a hearth they hadn't been able to see. Thick clouds blocked most of the sun's glow and all of its warmth. The snow didn't come immediately, but Dashi knew it was there, gathering behind the clouds, weighing them lower and lower until they'd nearly impaled themselves on the sharp tips of the trees. The animals knew it too. Spit kept his head down, his ears occasionally flattening against his skull in the blustery wind. Only the yaks remained unperturbed, their thick coats dancing as they trudged onward.

The banks on either side of the Purek road rose around them until, eventually, they found themselves riding in a canyon with steep, bare sides. The snow began then, not soft, peaceful flakes but sharp crystals flung by the wind. Dashi squinted at the horse in front of Spit, wondering where the river was and if the distances on the map were accurate. On cue, her ears picked up the sound of water, an unceasing frisson of sound that spoke of power and breadth.

The canyon walls disappeared, subsumed by a curtain of white as the driven snow mixed with the frothy spray from the river. The river cut through the canyon at a perpendicular angle, just as the map had depicted, barreling along without a trace of concern for those who would have to cross it. Moisture hung thick in the air, seeping into every seam, clinging to each hair, needling its way down collars and up pant legs, until they were frozen from the inside out.

The soldiers in front of Dashi halted a safe distance from the water, sliding from their saddles in a flurry of dislodged snow. The stamp of their boots echoed up the canyon and Dashi, out of long-curated habit, winced at the unnecessary noise. Snatches of conversation filtered through the roar of the river.

"—have to go first."

"Not a chance."

"—crossing that."

Even Ese pushed to the front of the crowd, eschewing his normal role of lurking among the horses and yaks, to survey the latest obstacle held up by the taiga. He studied the slate-colored water with an oddly meditative expression. The khan brought his horse nearly to the river's edge and plunked his boots into the snow. Dashi tensed. He had dismounted alarmingly close to Ese. He had only to look to his right—

But the khan turned away from the water, his soldiers following. Ese, tight-faced, watched him retreat.

"At least I'm not going to have to kill myself trying to carry everyone over," Solongo said, landing beside Dashi with a soft puff of snow. "There's—well, I don't know if I'd call it a bridge, but there's *something*."

Dashi studied the white layer that covered the river. "Where?"

"Do you see?" Solongo pointed to a piece of white that looked a little more solid than the curtain of snow and river mist.

"I agree," Dashi said after a moment. "I don't know if I'd call that a bridge either."

But it *was* a bridge, or at least that's what the owl and the moth reported after several fly-bys. It just didn't reach their shore. Instead, it was a cantilevered affair, with anchor points at both the far shore and a center column. Mid-span, the bridge hinged upward, pointing at the sky. *A drawbridge,* Dashi thought, when she heard the report. *Already raised against intruders.*

"Heralds!"

Dashi's attention snapped to the khan, but it was Zayaa who pulled the muff away from her mouth and spoke. "The bridge is lowered and raised by a triggering mechanism. It will be hidden somewhere on this side of the canyon and it will be hidden well. You will call me if you see anything that looks remotely manmade. A vertical cut in a rock. Anything metal. Any stone that has been etched, shaped or sculpted. Any human remains." A soldier standing behind the khan made a sign against evil.

The khan repeated Zayaa's directions, turning them into commands, and Dashi turned into the driving snow, spreading out with the other heralds to canvas the sides of the canyon. Snow-covered rocks crowded at the foot of the canyon walls, evidence of past rock slides. *Most of which probably occurred* after *the Purek empire,* Dashi thought, *which means we have no way of knowing what is underneath.* She began pawing through the rocks anyway.

The soldiers were also pressed into service, searching the lower parts of the canyon, while the heralds scrambled to the higher reaches. The Yassaris shuffled some of the rocks, but there were only five of them left and their efforts were distinctly unenthusiastic. An hour passed without success. The cold settled like a weight on Dashi's limbs, slowing her footsteps and making her hands fumble. Her stomach growled. She brushed snow from an odd-shaped boulder but found nothing more interesting than a rock masquerading beneath a layer of white. Another half an hour crept by. Finally, the khan, who had been pacing impatiently, recalled both heralds and soldiers.

"We will pull the bridge down," he said, his words muffled beneath layers of fur.

Zayaa didn't argue, instead conferring with several of the soldiers. It was decided that the owl and the moth would fly Dashi and the stag onto the end of the bridge where they would attach ropes and, using a combination of the heralds' weight and the strength of those on shore, they would force the bridge section into a recumbent position.

Dashi's gaze drifted to the raised end, which was covered by an enormous, rounded face of ice. Icicles as long as swords dangled threateningly. Dashi could tell, from the pinched look on Zayaa's face, that she did not like this plan. She also knew why: the Pureks had been paranoid about invaders. There were often extra surprises waiting for those who tried to force their way through.

"I'm sorry."

Dashi turned her head slightly, eying Ese without appearing to do so. "You think it's suicide, then?"

His gaze was fixed on the dark, swirling water. "I meant for before...for the belt."

There was a long pause. "I did not expect you to say that," Dashi said. "Ever."

Ese's mouth twisted with wry humor. "Neither did I. But the truth, however uncomfortable, is that we are each a sum of the choices we make and, by taking *your* choices away, I acted like the person I hate most." His eyes flicked to the khan. "Jochi would never have condoned what I did, even if it was done on his behalf. I wanted you to know that."

Dashi swallowed. She was still deeply angry about the pyrothrite belt, both at Ese for forcing her to wear it and at the Yassaris for creating such a thing in the first place. "I—"

"Heralds," the khan's voice boomed a second time.

Dashi turned away from Ese. Zayaa handed a heavy coil of rope to the stag. A second one went to Dashi.

"Owl and Moth, you'll deposit the stag and the ant on top of the bridge to weigh down that end. Affix the ropes and bring the ends back so that the soldiers can pull from shore." The khan motioned toward the upraised bridge. "Go."

"Yes, Most High," Dashi answered, along with the others.

The stag disappeared in the thickening snow, reappearing a moment later, his graceful bounds barely disturbing the newly fallen powder. A dark shadow glided just above him, connected by the straps of the harness. With three powerful wingbeats, the owl had them both in the air.

Dashi burrowed deeper into her furs, a vain effort to store warmth. Idree offered her a tight-lipped smile. Ese met her eyes and nodded. Practically a fervent blessing, coming from him. He was standing too near the khan again, but Dashi had other worries that took precedence.

Pursing her lips, Solongo said, "You're not going to look graceful like the stag."

"And you're not going to be fast like the owl. Just get us up there."

The moth gave her a pointy smile and, with no further warning, she caught Dashi in her arms and started over the river. The raised bridge loomed larger and darker as they approached and Dashi shuddered as the heavy, moist air pushed down into her furs. Above them, the stag touched down on top of the bridge, his hooves sliding precariously on the ice. A moment later, he unhooked the harness, gingerly settling into position while the owl alighted beside him.

The moth set Dashi down with surprising gentleness, but Dashi started sliding backward over the ice almost immediately. She'd had the forethought to bare her hands despite the cold. Now she clamped down with all her strength, feeling the strange bristles rise from her palms to arrest her fall. The moth hovered over her shoulder, waiting to see if she'd need help.

The stag lost his footing, then regained it again. "Hurry up," he ground out.

The shore was a hazy outline, only discernible because of the contrast between the white riverbank and the slate-colored water. The moth wrapped the ropes around the upraised portion of the bridge, then ferried the ends back to the shore, where the soldiers and several teams of yaks were waiting to pull. Voices drifted over the water. The ropes snapped taut. For a moment, it seemed like it wouldn't be enough. Then, Dashi felt a tremor in the ice.

"Brace yourselves," said Solongo, who'd returned to land on the lip of the bridge. Her wings tilted back and forth, balancing her as she added her weight to the top of the bridge.

The bridge creaked, its movement barely perceptible except when Dashi looked at the shore. She'd been able to see only layers of snow before, but now she could see shadowy figures. Some strained against the ropes. Others huddled like livestock weathering a storm. The bridge crept forward. Zayaa and the khan came into focus. Dashi could even make out Ese, moving quickly, his spectacles flashing. For a moment, it looked like he was dancing, his typically sinuous gait transformed into a series of spins and swipes. Then his leg whipped left and a soldier went down. Two more followed suit as Ese lunged toward them and Dashi felt a knot of uncertainty and hope in her chest.

Ese had timed his attack well. No one saw him transform from a lowly, bespectacled servant into a steppe adder, not even the soldiers who encircled the khan, their ranks now thinned by casualties. All eyes were focused on the descending bridge. The heralds, who should have provided the khan's staunchest defense, were too far away to do anything.

The tether flared inside Dashi, a white-hot pain that urged her to protect the khan, even as her mind begged Ese to succeed. The tether didn't compel her to leap from the bridge. There would have been no point. She was over the center of the river, where the current would sweep her away before she could do anything. She leaned forward anyway, her body ready to intervene as soon as it could. Driven by the same command to protect the khan, Solongo launched from the end of the bridge, her wings fluttering mightily as she tried to summon speed.

She won't get there in time. Elation filled Dashi, quickly replaced by dread, as the owl threw herself into the air. Unlike the moth, she was built for hunting. Wings beating soundlessly, she delivered, halving the distance to the shore in the space of a heartbeat.

Ese burst through the line of soldiers, felling one and hitting another hard enough to make the man's head rock back. Zayaa's legs bent, but she neither leaped to the khan's defense nor ran away. The remaining soldiers turned toward Ese, a half dozen hands drawing weapons. Everything seemed to slow, as if the weight of the consequences dragged at the participants, a subtle friction that made the owl's wings beat on a half count and Ese's arm unfurl like a slow-blooming flower.

The khan froze, half-turned toward Ese as he finally reacted to the commotion behind him.

The owl screeched, the primal cry of a hunter with prey in its sights.

Ese's feet left the ground, his back arching with effort. It wasn't his spectacles that glinted now—those had fallen away, suddenly unnecessary. It was a dagger.

The owl's wings flared, bringing her to a near stop. Her spiked boots swung out, colliding with Ese just as he slashed at the khan's chest.

Chapter 22

The owl hit Ese, knocking him to his knees with what sounded like a clap of thunder. A soldier tried to tackle Ese, but Ese twisted away, using the man's momentum to throw him into the flapping owl. Ese dove for the khan. He flipped him onto his back and swiped the dagger across his throat without a moment of hesitation.

Dashi inhaled sharply. She expected Ese to flee, or perhaps give in to his hatred and keep stabbing, but he only crouched there, pulling his furs away from his face to murmur something to the khan. Then he straightened and, with savage vehemence, spat into the khan's face.

A rivulet of blood fell from Ese's furs, dappling the snow, but he moved easily. He spun to avoid the sword of a charging soldier and then, with his elbow, knocked the man out cold. Ese swept up the sword, parrying another attack and disarming a second soldier with equal precision before engaging a third. The soldiers formed a semicircle in front of him, with the river as a natural border at his back. Ese smiled as his sword moved, belying the hopelessness of his situation. His fighting style had a smooth ferocity to it, equal parts dance and malice.

Finally, however, the inevitable came to pass. Turning to block a strike, Ese didn't recover quickly enough. He rolled right, taking the blow across the shoulder instead of the neck. It wasn't a fatal wound, but the force of it pushed him into the river. The rapids swallowed him eagerly. He bobbed up a minute later, his dark hair blending with the dark water. His eyes swept over the khan's prone form. With an air of great deliberateness, he turned away and gazed downriver. He paddled once, then stopped, as though the cold—or the effort—was too much. Dashi's fingers twitched toward him, but the river swept him into the snowy maelstrom and out of sight.

She glanced back at the shore, half expecting Solongo or the owl to give chase, but they were preoccupied with the khan. There was blood in the snow. Dashi hadn't thought she could feel the tension more acutely than she already did, but her muscles wound a notch tighter and her tongue turned to sandpaper in her mouth. *Was the khan...?*

Something sparked in the corner of her eye, an eerie phosphorescence that disappeared when she turned her head to stare. Beside her, the stag muttered a guttural string of words. She caught the word "ancestors" and then, clearer, "What is *that*?"

The soldiers had stopped hauling on the ropes when the khan was attacked, but the bridge had acquired its own momentum and it crept closer to shore with each passing second. Dashi stared straight ahead, careful not to look directly at the gleaming lines that emanated from the khan. Two went to the moth and owl, still kneeling beside him. Others went to the sledges, disappearing beneath the furs that covered the prone bodies of Okron and Idree's recent patients. The last two stretched toward the bridge. Dashi dragged in a great shuddering breath, but the line that plunged into her chest didn't vibrate.

"Can you feel it?" she whispered.

The stag grunted. "No."

Her fingers touched her chest cautiously, probing through her winter layers. The glowing line felt vaguely electric but also warm, like her fingers had crossed a beam of sunshine. She raised her head. She could *see* the magic that bound her to the khan's will.

"If a cart driver dies," Sevlin's scroll had said, *"the oxen will run off, the whip cast aside and the reins left to trail. So too with the half-torn."*

A soldier, who'd been bent over the khan, straightened. He took a step back, boots sinking into red snow, and slowly shook his head. As though awaiting this official confirmation, the tethers began to blur where they met the khan's chest. One by one, they floated away from him, each loose tether waving gently on an unfelt breeze. Solongo raised a hand to touch her own chest, her incredulous expression mirroring Dashi's. The owl's feathers puffed in alarm. She stood stiffly, braced for an explosion of pain from the tether. The soldiers had been oblivious to the tethers before. Now, they stumbled back, falling over each other as they tried to put as much distance between themselves and the lines of light as possible.

"We're free," Dashi breathed. She turned to the stag, almost babbling with excitement. "He's dead. We're free!"

From below came an exultant cry, and then Zayaa's familiar voice. "Kneel."

Dashi's attention snapped to shore, in time to see Solongo drop obediently to her knees. The soldiers, servants and Yassaris had backed away, pressing against the canyon wall. Zayaa towered over Solongo in an ocean of space. There was a triumphant expression on Zayaa's face and a tether in her right hand, its light bathing her sleeve in pale gold. As Dashi watched, the light flickered, then went out entirely, rendering the tether invisible.

No. The reins would be left to trail, the scroll had said. It hadn't mentioned what happened if *someone else* picked them up.

The other tethers continued to glow, beckoning from where they floated. The tethers belonging to Idree's recently stitched patients flopped just above the snow, lank and disspirited. Zayaa scooped them up without effort. But when she reached for Okhron's, it bounced out of reach, a thistle spinning on the wind.

Dashi's hand dropped to her own tether, trying to jerk it toward her, the way one would play a fishing line or rope, but it didn't move. Although she could feel it, it had no weight of its own. Her hands sped futilely while the tether refused to reel out of Zayaa's reach.

Sickening despair bloomed inside Dashi. The bridge was still creeping downward, but it was too far to make the leap to shore. *I could jump anyway*, she thought, wondering if desperation could propel her through the water before the current swept her away. *If I'm wrong, if I miss the shore and drown with Ese, Idree will be alone.*

"Kneel." Zayaa's voice rang out again. There was an audible gasp from those below as Okhron flopped weakly off a sledge and into the snow, his body trying to obey its master even though it lacked the strength. Zayaa glanced up, sparing a moment to see whose tether she had captured.

"No!" Idree rushed to Okhron's side, trying to lift him back onto the fur-draped sledge. "He's too weak!"

Think, Dashi screamed at herself. She longed for her bow. There'd been no reason to bring it onto the icy drawbridge, where it would've been in the way. *Knives*, she thought, desperate, but she was too far to throw with any accuracy.

Zayaa's attention had moved to another tether, dancing just out of reach. She dove for it and missed, sliding on all fours. Her thick hair, wet with melted snow and the khan's blood, fell in glistening ropes over her face while she scrabbled on the ground, heedless of the red that stained her hands and knees and elbows. She looked depraved. *Rabid*. Her gaze darted around, too preoccupied with the hunt to notice the indignity of the moment.

It was enough to keep most of the onlookers at bay but not all. A squat man, the khan's remaining advisor, took a step forward, watching as a tether floated overhead, riding whatever currents affected the magic. His arms stretched out eagerly. Suddenly Zayaa was there, a knife flashing in her hand. The advisor stumbled, then went over backward, his hand pressed to his throat. The Yassari convoymaster crossed his arms, watching impassively.

Zayaa surveyed the other onlookers. "Stay. Back."

"Don't listen to her," Dashi yelled. She saw Tuya flinch at the sudden noise. "She's not even Karak. Are you going to take orders from a Tyvalaran?"

Zayaa whirled toward the bridge, hatred transforming her features from beautiful to terrifying. Behind her, Idree stood up and stepped over Okhron.

"If you catch a tether, *you* can be in control," Dashi shouted. "Haven't you ever watched the khan and wished you had that kind of power?"

If she could spur one of them to action, if she could distract Zayaa for a little longer, Idree might be able to get to her tether. Dashi glanced at the stag, wondering if he was also contemplating jumping.

He shook his ponderous head. "I can't swim."

Just a little closer, Dashi begged the bridge.

The remaining tethers bobbed above Zayaa's head, corkscrewing together. She slunk toward them, Idree following silently. *Zayaa needs Idree*, Dashi reminded herself. *She won't kill her.* The tethers drifted apart again. Zayaa veered toward the one on her right, interposing herself between it and the others like a wolf culling a weak member of the herd.

Dashi swallowed as she traced the tether that Zayaa had selected. It led to her own chest. Her legs tensed. The shore was farther away than she would have liked, but she couldn't bear the thought of watching while her fate was delivered from one tyrant to another. She might not be able to get there in time, but maybe she could provide a distraction for Idree.

She jumped. There was only a moment of fear—to think of Ese's frozen body washed up downriver, to remember what it felt like to nearly drown—before the cold bludgeoned her, so shocking it felt like her skin would shatter. Her head came up, arms instinctively reaching for shore, one stroke after another. The river crushed her chest and surged around her legs, turning them wooden as the seconds stretched. Water pushed into her nose and mouth. Something crunched under her fingers and she grabbed for it out of delirious instinct, opening her eyes to see frozen reeds, their roots pulling loose beneath her weight. Dashi grabbed another handful, levering herself out of the river, not caring as she landed face-first in the snow.

The icy grip of the river clung to her body, phantom fingers that robbed her own fingers of feeling and dug into her chest, transforming each breath into agony. She looked up, blinking slowly as ice crystalized on her lashes. Large snowflakes were falling now, hitting her numb cheeks. They disappeared into the khan's still-warm blood and dappled Zayaa's dark hair.

The cold had numbed Dashi's mind as much as her body, but the sight of Zayaa jolted her into action. She pushed to her feet, lurching over the gentle slope as if it were difficult terrain. Zayaa stretched out a hand toward the tether. Dashi's hands were trembling from the cold, but she let her knife fly anyway. The blade sliced harmlessly into the snow at Zayaa's feet, startling her into jumping backward. Dashi's tether lurched upward, once again out of reach.

Zayaa swore, wheeling in Dashi's direction just as Idree threw herself into the fray. Zayaa was a tall woman, but the surprise of Idree's weight was enough to make her stumble. Idree tangled her legs around Zayaa's. They both slammed to the ground.

"The knife," Dashi croaked. She'd fallen to her knees again. Idree was back on her feet, her face upturned as she tracked Dashi's tether. She took two steps after it, before Zayaa grabbed her ankle, pulling her to the ground and doling out a single, sharp strike to Idree's temple.

Zayaa straightened, puffing a little. Her gaze swung around her. "Moth, keep her from interfering. If anyone else moves toward the tethers, drop them in the river."

Solongo moved obediently, squatting next to Idree as she scanned the line of soldiers, servants and Yassaris. Her face was an emotionless mask, except for the quick dart of her eyes toward the owl. Dashi followed her glance. Unlike the stag, the owl wasn't stranded on top of the bridge, nor was she stunned by the cold like Dashi. Yet, she didn't move. Her head was burrowed into her hunched shoulders, which quaked so hard that a few feathers had come loose.

"*Owl.*" Dashi's voice came out as a hoarse whisper, but she knew the owl could hear her. "Get the tethers. Save yourself."

The owl shuddered harder.

Zayaa cried out in triumph. On the icy bridgehead, the stag jerked, shock written across his face.

Dashi crawled forward, trying to focus on the two unclaimed tethers. Her thoughts were dull. Her neck was wobbly. *My head.* Reaching up a hand, she found a slick sheath of ice coating both antennae. She gritted her teeth and snapped the ice off. Pain spiked into her head, subsiding into a dull throb at the base of her antennae. She immediately felt clearer and less dizzy.

Her heart thudded as a tether drifted in front of her. She stretched out an arm, her eyes focused on the slow waltz of light. Her fingers opened infinitesimally, careful not to disturb the air.

"Moth," Zayaa's voice rang out. "Remove one of the seamstress' fingers."

"*No!*" Dashi half-turned before she could help it.

Solongo yanked Idree's mitten off and, blank-faced, closed her sharp teeth over Idree's remaining pinkie finger. Idree's scream sliced into Dashi as effectively as any sword. It was wordless with pain at first: a pure, audible incarnation of agony. The wail ended abruptly, as Idree clamped her jaw and stared down at the ragged, bloody stub above her knuckle. Solongo spat the finger out into the snow, then doubled over, retching.

Idree drove her elbow into Solongo's side, sprinting back up the canyon before the moth could recover. As the curtain of snow closed around her, she turned, screaming a single word.

"Dashi!"

Not a plea for help but an exhortation. Snapping out of her horrified trance, Dashi whirled. The snow masked the angry thud of her boots, turning the sound gentle and soft. The tethers had moved again. Zayaa was close, but Dashi was fueled by fury and each stride ate into the ground that separated them. Zayaa glanced over her shoulder. Her steps faltered as she screamed at Solongo, who'd decided to follow Zayaa's order to the letter and hadn't moved to pursue Idree.

Dashi covered the last few strides in a single leap, one hand closing around Zayaa's elbow. A dagger appeared in Zayaa's hand. She slashed, backhanded, as Dashi planted her feet, swinging Zayaa into the snow. Dashi glanced down. Reddish liquid—too thin and translucent to be called human blood—seeped from her arm, but she felt no pain.

To Dashi's right, the drawbridge was nearing its closure. The stag clung to the edge, staring at the approaching land. Zayaa jerked upright, clutching her dagger. Snow covered one side of her head. Wordlessly, Dashi palmed her last knife. Looking past Zayaa, Dashi watched the two tethers. They'd returned to the khan's body, hovering faithfully over the cold chest like a pair of hunting dogs waiting to be let back into the kennel. Her fingers tightened around the knife.

"Come," Zayaa said, command ringing in her tone. "You know who will win this contest. You know who will become your next master. You know what I am capable of, and what will happen to your sister if I'm disobeyed. Join me voluntarily, right now, and your sister will be free."

Dashi's lip curled. "You know me, Zayaa. Do you really think I'll believe that?"

"I *do* know you. You'd use your last breath to spit in my face, but most people aren't that stubborn if a loved one hangs in the balance."

Zayaa's eyes narrowed as she smiled. It was a familiar expression; whatever Zayaa was about to say would be sharp enough to draw blood. Dashi, impatient with talking and wary of wasting Idree's hard-earned distraction, lunged. Zayaa pivoted, her dagger rocketing toward Dashi's ribcage. Zayaa had always been quick, but Dashi's skills had been strengthened by a year of sparring as one of Ejen's guards. Desperation honed them to a finer point still. She caught Zayaa's dagger against her knife and pushed it aside, dipping her head to avoid the punch from Zayaa's other hand. She drove forward, her own blade flashing, exacting blood from Zayaa's shoulder, her wrist, her side. Not enough to kill—not yet, anyway—but enough to distract. Zayaa, busy blocking, didn't see Dashi's fist. Zayaa's head snapped back. She toppled onto her buttocks, her dagger still held in a defensive position.

Zayaa didn't plead or bargain, only gave Dashi that sly smile, as infuriating as ever. Dashi loomed over her. She couldn't fix Idree's fingers, but she could prevent her sister from being used as a pawn again. She couldn't bring Altan and Baris back, but she could keep Zayaa from betraying anyone else. She raised her knife. A shadow fell over Dashi. She started to turn as, too late, she realized her error. Zayaa's talk of sisters and loved ones, the threats of punishment, and the exhortations to obey hadn't been directed at Dashi at all.

The owl hit with the force of a charging yak. The pronged spurs on her boots raked up Dashi's side and into her shoulder. Dashi fell back, instinctively curling up to protect her face and neck. The owl dove again, but Dashi got a foot up, pushing off the feathered body so that the spikes slammed into the side of her boot, gouging leather instead of flesh.

Zayaa was calling the stag as Dashi flipped to her feet. She looked at Dashi and laughed. "Your sister may not be expendable, Dashi, but *hers* certainly is," she said, jerking a thumb at the owl.

The tethers still hugged the khan's body. Zayaa flew toward them, Dashi sprinting behind her. The wound in her side seared, flames that gyrated with each heartbeat. The scent of her own fear and blood flooded the air. Suddenly the great, swinging head of the stag was in front of her. Dashi veered left as antler tips skated in front of her face, missing it by a finger. She thrust her knife out, but its reach was pitiful compared to those enormous antlers. The stag snorted, the sound billowing out of him in a chalky cloud. His mannerisms were so closely matched to a real stag that, for a moment, Dashi forgot he had a human face and torso. He waited, watching her with dark, sorrowful eyes. Behind him, the tethers rolled playfully over the khan's body, begging to be claimed.

Anyone but Zayaa, was all Dashi could think. Anyone but the woman who'd killed her friends. Her gaze drifted to Spit, to her bow and her sword belt, draped carelessly over the saddle.

Dashi lunged. An antler tip grazed her shoulder, but she wrapped her legs around one of the stag's long, delicate ones and twisted. He stumbled, a hoof jabbing into her back. An antler caught Dashi in the hip, this time tearing through her furs and into her toughened skin as she drew back her hand and threw.

Zayaa fell onto her hands and knees, a few steps from the tethers. The knife handle stuck out of her calf.

Dashi surged to her feet, kicking wildly at the stag. He bellowed in pain, but she didn't care if she hurt him, didn't care if he was being coerced. She was so close to freedom, so *uselessly* close. Wings beat Dashi's face and back. Through the mess of limbs and feathers, she saw Zayaa take one last, limping step toward the khan's body.

Dashi flung herself forward, hands grasping at empty air. Zayaa's clear, cold laughter washed over her.

"Kneel."

Dashi's knees sank into the snow.

Chapter 23

Dashi expected retribution. Blood dripped in a steady rhythm from Zayaa's calf, speckling the snow with crimson and matting the fur lining of her pants where it poked through the torn fabric. The skin across Zayaa's cheekbone was lumpy and pinpricked with purple. Blood pooled in the corner of her right eye from a burst blood vessel.

As Zayaa lifted the golden chain from the khan's neck, Dashi caught the scent of blood. *Idree. Solongo.* The moth touched down, silent as a snowflake with Idree held in her arms. Red furrows crisscrossed Solongo's face, and her bottom lip was split. Idree had put up a fight. The thought pierced Dashi's heart more than her sister's compliance would have.

Idree, for her part, appeared unharmed, if Dashi discounted the finger missing from each hand. Her sister's cheeks were pallid, like the wound on her hand had drained all the blood from her face. Blood covered one of her sleeves, but it wasn't continuously seeping through the mitten so her hand must have been bandaged. Dashi glanced at Solongo, but the other herald wouldn't meet her gaze. Her eyes moved to Idree's, holding them in unspoken conversation.

I'm sorry.

Don't be.

Your finger—

Don't worry. Idree's bloodless lips quirked. *I still have eight more.*

Dashi gave a slight shake of her head. *Don't, Idree.* Her glance snagged on Idree's mitten. Without the full scaffolding of fingers to hold it up, the material sagged. She looked back at her sister's face. *Don't make light of it.*

Are you telling me to wallow?

Dashi's shoulder twitched upward. *If you want to.*

Now it was Idree's turn to shake her head. *No.*

Zayaa gave Idree a suspicious glance and shoved her toward the horses. "Clean your wounds. Get something to eat." She turned to the other heralds. "The same to you. The bridge is down. We leave soon."

Solongo and the stag started toward the horses. The owl followed in their wake, shoulders hunched. Her beak dipped, nervously grooming a section of feathers she'd already worn thin.

Dashi got to her feet, but Zayaa stepped in front of her. "I've got you under control now," she said, pleasant-voiced, "but as soon as I don't need you, I will kill you. And before this is over, I'll kill your sniveling sister too."

"*You're* angry?" Dashi scoffed. "Because your pretty face got smashed?"

She'd been leery when responding to the khan, but Zayaa was too familiar for her to hold her tongue. Her eyes flicked to Zayaa's neck, where two chains—one for the amethyst necklace and one for the golden needle—were now visible.

"Will that face scare away the next man before you can seduce him? Altan, Baris and the khan: your bed doesn't go cold, Zayaa, but the people in it do." Anger was boiling over inside Dashi. *Idree's finger. Idree's face.* "Or maybe you're angry because, even with the other heralds' help, Idree and I almost beat you."

"*Almost* counts for nothing, Dashi."

"You—"

"Don't speak to me unless I ask something directly."

Dashi's mouth snapped shut.

Zayaa smiled. "Get my horse."

The urge to strike Zayaa writhed under Dashi's skin, but her body turned and went to collect Zayaa's coal-black mare. She knew Zayaa reveled in watching her stalk away, so she tried to picture Sevlin, always cool and collected. But nonchalance, both feigned and real, was a losing battle. Anger leached out of Dashi, flavoring the air so strongly with bitterness that even she shivered with discomfort. The mare picked up on it too, snorting and pulling against the reins as she leaned away from Dashi.

"You have to serve her too," Dashi muttered. "You should be on *my* side."

She held the reins out, trying to ignore Zayaa's knowing smile. Zayaa took the reins in one hand and, with the other, peeled back the torn flaps of Dashi's furs, inspecting the damage from the fight.

"Everything looks survivable," she said, "so no need to tend your wounds right away. Change into something dry, then check the bridge for traps. Disable any you find."

Dashi changed into her extra set of clothes. She only had one fur coat, now sodden and ripped, so she went to the body of the khan's advisor and unceremoniously stripped him of his. The collar and edge of the hood were covered in thickening blood from where Zayaa had cut his throat. Dashi wiped it gingerly against the ground, leaving red-brown streaks in the snow. A whisper of scent split the air, and her antennae twitched as she tried to place it. *Ants.* She relaxed a moment later: not giant taiga ants but normal ones, waiting out the winter in their lairs.

The advisor's feet were very large, but the khan's weren't. Dashi helped herself to his boots, half-surprised when no one protested.

Word that the bridge might be rigged with traps had gotten out, and the soldiers were giving it a wide berth. Zayaa flashed them a smile, her battered face not quite as charming as it usually was. She pointed at the canyon and then the bridge, issuing a series of commands that Dashi didn't quite hear. Whatever she said put them at ease, however. Their eager nods reminded Dashi of her younger self, when, standing near some Purek ruin, Altan would brief her on what they were after and what they might encounter inside.

Not eager, Dashi corrected herself. *Relieved*. With her parents gone, it had been a relief to know that Altan was in charge, that he had a plan. Now that the khan was dead, Zayaa was the highest-ranking official, at least until the messy problem of Karakal's succession was sorted out. To have orders, to have someone in charge, must fill the soldiers with a similar sense of comfort. Dashi sighed. She'd hoped they might push back against Zayaa's leadership, but it was clear that they wouldn't, at least not while they were in the taiga. The last thing Dashi saw as she clambered up the slippery bridgehead was the Yassari convoymaster, solemnly grasping Zayaa's hand.

The body of the bridge was coated in ice, though not as thickly as the end had been. Halfway across the river, the bridge disappeared, hidden by a collusion of river mist and snow. Dashi's progress was slow, every step carefully laid and every sense focused on the bridge. She'd seen traps manifest seemingly out of the planks, reaching up from below. Sometimes the only warning she'd had was the touch of moving air or the barely perceptible whine of gears. Sometimes it was less than that: a hunch, a stroke of luck, the breath of the ancestors.

She glanced over her shoulder. The soldiers had shifted subtly, encircling Zayaa as they'd once done to the khan. Zayaa was watching Dashi. She wore a slight smile.

The river rushed frantically below, surrounding Dashi with its cacophony. The bridge had no railings, though this was of little importance. She wouldn't have touched them anyway, for fear they hid traps. Beneath its layer of ice, the planking had an odd, faintly metallic, gleam. Through the spaces, she glimpsed a pillar-like substructure that descended into the water, marking the midpoint and the axis of the drawbridge. More metal glinted beneath—chains? gears?—but the mechanism that raised and lowered the bridge remained shrouded.

The opposite riverbank drew into sight, gliding out of the snowstorm. Spindly trees clung to a cliff face, sticking out like bony arms, and dark rocks jutted defiantly into the world of white. A swath of clear ground wound away from the river: the road, continuing beneath the snow.

Drawing a breath, Dashi stepped over the end of the bridge and eased one foot onto solid ground. She waited, the snow and wind stinging her eyes. Logically, she knew the Pureks might *not* have placed traps here. Perhaps the Pureks had considered the raised bridge deterrent enough. But she'd crossed swords with too many Purek traps to be complacent, so she turned her attention to the rocks bulkheading the bridge.

Her boot slid on the first step, and she had to grab a boulder in an ungainly hug to keep from falling. The movement pulled at the cuts on her side, wrought by the owl's spurs. Muttering curses, she eased herself the rest of the way down until she stood below the bridge. It was dark here, a contrast to the white turmoil in the atmosphere above. Hanging shards of ice threatened her scalp. Magnified by the bridge overhead, the river roar was almost deafening.

"There you are," she murmured as her eyes found the wire stretching beside the bridge supports. Frost reared off the taut surface in minuscule stalagmites.

The wire followed the bridge lengthwise, disappearing partway across. Dashi considered it for a moment, then drew her sword and cleaved it in two. A splash echoed from the center of the river, almost obscured by the din of the current. Finding nothing else, she returned to the top of the bank, where she began painstakingly excavating the snow and frozen soil at the front of the bridge, checking for traps.

The sudden, shrill cry of a horse pierced the air. Dashi leaped onto the bridge, her mind going straight to the taiga rats. There was no scent of rat, but the air coming off the river obscured all else, so that didn't necessarily mean anything. Ignoring the throb of her wounds, Dashi's pace quickened, propelling her through the white shroud that covered the river. She paused at the bridgehead on the other side, surveying the scene. A handful of horses were bucking wildly, defying any attempts to calm them. A black mare—Zayaa's—ripped at her flanks with her teeth, her neck twisting like a snake. Zayaa stood nearby, dazed. Snow covered her side and leg from where she'd fallen from the horse.

A soldier caught the mare's reins, while another threw a blanket over her head. The mare calmed a bit, though her hindquarters kept jolting uncomfortably.

"What's gotten into her?"

"What is—are those *ants*?"

"I've never seen them swarm like that in the winter."

The ants were impossible to see against the horse's black coat, but Dashi glanced at the mare's stockinged foreleg and saw a dark line winding upward. They were in the snow too, struggling over the frozen surface by the hundreds.

"They must be biting her." The soldier swiped at the mare's side with the flat of his hand.

Dashi's antennae whipsawed back and forth, tasting the air and finding both the lingering scent of her own anger and pain, and that of the ants as well. Their scent positively crackled with alarm, making her muscles bunch with the urge to move. They were here for her, she knew. She must have called for help—or whatever the ant equivalent was—when she was fighting for her tether. They'd responded.

Zayaa was also studying the ants surging out of the snow. She looked up at Dashi. "Tell me the truth: did you order these ants to attack?" The soft tone of her voice only made it more dangerous.

"No." Dashi's voice was calm despite the line she walked between truth and lie. She had not *ordered* the ants to do anything. They'd responded to the scent of her distress, the same way the ants in New Osb had responded to her hunger.

Zayaa was silent, watching the soldiers shake out the saddle blankets and smooth their hands over the animals' sides, searching their thick winter coats for stragglers.

"The bridge?" Zayaa asked.

"I located and disabled a trap."

"One?" At Dashi's nod, Zayaa's mouth pursed in displeasure. "Nothing else?" Above all else, the Pureks revered a sense of balance, meaning that traps were usually found in pairs, not singles.

"None that I saw." Dashi hesitated. "Maybe they counted the raised bridge as—"

Zayaa waved the idea away before Dashi could finish articulating it. "That's not a trap." Her eyes moved from the bridge to the soldiers, who were grumbling impatiently. "You checked the underside?"

"That's where I found the one."

"Its complement might be weight-triggered."

Dashi nodded. It hadn't been a direct question so the tether didn't allow her to speak.

Zayaa turned away and began issuing orders. The sledges were readied. A handful of soldiers took up ice axes and began to attack the bridgehead, smoothing a path. Once a ramp had been formed, dead grass and clumps of dirt were harvested from beneath the snow and laid over the ice to give the draft animals better footing.

Dashi watched the chips of ice fly into the river, slipping away in the current the same way Ese had. She wondered if he'd managed to claw his way to shore. It didn't matter, she supposed. With no supplies and no way to warm himself, he would freeze if he hadn't already drowned.

"The ant and the stag will lead," Zayaa announced. "Then a sledge, then a few riders, then another sledge. We'll alternate like that, but I don't want more than three sledges on the bridge at a time. They're heavy, and we don't know how much the bridge can hold."

A neat sidestep around the truth, Dashi noted, without panicking the soldiers over traps.

Zayaa turned to the heralds and reiterated the khan's commands: they were not to raise their hand to anyone unless Zayaa ordered, nor could they leave or help anyone else leave. In an emergency, they were to protect Zayaa first, followed by Idree. *Curious*, Dashi thought. Zayaa must think the khan's death severed any commands he'd previously given.

"Once you're over the bridge, your job is to protect the sledges until enough soldiers are there to do the job," Zayaa said to Dashi and the stag.

Dashi glanced involuntarily at her sister.

"Idree and I will cross by air," Zayaa said. "Now go."

Dashi urged Spit up the ramp, pausing at the top to wait for the first sledge. Behind it, she could see the khan, lying where Ese had felled him. The mess of red snow was already papered over with clean white. Snowflakes landed on the khan's face, clinging to the cold skin instead of immediately melting. His toes, bare now that Dashi had stripped his socks and boots, were beginning to darken. Ese would like that, she thought, turning away: his enemy's body left out, payment for the way Jochi's had been desecrated.

The trip across the bridge was uneventful. She watched over the first set of sledges and riders as they crossed, each spaced several minutes apart. Leaning into Spit, she tried to quell her shivering. She hadn't been able to warm up since her dunking in the river. Only her feet were snug. The khan's boots were of unparalleled quality.

As the sixth sledge maneuvered off the bridge, Solongo floated out of the milky gloom, her arms locked around Idree's middle. They both looked shaken.

"Rats," Solongo said succinctly as they touched down. "They came straight down the canyon walls. It's a panicked mess over there. Everyone trying to force their way onto the bridge instead of grouping up to fight."

Dashi's hand jerked to her bow. "How long can you hover if you're holding me?" she asked Solongo.

Solongo shook her head. "The consul is on her way over now."

Dashi dropped her hand, understanding immediately. Zayaa had everything she really needed on this side of the river. There would be no attempt to save those on the other side.

"Okhron is here," Dashi said, touching Idree's sleeve and pointing in his direction. "He's safe."

"But the others," Idree said, "we can't just leave them. The Yassaris too." She turned to Solongo. "You and the owl could go back—"

"They didn't lift a finger to help when your sister tried to claim her tether," Solongo said, her expression hard. "They didn't intercede when the consul ordered me to bite off your finger. Even if she *hadn't* commanded me to stay with you, I wouldn't go back to help them."

"They're people," Idree said plaintively, as Solongo stalked off.

Dashi grunted noncommittally. Though her initial impulse had been to reach for her bow, she understood Solongo's point well.

A shout from the direction of the river saved her from answering. It was Zayaa and the owl, swooping silently through the falling snow.

"Get the sledges moving. Stag, lead them up the road," Zayaa shouted as she touched down. Hurriedly extracting herself from the harness, she turned, scanning the assembled sledges. "Where is the Yassari sledge?"

"It didn't make it over yet," Dashi said.

"Not possible," Zayaa snapped, glaring at the empty bridge. "Tuya started over just before the rats came."

Now that she was thinking about it, Dashi realized nothing had come off the bridge in several minutes.

"Maybe a sledge broke and is blocking the way," Idree suggested, peering at the swirling snow.

Maybe the rats followed them onto the bridge, Dashi thought grimly.

A loud crack sounded from the river, followed by an ominous moment of silence, during which they all stared at each other. When the silence was broken by a series of loud reports, Dashi wasn't the only one who jumped.

"Look!" Idree pointed at the bridge. A smudge of yellow, made indistinct by the weather, lumbered into view.

With an ear-splitting creak, the bridge tipped sideways, pouring the Yassari sledge and a screaming horse and rider straight into the river. The rider stretched an arm toward the bridge and Dashi recognized the neat, gray beard of the convoymaster. Then the hungry current ripped everything out of sight. Another sledge, partially submerged with a taiga rat clinging to its side, spun into view before also being whisked downriver. *So the bridge* was *a weight-triggered,* Dashi thought. A scream echoed over the water, then fell silent. Idree pressed her hand to her mouth.

Swearing under her breath, Zayaa turned on her heel and stalked away. "Moth and Owl," she called, "fly ahead and scout for signs of rats. Or anything else."

The moth leaped into the air. The sudden snap of her wings sent the already jittery horses prancing.

"I attacked her when she recaptured me," Idree said quietly, watching Solongo's silhouette grow smaller.

"I know. I saw her face when she brought you back."

"I elbowed her in the head, kneed her in the groin, gouged her throat. She didn't even lift a finger to defend herself." Idree sighed, the sound a sad one. Her eyes were dry, however.

"Idree, I—"

"Don't you start apologizing too." Idree swung around to glare at Dashi.

Dashi shifted. She had the sudden urge to put her arms around Idree, but she could tell by the way her sister was standing that she would see it as patronizing.

"If *I* were the herald, you would have helped me try to free my tether." Idree's shoulders squared with an uncharacteristic bellicosity. "*You* wouldn't have blinked at losing a finger if it gave me a chance, so don't you dare apologize."

"I won't," Dashi said, curt to hide her own pain. She forced a calmer tone. "You've bandaged it?"

Idree rolled her eyes. "Solongo did it for me, *while* she apologized."

A sudden gust of wind had them both squinting.

"Dashi, look." Idree pointed at the bridge, still tilted sideways over the river. "I think...is that Tuya?"

The wind had temporarily pushed aside some of the falling snow, revealing a thin dark shape clinging to the edge, suspended over the rushing water.

"Everyone, mount up," Zayaa called.

"We have to help her," Idree said.

"I can't, Idree, not unless Zayaa says so." Dashi picked up Spit's reins. "I'm also not allowed to speak to her unless she asks me something, so if you want me to do something for Tuya you'll have to go ask Zayaa yourself."

Idree darted off, disappearing among the somber soldiers. The sledges began moving, and Dashi fell in with them. After a few minutes, Idree returned, now astride a horse.

She gave Dashi a quick, devastated glance, then stared straight ahead. "No," she reported. "We've 'wasted enough time' and, with the pyro-tips lost to the river, Tuya 'isn't important.'"

Chapter 24

They followed the Purek road away from the river. When a side canyon split off to the northeast, the road plunged inside. The new canyon was shaped like a wedge: wide at the top where it skimmed the forest but so narrow at the bottom that Dashi could ride down the center and, extending her arms, touch both sides. Large rocks were strewn over the road where the canyon walls had crumbled. Every few minutes, they had to stop and clear a path for the sledges. Even as she labored over the roads, Dashi kept her eye on the forest above the canyon. The trees poked their roots over the edge, like children curling their toes over a riverbank just before jumping.

Between the commotion of the khan's death and the bridge crossing, a considerable amount of daylight had been lost. As soon as the canyon widened, Zayaa grudgingly called a halt for the night. There were only twenty-one of them left, a number that felt even smaller in the forest-crowned canyon. A few snowflakes sprinkled on Dashi's shoulders and hood, so sparse she barely noticed. The temperature had continued to drop. Spit's head sagged beneath the combined onslaught of physical exertion and the cold.

"Chin up, old man," Dashi murmured, giving him a sympathetic pat as she began to untack him. "At least you're not covered in cuts and bruises."

Adrenaline had long since seeped out of her, leaving Dashi acutely aware of every place she hurt. Between the cold and the steady thrum of pain, she was miserable. She pulled up her sleeve to examine the cut on her forearm. It was shallow, thanks to her toughened skin, but wide, and in any other circumstances Dashi would have bandaged it already. The fact that she hadn't—because Zayaa had ordered her on to another task—brought Dashi's failure to claim her tether into simple, crystalline focus.

There won't be another chance like that any time soon, she thought. It wasn't every day that a khan was assassinated. They had wealth, power, soldiers, and now heralds, to protect them. Zayaa, who was more ruthless and cunning than the khan—more so than anyone Dashi knew, in fact—would only grow in power. Still staring at the oozing cut, Dashi let her forehead fall against Spit's neck.

Her mouth was overwhelmed by a sudden influx of bitter liquid. She turned and spat into the snow, alarmed when she saw yellow splatter against the white. Had she been injured more than she realized? But no, an internal injury of any magnitude would have made itself known by now. She spat again, her mouth puckering at the taste. Then, driven by some unknown instinct, Dashi knelt and pawed at the snow until she found the stalks hidden beneath it: blades of grass, rigid with ice, their vibrant summer hues leached away. Without stopping to doubt the impulse, she shoved a fistful into her mouth, working the grass into a soft pulp. Somehow she knew that when she spat the pulpy mass out and applied it to her arm it would harden into a fibrous cast, identical to the poultices the taiga ants had applied to her wounds after the khan's race.

She felt a surge of shame at this strange, inhuman endeavor, and briefly contemplated spitting the grass into the snow. Practicality won out, however, accompanied by a measure of pride: she could heal herself, even when Zayaa had told her she didn't need to.

Leaning against Spit's broad side for warmth, she shrugged out of her furs and spat the poultice material onto her forearm, pressing it over the edges of her wound. Minutes later, she'd also tended to the gashes left by the owl's spikes. Shaking from exposure, Dashi yanked her furs back on, hiding the poultices from sight. When Zayaa walked by a few minutes later, glancing at her with that familiar gloating expression, Dashi smiled back.

"No sunset tonight," Solongo said, considering the sullen sky, "but I can look at your face and see all the colors of one."

"Funny." Dashi touched a lump along her cheekbone. Not wanting anyone to see how she'd bandaged herself, it was the only injury she hadn't patched. "It's nothing compared to Zayaa's face."

Solongo cracked a sharp-toothed smile.

"I assume Zayaa wants one of the heralds on watch at all times tonight?" Dashi asked.

"I think the soldiers would demand it even if she didn't. They've warmed to us since the rats."

Dashi huffed a laugh. "Didn't I tell you there were worse monsters than us out here?"

Solongo shifted on her log. "The worst monsters came with us."

A familiar scent forestalled Dashi's response. Raising her head, she squinted into the darkness. *"Tuya?"*

A figure stumbled toward them, falling beside the fire. Tuya's face was red with the cold. Despite the exertion of having walked from the bridge, she was trembling.

Dashi pushed her into an upright position closer to the fire and tucked a saddle blanket around her shoulders. She appraised Tuya for a moment, all glassy eyes and cold-cracked skin. "Here," she said, grabbing a hard cake of bread from where it was warming next to the fire. "I guess it's lucky for you we had to stop and clear all those rocks. You wouldn't have caught us otherwise."

"I followed...the tracks..." Tuya said, her words punctuated by her chattering teeth. "Couldn't stop walking...or the cold..."

"Did anyone else make it?"

Tuya shook her head. "The sledge fell off the bridge...I held on to the edge..." Unable to ignore the bread any longer, she sank her teeth into the crust, chewing ravenously.

Dashi nodded. "We saw you."

Tuya swallowed, eyes wide. "But why didn't—"

"Why *should* we have helped you?" Solongo snarled. "You didn't help us against the consul."

"I was hoping you—"

"Hoping but not *doing* a blessed thing," Solongo said. "You could have pried yourself off the canyon wall and grabbed a tether at any time. You could have grabbed it for yourself even." Her voice dropped to a whisper. "*Anyone* would be better than who we've got now."

"Yassari neutrality—"

Dashi snorted softly.

"Where did neutrality get you today?" Solongo asked. "The consul left you clinging to the side of a bridge and she ordered us to go on. Without your pyro-tips, your life wasn't even worth a twenty-minute pause to her."

Tuya turned to Dashi. "You were going to help me?"

Dashi shrugged. "Idree thought I should."

"She was the only one," Solongo added viciously.

Tuya glanced uneasily at Dashi. Dashi could tell that Tuya thought she was angry; in truth, she was too exhausted to feel anything. Her brain had spent the day generating one what-if scenario after another, thrusting them before her like a series of tantalizing desserts. What if she'd gone straight for the golden needle instead of her tether, throwing it into the river before Zayaa could get it? What if she'd brought her bow onto the bridge with her and been able to put an arrow through Zayaa's eye? The thought of adding one more—What if Tuya had helped them instead of staying neutral?—made her want to weep.

"Maybe you should go find Idree," Dashi said finally. "She'd probably like to know you're safe."

Solongo spat into the fire as Tuya walked away. "Spineless little mouse."

"I saw you talking with the owl," Dashi said, leaning forward to add a log to the fire. "You forgive her but hold it against Tuya and the soldiers?"

"The soldiers and the Yassari whelp don't have family members being held as collateral."

"The soldiers and Tuya don't know what it's like to be a puppet, forced to hurt someone they love," Dashi countered. "The owl knew the stakes. For all of us."

"She freezes sometimes," Solongo said, "like in Tyvalar. When she's focused on something, or frightened, she becomes very oblivious. It's a sort of tunnel vision."

"She didn't *freeze*. She attacked me as I was fighting with Zayaa."

Solongo looked up sharply.

"You'd flown off after Idree. Zayaa was on the ground. I had a knife in my hand, and the owl raked me with her spiked boots. Because Zayaa told her to. *Told her*, not commanded. Her tether was still loose. I could have…We could be…" Dashi trailed off.

The fire crackled into the silence.

"I don't believe it," Solongo said finally, but her tone said she did.

"I knew Tuya couldn't be counted on," Dashi said, "but I'd thought the other heralds could. At least with this."

"Zayaa told us that she'd given orders to have our family members killed if she didn't return from the taiga. Her way of insurance in case she was about to get left behind, I guess." Solongo said. "But if we'd escaped the tether, the owl and I could have surprised them..." She shook her head, incredulous.

"Who's holding your son?"

"He's in the prison camp still." Solongo stared unseeingly at the fire. "He's been treated better since I was changed into a herald. At least, if you discount that time the khan had me use a horsewhip on him." She gave a bitter laugh. "The last time I saw him he'd put on some weight. Had better clothes too. I guess it wouldn't be smart to let the *collateral* freeze or starve to death before they could be used as leverage. The owl's sister and the stag's mother are the same. The three of them share a tent and work shorter shifts than the other prisoners."

"How did you end up there in the first place?"

"Radku's father left just before he was born. It's been the two of us since I was about your age. I wanted him to have a good life. Better than mine anyway." She made a face, her delicate nose wrinkling. "I wanted to get him an apprenticeship at a saddlery. I didn't know anyone who could recommend him so I tried to bribe his way. When the owner took my money and laughed, I picked up one of his awls and threatened to gouge out his eye."

Dashi gave a low whistle, impressed.

"Unfortunately for me, a prefect walked by just then."

"They shipped you all the way to New Osb for making a threat?"

She nodded. "And when the prefects were arresting me, Radku tried to stop them. So they arrested him too."

"Ancestors above."

Solongo's mouth puckered. "The ancestors are no better than Tuya: standing by and watching."

"How old is your son?"

"Ten, now."

Not much younger than Idree.

Solongo's thoughts must have run in the same direction because she asked, "How is your sister doing?"

Dashi's eyes went to a nearby fire, where Idree's scent hovered. "Busying herself with Okhron. I can't tell if she's avoiding thinking about her finger, or if just it's easier the second time around."

"Probably some of both. The soldier looks like he'll make it." Solongo's tone was neutral.

"I don't know much about these things." Dashi thought of Idree's ten other patients, abandoned to the rats beside the river. Maybe Idree's silence had more to do with that than with her finger. "Have you ever been able to...communicate with other moths?" she asked Solongo.

"No." Solongo gave her a long look. "Is that what happened back there?" She held up a hand before Dashi could answer. "Never mind. Don't tell me. The less I know, the better."

Dashi nodded, remembering Zayaa's face when she'd accused Dashi of ordering the ants to attack.

"What do you think the new one'll be if he lasts?" Solongo asked, turning the subject back to Okhron.

"A wolf, maybe? Last I saw, he was growing gray fur on his ears."

Solongo huffed a laugh as the stag approached. "Those two should get along well."

The stag stepped into the circle of firelight, his hooved feet sliding daintily in and out of the snow. "The consul wants you," he said to Dashi.

Dashi stepped away from the fire, wincing as the cold assaulted her. Unlike the khan, who'd always been surrounded by advisors and servants, Zayaa was alone. She sat in front of a roaring fire, her eyes fixed on the dark road, straining in the direction they'd take the following day. Dashi wondered if she was thinking about the Wellspring. Of all the lines of Purek she'd translated—nature's balance being shifted and sparks dancing from a seamstress' fingertips—nothing seemed like it had anything to do with Zayaa's goal of revenge. But, whatever it was that Zayaa had planned, she'd shown no sign of slackening since the khan's death. If anything, she'd been consumed by a grim determination to push them faster, even going so far as to dismount and shift rocks from the road herself.

"I had intended to use the pyro-tips as a backup, in case you couldn't get through the Gateway," Zayaa said, without preamble. Her fire was so large that she'd shrugged out of her furs. Dashi had a brief glimpse of the scars along the back of her neck before she turned her head.

"Now that they're gone, there is no contingency plan." Zayaa paused, giving her a lingering look. "Don't fail or Idree will lose an eye, not a finger."

Dashi inhaled sharply, unable to respond more since Zayaa hadn't asked a question.

Zayaa's gaze shifted to Dashi's bruised cheekbone. "We should arrive at the Gateway tomorrow. Pack what you'll need tonight because you'll be going in right away."

The canyon widened as they traveled. Trees began to colonize the canyon floor, and Dashi had a strange sensation of a multi-layered forest, one crowding close enough to brush her shoulders, while the other leaned over her from above. Zayaa looked neither right nor left, leaving the riders and sledges to straggle behind her. Tuya hitched a ride on a supply sledge, though she had to get off and walk whenever the path became steep.

Dusk fell in earnest, bleeding seamlessly from the overcast sky and turning distance and time into something circular and unending. Spit's head jerked up, wary of the echoes that bounced around them.

"Save your energy," Dashi told him through cold-stiffened lips. "Zayaa may have us riding all night."

The words were no sooner out of her mouth than the trees began to change. The black serrated figures, a shade darker than the evening sky, no longer stooped over them but retreated, suddenly wanting to keep the trespassers at arm's length. Dashi glanced around her. The canyon walls splayed wide now, and the echoes changed again. She studied the placement of the shadows, the dark lines that were too regular, too symmetrical. It was a building. Its stone facade was so dark it could have been knitted from the encroaching night.

Without sunlight, it was difficult to see the details, but what she could see was impressive. It towered, nearly as high as the canyon wall. Parallel lines of darkness made her think of the space between columns. An arched space in the center, black as pitch, might be a doorway. Her attention swung around her, finding more shadowy patches of manmade design, though it was impossible to tell how many structures there might be or where one ended and the next began. Her fingers began to drum against her thigh, the cold momentarily forgotten. *The Gateway*. They had finally reached it.

Zayaa's voice reached back, high and clear. "Make camp."

Leather creaked and clothing rustled, relief somehow conveyed in those mundane noises. Dashi's legs had become stiff rods in the cold, but she busied herself with Spit's care, her hands working methodically while she studied what she could of the ancient edifices, gauging height and width and style.

Idree fell into step with her as she emerged from the scrum of equine bodies.

"When do you think she'll send you in?"

"Soon, I expect." Dashi glanced to where Zayaa was mechanically working her way through her meal. Her face, lit by the nascent flames, was harsh and beautiful and decisive as she rattled off orders to those around her.

"In the dark?" Idree's hands chafed restlessly over her arms.

"Yes." It wouldn't be the first time she'd gone into a Purek ruin by lantern light, as Idree well knew. "How's your patient?" Dashi asked, looking for a distraction.

"He's awake. Eating." Idree sighed contentedly, the sound at odds with their surroundings. "How much farther is the Wellspring?"

"I can't answer—" Dashi broke off as she realized something: Zayaa had not renewed the khan's command of silence when it came to the Wellspring. "The Wellspring is probably two days away," she said, testing the words to see if they would stick in her throat. "Assuming I open the Gateway quickly."

"You will."

"Mmm." Her sister's trust was both gratifying and saddening. *Someday*, Dashi thought, *I will fail it.* "Idree," she asked in a low voice. "The Wellspring—what do you know about it?

"You can talk about it, now that the khan is dead?"

Dashi nodded. "His commands must have died with him. Zayaa renewed the other ones—not to hurt anyone unless she says, not to try to escape—but she must have forgotten that he'd given me additional commands." *Or she's close enough to her goal that she's not worried about me talking.*

"I heard the khan saying he could unlock power there," Idree said. "I think he was hoping it would heal him."

"He's beyond healing now," Dashi said dryly, "and in any case, I think Zayaa made that part up."

"So there's no power?" The twilight accentuated the size and darkness of her sister's eyes, making her look oddly nocturnal.

"Not entirely. When she was translating for the khan, Zayaa made it sound like *anyone* could access the power, but the scroll I saw only mentioned a seamstress."

"What do you mean?"

"I think it said 'sparks of power.' I can't remember the exact words, but they were supposed to have come from the seamstress' hands when the needle was dropped into the Wellspring."

"Do you think I could stitch without the needle—" Idree began, then stopped. "Why would Zayaa go through all this," she waved a hand at the camp and the taiga beyond, "for *that*? That's not much different than what she has now."

"That's what bothers me," Dashi said. "There must be some other advantage in it for her, but I can't think of what."

"Maybe I could stitch multiple people at once? Or maybe the survival rate improves?"

"Maybe." Dashi's tone was doubtful. "I heard them talking though, and it sounded like the heralds were only part of their plan. And that just doesn't seem like enough of a reason for Zayaa."

"Then what—"

Zayaa's voice rose above the stamping feet and soft chatter.

"Dashi."

Dashi's body responded automatically, turning away from her sister. From her seat next to the fire, Zayaa watched her approach, the flames turning her eyes amber.

"I hope you're ready."

Dashi was silent.

Zayaa made an exasperated noise. "You may speak freely."

Swallowing her retort, Dashi nodded toward the encircling canyon. "I'm ready but it will take time. There are a lot of buildings and a lot of doorways."

"Sit down."

Dashi sat.

Zayaa pulled something from inside her deel: a tiny case meant to safeguard the short missives carried by Purek messengers. From the yellow-white material, Dashi could tell it was made from bone. The lines and symbols carved into its surface had gone dark with age. Zayaa uncapped it, dropping two tiny scrolls into her hand. She replaced one and unfurled the other against her thigh, holding it carefully. It was in poor condition, its tattered edges curling back on themselves. Dashi felt her heart accelerate.

"No one has seen this," Zayaa said, watching her intently. "Not Sevlin, with all his spies and machinations. Not even the khan," her lips quirked ironically, "may the ancestors keep him."

"The Pureks *never* made temple maps," Dashi exclaimed, drawn in despite herself. "To copy down the sacred on something so fragile...It would have been sacrilegious." She looked up, open-mouthed. "*Illegal.*"

"Yet here it is." Zayaa's eyes twinkled.

"No scribe signature," Dashi mused, thinking about the other two anonymous scrolls. "I guess no one wanted to sign their own death warrant."

"Renegades always face opposition," Zayaa said. Her eyes were still crinkled with pleasure, but something about her tone told Dashi she wasn't just speaking about the Pureks.

"Holding a candle and calling yourself the sun doesn't make it so, Zayaa," Dashi said. "You're a traitor, not a renegade."

The congeniality dropped from Zayaa's face so quickly that Dashi took a step back. It was like watching a street charlatan make coins appear and vanish on a whim.

"The scroll," Zayaa said, her voice curt. "Look at it." Dashi's neck bent. "All the buildings built into this canyon are facades, designed to distract and waste time. Except one."

Zayaa's fingernail traced the curvature of the map, crossing each hand-drawn facade. Windows, columns and stairs were meticulously marked. Behind each doorway was a shallow entrance hall, with a heavy line at the rear to indicate a solid wall. The word "gateway" had been written in Purek in front of one of the facades. *No*, Dashi realized; *it wasn't a facade at all*. The entrance hall went deeper than the others. Two lines in the rear wall indicated a doorway.

"Fifth from the left," Zayaa said.

Dashi pointed to the door set into the rear wall. There was nothing drawn behind it, just blank space. "What's in there?"

"That's for you to find out. The way to open the Gateway, I expect."

There was some discordance in the illustrations, Dashi noticed, differences in color and writing utensils. As if the mapmaker had explored the canyon over weeks or months, looking for the correct entrance. Dashi stared at the slant of the Purek characters. It wasn't much to go on—only a few slashes of ink, after all—but the handwriting looked similar to the two unsigned scrolls.

Zayaa snapped the scroll shut and returned it to the thin case. "You will open the Gateway and return to me," she said. "You will be prudent. You will be fast. No unnecessary risks. No lingering. No treasure-hunting. Do what you're there to do and then go."

Dashi went to her saddlebags and retrieved a small leather pack. In it was everything she thought she'd need: food and water, flint, rope and grappling hook, an extra knife and several other things she'd found to be useful in Purek temples in the past. She'd set aside two of the sturdy travel lanterns for herself too, both full of fuel. When she finished gathering her supplies, she followed Idree's scent to Okhron's pallet, which had been pulled close to the fireside.

Idree looked up, her smile dying as she saw the pack in Dashi's hand. She stood up, her eyes instantly teary, and grabbed Dashi in a hard embrace.

"Go with the wind, come like the wind," Idree murmured. It was the traditional greeting of their father's people.

Dashi smiled. Idree didn't speak Mori; Dashi hadn't thought her sister knew the expression at all.

Wary of coming too close to anything Purek-made, the soldiers had erected the camp in the very center of the canyon. *Fifth from the left*, Dashi thought, making her way to where the line of facades began so that she could count properly. The edifices gazed down at her, shadows flickering over their faces as she passed with the lantern. Her tread changed from purposeful to cautious as she stopped before the first Purek ruin. Pillars framed a circle of darkness that she took to be a doorway. It reminded her of a taimen, with gills framing its gaping, hungry mouth.

The longer she looked, the more she thought *ruin* might not be the correct word. The front of the building was pristine, the edges sharp and unweathered, as though the craftsman had finished their work only yesterday. *Building* wasn't the correct word either. It looked like a tall temple that had been partially swallowed by the rocky cliff at its back. She eyed a curving staircase, which led to a covered entryway. Without the map, she might have spent days investigating each of the facades, probing for secret passages or concealed entrances and finding only traps instead.

She moved down the line of facades, Zayaa's command speeding her steps when she might have lingered to gawk. The lantern light seemed to bend around the fifth temple, but the details came into focus as she edged closer: a screen of massive columns, images of vines and cavorting animals. Dashi took another step. The pool of light caught arches, rising gracefully above the apertures on the upper stories. The heads of foxes and deer and snakes marched across the frieze.

Dashi raised the lantern overhead, trying to direct the light, but it would go no farther. Her hand brushed the straps of her pack, then moved to each of her knives, reassuring herself that she wasn't alone. She didn't need to touch the bow. The wood curved against her back like the arm of an old friend.

She drew a breath and started forward.

Chapter 25

She decided not to use the stairs. Only the bottom quarter was visible from where she stood, but in that section alone, Dashi counted four tripwires. For once, the razor-thin wire was easy to pick out. Edged in silver frost and limned in golden lantern light, they looked almost decorative. It was the ice that made up her mind. It flowed over the edge of each stair into long, drooping icicles, concealing the signs of any pressure plates or other traps that might be there.

Dashi uncoiled her grappling hook and threw it over the railing next to the top of the steps. The stone was slick and her feet slid out from under her several times as she climbed, leaving her dangling like an autumn leaf. In a few minutes, however, she had muscled her way up, bypassing the staircase to perch on the wide brim of railing. Protected by the overhang of the upper stories, it was largely free of ice.

"Ancestors above," she muttered, eying the fine weave of traps that covered the floor.

She leaned back, craning her neck to see the upper levels of the building. Despite being formed from living stone, the imposing walls reminded her of the nobles' homes back in Karak City: tall, stately and insular. There looked to be four stories in all.

She picked her way along the railing until she stood below a promising spot, but her first try with the grappling hook didn't catch. Neither did the second. Each clank of metal against stone made her wince inwardly.

She had no reason to be clandestine, but the hush of the place was contagious: the muffling, gray sky that had dogged them all day; the frozen canyon that ate the sounds emanating from camp; the soundless, white taiga, not dead but waiting. Behind her, the campfires dimmed as snow began to sift from the sky.

The metal prongs of the grappling hook clanged again, but this time when she tugged on the rope there was resistance. She tied the lantern to her pack. Then, gripping the rope with her hands and pinning it between her boots, she pulled herself up. The wind burst into life as she climbed, pushing her hood back from her face and swinging her like a weighted pendulum. Dashi pulled herself higher, hand over hand, pushing up with her legs. Another gust shoved her toward the wall. The hairs of her fur coat brushed ominously against the unforgiving surface. Metal creaked against stone, warning her that the grappling hook was shifting. Dashi's hand shot out, grabbing an overhead sculpture.

Breathing hard, she swung herself onto the cold stone and reached back to haul in the rope, which was now dangling precariously by a single prong. A glance revealed the small constellation of campfires in the center of the canyon, a counterpoint for the starless night. Was Idree watching, monitoring the slow ascension of her lantern?

High-relief sculptures jutted from the front of the edifice: a frog, a dragonfly, a boar and a stoat, frozen in the act of leaping to their deaths. They were interspersed with blank, black spaces, which was what had convinced Dashi to climb up in the first place. They were too narrow to be called windows. Perhaps they had functioned as viewpoints for archers or lookouts, she thought, or a ventilation shaft.

Humming under her breath, she edged onto a thin ledge that ran beneath the openings, leaning back slightly to search for handholds in the stone decorations above her head. The Yassari boots would have been nice for this task, but having an ant's traction on her hands made up for the lack; when one foot inevitably slid, she steadied herself with relative ease.

Upon reaching the opening, she found it to be slightly wider than her head but wedge-shaped. If she could get through the narrowest part, she would have little trouble. After some consideration, she decided to take off her furs and pack and stuff the lot, along with the lantern, inside first.

A row of stone finials jutted above the opening, so convenient that she felt compelled to check—and then double-check—for traps. Grabbing the finials, she maneuvered herself up to the slot, fitting her boots and legs through the narrow aperture. Without her furs, the frigid stone bit through her deel, the cold nearly as pervasive as it had been in the river. Shivering, she pushed against the finials, wriggling awkwardly until the resistance suddenly gave way and her hips slipped past the narrowest point.

She landed on her knees with a painful thump that sent something clattering across the stone floor. Dashi hissed in a breath, instinctively rolling sideways. She forced herself to lay flat and still, her face pressed against a bristly floor covering. What kind of trap had she just triggered? The lantern was mostly blocked by her pack and furs. Only a fingernail of peach-colored light shone against the far wall. The floor lay in darkness.

Something was still rolling. The sound was uneven, as if the thing was oblong or maybe only partially finished. It turned slower and slower, the last echo fading away until only the howl of the wind and the smell of dust remained. For several minutes, Dashi stayed that way, motionless except for her antennae, which poked tentatively into the darkness. The mat was lumpy beneath her. The coarse weave itched her cheek and stuck into her nostrils, threatening her with a sneeze. She hadn't seen any rugs or mats when she peered through the opening. How far had she rolled?

After another long minute, Dashi let out a breath. No arrows had swished by overhead. The room hadn't turned into a giant oven or been submerged beneath an unexpected wall of water. She got to her feet, careful to only stand on the section of floor where she'd already been. The room held its breath. She took a cautious step toward her pack, knees bent, weight on the balls of her feet in case she needed to move suddenly.

Light flashed over the room as Dashi picked up the lantern. She looked down and her breath fell out in a screech. The floor was strewn with bodies; that wasn't uncommon for Purek ruins. The magical cataclysm had left some ruins intact but empty, while others were densely populated with bones. Skeletons didn't rattle her anymore—not enough to be noticeable, anyway—but these weren't skeletons. They were....gro tesque. Haunting. She held her breath, keeping the scream inside by sheer willpower. *Emotions are about as useful as armor on a fish*, Altan's voice chided her. *Flashy, but hampers everything useful. That's not how we think. We study. We learn. We strategize.*

Dashi forced herself to exhale, to inhale, to study. Her eyes moved over the litter of human remains. She'd trampled the body, her uncaring feet breaking it into several sections: an arm over there, the hand nearly twisted off; a hole punched into the torso where she must have stepped down in the darkness. The odd rolling sound had been the skull of a second skeleton, now kicked halfway across the room.

Not skeletons. Skeletons didn't still have skin, blackened with age and sucked in around bone, a garment that no longer fit. It reminded her of the tanners in Karak City, stretching hides over wooden frames to dry in the sun. Skeletons didn't have fingernails. They didn't have—she gulped, her eyes going to the coarse mat she'd been laying on—*hair*. The swath of dead hair she'd pressed her face against must have been luxurious once, reaching the person's waist. Now it was an unnatural dusty color: part gray, part brown, part black, without really being any of those colors. The clothes had disintegrated in spots, giving Dashi more glimpses of that leathery, too-tight skin. In other places, it remained intact, incongruously hued in joyous yellows and bright greens.

She forced her gaze up, taking in the rest of her surroundings. The room was small, lined with more narrow shafts like the one she'd come through. Though the absence of the wind made it noticeably warmer inside, Dashi's teeth were chattering. She reached for her furs, telling herself that she would stop shaking once they were on.

Outside, the wind whipped by the openings, creating a peculiar, deep-toned whistle that sounded almost human. In the daylight, those slot-like windows would look out over the canyon, providing a vantage point for guards while shielding them from both sight and the elements. At the thought of guards, Dashi's attention returned to the heap at her feet. There were three more piled beneath the windows, shriveled and blackened. She did her best to ignore them, moving the lantern to the floor to check for traps. There were none, which fit with the evidence that the guards had died on duty, instead of rigging their posts with traps as they beat a hasty retreat during the cataclysm. The door on the opposite side of the room was a different matter, however. She never trusted Purek doorways.

This one was plated in hammered bronze. A circle of wood stared at her from the center like a single, blackened eyeball. It was a formidable door, something capable of keeping intruders at bay. She caught a glint of metal beneath one of the shriveled corpses and, stealing herself, retrieved the spear, studiously ignoring the way the arm of its previous wielder had stiffened. Holding the spear in one hand, she used it to hook the door handle and pull. There was a loud click of protest as a locking mechanism disengaged, though no lock was visible from this side.

Dashi stepped away, waiting as the door crept toward her on silent hinges. She wasn't sure what the penalty would be for opening it, only that there would be one. The rapid *thunk-thunk-thunk* of arrows hitting the black circle of wood in the center of the door would have made most people jump, but Dashi felt her tension decrease a notch. It was the traps she *couldn't* see that made her nervous.

Darkness yawned on the other side, barely dented by the lantern. Even when Dashi stepped over the threshold, holding the lantern aloft, she could see nothing but a chest-high railing, a wooden square of protection folded around her. Blackness stretched on the other side and lofted overhead.

She peered over the railing, careful not to touch it. Was this a second-floor gallery for the guards? A ladder dropped down on one side, invisible below the first few rungs and rendered inaccessible by the railing that surrounded her. Dashi squatted down, her fingers tracing over the spindles as she searched for a way to reach the ladder. She could always climb over the railing if she had to, but—

Her thumb found a knothole, the wood around it worn smooth by the probing fingers of long-dead Pureks. She thought about the desiccated bodies in the room behind her, the skin wrapped so tightly it looked like the people had died from its constriction. When the railing sprang open, she bolted through it, then sheepishly came back for her pack.

Partway down the ladder, she paused, her eyes touching the details illuminated by the lantern. Delicate metal sconces emanated cobwebs instead of light, but the rough-hewn walls were still smudged with forgotten smoke. The floor, mercifully, was free of bodies. Two rows of pedestals ran down the center of the room, fading into the darkness. Each was topped with the sculpted bust of a famous Purek: religious leaders, war heroes and the like. She could see more than one headdress, the mark of a khagan. Between the lines of pedestals was a long pool, somehow still filled with water despite the intervening centuries. It must have a source below ground, the rational part of Dashi's mind supplied, but she knew she would try to stay as far from the pool as possible. The memory of a giant mouth lurking in the bottom of one of those wells was too strong.

A faint sound reached her, there and gone again. Dashi twisted toward it, muscles rigid as she searched the shadows. Her antennae twitched, trying to wring clues from the still air; if there were any scents, they were close to the floor, not halfway up a ladder. She hung there for a moment, weighing the risks, but when another noise came—the scuff of a boot against stone; she was almost certain of it—Dashi made up her mind. Hooking the lantern's handle over a rung, she let go, leaping away from the ladder and the light that would make her a target.

The floor slammed into her feet, the impact rattling her knees. She kept moving. Now, she wanted the shadows to close over her, wanted that cloak of near-invisibility. *Shift.* Her foot landed on a pressure plate and sank slightly, warning her what was coming. She dove right. An arrow clattered against the stone where she'd been standing. *Shift.* Another pressure plate, another arrow, this one passing close enough to nick the top of her ear. Her brain acknowledged the hit but nothing else, not pain or fear, only the need to keep moving. *Shift.* She veered right, dodging around a bend in the wall. The arrow hit behind her, bouncing off the stone with the sound of cracking wood. She crouched against the wall, heart thundering, while the thud of her boots echoed around the chamber, a clarion call announcing her presence. Dashi squeezed her eyes shut in annoyance.

A minute passed. Nothing moved except the nervous energy skating up and down her limbs. Logic told her that she might have been mistaken. Rattled by the sight of grotesque bodies and the feel of dead hair against her cheek, she might have imagined the sound. *Proof*, Altan said in her head, *you have no proof,* but instinct overpowered his insistence on evidence.

When the echo of strange footsteps returned moments later, she was already reaching for an arrow.

Chapter 26

Dashi crept forward along the wall, its solid presence a reminder that nothing could attack her from that side. Nothing alive anyway; there were always traps.

She kept her eyes on the lantern, torn on how to best move through the ruin. Being bathed in lantern light felt like an enormous vulnerability. On the other hand, she couldn't explore blind. Sooner or later she'd stumble into one of the Purek's more dangerous welcomes.

The footsteps came again, a measured rhythm that sounded like it was just in front of her. Dashi frowned at the darkness. How could anyone move that confidently without a light? The memory of matted hair against her cheek made her shudder. *What if—No*, she told herself firmly. *Logic, not superstition.*

Dashi stopped at the demarcation between shadow and darkness. Moving any further, when she could not see what obstacles lay ahead, would be dangerous. The footsteps started up again, directly overhead now. *Impossible.*

The ceiling of the chamber was high enough that it remained hung with darkness, even directly above the lantern. The light did reach partway up the walls, however, revealing dozens of doors set into the sheer face. A person who stepped through incautiously would have a long fall. The doors, and the thought of unknown rooms on the other side, gave Dashi a hunch. She waited for the next sound, searching the dark ceiling until she'd pinpointed the origin: a corner that was a little blacker than the rest.

She let out a breath, losing some of her tension. *A ventilation shaft.* There was someone else in the ruin, alright, just in a different part. The footsteps she'd been hearing were echoes, piped in from overhead so that they sounded unnervingly close.

Feeling a little foolish about her hasty dive from the ladder, she retrieved the lantern, glancing at the pool and the twin rows of pedestals as she passed. Normally, she would have investigated each sculpted bust, combing them for clues that could help her navigate but also out of simple curiosity. Altan had always made it a game, testing her to see if she recognized any of the subjects, to see if she understood what the artist was trying to say, and that spirit lingered every time she came upon a Purek relic. *Zayaa is wrong about him,* she assured herself. *He cared about me. He was a good person.*

The chamber was a long one, a knife thrust straight into the heart of the cliff rock. In contrast to the doors uselessly located at the top of the wall, she did not see any exits at floor level. She had just decided to start over on the room's perimeter, when her antennae went rigid, shocked by a familiar scent. She eased toward the center of the room where the trail lingered, smudging the air. *No. That can't be.*

She followed it anyway, tracing it to one of the walls with a door set on the upper level. Had he come through one of the doors and rappelled down to the floor? Unlike Dashi, he'd gone straight for the pool and the rows of pedestals. She followed, less cautious of the pool now that she knew someone had already walked by and lived. He'd crisscrossed meticulously amongst the pedestals, checking each one, before coming out the other side. After that, he'd gone to the chamber's far wall, opposite the entrance. The scent had settled thickly here; he must have paced back and forth dozens of times. He'd veered off to examine a few items of interest—a mural, statues, columns—but always come back to this spot.

Dashi pulled her attention back from the scent, trying instead to look at the chamber around her, to see what he might have seen. It took effort, like focusing on a single arrow in the midst of a chaotic battle.

Flower petals had been sculpted into the wall, scalloped and delicate where they protruded. The proximity of the lantern washed out the colors, replacing everything with gold, but when she stepped back, she could see that each petal was painted a different color, increasing in brightness as they flared outward. From the corner of her eye, it resembled a giant, ostentatious flower.

Bouncing thoughtfully on her toes, Dashi stepped closer again, refocusing on the scent trail. He'd stood here, where the colors were darkest, at the center of the flower. She ran her hands over the stone petals, searching for a trigger mechanism, imagining him doing the same, his eyes and mouth narrowed in concentration. A petal near the floor shifted upward, immediately followed by a grating noise on her left. Dashi straightened, smiling triumphantly as a statue split neatly down the middle, revealing a narrow, arched doorway cut into the stone.

The statue was male, holding what appeared to be a bolt of cloth beneath one arm. He was dressed as a commoner, but the mantle of leaves around his shoulders indicated some form of natural blessing or favor of the ancestors. *A seamstress, perhaps*, Dashi thought, considering the cloth.

Moving carefully, she stepped between the halves of the statue. The scent was stronger here, more recent. Dashi closed her eyes for a moment, letting it wash over her, even as the rational part of her mind cast about for another explanation. She *wanted* him to be here. Perhaps the strength of that want had driven her to imagine the evidence.

The room on the other side was many-sided, with walls that turned and tacked without reason, and corners that appeared where the eye least expected them. The floral motif continued: blossoms carved into wooden paneling, floor tiles resembling a field of flowers. Dashi leaned through the doorway, careful not to touch the tripwires. Silver flashed from the floor tiles: a needle protruded from each flower design. They were thin, the width of a hair, but Dashi was certain they were strong enough to puncture the sole of an unsuspecting boot. They might do worse than that, she thought, noting the green sheen on the tip of the closest one.

The rest of the room was awash in rich, dark wood, miraculously preserved. Panels covered the walls and carved chairs lined two sides of the room. There was even a wooden chandelier, waiting to hold torches. How someone could make wood curve and curl that much without cracking it, Dashi didn't know.

She could see no exits in the room's shadowy reaches, but the scent trail beckoned her inside. Ducking between the wires that strung the doorway, Dashi balanced on the threshold. The tiled flowers were easy enough to avoid. They were brightly colored, for one thing, and were congregated in the center of the room, for another. What bothered Dashi was the thought that the flowers were designed to distract from something else. It was artistic sleight-of-hand, the Purek equivalent of the way Baris used to feint with his right fist, only to catch you in the jaw with his left.

Accordingly, her progress was painstaking. She kept to the edge of the room, following the scent, coming close to the rows of chairs and then to one of the sharp corners of the room. Her eye picked up the sudden glint of silver and she halted. Here, the floor tiles were the exact shade of silvery gray as the needles they camouflaged.

Careful of her feet, Dashi leaned forward to see around the corner. There was a shadowed gap on the other side, so low it was almost child-sized. An arrow, broken at a right angle, lay in her path. She saw no blood, either on the tip or on the floor, nor did she see what had triggered it in the first place. Although the lantern light illuminated several wires strung across the passageway, all were intact.

A puff of air alerted her a second later: a test, designed to feel out trespassers even now, centuries after its creation. If something—a human body, for example—blocked the moving air from reaching the complementary crevice on the opposite wall and pushing the tiny, feather-weight gears embedded there, an arrow would be released.

Dashi skidded to a stop. The arrow hit several paces in front of her, designed to target the intruder who thought they could dash straight through, using speed to stay ahead of the threats. It had been a long time since she'd seen this kind of trap. *An air kiss with a stinger,* Altan had said. It had been just Altan and her then, together in the bowels of a half-collapsed Purek theatre. He had said she was too young to go first, so it was Altan who'd entered a similarly skinny hallway, Altan who'd gotten an arrow in the shoulder, and Altan who had shown her how to remove a projectile, staunch the blood, and clean the wound.

Dashi stepped into the next doorway with a sigh of relief. The new room was octagonal and sand-floored, with a faux window in high relief along each wall. At the opposite end of the room, a door swung slowly closed, moving under its own power. Through the dwindling gap, she glimpsed a lantern, shining like a second sun. Then the door clicked shut, leaving her staring at the unfeeling bronze. *So close.* She could taste his scent on the air, pushed across the room by the door's momentum. It was overlaid with something else, too. *Something strange. Metallic.* Dashi tried to still her rapid breath, tried to think practically about the room that lay before her. *This is your immediate problem,* she told herself, staring at the sandy floor. *Solve* this *first.*

But it was hard to get the image of the lantern out of her head. It was still lit—the interior chambers kept the fuel from flooding the flame no matter the angle—but it had been on its side. If he'd accidentally kicked it over, it would have been second nature to right it. What had happened so quickly that he'd been unable to—*If you've lost focus, you've already lost,* Baris said, a warning in his voice. Dashi blinked, trying to concentrate on what was in front of her.

Her eyes roamed the perimeter. The sand abutted the walls directly on all sides, with no ledge or border, except the tiled lip in front of her and, on the far end, another to match. The sand had been combed into a swirling pattern, a complicated, spiraling dance that made Dashi dizzy the longer she stared. Dizzy...and suspicious. How could it have stayed perfectly coifed? No footsteps marred the pattern and, although she could both see and taste the swirls of scent on either side of the pit, they didn't seem to touch the sand itself. She narrowed her eyes. *How?* The ceiling was smooth, with nothing to which she could affix a rope.

She looked down at the line of tile in front of her boots. Each square was decorated with an image. *A pattern of suffering,* she thought, as she absorbed the depictions: a child with one leg; a man standing on a sword with droplets of blood spewing from his feet; two women, holding hands and falling from a great precipice; a man swarmed by rodents, which appeared to be eating his wounds. They were a distinct departure from the usual designs found in Purek ruins, which tended to be stylistic glorifications of the natural world.

She inched along the relative safety of the wood strip that bordered the tile, watching the pattern repeat but gaining no new insight until she noticed a slight distinction in one of the pictures: the man standing on the sword. Her eyes went back to the previous tile of the same design.

There were twelve different tile designs and the overall pattern repeated twelve times—a doubly sacred arrangement, by Purek standards. Each of its eleven partner tiles was identical, a careful rendering of agony. *This* tile, however, showed no blood coming from the man's feet.

Dashi stared at the anomalous tile, sifting details. There was another difference, so slight she hadn't noticed it at first: the tiny line that denoted the man's mouth was straight across, not so much a grimace of pain as it was an expression of...concentration? His feet—she squinted, leaning closer—appeared to be set *on top* of the sword, rather than pierced by it. Dashi shifted on her feet, trying to decide if she was inferring too much. She thought she caught a fragment of scent, sharp and masculine, wavering in front of her.

She put one foot on the unique tile. Nothing happened. *A good sign*. She transferred her full weight onto it, still tensed. No reaction from the Pureks. *Fine*, she thought at her imaginary Purek spectators, *I'll do it*. She slid her boot over the edge, pushing with gradually increasing force onto the sand. The sand—or whatever was beneath it—held firm. She rolled her foot gently, trying to suss out the shape beneath those granular layers. It was perilously thin, she could tell that much. A sword blade might be a bit of an exaggeration but not by much.

Stepping onto such a thin support was counterintuitive, flying in the face of her instinct for sturdy footing, or at least footing she could *see*. Dashi pushed the feelings aside, reaching instead for the scud of her pulse, the drop in her stomach, the strange calm that always fell over her mind—before sliding both feet onto the invisible path beneath the sand. Her posture was erect, her gaze angled a few steps ahead, but her focus was inward, feeling the pressure that cut a straight line from her toes through the center of her heel. She slid her boots forward, not even daring to lift her feet for fear she wouldn't be able to find the exact center of the thin rail again.

Movement flashed at the edge of her vision. Grains of sand trembled along the spine of a furrow, rolling down the hill in a miniature avalanche. A low hum reached her ears, rising in volume until Dashi could make out the individual components. It clacked, she thought, like teeth. The comparison lingered uneasily in her mind. She took a sliding step forward. More sand grains jumped down the spiraling ridges. The clacking grew louder. Then, steel flashed. *Teeth*, Dashi thought again, as jagged silver peaks thrust up from the sea of dunes. Some of the teeth were serrated, while others were long and sharp as incisors. They moved up and down, undulating in a pattern she couldn't discern. The spirals in the sand had not been art but the settling of sediment over an underlying mechanism.

Clackaclackaclackaclack.

Halfway across.

Out of nowhere, air buffeted Dashi, nearly knocking her over. *Another air kiss*, she thought in a panic, narrowly righting herself, but the air that galloped at her was wild and lawless, rolling over her from both sides, rather than a controlled puff from a single direction. She crouched, trying to make the smallest target for the wind's punches. Sand rushed in waves over her boots and slopped over the invisible rail in front of her, obscuring her own scent trail just as it had done to the one she was following. Her legs burned with the effort of staying low while still moving. Sweat dripped from the end of her nose, gobbled at once by the sand.

Clackaclackaclackaclack.

Almost there.

A flashing metal tooth leaped higher than the rest, a fish breaking the surface of the water. She was crouched so low that it came up beneath her elbow, catching her with a flash of pain. Dashi flinched, a movement as involuntary as it was dangerous. She teetered, perilously close to falling.

Clackaclackaclackaclack.

Her toes curled against the inside of her boots, feeling for the rail through her soles. She slid forward, lurching at first, then smoother as she regained her equilibrium, though it took her several seconds before she stopped swaying completely. After that, she kept her elbows tucked close to her body.

A row of tiles greeted her as she neared the other side of the sand pit. Dashi jumped to safety, stamping hard on the image of the man balancing on a sword blade. Behind her, the rushing air died. She would have liked to catch her breath, but the bronze door swung open, silent and ominous.

The doorway was set at the end of a turned hallway. Dashi could see nothing, save for two walls of carefully pieced stones. Darkness stretched on the right. His scent splayed across the threshold where he'd lingered before stepping through. The lantern was still there, deserted on the stone floor, and the sight filled Dashi with unease all over again. *No one leaves a lantern behind on purpose.*

She stepped through before the door closed again and picked up the fallen lantern, holding it in the same hand as her own so that one hand was free. Even with two lanterns, the light didn't penetrate the darkness. The door swished closed behind her. She caught that strange, metallic smell again but not the scent trail she'd originally been following. *Odd.* He'd certainly come this way; she was holding his lantern.

The walls of the hallway were free-standing, with no attached ceiling, but she could not see over them. The floor wept moisture, cavelike and clammy. Eyes on the floor, Dashi edged forward, each step bringing her closer to the end of the hallway. She paused where the walls terminated, staring into a black void of space. There was still no scent trail.

A single, melodic plink reached her: the sound of something dropping into liquid. Dashi stiffened. She hadn't broken a tripwire, nor had she felt the telltale shift of a plate beneath her feet. Yet something had changed.

Light flared suddenly over her shoulder, warm gold that transformed rapidly into an aggressive orange. *Fire.* She didn't have time to be frightened or to be pulled under by the old memories. The fire was coming too fast, ripping over the stone as if it were a field of dry grass. The seeping moisture, she realized belatedly, must have been a fuel source.

She ran blindly out into the open space, the fire galloping behind her. The lanterns, slapping together with each stride, revealed the floor only a few steps ahead. Her voice rose, inarticulate with panic, and she heard another voice answer, but her mind was too absorbed in survival to comprehend the words. Her breath came hard, rasping in her ears.

The amber circle of light cast by the lanterns now seemed barren and empty of options, rather than warm. *Left. Right.* More empty stone floor. Somewhere in the back of her mind, she realized the absurdity of this. The room must be made of something more than darkness and an endless, open floor. Where was a creepy pool when she needed one? *Think, Dashi,* Altan shouted. *There* have *to be walls. They're just too far to see.* She glanced up, thinking to use her grappling hook to swing above the fire, but the ceiling was high and lost in the darkness.

She knew without looking that the fire was gaining. The skin on the back of her neck grew dry as it ate her sweat. Then, with no moisture left, the skin itself tightened and parched, painfully hot. Suddenly, the floor in front of her met black emptiness. Dashi veered right, following the line where stone met plunging space. The two lanterns, still held tight in her left hand, dangled over the abyss of the manmade cliff, their light flashing against silver far below.

Water? Her eye caught the reflection again. *No.* She recognized the hue. *Acid, like in the Purek maze.* These were her choices, she wondered indignantly. Burned by acid or burned by fire? The Pureks *always* left a way out, even if it wasn't immediately obvious. On cue, the lanterns picked up something else in the abyss on her left: great vertical cylinders, varying in size, rising out of the flat, silver surface below. Platforms encircled the cylinders and there were other odd marks she couldn't understand. She glanced upward, a difficult task while running; she couldn't see the top.

The edge of the floor turned, and Dashi started to turn with it, only to find that the fire had flanked her. It was now speeding toward her on three sides, herding her toward the edge. She heard a masculine voice, an eerie combination of her present and past, yelling for her to jump. A cylinder loomed out of the darkness on her left. An empty platform, big enough for several people, girded it like a belt, a clear invitation. She gathered herself, meting out her remaining strides, and leaped.

The gloom made distance a difficult thing to judge, but she landed on the platform with a precise thump. The fire raged behind her, pushing up to the edge and leaning over the dark expanse, angry that it couldn't reach her. The flames were all she could see, all she could smell. Her breaths came rapid and shallow. She wrapped her arms around her middle and, for a brief moment, she let herself think of what might have happened, of what *had* happened to her mother. Fire was her weakness, the doorway that returned her to the single most devastating moment of her life.

Below her: a window ledge, her hands gripping the wood so hard it cut into her palms.

Behind her: her mother's screams, as flames ate everything in sight.

In front of her: Altan, calmly instructing her to jump.

Eventually, she realized that the present-day fire had died, the flames sinking back into the fuel-soaked stone from which they'd arisen. She was curled on the platform, knees tucked to her chest. Dashi forced her breathing to slow, shutting her eyes so she wouldn't see the plumes of smoke hanging in the air. She tried to pick up the lanterns, but her hands were still shaking violently. She set them back down.

She still hadn't been able to recatch the scent trail, and a small, mean part of her mind insisted that he wasn't here, that he'd died in the fire or the acid. Or that he was a figment of imagination and desire and had never been here in the first place. *But the lantern,* she thought. *I found his lantern.*

"Sevlin?" she called into the surrounding darkness. "Are you here?"

Chapter 27

"I'm here." His voice came from the darkness on her left.

She let her eyes drift closed as the familiar timbre washed over her. He must be on one of the other cylinders, one she hadn't yet passed when she'd been forced to jump.

"Didn't you hear me?" he asked.

"I couldn't hear anything but the fire."

A pause. "How did you know it was me then?"

"I picked up your scent in the first chamber and followed it here."

"Ah." Understanding colored his voice.

She felt the urge to twitch her antennae out of sight. "I have your lantern," she said.

"I saw."

"You didn't bring a backup?" There was a note of incredulity in her voice. *Sevlin*, underprepared?

"That *was* my backup. I dropped the other as I was climbing down into the canyon." His voice turned wry. "Anyway, the fire provided plenty of light to see by, at least until I got onto this platform."

"You *climbed* into the canyon?"

"I knew the Gateway was east of where we'd traveled before. Without the map, I had to retrace our route from the khan's race, ride up the riverbed, and then cut eastward from there. I was hoping to find the road when it was still on level ground and then follow it to the Gateway, but I...overshot a little and ended up on top of the canyon. I've been rappelling down from the top of the canyon and exploring a building every day. I thought there would be fewer traps if I entered through the upper story, but yesterday a chute opened up in the floor as soon as my feet touched it. If I hadn't still been holding the rope, I would have gone down. The lantern though...there was no rescuing that."

Dashi felt her eyebrows rise. That explained why she hadn't caught his scent outside. "That's..."

"Mad?" One side of Sevlin's mouth had pulled up into an al-most-smile. She knew it without seeing him.

"Yes. You came into the taiga yourself?"

"I didn't say that." He kept his voice casual, but she heard the reserve in it.

"See anything interesting?"

"A giant beetle, but it was more interested in eating the trees than me." There was a rustle from the other platform.

"You have a grappling hook?" Dashi asked.

"Of course." Amusement lined his voice, a thread of shared experience and past danger.

"Are we close enough?" The platform was made of hammered sheets of metal, with no lip or edge that would hold the grappling hook. She would have to catch it.

"I think so."

She heard him grunt with effort. A moment later the metal claws came tearing through the air toward her. Her hand shot out to catch the grappling hook before it skidded off the platform. She tilted the hook, maneuvering it through the handle of the lantern several times, before tying it off securely.

"Ready?"

"Yes."

She let go of the lantern, feeling that strange magic of familiarity flare, as if they'd planned and practiced. The lantern's glow plummeted through the darkness until the rope caught, before rising in fits and starts as Sevlin hauled it up. She caught the shape of him first, shadowy and broad-shouldered as he bent to retrieve it. As he lifted it, the light cast the planes of his face in sharp relief, light and dark warring everywhere. He stared back at her, both of them motionless while the moment stretched, growing and thickening until it became something else entirely.

Dashi cleared her throat and jerked her thumb at the column rising above her. "We're meant to climb."

"I surmised as much. I had been working out how to do it in the dark when you showed up to rescue me."

"You're not rescued yet. So far I've only succeeded in returning your lantern."

Despite the distance, she caught the quirk of his lips. She forced herself to turn away so that she wouldn't stare.

"Some of the handholds and footholds will be false," she said, "either deliberately weak or rigged with spikes. And Purek pillars and obelisks typically have blades that slide in and out, so don't position anything over a crack, unless you don't mind losing it."

Sevlin muttered something, then said, louder, "There's a trickle of fuel running down the side of this pillar."

Dashi leaned around the edge of her platform, moving her lantern systematically until she caught sight of the damp line wending its way downward. "I'd avoid that too."

"What happens when we get to the top?"

"Maybe there's some way to cross up near the ceiling?"

He looked at her. "Why didn't the khan send one of the winged heralds with you?"

"The khan is dead. Zayaa is in charge now."

His head jerked. "Of you?" He glanced at her chest like he could see the place where the tether plunged inside.

"Of me and all the rest. As for why it's just me, I think I'm the most expendable. She'd probably want to keep the winged heralds in case there's another river crossing." She wanted to tell him about Ese and the khan, about her fight with Zayaa and Idree's blood in the snow. She wanted to ask him about Baris and Altan, about Zayaa's dead family. But restlessness chafed beneath her skin, and it wasn't just Zayaa's command to hurry. If the fire was on a timer, the cylinders might be too. This was not the place for a lengthy conversation, no matter how overdue.

She tied the lantern to her pack and jerked her chin upward. "I've found my path up. You?"

He nodded but didn't move right away. His eyes lingered on her face. In the uncertain light, she fancied she saw that same intensity, that same hunger she'd glimpsed when they parted in the Purek maze. She remembered the feel of the metal bars crushing into her as their lips met, a cold counterpoint to the heat.

"Luck," he said in a low voice, then started climbing.

He moved surely, strong legs levering him upward, his hands nimble as they tested each hold. Stretched out to his full height, he looked enormous against the light-colored stone; in only a few minutes, he'd covered a considerable vertical distance.

His voice drifted down through the open space. "I thought you would be the type to compete, not spectate."

"Waiting to see if you'd need to be rescued again." She grinned as she dragged her gaze away.

Her path upward was pocked with obstacles. Moving as far away from the trickle of fuel as possible, she grasped the base of a metal spike and pulled herself up. From there, her movements became almost mechanical: search for the next handhold, search for signs of danger, try to reach the former while avoiding the latter. Her shadow, projected by the lantern strapped to her pack, spooled out above her, scrambling maniacally with elongated limbs.

Dashi stole a glance at Sevlin. His head was tipped back as he searched for the best path, the pillar of his throat as straight and strong as the one he climbed. He stretched upward and grasped a knotted piece of metal that protruded from the stone, covering a distance in a single move that would have required several from her. Still, it only took minutes for Dashi to close Sevlin's lead. Her reach might only be half of his, but her decisions about where to move came faster, sturdily underpinned by years of experience. The bristly scales that normally lay flat on her palms stood at attention, making each handhold surer.

It wasn't until the platform below had been completely swallowed by darkness that they began to experience real trouble. Sevlin grunted in pain, and Dashi turned in time to see a silver blade slither back into the pillar.

"Sevlin?"

He held up his hand, displaying a thick line of blood edging one side. He made an experimental fist.

"Just flesh," he called.

Dashi let out a breath, nodding to show she'd heard. A serious injury to the hand would make it nearly impossible to continue climbing. She reached for the next handhold, testing it while she clung with one hand. Her muscles were starting to feel the strain. She stared upward, where sand-colored stone tapered into shadow. How much farther did they have to go?

A sudden line of fire shot toward her face, racing down a trail of fuel she hadn't noticed. Dashi slung herself sideways, somehow still holding onto her perch. The pillar sucked the flame back inside a moment later, but the stench of singed hair lingered, filling Dashi's nostrils. She patted the side of her head with her free hand, cursing as she encountered smoldering strands. Fuel began to trickle out of the pinprick hole above her, laying a winding path for the next flame. Dashi hazarded a downward glance, watching as fire mushroomed to life from a different location. Avoiding the handhold that she'd touched directly before the flame, she reached instead for a loop of metal anchored into the stone. She placed her fingers carefully between the barbs.

"The cracks are so thin I can barely see them." Sevlin's words were punctuated by a pause as he dodged a flash of silver. "The blades are coming from everywhere."

"Did you trigger anything?"

"I've barely moved!"

Flame spurted near her again, though this time she was safely out of the way. Like Sevlin, she hadn't noticed any obvious triggers. There'd been no warning click of gears, no telltale shift as a mechanism switched into motion.

"They're coming faster," Sevlin shouted a few minutes later.

Dashi hadn't made the connection, but as soon as he said it, she knew it was true: more gouts of flame, more flashes of spikes and blades. The pillars had come alive, placid nags transformed into writhing beasts.

"A timer," she shouted back, pulling herself up. "Everything is on a timer in this room."

Sevlin's limbs kicked into motion, moving up the pillar in a series of great pushes and leaps. Silver and bronze glinted faster and faster, needles flashing through stone cloth. The flames on her pillar were slower. *Then again, I jumped on my platform later than he did*, she thought. She would bet the timer for each pillar started the moment a person's weight landed on the platform.

A belch of flame reached for Dashi's foot. She kicked away from it, then had to pause to rub her pant leg against the stone, snuffing out the sparks that had taken root. She stretched out for another handhold and pulled herself up, flinching as the pillar erupted again, close enough that heat caressed her cheek. *Faster.* A glance upward revealed only darkness, with no end in sight. Sevlin's light bobbed beside her.

Dashi reached for one handhold after another, trying not to think of the pillar stretching above her or the acid waiting below. Flames spurted everywhere, sometimes staying even with her, sometimes edging ahead but never falling behind. *Faster.* She selected a handhold, then snatched her hand back as a flame appeared, blistering her knuckles. She went sideways, scrabbling halfway around the pillar before she found another way up. She cursed the delay, then cursed again as she put her hand on a barbed loop of metal, shredding the skin between two fingers.

From her right came a whoop, a sound of relief and encouragement combined. Her sideways detour had cost her time; Sevlin was near the top. Dozens of stalactites glistened overhead. Their sharp tips brushed the bubble of lantern light, threatening to puncture it.

Minutes flew by as she climbed, dodging the shooting flames. Her hand, both cut and burnt, radiated pain. Sevlin was hidden by the stalactites now, but the glow of his lantern was still visible, backlighting the limestone teeth. It was a deranged version of the taiga: tree trunks made of limestone instead of wood, sprouting from a stone sky instead of soil.

"Don't wait," she called out, her ragged breathing precluding more words. "Timer."

But Sevlin's light lingered, either oblivious to her words or ignoring them. Fire flew from beside her. Dashi held on, gritting her teeth and swinging herself up as soon as it was gone. Her hands were cramping. She almost didn't care what the Pureks had in store next, as long as she was done climbing.

The pillar flowed seamlessly into the ceiling. Like the forest of stalactites, it looked to have grown there naturally. The circular metal hatch, on the other hand, was obviously manmade. Head canted sideways to avoid a stalactite, she reached for the ceiling hatch, fitting her fingers in the semi-circle of indentations along one side. She drew back in alarm when the round door popped open.

"It's alright," Sevlin called.

Stretching out, she grasped the edges of the opening, ignoring the sick, spinning feeling of space below her.

The room she dragged herself into was cool, with a rough floor that abraded her palms. Sevlin's light was closer but obstructed, like she was seeing him through a screen of branches. She couldn't quite see what was blocking him, but his presence drew her steps the way a flue draws air. She wouldn't be *safe*, exactly—she was still deep in the bowels of a Purek construction—but she would be with Sevlin. There was comfort in partnership, in the knowledge that she could lean her back against his and rest, that he would watch where she could not. More than a partnership, she thought, again remembering his lips against hers.

His figure remained partially obscured even as she came closer. He raised his arms to push at something, backlit by a halo of lantern light. Dashi paused, squinting. That was no flimsy screen that hid him from view. It was a work of art, the details worked so finely that it resembled a curtain of lace. She stepped forward, her outstretched hand trailing over the intricate lattice of vines and flowers illuminated by the lantern light. It was cold beneath her fingers.

Stone.

Sevlin's fingers were hooked into the filigree, his neck bowed in a posture of defeat.

Dashi craned her neck. The stone curtain extended around both of them, creating two large cells with no possibility of climbing over, around, or under. Despite its appearance of delicacy, it was thick. She could thread her fingers through and he could do the same, but they still wouldn't touch. His scent drifted toward her slowly, smudging the air where it meandered through the stone filigree.

She shook her head. "There must be—"

"I couldn't find any openings. It looks like the only way out," Sevlin gestured at the hatch behind her, "is the way we came."

Chapter 28

The stone cell was fifteen strides across and ten long. Sevlin's was to the left of hers. There was another on the right. The back wall was solid rock. The front wall, made of the same stone lattice as the sides, was slightly convex. Dashi squinted through the openings in the lattice, but her lantern illuminated little on the other side.

"One cell above each of the columns?" Dashi suggested, eying the hatch. The floor was free of traps, at least.

Sevlin grunted in assent. "There's a vertical crack on the front side," he said eventually, "but I don't see a mechanism for opening it."

Dashi, who'd been examining the solid stretch of the back wall, turned her attention to the opposite side. Sure enough, the lantern revealed a thin crack stretching from the floor to somewhere overhead. Her fingers quested over the stone flowers and leaves, pushing and prodding.

"Maybe it's on a timer too," she suggested.

"It better be." Frustration threaded Sevlin's normally even voice. "Because I can't find anything."

"It seems impossible after all *that*..." Dashi gestured at the hatch.

"That I won't be able to kiss you," Sevlin finished.

Dashi grinned, wolfish. "A kiss is unambitious. You should try for more."

Sevlin chuckled, and the sound warmed her. When had that happened? When had he become part of her, like Idree and Spit, Altan and

Baris? Their names hit her in shards of ice, recalling the niggling doubt from her conversation with Zayaa.

"Sevlin, I need to ask you something."

"You don't usually warn me."

Dashi looped her fingers through the lattice between them wishing it was thin enough that they could touch. The stone filigree only gave her parts of his face: the corner of one eye, a sliver of cheekbone, the pulled-down edge of his mouth.

"No," she agreed, "but I want to know the truth about this."

"Your tether—"

"It's nothing I could report to Zayaa. Or at least, I don't think it would matter if I did. I want to ask about something that happened a long time ago."

He waited. What she could see of his expression was carefully blank and unencouraging.

"Zayaa told me you're the Tyvalaran spymaster." No response, not even the flicker of an eyelid. "Fine, don't answer. I don't need you to." The corner of Sevlin's mouth twitched upward. "I saw the nest of papers in your tower and I'm a fool for not realizing it earlier. It explains why you came to New Osb for the Founding Day feast, even though Prince Zevi was already there representing Tyvalar. It explains how you found out about the khan's race in time to travel all the way from Tyvalar. It explains how you knew so much about the golden needle and the first seamstress. That story you told Idree and me...you knew every last detail. The Queen didn't tell you about its power and then order you to find it; *you* told *her*. So it doesn't matter if you confirm what Zayaa said or not. I already believe it." She realized she was taking a convoluted way to arrive at her point, babbling even, but she couldn't make herself stop. *You don't want to ask*, her mind sneered. *You're afraid of the answer.*

She drew a breath, steeling herself, but Sevlin mistook her pause for an invitation.

"I became spymaster after the attack on Queen Lyazzat. The previous spymaster was a holdover from Lyazzat's mother's reign, someone we thought could be trusted. Chaimak." His voice dropped a fraction, a thread of bitterness that was the only deviation from a calm, cold recitation of history. "Chaimak knew everything and everyone, it seemed. He helped Lyazzat's mother run Tyvalar in the last years of her illness, sending out missives in his own name, filling advisory positions with his own loyalists, presiding over squabbles between nobles so that he could curry favor with the least scrupulous and the most powerful. But after Queen Ariat died, Lyazzat proved to be less tractable than he'd anticipated. She had her own ideas about how to lead Tyvalar, and she refused to give in to Chaimak. So he made a pact with a group of separatists from the Kurlar region and with our enemies in Karakal. Lyazzat would be overthrown. The Kurlaran separatists would get independence. Karakal would get a weakened neighbor. Chaimak would get what was left of Tyvalar."

Dashi swallowed. This was sounding too close to Zayaa's recounting. *No*, she thought, *Altan would never—*

"After the attempted coup, we—Lyazzat, Zevi and myself—knew that we could trust no one. Zevi became Prime, the queen's head advisor. I became spymaster."

Sevlin would have been unbelievably young, Dashi thought, astonished. Still a teenager.

"And Chaimak relinquished his position?" she asked.

"Chaimak had already gone to the pyre," Sevlin said. His tone left little doubt as to who had sent him there.

"You lied," she said softly, "when we first met. You said you didn't know Altan and Baris." The knowledge hurt, not because she believed in honesty as a virtue, or even because she insisted upon it between herself and Sevlin, but because she vividly remembered the disappointment she'd felt when Sevlin had denied knowing her friends.

"I did not know you then, Dashi." His voice was hushed, a mixture of apology and resignation: sorry that he had done something, certain that he could've done it no other way. "I did not know the nature of your relationship with Baris and Altan. I only knew that two of my countrymen—the two who had rushed to my side during the coup—had been betrayed. You admitted to knowing them and to knowing Zayaa. You were familiar with the Purek language and culture. You'd even been with Altan and Baris when they were killed. And there you were, riding in the khan's race, pursuing the very thing I was after."

"And you don't believe in coincidences."

"Not in coincidences, no. But I do believe that you would never betray those who've earned your loyalty." Sevlin hesitated, choosing his words. "For all of our differences, I think we are very alike in that respect. My loyalty is to my country which, according to you, is misplaced naivety." He gave her a half smile. "But I have sacrificed much in service to Tyvalar and I would again. Your circle is much smaller, but you would meet death in Idree's place, and now I know the same was true about Altan and Baris."

"And Zayaa," Dashi said bitterly. "It used to include her too."

"Yes, well, I did not say that we never make mistakes with our circles of loyalty."

"Circle of loyalty," she murmured, liking the phrase. She glanced up at him through the stone lattice. "It includes you too, you know. In my nightmares, I have to leave you bleeding in that ancestors-cursed maze over and over."

Dashi's fingers dug at the stone. She would have liked to kiss him. She would have liked more. But even the thought of pulling him down on top of her, while appealing, was not the totality of what she desired.

She didn't want to have one taste and then never see him again. She wanted to take all day with him if she wanted. She wanted to watch his sword flash as he trained, a mercurial counterpoint to the stillness of his expressions. She wanted to ride beside him during the day and sit across a fire from him at night, watching the shadows transform his face into something mysterious. She wanted his stories of the past, those meaty tidbits he doled out a little at a time. She wanted his plans for the future. She wanted to stand watch over him while he slept, ready to put an arrow through anyone who would hurt him again.

"I wish I'd trusted you," she whispered. "I wish Idree and I had gone to Tyvalar after the race. I wish I'd gotten the seamripper. Just a few more minutes at the end of that maze and I...I could have—we could—" Her voice cracked.

"Dashi."

Slowly, Sevlin kissed the tips of his fingers. Without taking his eyes from her, he threaded them through the stone lattice across from her hand. He didn't touch her—the thickness of the stone prevented that—but a strange awareness sparked in her fingers anyway.

"Do you trust me now?" he asked.

She nodded, mute with emotion.

"Good," he said quietly. "Because I swear that I will see you and your sister free, or I will die trying."

"I...don't think that's as comforting as you mean it to be." She'd meant her tone to be light, but the pitch was wrong, an instrument with strings wound too tight.

He gave a low chuckle. "That's where the trust comes in."

She sighed, leaning her forehead against the stone.

"Did I answer your question?" he asked.

"I didn't even ask it yet." She smiled, but it felt tight. Sevlin never volunteered to answer personal questions and, now that he was being amenable, she dreaded the answer. "Zayaa said that Altan and Baris set her home on fire *with her family still inside*." She didn't bother trying to disguise the way her tongue tripped over the last five words. "She sounded"—Dashi swallowed—"like she was telling the truth, and I wanted to know—"

The corner of Sevlin's eye pinched.

"*No*." It came out as a gasp. "They wouldn't—They were the kindest—" She shook her head as words abandoned her.

"After the attack, everything was in shambles, Dashi. Hundreds of palace soldiers had been killed defending the queen, men and women we'd shared rooms with, shared meals with, sparred with. Everywhere I looked there was blood and death and the charred remains of things. Dozens of other soldiers had turned on us, had been embedded in our ranks, just waiting for the signal. There was this palpable fear and distrust, the sense that another attack was imminent and that it could come from a friend rather than an obvious foe. It was...hideous." Sevlin's eyes glazed over with memories. "I had to safeguard Lyazzat, but I didn't even know how big the conspiracy was. Chaimak was dead. I hadn't thought to question him." His mouth pinched inward in self-recrimination. "So I sent Altan and Baris to the Kurlar region to see if they could root out the depth of the conspiracy."

"I thought you'd decided to only trust Zevi and Lyazzat?"

"Baris and Altan's commanding officer had been one of the betrayers. Before the attack, he'd ordered his soldiers away from where the action would be, but Altan figured out what was going on. He and Baris flouted orders and came charging in, swords raised, at the proverbial darkest hour." Sevlin reached into his pack and pulled out his waterskin, leaning one forearm against the lattice while he drank. "I'd crossed paths with the two of them before that, in training and in the barracks, but we weren't friends. Even afterward." A shrug of one shoulder. "I am the half-brother of the queen. That is a difficult thing for people to compartmentalize. But they'd single-handedly turned the tide against Lyazzat's attackers. If they'd been part of the coup, they would have killed her then. So when I needed someone to go to Kurlar, off they went."

Desperate to be doing something while she waited for his verdict on Altan and Baris, Dashi flipped onto her hands. Pain coursed through her palm, and she dropped back to her feet.

"You're hurt," Sevlin said.

She kept pacing, but Sevlin remained pointedly silent until finally she slanted him an exasperated look and went to her pack for salve and a bandage. The urge to find grass pressed against the back of her thoughts, but no plants grew in a dark ruin. Even if they had, she didn't think she would have made an ant-style poultice in front of Sevlin.

"Your story?" she prompted. She held up her hand as proof that he could continue.

"Altan and Baris spent several days in Kurlar before they discovered who'd been behind the attack. There were many people involved, but the masterminds were a prominent family of merchants, with several estates along the river. According to the locals, the family had fled when the coup failed. Baris and Altan called for reinforcements and, after more searching, they found the tunnels that had been dug beneath the river to smuggle men and weapons from Karakal.

"I had told them—" Sevlin scraped a hand over his face. "I had *ordered* that no safe harbor was to be left for the conspirators. All property and holdings were to be destroyed or confiscated in Queen Lyazzat's name. There would be a trial in Rucharla for anyone who was captured, but most of the conspirators had fled across the border, and I didn't want them to be able to reap the benefits of their estates from outside of Tyvalar. Not when they'd tried to destroy us. There would be no home left for them. They would be struck from the fabric of our country."

Dashi pictured Ese's estate: the big house burned, the gardens uprooted, all traces of his life extinguished.

"Altan and Baris went to each estate owned by this Kurlaran family. The houses were empty, the livestock loose. The neighbors either didn't know where they'd gone or else they weren't saying. Baris and Altan said they checked each house, then set a torch to them."

In her mind, Dashi saw the story play out. Zayaa would be curled on the floor, sleeping peacefully beneath a creeping tide of smoke. Altan and Baris were in the yard, relieved to have accomplished the mission set for them by the new spymaster, slapping each other on the back for a job well done. Then came the churning flames, the blackening timbers. Her family dead, Zayaa crawled out into the clean night air just in time to glimpse Altan and Baris leaving. It was the beginning of a braid, the strands tightening over days and months and years, incorporating strangers and ancient treasures and the fate of nations.

"Do you believe—" Dashi stopped. Cleared her throat. Tried again. "Do you believe that's how it happened?"

Sevlin was quiet for a long moment. "I only know what they told me afterward. But I never witnessed any wanton cruelty from them, and I have no reason to think that they were lying."

"They didn't hear anyone?"

"They said no. After they'd returned to Rucharla, word reached us that bodies had been found, buried beneath the burned timbers. One of them was a child, a cousin of Zayaa's, maybe, or a young servant."

Dashi sucked in a breath. "They *all* had hidden rooms? Each house?"

"They'd been planning it for years. I should have thought of it. Baris and Altan should have looked; they'd just found the hidden tunnels, after all. But we were, all of us, so green. Only weeks on the job."

"And afterward...Baris and Altan...?"

"Baris never spoke of it after that initial report. He had always been good with a sword and with soldiering in general, but he became a man obsessed after that. When he wasn't training, he was drunk. Always. Altan once told me that Baris had several younger siblings and that the thought of that small body…" Sevlin laid his hand over his chest and squeezed it into a tight fist: a heart constricting. "Altan was pained by the knowledge of what they'd done too. To him, it was caused by a failure of information and a lack of experience, one which he was determined to correct. He dedicated himself to spy work, going all over the continent on my orders."

"And when he had the opportunity to save another child from a fire, he took it." She saw Altan then, so clear in her mind's eye that she might have touched him: arms outstretched, his face painted orange by the proximity of the flames, his eyes streaming from the smoke. "Zayaa's family died by accident."

"That is what I believe."

Dashi had expected relief, to be able to absolve Baris and Altan in her mind, but somehow the truth did neither. Their motivations might be clearer, but the fact remained that people had died, some of them children. The image of Altan broke apart, reconfiguring itself so that now it was Altan who held the torch to the dilapidated wall of Dashi's childhood home.

The fire that killed Dashi's mother had been sparked by rioters panicked over the plague spreading through the dirt circle. The mob had torches, whether by design or because it was evening, she never knew. The fire had grown out of control almost instantly, Altan told her later, jumping from shanty to shanty like a hot, orange monster, until it had consumed a quarter of the dirt circle. Maybe whoever had lit that first flame hadn't meant for innocents to die. But die they had. Motivation only mattered so much when it was your loved one who'd been taken.

"Zayaa never talked about it?" Sevlin asked.

"Not before this. She has scars on her shoulders and the back of her neck, but she was always discreet, almost embarrassed, about them. Altan told me not to ask because she hated talking about it." Dashi paused, thinking. "It didn't seem strange at the time. Zayaa and I...neither of us are the chummy type, so there were no confessions of the heart or late-night stories. I was barely domesticated when Zayaa came to Karak City. I slept in a blanket beneath the window so I could come and go as I pleased. Zayaa was always...prickly isn't the right word, exactly. She was very charming, but she held you at arm's length at the same time. She was close with Altan, of course—and Baris too, apparently—but I do not think they ever knew the truth of her burns."

Even with the stone lattice between them, she could feel Sevlin's interest sharpen. "She was with both of them?"

"Yes."

"Did they know about each other?"

"Well, Baris definitely knew about Altan. I don't know what Altan knew, but the weeks before the ambush were...tense."

The days before their deaths had become strangely golden and crystalline over the intervening months, a granulated honey that could be spread thin and examined in the light. She recalled Baris, leaning one heavy elbow on her shoulder as they recovered from a particularly brutal bout of training. When she'd teased him about needing to keep his skills sharp in case any jilted husbands came calling, a common refrain between them, he'd shoved off of her and stalked away. Altan had been jittery, wading out into the snowy slop each morning without saying where he was going, and not returning until the moon was high. And Zayaa...Zayaa had been like the sunshine incarnate.

"At the time I thought it was the winter," Dashi said. "I get restless like that when I'm penned up for too long. After I found out they'd been spies, I thought the tension stemmed from something to do with that. Maybe they suspected they'd been discovered, or they were itching to follow up on a lead."

One they didn't share with me. The words flowed into her head automatically, footsteps following a well-worn trail. She'd honed that path for months, each doubt, each painful whisper of "*Why not me?*" grinding it deeper into the embankment of her mind. So it was with no small amount of surprise that she realized the sting of betrayal was...gone.

"And now you wonder if the tension had another cause," Sevlin said.

Dashi nodded. "It's hard to know if Zayaa planned it all along or if that's just how things fell into place." Baris was a notorious womanizer and, though he'd loved Altan like a brother, Dashi couldn't imagine that Zayaa had needed to work very hard to make him stray. "I suppose the details of what everyone said and thought only matter to me at this point. It must've served Zayaa's purposes, or she wouldn't have done it."

"A distraction before she made her move."

"Exactly."

Dashi flexed her hand experimentally. The burn felt better already, but the lacerations from the wire still throbbed. The urge to find grass hit her again, stronger than before. It was all she could do not to paw at the floor. The press of another compulsion was there too: the tether, telling her to hurry. She got up, stowed the wound salve, and began rechecking the stone lattice for a hidden mechanism.

"How is Idree?" Sevlin asked, doing the same.

"Oh, she's holding up well," Dashi said, "considering she's down another finger."

"What do you mean *down another finger?*"

"The price of defiance, according to the khan." Dashi pictured the blood-splattered floor. "I thought it would be me who was punished. I didn't realize that Zayaa keeps a family member to use against each herald." She explained how she hadn't wanted to admit to Sevlin's involvement in hunting for the seamripper and what she'd been made to do as a result. She told him about fighting Zayaa for control of the tethers and the loss of Idree's second finger.

"I am sorry, Dashi. More than..." Sevlin exhaled slowly. "More than I can put into words."

"Well, if you see Idree again, don't tell her that," Dashi warned. "She won't thank you for it."

"I wouldn't dare."

Dashi straightened, looking up at the latticed ceiling. "Maybe the way out is up there."

"Mmmm," Sevlin agreed. "It's the only place we haven't looked. I kept thinking this room is timed, but we've been here for half an hour and there's been nothing."

"There were nearly a dozen columns. Maybe we chose two that don't lead anywhere."

He eyed the hatch they'd come through. "We couldn't retrace our steps even if we—"

Light flared suddenly. Dashi recoiled from the front of the cell as a fire jumped to life on the other side. It put out enough light to illuminate the central space in front of their cells: a circular arena. One end of the arena was lined in walls of stone lattice—more cells like theirs—while the other end had large wooden doors set into stone.

"I guess it *was* timed," Dashi murmured.

"Look." Sevlin pointed to the center of the pit, where a line of Purek characters had been chiseled.

For once, the translation was a simple one: *The Gateway.*

The wall of the first cell slid open. No one came out. The fire at the center of the room continued burning.

"It almost looks like a gladiator pit," Dashi said softly, one hand rubbing her bow.

"There are no other combatants."

"There might have been at one time." She wondered if the doors hid the skeletons of bears and lions, forever waiting to vanquish their foes.

"Shouldn't the big doors also be opening then?"

"Hmm. Maybe it takes someone stepping into the ring to trigger it. Or maybe it won't start until all the cells have opened. Maybe everyone faced each other at once."

"Bloody," Sevlin murmured.

They waited, watching the fire flicker in the center of the arena, until the first lattice door closed and the next one opened.

"So you can read Purek," Dashi said conversationally. She squinted at several circular outlines in the floor to either side of the fire.

"I used to rely on Altan's translations. I've spent every spare moment since his death pouring over crumbling scrolls. I can decipher it passably now. I was not nearly as competent when we first met."

She glanced at him, eyes darting over the parts of his face that she could see, trying to determine if he was telling the truth. He sighed, and she saw his hands spread in a gesture of openness.

"I'm not foolish enough to think I can always count on the truth from you," she said.

"I didn't think you were," he said. "I have no reason to lie about when and how I learned to read Purek. You're better at it anyway."

Another cell opened.

"Only one more door before yours," Sevlin said.

Dashi nodded, anticipation coiling in her legs. "The Wellspring," she blurted, suddenly recalling that she could speak of it now that the khan was dead, and Zayaa hadn't renewed that particular command. "Do you know what it does?"

"I know what the scrolls say." Sevlin's voice was guarded.

"I'm not sure if you're here to stop Zayaa or if you have another plan—and I'm not asking you to tell me. I meant it when I said I trusted you." Dashi took a deep breath. "Zayaa told the khan that the Wellspring's magic could be wielded by anyone—whoever was closest—once the seamstress and the needle were brought there. But that's a lie; the scrolls I read said the magic came still from the seamstress. I can't figure out why she would want to go to the Wellspring if all she had to gain was making Idree more magical." She glanced in Sevlin's direction. "Idree thought it was about the heralds, that maybe Zayaa wants the army to grow quicker, but...I think she's planning something else. I have a bad feeling about it, Sevlin."

The cell next to hers opened, smooth and silent.

"I came here for you, Dashi. For Idree, too. I can't tell you anything else until—" She heard the quick, hard scrape of stubble as Sevlin rubbed his jaw. "Until you're free." Through the carefully shaped holes in the lattice, she glimpsed the corner of his eye, pinched in pain. It was a veritable deluge of emotion for Sevlin.

In moments, her cell would open.

"I don't want to leave you like this again," she said. The similarities between their goodbye in the maze and this one were striking: the physical obstacle between them, the same sense of longing and uncertainty. The Pureks' presence stretched over it all, manipulative and mysterious.

"It's not like before." He raised one leg. "No spike."

She'd wanted to ask how he'd gotten out of the maze, and out of the taiga, while injured. She'd wanted to talk to him about countless other things too, but there was no more time.

"Be careful," she said, pressing her lips together before she hemorrhaged the worries inside her head.

One side of Sevlin's mouth hitched upward. "I won't waste my breath telling you to do the same."

She recalled a different moment, a different Purek puzzle. This felt like when Idree had been trapped behind the moving wall in the temple. Not because her sister and Sevlin resembled each other in their experience or skills—Sevlin was plainly a very capable man—but because the thought of something happening to either of them was enough to level her. *Circle of loyalty*, she thought shakily. The more people who were in it, the more people who could be lost, the more likely she was to fall back into the crater of desolation she'd been in after Altan and Baris died.

"Sevlin." She brushed the cold stone lattice near his face.

If not for the stone lattice, she would have kissed him, long and hard. But its existence meant that goodbyes had to be done with words, something at which Dashi did not excel.

The front of her cell opened. The firelit arena beckoned. She gave Sevlin a cocky salute and stepped out.

Chapter 29

Fire clung to the walls in precise angles, following the lines of fuel that dripped down to feed it. The floor immediately in front of Dashi's cell was made of great stone blocks. Halfway to the center of the arena, they changed, becoming a bizarre mishmash of shapes. *Easy enough,* she thought. *I'll stay away from those.* She headed toward the doors on the opposite side of the arena. Sevlin shifted behind her, a nervous rustle of fabric.

She reached the nearest door without anything happening. It stretched above her head, an imposing display of aged wood planks, banded with metal. There was no handle, but each plank was decorated, top to bottom, with carvings. Like the pictures on the tiles in the sand room, these were not the typical Purek depictions of the natural world but images of destruction. Fires. Floods. Pestilence. These were the disasters that would occur, the Pureks believed, if the proper rites were not administered at the Wellspring. She studied the scenes without touching them.

There was a soft snick behind her as the door to her cell closed. Dashi glanced over her shoulder, waiting for Sevlin's to open. Minutes ticked by. Nothing in the circular arena moved. Sevlin swore. The sound was cut off by the hiss and crackle of new flame. Dashi spun around. A line of fire was spreading from the opposite side of the arena, racing rapidly around the perimeter. She jumped back from the door as the flames crossed in front of it like a line of waving sentries.

Dashi had a moment of panic as she considered the possibility that the rest of the arena was about to be engulfed in flame, but other than the sudden inrush of orange light, it remained unchanged. She looked to the center. Even with the extra light, she could not discern a pattern in the oddly shaped stones of the floor. Along the upper reaches of the walls, just above the flames, a strange spiraling design was now visible. It unspooled around the circumference, etched deep into the stone.

"Dashi!" Sevlin's voice was taut. The flames stretched past the door of his cell, blocking his view of her.

"I'm fine. The flames are only along the outside of the arena. Barring the exits, I guess."

There was a pause. She pictured Sevlin bracing his arms against the wall of his cell, head tilted thoughtfully.

"There *was* no exit," he said finally.

"Not yet." Her fingers strayed to her bow, seeking reassurance from the smooth wood. "I have to earn it."

"Dashi...I—"

But Dashi had stopped listening to anyone other than the Pureks: the soft whine of gears, long dormant; the whoosh of air as something shifted out of sight; a rhythmic bumping, deep and far off, like a barrel being trundled along an alley. The floor at the center of the arena began to shift, creating a disjointed topography as some stones rose above the rest, revealing themselves to be narrow obelisks. The smooth planes of their sides gleamed in the surrounding firelight. Many were taller than she was.

"Dashi!" Sevlin's tone told her he'd been saying the same thing over and over. "What's happening?"

"The stones around the fire pit are moving," she shouted back.

"Moving where?"

"Straight out of the floor. Twenty-four of them. They're tall, Sevlin."

The stones stopped moving. The trundling noise increased in tempo, growing louder.

"Now what's happening?"

"They've stopped rising. There's something in the center." She leaned sideways to see around an obelisk. "It looks like a pit. Or maybe a well? There's a low wall around it." Dashi's eyes moved over the field of obelisks. She could still see no pattern to their stance. A few were grouped close together, while others stood apart. Their sides were covered in Purek characters, but she was too far away to read them. She felt dangerously exposed, despite the perimeter fire warming her back

A dark shape burst from the flames on the opposite side of the perimeter. Dashi dropped into a reflexive crouch. The thing hit one of the standing obelisks and bounced off, rebounding into a second and then a third, before sailing into the dark pit. A gong sounded, reverberating across the floor and up through the soles of her feet.

"That was..." Dashi paused. "Actually I don't know what that was. It reminded me of a goathead ball but wooden. It bounced between the obelisks and landed in the pit."

Before Sevlin could respond, another ball, nearly as big as her head, flew from her right, once more bounding between the obelisks before landing in the center pit. The gong played again, dirgelike. A third ball shot out from a different direction than the first two. They didn't come from the fire, as she'd first thought, but from the etched lines that encircled the walls. She could tell by the way each ball hit the obelisks that it was heavy. Was it a trap? It looked more like a game.

"Dashi, look up!"

She did, her mouth falling open at the sight of a circle of stone spikes on the ceiling above her. *Stalactites*, she thought at first, but they were too perfectly shaped and evenly spaced to be anything other than manmade. Before she could summon any other observations, the ceiling moved, sliding a little closer to the floor.

Closer to her.

Each spike was as long as her arm. They were clustered so closely together that there would be no escape if they reached her.

"I didn't trigger that," she shouted to Sevlin, sounding like a child trying to shift blame. "I haven't moved."

"Maybe you're *supposed* to."

Another ball launched itself from the wall and bounced between obelisks. Dashi focused on the ceiling instead. As the final reverberations of the gong died away, the entire circle of spikes moved again.

"It's the gong," Sevlin said.

"Yeah." Dashi was still leery about stepping amongst the obelisks—the strange pattern of the floor could hide any number of traps—but she forced herself to do it anyway. She made it safely to the center of the arena and, after a glance to verify that the pit was indeed just that, she positioned herself in front of it. She shifted her weight, sword in hand. *Ready.* The pack jostled against her shoulder blades. She didn't dare take it off for fear of being separated from the lantern and supplies.

A ball burst from the wall in front of her, immediately meeting the side of one obelisk and bouncing off in the direction of another. After several more ricochets, it sailed toward the pit. Dashi met it with the flat side of her sword. She'd been right; the ball was extraordinarily heavy for its size. The impact shook her arm, but the ball thudded to the ground, rolling to a stop against the base of an obelisk. The flames along a section of the arena's perimeter shuddered and went out. No gong sounded. The spiked ceiling stayed where it was.

"I stopped one from going into the pit," she informed Sevlin. "They're heavy." She glanced up at the ceiling. The spikes were only positioned over the arena. Inside his cell of stone lattice, Sevlin would be safe—at least, until *his* turn.

"So you're supposed to defend the pit?" Sevlin asked.

"I think. A small section of the perimeter fire went out too, directly across from your cell. I'm not sure what that means."

The trundling noise increased again. Another ball whipped toward the circle of obelisks. Dashi caught it on the third ricochet, pushing it out of its orbit like a discarded moon.

"Stopped another," she panted.

The sound of another ball rolling down its chute precluded Sevlin's response. She dispatched this one after two ricochets. The trundling began again.

"They are coming closer together," Sevlin said.

"I noticed."

"What else is happening?"

"Nothing."

The next ball came at her from behind. Dashi threw herself flat, narrowly avoiding a blow to the back of the head. *Smack. Smack.* It flew between obelisks, working its way closer to the pit. She batted it aside before it could go in.

Sevlin's voice rose to be heard over the thunder of the next ball. "You once told me there's a point to everything in the Purek ruins. What's the point of this? You're not here to play a game against the Pureks."

You're here to open the Gateway. The words were drowned in the smack of wood against stone. This time, two balls flew from the walls of the arena. Dashi swore, swatting the first ball to the ground and diving toward the second as it zigzagged between obelisks. She stopped it just before it dropped into the pit.

"Two at once," she said to Sevlin, gulping for air.

Two more launched from opposite sides of the arena, and she stopped them both. On the next round, there were three. This time, she didn't even have time to curse. She stopped the first and third but missed the second. The gong reverberated through the chamber. The spikes glided nearer. They were close enough now that she could see the scars of their creation, left by chisel and hammer.

Breathing hard, her gaze snagged on the darkened section along the arena's perimeter. The fire had not rekindled there, and it stood out among the lively flames like a punched-out tooth. She'd forgotten about it in her efforts to keep the spikes from descending. Now, she saw a space had opened between the floor and the bottom of the nearest door. The crack was barely wide enough for her finger. It would, she hoped, get larger as she continued to play the Pureks' game. She glanced once more into the pit at the center of the arena, her only other exit option. A sphere of darkness stared up at her. Dashi swallowed.

A ball shot from the wall. Dashi turned toward it, deflecting it just as a second ball slammed into her stomach. She fell to her knees, oxygen whisking out of her. The gong sounded as the third ball dropped into the pit. She pulled herself up in time to slap down a fourth ball. The spikes slid closer. When Dashi glanced at the door, she saw that it had opened a little more.

"Are you alright?" Sevlin called.

"I got hit, but I'm fine. For each ball I keep out of the pit, one of the doors raises a little."

"How big is the opening right now?"

"It's the perfect height if the only thing I want to save is my arm."

The next ball came and the next. Dashi grunted, knocking as many aside as she could. The floor was littered with them now, adding another obstacle for her to dodge. The spikes lowered too quickly. The door crept up too slowly. It still wasn't high enough for her to squeeze her head and shoulders through.

The arena spat so many wooden balls at her that there was no time to catch her breath. It was a whirling dance from one target to the next. She wasn't even sure how many she was dealing with at any given time, only that there were always too many bouncing between obelisks and too many swishing past her into the pit.

Dashi glanced upward. If she stood on her toes, she could almost touch the spikes. Soon she would have to be careful about jumping. Due to his height, Sevlin would have an even harder time when his cell door opened.

"Sevlin, the spikes—I don't know if you'll be—"

"Just concentrate on getting out, Dashi." He still couldn't see her behind the wall of fire. His voice sounded strained.

The height of the raised door was a tricky thing to judge from across the arena. Glancing at it again, Dashi thought she might be able to squeeze through. Sheathing her sword, she sprinted in the direction of the opened door. Her arms and head slid through easily enough, but the door dug into her as she tried to maneuver the rest of her body inside. She wasted a fruitless second squirming and cursing, before reversing course. Rising to her knees, she grabbed her bow.

The gonging had become a more or less steady sound since she'd given up trying to keep the balls out of the pit. The spikes grazed the tops of the obelisks, and she saw the carefully shaped spaces where they would fit into the lowered ceiling. Dashi drew her bow and let two arrows fly in quick succession. There was a swift *crack-crack* as they bounced off a wooden ball barreling toward the pit. The impact was slight, but it was enough. The ball hit the outer edge of the pit's wall, landing harmlessly on the floor. The door at her back rose infinitesimally higher.

She wedged herself beneath it, pulling her pack in after her.

"Sevlin," she yelled over the gong. "I'm through."

Chapter 30

Dashi had barely scooted free of the door when it slammed shut, vibrating the stone floor. Wondering if the spikes had fallen with the same velocity, Dashi shuddered; Sevlin would be in that room soon. She sat up, her breath coming hard. The lantern illuminated a small chamber with a narrow staircase spiraling off to her left.

She took out her waterskin, then checked her bandaged hand and the recent crop of bruises accrued from flinging herself between the obelisks. The gong started up again. Though the sound was muffled now, it still set her teeth on edge.

Zayaa's command to hurry prodded her, but Dashi didn't move. *Come on, Sevlin.* She stared at the bottom edge of the door, willing it to rise. Another peel of the gong sounded. Pain surged in her chest and sizzled out to her limbs, the punishment for ignoring the tether. From the intermittent tempo of the gong, Sevlin was still stopping most of the shots coming from the arena walls. The door didn't move.

The gong increased its pace. He must be nearing the end of the ordeal, when the wooden balls flew from the sides like bees from a hive. *Bonnnng. Bonnnng. Bonnnng.* Finally, Dashi heard the muted thud as a door crashed shut and the spikes made their final descent. No Sevlin.

As she started up the staircase, Dashi tried to think of the sound as a positive thing. She'd heard a door slam shut, but that also meant a door had *risen.* There was a good chance Sevlin had escaped the room. Still, disappointment curdled her stomach. There was no telling where the other doors led or if her path would cross his again. Their brief reunion had not been nearly enough.

Zayaa's commands drove her onward. Dashi inspected each step until, finally, she reached the top of the staircase, where an open space beckoned. She thought it might be larger than the arena, though it was difficult to tell with only a single lantern. A breath of cold air tickled her scalp, and Dashi looked up, her legs automatically tensing for a sideways leap. This time, however, the air was nothing more nefarious than the wind, bustling across an opening in the ceiling. The opening was circular—a representation of nature in its cyclical form—and through it, Dashi could see a slice of the night sky.

A forest of pillars rose in front of her, shadowy and erect. Her lips puckered; she wasn't eager to climb one of those again. These pillars were directly below the opening in the ceiling, though they were much too short to reach it. There was something strange to their arrangement, she thought, skirting a suspicious-looking pockmark in the stone. Like the overhead window, the pillars were grouped in a circle, but they varied considerably in size. The one nearest to her was no thicker than her bicep. Another was wider than her waist. Lines branched away from the main body, spreading into the dark.

Her steps faltered. These weren't pillars. They were white, ghostly *trees*. The Pureks were excellent craftsmen, but as she got closer and the finer details began to come into focus, Dashi's eyebrows rose higher and higher. Pearly swirls on the tree trunks resembled wood grain. The twigs at the end of the bare branches were hardly wider than a hair. Hundreds of stone leaves were spread around the base of every tree, each one dusted with snow that had sifted through the window overhead.

An entire garden made of stone. The living trees of the taiga were discomfiting enough; trees that looked like ghosts sent shivers racing along her skin.

She came even with the first tree and sucked in a breath. This one had evidently been designed as an evergreen; around *its* trunk, thousands of stone needles lay scattered. Dashi picked one up. She'd never seen stone worked to such a delicate point. She pressed her fingers together, hardly surprised when it snapped.

Stone grass showed beneath the pine needles, each blade sharp enough to cut. A half moon of indentation—the heel of a footprint, perhaps?—bent the stone grass at the edge of the garden. Careful not to touch anything else, Dashi leaned forward, holding her lantern close to the tree's trunk. The swirls of wood grain weren't painted on; they were *part* of the stone.

Dashi cut a careful path along the garden's periphery, only to realize that the cavern ended on the other side. *The garden,* she thought, and turned away from the walls rising out of the darkness to meet the rock ceiling. The garden would have been—and still *was,* despite its inherent creepiness—a jewel of Purek creation. It was a balance of inside and outside, light in the dark. It was lifelike but dead. *Anything worth finding will be there.*

Dashi hovered at the garden's edge, debating how to proceed. She couldn't stop staring at the extraordinary level of detail the artists had included. The fallen foliage was mostly deciduous on this side, and she could see intricate webs of veins scrawled across the surface of each leaf. Dashi shook her head, forcing herself to focus on what might hide *beneath* the leaf litter. She could think of only two ways to navigate the traps that inevitably lay in wait. She could meticulously excavate each place where she wished to step, removing all leaves and needles that might hide a trap. Or she could attempt to leap from tree to tree.

She selected a likely tree—sturdy and not too far from its neighbors—then noticed a strand of wire entwined among its branches. It was the same kind that had cut her hand as she ascended the column. Almost simultaneously, she recalled the half footprint in the stone grass on the other side of the garden. Buoyed by the possibility of having found one of the Purek's hints, Dashi circled back to the other side of the garden. She located the first footprint and several beyond it. They zigzagged between trees but ultimately angled toward the center of the garden, disappearing where they eluded the lantern light.

Gingerly, she placed her foot on top of the first print, surprised to find that the delicate stone grass did not crack beneath her weight. The spike of adrenaline and the prickle of danger always made her feel giddy, but she forced herself to move slowly to the next foot-shaped indentation. The footprints were small, she noted and wondered if that was significant. Some sort of artistic representation of innocence, perhaps? Dashi hopped another step, passing directly beneath one of the bone-colored trees. The stately spread of the limbs only made them more naked and pitiful somehow. She leaned away so her shoulder wouldn't brush the wire looping around the trunk.

A pool encompassed by a low rock wall revealed itself in the lantern light: a perfect circle surrounded by clusters of expertly formed stone flowers. Four trees stood sentry around the pool, and Dashi knew without checking that each marked a cardinal direction. The pool was shallow. No taiga giants lurking beneath these waters, she thought gratefully. The swirl of clouds reflected on the surface made her glance up. She was directly below the hole in the cavern roof.

The pool's presence did not surprise Dashi. The garden had a predictable sense of symmetry and use of natural elements: a circle of sky, a circle of grass, and a circle of trees. Each tree had a circle of foliage beneath it. What *did* surprise her was that the footprints continued *past* the pool, veering off between two of the sentry trees and disappearing into the shadows. Dashi frowned. Though she thought the garden was spectral, she could tell the Pureks had meant it to be spectacular. The pool was at the garden's center. Ergo, there was a good chance the pool held some significance. Maybe a clue of some kind, or a way to open a passageway to another room.

Dashi slid another look at the footprints, her fingertips still drumming their concern into her thigh. She would continue following them, she decided. She could always turn around and reexamine the pool.

The footprints crossed behind the pool and between two trees before stopping in front of a third. Stone flowers clustered at knee height around the trunk. The final footprint was set directly in front of them, the toe of the boot partially concealed beneath the immobile foliage.

Sliding her own foot on top of the print, Dashi found herself nose-to-trunk with the tree. Reaching as high as she could, she swept her hands downward over the cold stone. Any irregular marks or textures were investigated, but she found nothing. Without stepping out of the footprints, she bent to get a better look at the base of the tree, pausing to examine a stone flower. Its spade-shaped petals were familiar, despite their lack of identifying color. They would have been bright red in life. The red of blood. The red of a poisonous snake. Had this plant been alive, just brushing against its velvety petals would have meant death.

Undaunted, Dashi snaked both hands amongst the wide, strap-like leaves, feeling for any anomalies. The sharp edges caught at her wrists and snagged at the bandage on her hand, making her hiss in pain. Although most of the leaves were solid gray, the few closest to her were marked with darker splotches, which dotted the surface at irregular intervals. Lichens, Dashi thought at first, but as she brushed her finger over the nearest spot, she realized that the texture, while slightly raised, was too smooth. Seeing the smear of blood she'd left behind, Dashi glanced down at her hand.

Blood dripped from her bandage where the stone leaves had reopened her earlier wound.

Something white slithered at the sides of her vision. The sound of breaths echoed in her ears, foreign and out of sync with her own. Stricken with a sudden bout of vertigo, she put out a hand to steady herself and caught the cold, lifeless bulk of the tree. A strange dual-vision gripped her. She was moving. She blinked. No, she was standing still, holding on to the tree. In the next second, the duality of sensations condensed into a single stream, one which couldn't actually be happening, Dashi knew, but which was in front of her nonetheless.

Feet hit the ground under her, silent in the thick grass. The shoes themselves were a strange confection of golden straps, which crisscrossed over the top of her foot and wrapped up her ankle. She felt a surge of unease—these were emphatically *not hers,* just as the feet inside them were not hers—but it was gone before she could dwell on it, pushed away by all that was happening around her. Trees whipped by on either side, green with the bounty of summer, interspersed with splashes of color that she recognized as flowers. Shouts came from a distance, but they were far behind, too far to catch her. She knew this, not from her antennae, but with a detached certainty, like she was reading it over someone's shoulder or eavesdropping on a stranger's conversation. Her pursuers still had to navigate the whole Gateway, whereas *she* was almost through. She would soon be free.

It was nearing noon. Warm sunlight streamed through the hole in the cavern's ceiling, striking the pool at the garden's center and bouncing off the water and the white stones beneath in a blinding display. The light caught the sleeve of the deel she wore. *Something else that's not mine,* Dashi thought. The image of the stags locked in combat, stitched in purple iridescent thread, was fancier than anything she'd ever owned.

The body she was in veered around the pool, stepping carefully to avoid the traps hidden beneath the grass, knowing that her goal was the tree standing to the west of the pool and the Gossip's Tongue at its base. That's what the builder had said before he died. The knowledge floated through Dashi, sure and serene.

"West like the setting sun, the end of the day, the completion of a cycle. The end that marks a new beginning." The words came to Dashi in another language, one she'd never heard spoken fluently, yet she understood their meaning on a deep, effortless level, without the labor of translation.

The woman skidded to a stop next to the tree and pulled out a bulky leather glove, adorned with colorful beads and tassels: a gauntlet, nearly as decorated as the khan's and scored by countless talons. The sight of bright red blood on the hand came as a surprise to Dashi. She had been so overwhelmed by the sensation of inhabiting another body that she hadn't realized the woman, whoever she was, was injured. Blood sheathed the side of her hand, covering the ring on her little finger.

The shape of the wound was familiar. It was the kind of jagged hole an arrow left as it punched through flesh. Pain flared in Dashi's palm even though the wound wasn't hers. The woman pulled on the gauntlet with obvious pain, leaving a generous smear of blood on the leather.

Crimson flowers, their velvety petals laden with poison, bobbed innocuously in the sunlight. With the glove as protection, the woman pushed aside blooms and leaves, probing with fingers made unwieldy by the thick leather. A pink dusting of pollen drifted from the flowers, falling harmlessly on the outside of the gauntlet. The woman's fingers found a ring near the base of the tree and tugged on it. Dashi felt it too, like it was her own fingers that did the work.

A grating noise filled the garden. The woman shucked the gauntlet from her wounded hand, her movements decisive and satisfied despite the spray of blood that fanned outward. Dashi watched the droplets splatter among the flowers, one shade of red quickly blending with the other. The woman straightened and, taking Dashi's consciousness along with her, stepped into a beam of sunlight. She tipped her head back in triumph, letting the sun fall on her closed eyelids. *Nearly free.*

Abruptly, Dashi's vision refractured, dividing into two scenes: the sunlight pressing against the woman's eyelids, and the ghostly stone tree in front of Dashi. There was a sensation of spinning, of falling, and Dashi braced herself to land hard. When the impact came, however, it was only in her mind, not her body. Her thoughts jolted as she looked down at her own hand, swathed in the bandage she'd recently applied. There were familiar brown boots on her feet. The grass beneath her was stiff stone once more. She jerked away from the stone flower, unconsciously rubbing her thumb and forefinger together as if she might find someone else's blood on her skin. It was her own blood that slicked her fingertips, however, still dripping from where the plant had snagged her bandage.

What was that? A trick played by the taiga mist? Her eyes darted around the stone garden, but there was nothing there. She looked back down at the plant. *Gossip's Tongue.* It was not a name Dashi had ever heard used for the red-flowered plant. She said it slowly, her mouth clumsy with a language she knew only from dusty scrolls and sculptures: ancient Purek. The slightly raised circles marred the stone leaves, marking the exact spot where the woman's blood had fallen. Her own blood was smeared on top. Dashi itched with the deep-rooted instinct to conceal the evidence of her passage, but she couldn't wipe her blood away without touching the stone leaves again. She decided to leave it.

The woman's fear of pursuit lingered, making Dashi want to rush where she should be cautious. She shook her head, trying to remove the last vestiges of...whatever that had been. Dashi reached below the bloodied leaves just as the woman had. Her fingertips brushed cold metal. She pulled, feeling the resistance of the wire attached to the other side of the ring. The low growl of gears came from below her, more vibration than sound. *The pool,* she thought, grinning in vindication. *I knew there would be something there.* She whirled, retracing the footprints, excitement making her push aside thoughts about dead languages and a Purek woman's dash for freedom.

When she reached the pool, she saw that the entire thing had shifted sideways, revealing a sliver of space beneath it. She could just make out the top rung of a ladder descending into the darkness. The pool *should* have pivoted farther, but it had gotten stuck against the stone flowers. Dashi frowned. She'd never seen the Pureks make such an oversight. It only reinforced her confusion about what she'd seen in the strange vision where the garden had been alive.

She went around to the other side of the pool and surveyed the thick clusters of flowers. Altan, she knew, would have wanted to catalog which plants the Pureks had cultivated. Dashi sighed and, drawing her sword, used the pommel to smash the delicate stone flora. With each one she destroyed, the pool slid sideways, until finally there was enough space for her to clamber past its edge and down into the darkness. She held the lantern in her teeth, wanting both hands on the ladder in case the Pureks had any surprises in store. The ladder ended after only a few steps, however, and she found herself in a tunnel. She followed it slowly, stooping when the ceiling occasionally bulged with boulders. After several long minutes, the tunnel turned upward at a right angle and Dashi stood at the bottom of another ladder. The rock changed here, pink marble bleeding into milky green. *Lechitite.*

She started up, careful not to touch the green that surrounded her. One rung. Ten rungs. Eighty rungs. The air began to crackle. Sparks danced along the exposed skin of Dashi's face, neck and hands as the lechitite and the magic in her body protested their proximity to each other. She flinched as a spark erupted on her cheekbone, exploding in light and pain. The white lines of unknown minerals split the lechitite walls, like layers of fat splayed across freshly butchered meat. The ladder seemed endless. Her arms and legs moved mechanically, pulling her higher and higher. Finally, the lantern light bounced back at her, no longer swallowed by the darkness but reflected by a circle of hammered bronze overhead. She hesitated at the sight of the metal hand wheel on the hatch door, but there appeared to be little choice. The lechitite reacted angrily to her pause, showering sparks over her. After checking the rock walls on either side for obvious traps, she grasped the handholds on the wheel and turned.

Noise thundered around her, immediate and painful. Leaning into the ladder, Dashi managed to press her hands to her ears, but it was little help. The lechitite walls shook with sound; the ladder rungs vibrated with it. It ended suddenly and a simultaneous blast of wintry air made Dashi look up, dazed. The bronze hatch had popped open. She was staring up at the night sky.

Dashi poked her head cautiously through the opening, unsure what she might find. Cliff walls rose around her, dark and menacing. The snow glowed wherever the moonlight slashed down. Her ears were still filled with the atrocious grinding, but something made her whirl around. Campfires winked through the darkness. The wind from that direction carried familiar scents: Idree, Zayaa, Tuya, and the other heralds.

No. She didn't want to rejoin the expedition. She didn't want to leave Sevlin again.

Dashi peered back down the ladder, but everything below her was completely dark. If Sevlin's route out of the obelisk room ended here, there was no sign of him, nor would Zayaa's commands permit her to retrace her steps. Dashi hauled herself through the hatch opening and started toward the camp.

Chapter 31

Dashi heard the hubbub of the camp before she reached it. Figures crowded around sledges, ripping back the oilcloth covers and ransacking the contents. Saddles slapped onto equine backs as the horses were pulled from their well-earned rest and readied once more. One glance at the surrounding canyon walls told her why. One of the Pureks' carefully hewn facades had moved. The entire block of rock had shifted backward, creating a narrow opening between its portico and the adjacent building. It was just wide enough to allow a horse and rider.

The Gateway.

"What about this sledge?" Dashi heard one of the soldiers call.

"I told you: no sledges. Nothing that can't be moved easily," Zayaa snapped, turning back to her preparations.

Idree looked up from changing Okhron's bandages, a smile lighting her face when she saw Dashi. "You're back," she said. "How was it?"

"Full of surprises." Dashi wanted to tell her sister about Sevlin's unexpected appearance and the strangeness of the stone garden, but there were too many ears nearby.

"I was worried we'd leave without you." Idree glanced at Okhron. "I know Zayaa doesn't care if he's left behind to freeze," she said in a fierce undertone, barely pausing for breath, "but I won't do it. I don't care what she says."

With one of Okhron's soldier friends, Dashi helped Okhron into the saddle of a spare horse. He blinked feral yellow eyes at her. When he began listing in the saddle, Idree tied him to it. Seeing his injuries made Dashi remember her own. She pressed her fingers to the poultice-covered wounds from her fight with Zayaa. They no longer hurt.

The sledges squatted woefully, their coverings carved open and their innards spilling into the snow: a forgotten bedroll here, an unneeded section of harness there. Dashi frowned at the waste. They should be hanging the abandoned food from the upper floors of the facades, where it would remain secure from animals and ready for the return trip, but Zayaa seemed unconcerned with what was left behind.

A group of soldiers went into the Gateway first, followed by Idree and Zayaa. Dashi pushed in behind Zayaa, as close to her sister as she could get. Tuya and the other heralds came next, followed by the remaining soldiers. The rock-hewn passage was claustrophobic and unforgiving, but it soon transitioned from stone to packed earth and widened enough to ride two abreast. Wide timbers appeared at regular intervals, marching in lockstep as they shored up the tunnel's earthen sides and the ceiling. Zayaa's arm shot out protectively, grabbing Idree's reins and pulling her horse in close so that Idree wouldn't smash her knee against one of the support timbers.

"Oh, she's a regular mother hen now," Tuya muttered from Dashi's right.

The packed earth walls and wooden timbers whisked by as the minutes piled up, marked only by the regularity of the bobbing lanterns. The smell of dampness and decay was invasive, clinging to the roof of her mouth so that every breath and every swallow flooded her with more.

"Don't you think it's strange that we left the sledges?" Tuya asked.

"They couldn't fit through the Gateway opening."

"I mean the *way* they were left."

"We should have made a supply cache," Dashi conceded, "to pick up on the return trip."

"I heard the consul order the soldiers to load the pack horses at quarter weight."

Dashi blinked.

"We should have brought the food with us," Tuya continued. "A winter storm could necessitate holing up for days or even weeks. We might need it."

Dashi glanced at the other woman. "I thought this was the first time you'd left home." Yassar reputedly didn't even have a winter season.

"I was briefed on the continent's seasonal conditions to mitigate their impact on travel."

"Right." Dashi's gaze returned to Zayaa's back. "The only reason to partially load the horses is speed."

"Why does she need to hurry so much? She never mentioned anything to the convoymaster—"

In front of them, a horse screamed in fright. Dashi's eyes caught a blur of movement, many shades paler than anything else in the tunnel. Spit jerked to a halt, his ears flat against his head. The next horse jammed up against them, creating a bottleneck of trembling horseflesh.

"What was that?" Fear tinged the voice of the soldier behind Dashi.

Particles of dirt danced off the walls. When Dashi pressed her hand against it, she could feel the subtle tempo of vibrations even through the thick material of her mitten. The scent that swirled around them was fetid, a mixture of stagnant water and rotten vegetation. Spit sidestepped nervously, bumping into Tuya's horse, who then shied into the tunnel wall. Muttering in Yassari, Tuya rubbed her knee with one hand and stroked her horse's neck with the other.

The tunnel shivered again, sending down another shower of dirt and rocks. Dashi drew her sword—the bow was an inferior weapon for such close quarters—and tried to move closer to Idree. Dust sifted onto them, subsiding slowly over the uneasy mutterings of both horses and humans.

Dashi swiped at her dirt-covered face, her thoughts unexpectedly jumping to Sevlin: to his slightly intimidating height and to the way his movements managed to be both lithe and deliberate: lightning winding through the sky as it tracks a target. The hair on her neck rose. Sevlin was someone to have beside you when you were facing—when you weren't sure *what* you were facing. A minute ticked by, then another. Tuya let out a measured breath.

Suddenly one of the timbers bowed inward. The dirt wall behind it bulged, then partially collapsed. Dashi saw a flash of pinkish gray, undulating and slick, and then it was gone, leaving a pile of rubble and a dark hole where there used to be a continuous wall.

"Did you see that?" The soldier in front of Idree spoke in a whisper. "Was it...?" The question hung, unasked.

Dashi peered at the hole. She could see another tunnel on the other side, running adjacent to their current path. She and Sevlin had once theorized that the taiga's enormous animals had originally been small. Perhaps larger bodies reacted differently—poorly—to a tidal wave of magic. Perhaps larger animals had been better equipped to flee before they were inundated. Regardless of the reason, in all the time she'd spent in the taiga, she'd seen no sign of giant bears or wolves, no stags with antlers as thick as tree branches. And, though she *had* seen giant spiders, toads, birds, bats, ants and rats, she had never once thought about the living things that normally stayed out of sight.

The earthen walls shuddered again, racked by a subterranean storm that sent a deluge of soil down Dashi's neck. A mass of pinkish-gray shot from the wall of the tunnel, barreling into Spit's side and sending Dashi flying from the saddle. Her sword skidded out of reach.

Spit reared, caught off-balance as he lashed out with his front hooves. The long naked body of the beast wrapped around his ribs, twisting him off his hind legs. Everything was chaos—the cries of animals and people, dust clouding what little light the lanterns produced—but Dashi rolled forward, scooping up her sword and swinging it into the beast's flesh. The sections of muscle in front of her contracted, loosening elsewhere and dropping Spit onto his side. One end of the beast—*A head? A tail?*—rose upward, the shape of it almost indignant. Dashi flung herself sideways, thinking it was about to lash out at her. Instead, it retreated, making one final grab for prey as it went, its pinkish coils shooting straight for the nearest horse: Idree's. The beast curled itself around Idree's mount, then Tuya's. There was a nightmarish jumble of bent limbs and terrified eyes, before Idree, Tuya, and both horses disappeared through the hole in the tunnel wall.

Dashi lunged. "*Idree!*"

"Dashi, stop!"

Dashi's legs halted. She turned, disbelief making her eyes bulge slightly.

"Take a lantern." Zayaa pushed herself up from where she'd been knocked to the dirt floor. "Bring her back."

Solongo took a step forward, her face turned to Zayaa for permission to go, but shouts from the other end of the tunnel pulled Zayaa's attention away. The beast's thrashing had carved out one wall. The joists trembled uncertainly. The soldiers gestured frantically through the dusty gloom, trying to figure out a way to shore it up with limited tools. Dashi cast a final glance at the struggling joists before stepping through the hole. If the tunnel collapsed here, she'd be left without a way out. *Save Idree first,* she told herself as she settled the lantern in her hand. *Then worry about escape.*

As Dashi had guessed, the beast's tunnel ran parallel to the one the Pureks had constructed, before turning away at a right angle. It was lower than the Purek one, coming only to Dashi's forehead, and she had to stoop as she walked. Her thumb drummed worriedly against the lantern handle. It would be difficult to fight like this.

There were no wooden supports in this tunnel, but the dirt was densely, purposefully packed. The moistness from the beast's skin had rubbed off on the walls, leaving it to glisten in the lantern light. Dashi pinched at the wet track with her thumb and forefinger, then spread her fingers apart, staring at the shining strands. Mucus, maybe, or some other bodily secretion she didn't have a proper name for. Grimacing, she wiped it on her pants. She'd seen that long, limbless body and thought *snake*, but she'd been wrong. It was some type of worm, she thought now, remembering the lack of discernible eyes and the neat segmentation of its body. She didn't think worms had teeth, but having never made a careful study of them—at any size—she decided that she couldn't rule it out either.

Dashi shifted into an awkward jog. Her neck ached from bending to avoid the slimy ceiling. A side tunnel branched off to the right. She halted, tasting the air with her antennae and trying to ignore the overpowering earthiness of the worm. With the worm carrying them, Tuya and Idree hadn't actually touched the ground, but a diaphanous layer of their scents still tinged the air. She turned into the side tunnel, ducking to avoid the viscous discharge that dangled across the opening. More tunnel branches materialized out of the gloom. They angled in all directions, but her sister's scent was a blazing beacon, guiding Dashi through one intersection after another.

Soon enough, Dashi passed another marker. The first pile was old and nearly odorless. White splinters, riddled with holes, some as long as Dashi's boot, mixed with what looked like plant matter. *Omnivorous, then.* The bone splinters, especially such porous ones, suggested that it lacked the teeth to chew its prey but instead swallowed them whole. The thought was a grim one, but at least she had a better idea of what she was up against.

The tunnel sloped downward now and the walls turned rocky. The worm had slid easily over the places where boulders jutted inward, its slimy trail layering over the sharp edges and smearing over the colorful stria of the walls: ochre, rich brown, black, even a sickly whitish green. Layers of time, compressed into the earth.

Dashi's antennae twitched. Idree's scent was growing stronger. The droppings had also increased, the piles falling every few strides now. In some places they had decomposed completely, leaving behind a carpet of bone splinters to crunch beneath Dashi's boots, like pieces of pale straw.

A scream echoed down the tunnel. Dashi charged around the last bend, her heart pounding as she took in the tableau revealed by lantern light: a horse, hanging halfway from the worm's maw and, just below, Idree and Tuya trapped in coils of wet, pink flesh.

Chapter 32

Dashi skidded to a stop at the entrance to the worm's lair, momentarily aghast at the beast's size. She had seen only a portion of it during the attack but now pink segmented muscle seemed to be everywhere: piled in corners, draped over errant boulders, crisscrossing the lair floor. It was like peeking inside an abdominal cavity. Idree's horse hung limply from the worm's mouth. Tuya's horse lay near the entrance, its neck twisted horribly. The worm kept a loop of its meaty body draped casually over the horse's hindquarters, reassuring itself that its meal wouldn't bolt.

The worm didn't seem particularly concerned by Dashi's appearance, but Idree and Tuya both turned toward the lantern light, relief plain on their faces. Idree's hair was plastered to her face, glistening with the same mucus that had coated the tunnel. She'd managed to keep one arm free, but everything else from the chest down was wrapped tightly in the worm's coils. Tuya was even worse; Dashi could only see half of her stricken face.

For a moment, Dashi froze, unsure what to do. Even a slight constriction of the worm's coils could be fatal. If she *did* manage to free her sister, the worm could just capture her with a different loop of pink-gray rope, or catch them in the tunnel as they tried to flee. The best thing, she thought, would be to deliver a killing blow quickly, but her short sword and bow paled next to the worm's size.

Her eyes darted around, looking for anything that could be of use. The lair was part of a Purek ruin, she saw with surprise. The worm's tunnel had veered back in the direction of the dead-end canyon, though she couldn't tell if she was standing in one of the unexplored facades, or if she had reached some other, undiscovered, place. The intricate Purek craftsmanship had been destroyed when the worm moved in. Bricks and broken tiles, smeared a uniform brown, littered what ground was visible between the worm's fleshy folds. A line of toppled pedestals and pieces of unidentifiable sculpture lay against one wall. There was a ragged hole in another wall and a shadowy room beyond. Only the high ceiling retained any of its artistic glory: an exquisite design of the night sky, the tiles still pristine and bright. Just a little lower, the support columns were coated in the worm's secretions, shiny with freshness in some places, dull and dried in others.

She looked back to the worm just in time to see Idree's horse slide the rest of the way into its gaping mouth. The wet, sucking noise made Dashi's skin crawl. Idree met her eyes, her expression equal parts terror and fragile hope. The coil of flesh holding her shifted, moving her directly below the head.

The worm was lining up its next meal.

Idree leaned back, her shoulders gyrating erratically as she tried to free herself. Tuya's mouth moved, her dirt-streaked face canted toward Idree, but her words were inaudible. *Think*, Dashi ordered herself. Her sister's gaze was as heavy as a physical touch: that little hand, eternally tugging on the hem of her deel.

The worm lowered its head. Its wide, soft mouth cracked open. Idree cringed, trying to ward it off with her free arm. Dashi took a deep breath. She was out of time, and the only plan she'd come up with was to offer herself as a distraction.

She'd intended to attack close to the head, but as soon as she darted forward, the great pink-gray body moved to counter her. Coils were folded up and shuffled. Some parts retreated, while others rose in cresting waves. She hurtled left and right, dodging walls of segmented muscle. Abruptly changing tactics, she planted a foot in the worm's side, using her forward momentum to spring onto its body and from there onto an adjacent coil. The coil snapped open, and for a moment she teetered above the waiting snare, before regaining her balance and jumping away. A few slip-sliding steps later, she was within reach.

Dashi launched herself into the air, her sword flashing. The soft pink skin parted easily beneath steel as she sliced into the side of the worm's head. It reared back, the sudden movement flipping Idree out of the coil that held her. She landed on the floor on her back. Tuya disappeared entirely. The worm's head rose, higher and higher, a king surveying the single, paltry rebel who dared challenge it. Dashi could see no eyes in the folds of skin, but its posture—watchful, turned slightly away from Idree now—made her think it was watching her. It was silent, where any other animal would have been snarling in rage and pain. The sound of Idree scrabbling over the packed dirt stood out all the more.

"Leave me the lantern," Dashi shouted. It would be slow going for Idree in the pitch black of the tunnel, but without light, Dashi would only last a few seconds.

The worm's head plunged. Dashi rolled sideways, landing next to a different part of its body, which immediately spilled toward her in a wall of wet muscle. She jumped again, striking the worm as she moved to a patch of open space. Idree was crawling toward one side of the lair. At the entrance, she took one staggering step and stopped to look back.

"Go," Dashi yelled.

Part of the worm shot toward her, and she couldn't move fast enough. It clipped her shoulder, throwing her to the ground. The impact jolted into her elbows and ribs. She kept moving, ducking to avoid the next attack of pinkish gray. Neck? Tail? Middle? She didn't even know which part was after her. She changed direction, somersaulting and jumping to avoid the pink coils that rose to entrap her. It was all instinct, all reactive. It was all a matter of time before she lost.

She crawled behind a support pillar, hoping to buy a moment of safety. Her breathing never got a chance to slow. The worm wrapped around the pillar, its blunt head appearing above her. Her palm skidded on its slick mass as she rolled toward the rear wall of the lair. The folds of pink and gray flesh slid closer, a rapidly shrinking semicircle. She was cornered. *There's too much of it,* she thought, her mind spinning with panic. *And too little room to maneuver.* Feeling around, her fingers found the edge of the gaping hole she'd noticed in the back wall. *Open space.* Without pausing to second guess herself, Dashi launched herself through the opening and into the shadowy room beyond.

The lantern light was significantly diminished here, but Dashi could make out a line of altars marching down the center of the room, bracketed on each side by enormous, jewel-studded pillars. Then the worm thundered through the hole behind her in an explosion of stone and dust and brickwork. A shard cut Dashi's cheek. Pain blazed along her nape as a chunk of brick struck her. She dove for the nearest altar, but the worm got there first, flattening it in one move. Jewelry and coins flew into the air, precious offerings now discarded.

Its soft-lipped mouth was open, reaching for her. Scrambling to put something between them, Dashi moved for the next altar. The beast bludgeoned that one too. She danced sideways, striking it again and again with her sword, but it was like trying to chop wood with a kitchen knife: she could make contact with every strike and still not make a difference. Her foot slid in its purplish blood and, before she could regain her momentum, it struck her in the back, spinning her through the air.

Her shoulder hit a pillar. Her head followed suit. Dashi's knees buckled, slamming into the ground.

Remaining stationary was dangerous, she knew that, but it was suddenly hard to focus on what needed to be done. The impact was still reverberating through her jaw. *Keep moving*, Baris ordered. She staggered to her feet, the room spinning around her. A pressure plate shifted beneath her boot. She was too disoriented to move quickly, but she managed one lurching step sideways. A spear flew from the dark edges of the room, rifling over her shoulder and into the fleshy folds of the worm. The beast recoiled under the blow. The spear had hit with tremendous force; the shaft was almost fully buried in the worm's side. The injured segment of muscle trembled. Dashi held her breath. *Could it have...?*

The worm churned back into motion, crushing another altar and Dashi's short-lived hope. But it had also given her a strategy. *Patterns.* The Pureks were crazy about them. One spear hadn't done much, but if she planned it right, one spear might make a difference.

Trying to shake off the remainder of her dizziness, she broke into an ungainly run toward the next pillar. She knew the worm was following her. She could taste that horrible, dank scent. She could hear the whisper of wet flesh against stone, coming closer and closer to her back. She turned, staring as it rose, its shadow falling over her as it blocked the light from the other room.

Not yet, she told herself. *It's too high.*

A breeze rushed against the top of her head as the giant, wrinkled mouth dropped toward her.

Now. Just before it touched her, she stomped on the pressure plate and flung herself sideways.

The spear flew from the darkness, a gift from the Pureks. It hit the worm in the side of the head, embedding so deeply that it was lost from sight in the wet folds. The effect was akin to an electric shock. The worm bucked wildly, whipping around in wild gyrations. A wall of flesh hit Dashi and threw her partway across the room. Pieces of pillar flew after her. Above, the ceiling grumbled. Dashi scrambled to her feet, running for the worm's lair as pieces of ceiling tile fell around her in clinking raindrops.

The worm was long enough that its body snaked through the hole in the wall, occupying both rooms at the same time. Dashi vaulted onto it, sliding over the gooey mass as she tried to escape.

"Dashi!"

Her head whipped around. "Idree! Why—" She broke off, noticing Tuya hobbled against the wall, one leg still pinned in the worm's massive coils. Idree had stayed to help Tuya. *Of course she had.* Tuya was grime-covered and frantic as she tried to jerk her leg free from the knot of flesh. She looked up, her eyes meeting Dashi's across the lair. Dashi wanted to scream. She wanted Idree long gone.

She plunged toward them, climbing over the worm's body. As soon as she was within reach, she began hacking at the worm's slick body, carving away flesh to free Tuya's trapped leg.

"Run, Idree," Tuya warned in a strangled voice, her gaze focused over Dashi's shoulder.

Idree looked up and took a step back. Dashi had only an instant to register that Tuya's foot was free when the other woman dove sideways, grabbing Dashi by the arm. The worm's body convulsed, flinging them in opposite directions.

Dashi rolled to her feet, wiping slime from her face. A wall of worm blocked her from Tuya and Idree. On the other side of it, she saw Tuya bend over her dead horse, making a nonsensical attempt to salvage her saddlebags. Idree had almost made it to the tunnel mouth. Dashi tried to vault over the worm's back, but suddenly her entire leg was enveloped in a sinkhole of flesh. The worm's mouth came closer, soft and flabby as an old man's. The end of the spear was just visible, sticking out from its cheek. Grasping her sword in both hands, Dashi stabbed down with all her strength. The pink-gray trap twitched involuntarily and she shucked her slimy leg free.

Idree was just inside the tunnel entrance, one dirty hand over her mouth. Tuya, holding the lantern, tugged on her arm. Dashi gained speed as she slid over part of the worm's pink bulk. Idree's expression mutated, becoming even more horrified, and Dashi jumped sideways in response. The worm's head pummeled the ground where she'd just been, hard enough that Dashi felt it tremble beneath her boots. She reached the tunnel, hurtling after her sister. The worm slammed into the opening behind her, its pillowy mouth open and oozing purplish blood. *Faster*, she silently urged Idree. *Get out of its range*. Air rushed at her from behind, a tide pushed by the worm as it glided after them. Even as she tried to force more speed from her legs, Dashi braced herself for the blow that would flatten her.

Instead, a dull roar rose from behind them. The whole tunnel began to quake. Dashi stumbled, catching herself with one hand just before her knees hit the ground. In front of her, Idree and Tuya stopped, their hands gripped together.

"What was that?" Idree pushed grime-coated hair from her eyes.

The lantern illuminated enough of the tunnel that Dashi could see the worm stretched out, plugging the tunnel like a cork at the end of a bottle. It wasn't moving. A wave of dust filtered through the sliver of space between the worm and the wall, settling over its still body.

"I think," Dashi said, "that it knocked over one too many support pillars."

She walked backward to Idree and Tuya, not taking her eyes off the worm. She wasn't sure if it was dead or only temporarily incapacitated, but she would make sure Idree was out of danger long before the outcome became apparent. Idree's tight expression collapsed slowly into one of relief. Tuya turned away, abruptly bending over and putting her hands on her knees.

Idree glanced at Dashi. "Thanks," she murmured.

"You can't think I would have—"

"I knew you wouldn't leave *me*." A tip of her chin toward Tuya's back, made her meaning clear: Dashi might never leave *Idree*, but Tuya was another matter.

Dashi shrugged, looking away.

Tuya straightened and wiped her forehead. "Let's go," she rasped.

Dashi picked up the lantern in one hand and carried her sword in the other. She had nothing clean with which to wipe the blade, and Baris would come back from his ancestors to haunt her if she sheathed a sword while it was dirty. Idree's fingers, crusty with grime, wrapped over hers on the lantern handle.

After an interminable amount of time, light appeared ahead of them. Idree's steps quickened, but Tuya stopped.

"The pyrothrite wasn't supposed to be used like that," she said, not looking at Dashi. The earthy scent of the worm was strong on her.

Dashi snorted. "No need to charm me. I've already taken care of the worm."

Tuya adjusted the saddlebags slung over her shoulder and frowned. "No," she said firmly, finally meeting Dashi's eyes. "You should know. I *want* you to know. Every spring there are huge storms that wash up trees and rocks and sand and deposit them in a snarl at the mouths of our harbors. It takes weeks to clear. All trade is stopped. We're called to follow Mother Inspiration wherever she leads and not to think too much about the application of what we're studying. We're not supposed to worry how—or if—the Merchantry Council will market and trade it. But when I discovered how to make the pyrothrite and then time its detonation, it was so our harbormasters could safely explode the storm snags. The harbormaster would have enough time to get to shore, while the snag…" Tuya made a fist and then opened it suddenly, finger splayed. "I invented it to keep people *out* of danger, not to be put them in it. Not to coerce."

Dashi watched the other woman, uncertain what she was supposed to do with that information. It didn't make her like the Yassaris more.

"Thank you," Idree said. She touched Tuya's shoulder. "I—*we*," she amended, casting a meaningful look at Dashi, "know you're forbidden to talk about anything to do with Yassar, so that means a lot."

Tuya nodded, but her eyes were intent on Dashi. Idree was looking at her also, waiting for a response. What was she supposed to do, pat Tuya on the shoulder and say it was all fine? It wasn't, and not just because of the belt.

"Maybe you invented pyrothrite for a noble purpose and maybe you didn't know about the belt," Dashi said finally, "but you stood there as a Yassari representative and negotiated with the khan and Zayaa for the sale of the pyrothrite-tipped arrows. Those arrows won't just be used against giant rats. Someday soon they'll be used against people and, knowing Zayaa, they'll probably be innocent ones. You can hide behind Yassari neutrality all you want, but *that* will still be on your head." She turned back to the light ahead of them. "I have learned," she said slowly, "that the past is only important so long as it informs the future. Any regrets, any hopes to apologize, let them be focused there."

When they stumbled from the worm's tunnel, the look of unabashed relief on Zayaa's face might have been interpreted as worry or affection from someone who didn't know her.

"Good. We can continue," she said, dispelling the illusion.

Dashi glanced at the body of a soldier on the tunnel floor, his neck bent at the wrong angle. She wondered which one of the heralds had been tasked with putting down the soldiers' rebellion. Solongo's eyes slid to the stag.

"Did you kill it?" Zayaa asked Dashi.

"I'm not sure," Dashi said. "It might just be...stuck. But we decided not to wait around."

Zayaa took Idree by the arm, propelling her toward a new mount.

Dashi didn't move. Her eyes had caught another shape on the tunnel floor. Her feet were rooted in place. Her heart cracked in two.

Spit.

He no longer lay on his side, as he had when she'd left to find Idree but had rolled onto his belly with his forelegs outstretched, preparing to stand. Yet he remained there, unmoving, except for the heaving of his gray sides. His neck bowed so deeply that his nose touched the dirt. Someone had removed her saddle while she'd been gone, perhaps in a vain effort to help Spit get to his feet. His right rear leg was splayed out to one side. The length of it was horribly turned, a washrag that had been partially wrung out and left, limp and twisted, on the side of a bucket. Jagged bone poked out in two spots.

"Spit," Dashi breathed. Her stomach leaped to life, churning at the sight of that leg, so she tried to focus on his blocky head and wise, dark eyes.

At her voice, Spit made a game effort to rise, chest muscles straining as he tried to take all of his weight on the front half of his body. Dashi stepped forward, her hands outstretched to help.

"Leave the nag," Zayaa snapped. "I don't want to be here if the worm comes back for a second helping." She raised her voice. "Everyone mount up. We leave now." She turned back to Dashi. "Get your saddle and grab a spare mount."

Dashi's legs obeyed, moving toward her saddle and then to the nearest unclaimed horse, a stocky bay gelding with a white star on his forehead. Dashi hated him. She saddled him anyway.

Her gaze drifted back to Spit's leg, drawn by some magnetism she couldn't deny. Altan's voice, placid and unemotional, came to her. *Facts and logic, Dashi. Facts and logic. It is the only way to make decisions.*

Fact told her that Spit's leg was unsalvageable. Logic told her that the humane thing to do would be to end his life rather than prolong his suffering. An image of Sevlin's hand, swift against the throat of another horse, came into her mind. She pushed it away. Could she make a poultice for him? There was no grass nearby and Zayaa wouldn't allow the delay, she knew that. Could it be amputated? *No.* A horse couldn't get around on three legs and, even if it could be done, it couldn't be done *here*, in the taiga, next door to a giant worm.

Facts and logic, Altan insisted, but even he must have denied facts and given up on logic, or he would have realized that it was his lover who'd betrayed him. *Shut up*, Dashi told him roughly.

"Ride," Zayaa called.

Dashi swung herself into the saddle, her legs settling around sides that were too narrow, too unfamiliar. The remaining soldiers kicked their horses into a trot, needing no reminder that the worm might return. Spit heaved a sigh, his dark, liquid eyes fixed on the other horses as they left him behind. The bay followed, high-stepping in protest when Dashi slowed him.

She had determined, before, that the bow was an inadequate weapon for the cramped, poorly lit conditions of an underground tunnel. But she'd assumed a dynamic target, moving and lively. Spit was not. She wondered, detachedly, whether she would be able to do the job well, or if those unwieldy emotions she always attributed to Idree would finally befall her too.

When she pulled a crane-fletched arrow from her quiver, however, her hands were steady. Like many of her arrows, this one had already been used. A brown stain—the dried blood of a taiga rat—splattered partway up the shaft. She shoved it back in the quiver, searching until she found one of her few unused arrows, its fletching snowy white, the shaft pristine and smelling sharply of cedar.

She set it to her bow. Raised her arms. *Action*, said Baris, but the deep rumble of his voice was uncharacteristically hushed. *We are people of action.*

Dashi sighted on one of those familiar brown eyes.

Exhaled, slow and even.

No arrow flew.

Her horse—*a* horse, not hers, never hers—was desperate to follow the others. She held him to a slow walk, his neck arching with restrained energy. The distance between Dashi and Spit grew.

Still, her fingers refused to release the arrow. Shadows grew thick over his flanks as her lantern, swaying against the side of her saddle, abandoned him. Soon she would have no shot at all.

Spit raised his head then, looking at her directly. He gave a single, soft whuff, almost encouraging.

Dashi exhaled again, but this time it was neither slow nor even.

"Goodbye, old man."

The bowstring sang.

Chapter 33

The tunnel spat them out at the top of a ridge. Blinking, most of the soldiers sank to the ground, too fatigued and too relieved at being outside to care about the snow. Dashi dismounted, watching numbly as the horse she'd ridden moved as far away from her as the reins would allow. She didn't bother trying to acclimate him to her strange scent. *He can probably tell I hate him anyway.*

The trees at the mouth of the tunnel draped them with freezing shadows, counteracting the weak sunlight that rose over the rim of distant mountains. In front of them, the land sloped sharply downward, a bare bowl beneath a blanket of snow. More trees grew at the bottom of the bowl and, in the very center of these, was a lake. Dashi studied it for a long moment. Mist, rose-colored in the dawn, huddled over the lake's surface, a tight-fitting lid that allowed only glimpses of frigid teal water to peek out at the edges. In the middle of the lake, something dark and lumpy jutted upward, thinning its misty veil. *An island.*

Dashi's attention swung to Zayaa, but there was nothing celebratory in the other woman's expression. Instead, Zayaa had become hyper-focused, almost martinetish. She pulled two pieces of the Wellspring map from her pocket and consulted them.

"Scout the slope," she barked before the soldiers could get too comfortable. "Look for ruins. Look for obstacles. Look for signs of predators." She turned to the owl and the moth. "You two, into the air. Look for anything Purek-made." She stared at the mist-filled crater, one hand cupping her elbow, the other braced beneath her chin.

"Zayaa," Dashi began, pitching her voice low. "Idree is innoc—"

"Silence."

Dashi's mouth closed. She slumped back against a tree. Her eyes were gritty. Worm slime had dried into her hair. She felt hollowed out. Her other emotions were specks wavering on the horizon, their presence blotted out by her overwhelming despair. Spit was dead. Idree was still a pawn. Zayaa was exactly where she wanted to be, and Dashi still hadn't figured out why. She kicked at the snow, staring dully as her boot scuffed something hard. Spiked blades of grass looked back at her, pale and hard. *Stone, just like the strange garden.* The tunnel entrance seemed a strange spot for a second ornamental garden, but even that mystery failed to arouse her energy.

The owl landed near Zayaa, causing the horses to prance nervously. Immediately, Idree appeared at Dashi's side, forcing a handful of dried meat into Dashi's clenched fist.

"Eat," Idree said in the same firm, soothing voice Dashi had heard her use with her patients.

Dashi shook her head, silenced by Zayaa's order. She wasn't hungry, only tired.

"You haven't had anything since yesterday evening."

Zayaa's voice, full of giddy triumph, reached them. "Really?...cannot be that lucky."

Dashi glanced up, the food untouched. Zayaa's back was to her, but there was no mistaking the coiled excitement in her stance. She was still talking to the owl.

Idree ducked in front of Dashi, refusing to be ignored. *"Eat."*

Her sister's hair had gotten long. The fringe that usually covered her forehead could now be tucked behind her ears. It made her eyes look exceptionally dark and doe-like.

Dashi looked away.

"It's not over yet," Idree said, reading her expression.

Dashi rolled her eyes.

"We don't know what might happen," Idree insisted, "but we keep trying. We keep surviving. That's what *you* said."

A triumphant cry rose from farther down the slope. Idree glanced up in puzzlement. Zayaa was walking toward them. The wide smile on her face sent a tremor through Dashi. The owl ducked her head, darting a glance at Dashi.

A scrum of figures emerged from the trees. Dashi glanced at their drawn swords, thinking their shouts must mean they'd encountered some animal, but their blades were bloodless. Then the breeze shifted, bringing with it a familiar scent. Dashi's eyes widened. *No.*

Idree's gasp came a moment later. Her hand wrapped around Dashi's forearm. "Is that...it's not...*Sevlin?*"

Even without Zayaa's command, Dashi couldn't have responded. Despite the soldiers herding him, Sevlin strode with his shoulders back, moving easily despite the snow and the shifting scree beneath his boots. He stared at them over the heads of the men and women who had him at swordpoint, his scarred face devoid of emotion.

Zayaa stood regally, waiting for a prince of Tyvalar to be brought before her, but Dashi saw how she shifted onto the balls of her feet: an aggressive stance.

He can't be alone, Dashi thought. Her eyes and antennae scanned the land, searching for Tyvalaran forces. He'd said...she stopped, picking through their conversation in the Gateway. He hadn't said much, she realized, only that he intended to free her and Idree. She'd *assumed* he must have companions somewhere...*because who would voluntarily enter the taiga alone?*

The soldiers pushed Sevlin to his knees in front of Zayaa. The sun had risen fully now, turning the sky a deep, pitiless blue.

"We found him in the trees," said one soldier. His expression was satisfied, aware of the prize he'd captured.

"The inscription on his sword is Tyvalaran," another added, tilting it helpfully toward Zayaa.

"You don't say," Zayaa drawled. Not looking away from Sevlin, she flicked a hand at the soldiers. "Half of you go back and search for another tunnel opening. When you find it, make sure there are no Tyvalaran reinforcements lying in wait. You too," she said to the stag. "Owl, look from the air."

Dashi searched Sevlin's face for a telltale twitch of his lips or a shift in his eyes, but he was impossible to read, even for her. Half of the soldiers stayed to guard Sevlin, while the others dispersed to search. The owl took flight, whipping Zayaa's hair with a sudden wind. She brushed it back patiently, smiling at Sevlin. The silence stretched until Dashi longed to pace or balance on her hands, anything for a release of tension. Idree's grip tightened, enough that it started to hurt Dashi's hardened skin. Even the soldiers began to shift nervously.

Finally, the dispatched soldiers began to trickle back. They'd located another tunnel but had found no one inside. The owl landed, shaking her feathered head. The stag followed suit a few minutes later.

"The great Tyvalaran spymaster arrives without a contingency plan?" Zayaa's hand went to her neck, stroking the amethyst pendant. "How unlikely. There's always something churning in that convoluted mind, even if it's just the notion to burn a family to death in their home."

Sevlin was silent.

"No contingency plans and no response." Zayaa stepped closer, towering over the kneeling Sevlin. "Very unusual. If you have nothing to say, then there is no reason to keep you alive."

"You want me dead regardless of what I say or don't say," Sevlin said. He sounded calm, his Karakalese as exactingly pronounced as ever.

"Tarqn Dashi fulestik tere atak." Zayaa hissed the words in Tyvalaran. Sevlin blinked once, a quick, involuntary flinch.

Without warning, Zayaa brought her knee up, cracking him under the chin. Sevlin's head snapped backward, his body rocking, but he did not fall.

"Make sure he does not escape," Zayaa said to the heralds. "I've changed my mind. I want him taken to the lake so he can watch," she paused to smile at Sevlin again, "while I destroy everything he's worked for."

Dashi turned her back on Sevlin, walking toward her mount. Spit would have let her bury her shaking hands in his mane, but the new horse laid its ears back, cowering from her inhuman scent. So she stood there with her arms hanging uselessly, waiting for Tuya to lead her horse past.

"Do you...want to know what she said?" Tuya murmured as she drew even.

Dashi swallowed. She kept picturing the way Sevlin's eye had flickered shut, a subconscious retreat from Zayaa's words. Finally, she nodded.

"She said," Tuya's gaze dropped to Dashi's hands, "that she would make you be the one to kill him."

Chapter 34

The horses' fatigue and the slide of loose rocks underfoot made riding more treacherous than it was worth, so they started to the lake on foot. Sevlin was sandwiched between half a dozen soldiers, hands tied behind his back. Zayaa stalked behind him, her gaze boring into the back of his head. The moth and the owl drew circles in the sky, the only sign of life in the limitless blue.

Dashi lengthened her strides, catching up to Zayaa as she crossed a stream that cut across the slope. Beneath its sheet of ice, the water rushed along merrily, its melody loud enough to cover the tramp of boots.

Glancing at her, Zayaa bared her teeth. "Speak, Dashi. I can't wait to hear this."

"Don't do this, Zayaa. I'm..." She swallowed. "I'm begging you. Please. If you hate me so much, just kill me. Don't make me kill Sevlin."

"I hated Altan and Baris. I hate Sevlin. You," Zayaa flicked her hair dismissively, "are a game piece."

Dashi tried a different tack. "Sevlin didn't order them to burn your family."

"Did he tell you that? Or is that just the way you've decided to see him?"

They entered the trees that bordered the lake and Dashi's horse shied as a skeletal branch scraped its flanks. She tugged it forward, not answering Zayaa directly. It would only enrage her if she knew Dashi had seen Sevlin at the Gateway and not reported it.

"You've had your revenge on Baris and Altan. Can't that be enough?"

"What do you think would have happened to my family if Baris and Altan had known they were inside?" Zayaa asked.

"I know they wouldn't have burned them alive," Dashi said firmly.

"Of course not." Zayaa's voice was bitter. "They would have arrested them. Transported them to Rucharla. Tried and convicted and executed them. All very neat and tidy, but my family would be just as dead."

They were responsible for the deaths of hundreds of people, Dashi wanted to say. *For murdering Sevlin's mother. For the attempted assassination of Queen Lyazzat and near-overthrow of the Tyvalaran government.* Zayaa was arguing that her family's actions should not have been punished at all, but Dashi swallowed her thoughts, knowing they would not work to her advantage.

"Isn't that what you should do with Sevlin then?" she hazarded. "Take him back to Karak City and make him stand trial?" It was a dubious argument, one that still saw Sevlin held captive. But if his execution was postponed, there was always the chance that the calculus would change in his favor. Perhaps his half-sister would exert some pressure on his behalf. Perhaps he would find a way to escape on his own. He was a resourceful man who undoubtedly had a few allies in Karakal.

"You're so obvious." Zayaa cast her a snide look. "No, Sevlin is slippery. The sooner I land this particular fish, the less chance he'll slide back into the water."

Dashi swallowed.

"Besides," Zayaa continued, "he cares about you."

Dashi started, looking involuntarily to where Sevlin walked in front of them. They hadn't exchanged a word since he'd been captured.

"I could see it in the way he was determinedly *not* looking at you," Zayaa clarified, casting another sly glance in Dashi's direction. "It will cause him a special pain to know you are the one holding the knife."

Something about the satisfaction in her voice told Dashi she was speaking from experience. She was speaking about Altan. "It won't be the same," Dashi said fiercely. "Sevlin knows I would never do that on my own."

"But it will cause *you* pain, and watching that will hurt him as much as your knife."

As they ventured deeper into the trees that surrounded the lake, Zayaa's pace quickened, leaving Dashi behind. Beneath the boughs, the snow on the ground was noticeably shallower, only up to Dashi's ankles. It reminded her of the stone grass she'd uncovered near the tunnel entrance. She couldn't see any peeking through here.

Idree caught up to her, giving her a distraught look. Dashi grimaced; her own failings had been translated into worry lines on Idree's forehead.

"I asked Tuya to help me free Sevlin," Idree whispered.

"Will she?" Dashi glanced back to where Tuya walked. The Yassari's eyes were downcast.

"I think she's thinking about it."

"She better think quickly."

"She doesn't like the way Zayaa and the khan have done things."

"I'm sure it must be difficult to see evil up close when you're accustomed to provisioning it from afar. Anyway, what does it matter what she likes or doesn't like? I thought she was committed to being neutral, no matter what."

Idree shrugged.

"Even if she does help you, there will only be two of you against all of us. You need something to reduce our advantages," Dashi went on. "A distraction or a hostage or—" She glanced at her sister's furrowed forehead, at the way her eyebrows had puckered together. What was she *saying*? This was a disastrous idea, and Tuya's participation would do nothing to change that.

"Never mind," she said quickly. "Forget whatever you're planning and run instead. Don't go to the tunnel Sevlin used." Her words tumbled out, trying to form themselves into a plan. "There was slime caking his boots. Wherever he was, it must have been near another worm. Hopefully, the worm in our tunnel is dead, but even if it isn't, you have a better chance of slipping through with two people than you do with a large group. We left supplies and pack animals in the canyon at the Gateway so if you can make it there—"

"I'm not going to—"

"You wouldn't be abandoning us. You'd be keeping Zayaa from getting what she wants. Whatever it is, she needs *you* to do it, or you wouldn't be here. Besides," she added with more certainty than she felt, "if she's busy searching for you, she'll forget about killing Sevlin."

Idree was quiet, thinking this over. When she started to drop back to where Tuya trudged, Dashi caught her arm. "Whatever you come up with, Idree, you can't let on to me. I can't be trusted."

"It's not *you*—"

"I'm the one who took your finger, Idree, and I'd do more than that if Zayaa told me to, so just...make sure I'm occupied. The deadliest—"

"—strike comes from a hidden hand. I know, alright?"

Dashi nodded, swallowing the urge to lecture. If anyone had learned the seriousness of the situation—in the most brutal way possible—it was Idree. "And one more thing," Dashi said. She could see Idree preparing to roll her eyes. "I love you."

"I don't remember you ever telling me that before." The worry lines on Idree's forehead doubled. "I love you too, Dashi." She dropped back to where Tuya walked. Dashi could feel the weight of her worried gaze for several minutes afterward.

The slope grew steeper, speeding toward the water's edge. They emerged from the trees onto a snowy bank, where they were immediately bombarded by a wash of raw, moist air. Pale green where it touched the land, the color of the lake darkened precipitously to a striking teal before disappearing beneath the wall of mist. Several of the soldiers skidded down the bank, leading their thirsty mounts. The horses pawed at the water but unanimously refused to drink it.

One woman dipped her finger in, tasting it. She shook her head, mouth puckering. "It's salty."

Zayaa scanned the shoreline, ignoring them all. The island in the center of the lake was invisible now, fully cloaked by the mist. The banks, too, were only visible in the foreground, curling around them with uniform steepness, before the curvature was hidden beneath white.

Dashi leveled a pleading glance at the mist. If there was ever a time for the spirits that roamed the taiga to arise, this one would have been perfect. She knew from past experience that she and Idree would retain consciousness the longest, while the others fell to the ground. Because of Zayaa's command, Dashi couldn't help Sevlin escape, but perhaps Idree could rouse him—*no*, she thought in despair, remembering Zayaa's exact words. *Make sure he does not escape.* She would be forced to stop them.

Her thoughts turned out to be moot; the mist stayed where it was. Zayaa consulted the map. The others debated where to set up camp. Dashi kicked a rock in disgust.

"Tie him to a tree," Zayaa instructed. "No, facing the lake." She glanced at Sevlin, a smile on her lips. "As you die, you can watch me cross over to the Wellspring. Your last thoughts will be about what is coming for your beloved Tyvalar, for your sister and brother."

The soldiers pushed Sevlin, arms still tied behind his back, against the trunk of a sturdy larch and began securing him there. Dashi shut her eyes. Her mind scrambled for ideas, half-formed and improbable, before discarding them, one by one. Despair threatened to swallow her whole. Her antenna twitched, mimicking the agitation of her thoughts. She would have to watch Sevlin die. She would be the one to *make* Sevlin die. When Dashi opened her eyes, Sevlin was staring at her. Idree was too. Tears coursed down her sister's cheeks.

A scent tickled Dashi's antennae and, glancing down, she saw dark specks appearing next to her boots: ants, struggling out onto the snow. A few, bolder than the rest, found their way onto Dashi's boot, coursing up her calf. Scooping them gently into her palm, she returned them to the ground.

Sorry I woke you, she thought at them, because that was clearly what had happened. Before, Dashi had almost convinced herself that the ants crawling up Zayaa's horse weren't her doing. Now, however...she swallowed. It couldn't be a coincidence. She had summoned them from their nests.

Emotion. That must be the catalyst. She'd been so angry about Idree's finger before, a red-hot rage that blinded her to all else. Now, as she focused on Sevlin's plight, she felt...love. Despair. Pain. Sadness. Many emotions, but they twisted together to form a torch that burned just as bright as her anger had, creating a scent stimulus to which the ants responded. Her lips twitched bitterly. Intense emotion was something she had in abundance, but was it useful? *No.* Zayaa held the abilities of four heralds like tools in her hand, while she, Dashi, had ants who commiserated with her emotions. Even if she could direct them against Zayaa, something which was not a certainty—the tether prevented her from raising her hand against her master, and Dashi wasn't sure if using ants counted—what good would it do? The ants could bite Zayaa and her horse as much as they wanted, but they couldn't change the outcome.

"Dashi."

Her head whipped in Sevlin's direction.

"Come here?"

Dashi narrowed her eyes, glancing to where Zayaa stood studying her map.

"Don't worry," Zayaa said, a smile curling her lips as she looked up. "I'll make sure you have a proper goodbye. For now, Dashi, you're coming with me. The rest of you, wait here."

Dashi followed her, giving Sevlin a final glance over her shoulder.

He smiled, slow and enigmatic, with one side of his mouth.

Zayaa headed east along the shoreline, her long stride eating up the ground. "For someone who is supposedly so rash and wild, you are terribly predictable."

Dashi, who'd been about to speak, closed her mouth with a snap.

"Oh Zayaa, please spare him," Zayaa continued, transforming her voice into a decent mimicry of Dashi's. "He's so handsome and tragic with his scars and he kissed me, and now I will debase myself to beg for his life."

The desire to reach for a knife, a sword, an arrow—anything—made Dashi's fists clench. "It's not debasing to beg for someone's life," she said, then felt compelled to add, "and he hasn't kissed me." *I kissed him.*

Zayaa glanced down at Dashi's hands and laughed. "The tether stands in for self-control if nothing else. You would be a murdering savage, else."

"You're the one who wants to commit murder."

"But not the savage kind. That requires hardly any intellect at all." Zayaa's voice was light. Buoyant, even.

Once, Zayaa's good mood would have been contagious, morphing into banter between their friends. The backslapping, the side-aching laughter, the lazy conversations beneath a ceiling of stars: the memories flashed before Dashi's eyes like a series of paintings, still and surreal.

"I don't think *lack of intellect* is the normal objection to murder," Dashi said.

"Tell that to the men you killed in the brothel. Why is your revenge more acceptable than mine?"

"Because they—"

"Killed someone you loved? So did Altan and Baris. So did Sevlin, by dint of his orders."

"Sevlin didn't order your family burned."

"The results speak for themselves." Anger quivered in Zayaa's voice, banishing her earlier tone.

"And Idree?" Emotion made Dashi's voice come out hoarse. "What have *her* crimes been, Zayaa?"

"Idree is an innocent." Zayaa said coldly, "but sometimes innocence is lost."

Dashi opened her mouth, but Zayaa cut her off. "Enough. I brought you to help me locate the bridge to the Wellspring. Come."

Zayaa turned right, cutting back up the slope to duck beneath the trees. Limbs arched overhead, buttressing the sky. They intertwined so tightly that only a dusting of snow had gotten through. Dashi's feet followed, although her mind found it difficult to let their previous topic go so easily.

"The Purek high priests and priestesses made sacrifices at the Wellspring on both the summer and winter solstices," Zayaa went on. "Today is the winter solstice, so today a bridge to the Wellspring becomes available."

The summer and winter solstice: the two most sacred days of the Purek calendar. *Balanced*. Dashi replayed their journey—snow, deaths, delays, giant taiga animals. Despite everything, Zayaa had still managed to arrive on the exact day she needed to. It was admirable in its way, Dashi thought, wanting to punch something. It also explained Zayaa's inexplicable rush to enter the taiga in the dead of winter.

"Why not have the owl or the moth fly you across?" Dashi asked.

"Because the Pureks left waypoints—triggers, if you will—that need to be engaged, not just to access the bridge, but also to access the Wellspring itself. You know the Pureks: there's no skipping ahead."

"How will you know which trigger is a waypoint and which is a trap?"

Zayaa waved a hand. "That's for me to worry about, not you."

Dashi's eyes flicked to the pocket where Zayaa had deposited the sections of the map.

"The waypoint is on this slope somewhere," Zayaa said.

"There's only one?" Incredulity seeped into Dashi's voice. Balance underlined everything the Pureks did. That usually translated to even numbers, not odd.

"There are two," Zayaa said. "You triggered the first when you opened the Gateway. Didn't you wonder why I didn't use the heralds to fly me over the canyon walls?" She gestured at the trees around them. "I don't have a description, but I assume we'll know it when we see it. Go that way. Don't trigger it. Summon me if you find it."

Dashi's body turned where Zayaa had directed it. Her eyes swept the ground, determined not to miss anything, while her mind looped frantically back to Sevlin. Catching sight of a pile of rocks, her stride quickened. *A cairn*, she thought, but after she'd shifted dozens of stones and found nothing of interest, she moved on. She wondered if there was any possibility they were searching in the wrong place. *Let Zayaa's research be wrong, just this once,* she silently begged.

Dashi tracked downhill to avoid a pair of wide spruce trees, which had grown, twisted and crone-like, around each other. As she came around the other side, she let out a strangled yelp. A pale figure stood directly in her path.

Chapter 35

The figure stood in a snow-dusted dip in the land, rising from the center like a pillar waiting for the weight of the roof. Adding to the effect, her left arm was raised, empty-handed, toward the sky. Her right stretched toward the ground. Her face was turned away, hidden as she peered beneath her raised arm.

The statue was so lifelike that, for a moment, it fooled Dashi. Then, her brain began to assimilate the figure's details—most significantly the lack of scent—and she relaxed. The figure was a pure, bone white: not robed by moss or lichen, not defiled by dirt or bird excrement. Nothing alive could be that perfect.

The details that Dashi could see were incredible, even when measured against the legacy of talented Purek sculptors. The drape of the woman's deel fell exactly like real fabric, clinging at the hips and flaring out around her knees, blown by the momentum of her stride. Everything about her spoke of action, the tension of muscles and the fizz of adrenaline. The statue was short, Dashi noted. *Not much taller than I am.* The stone fabric managed to look tight across the shoulders and the ripple of biceps was visible through the long sleeves. Dashi sucked in an impressed breath as she edged closer; she could see the individual threads of the pattern embroidered from cuff to elbow.

Something about the pattern seemed familiar. She could almost imagine how it would look in real life: vibrant blues and cool greens; regal shades of gold and copper. Dashi glanced at the hem, where the pattern continued. The sensation of familiarity grew stronger, crystalizing into certainty. She *had* seen this before, shrouding the legs that ran through the Gateway, encircling the wrist that reached boldly among poison blossoms. She glanced at the statue's feet: fine sandals, their straps weaving around the ankle. Those, too, were recognizable, though when she'd last seen them—in the vision she'd had before opening the Gateway—they'd been gold, not white.

Dashi stopped moving, caution finally wresting her attention away from the improbability of finding a physical manifestation of her vision. Rigid grass stuck up around the statue's feet: stone, like the ghostly garden and like the patch she'd discovered near the tunnel.

Her gaze followed the path of stone grass down the slope. It meandered slightly, poking through the thin layer of snow, before disappearing behind a tree. Dashi stared at the oblong patch of white on the tree's trunk. Like the grass, it appeared to be stone, though the rest of the tree was living. How had the Pureks managed *that?* Unease stirred inside her, dark and superstitious. She *knew*, without any of the facts or logic that Altan had always insisted upon, that the path of stone led to death.

The stone grass encircled the statue's feet, spooling out to surround the base of a knee-height, pyramidal block of granite. As soon as she caught sight of it, Dashi raised her voice to hail Zayaa, the tether forcing her to ignore her sense of foreboding. She stepped over the line of stone grass, circling to the front of the statue. There was a narrow slit on this side of the pyramidal stone; she could just make out the gleam of a metal lever inside. It was either a trap—if it was, she'd bet on a poisoned needle in the cleft—or the waypoint that Zayaa said would raise the bridge to the Wellspring. The pyramid itself was dark, speckled granite, a stark contrast to the white hand of the statue that hovered above it.

Odd, Dashi thought; she would have expected the artist to use the same materials for both statue and pyramid. *Perhaps the difference in stone was meant to highlight—*

Her thoughts broke off as she squatted to get a glimpse of the statue's face, which was mostly hidden behind her upraised arm. Dashi bit off a startled cry, her feet backtracking so quickly that she nearly fell. The hawkish nose, the strong jaw, the wide cheekbones: all were familiar features. She'd seen them in her dreams. She'd seen them in the mist. She'd seen them on the face of the small, brilliant statuette that housed the golden needle. *Khagan Nuray*. Dashi stared at the familiar sandals, at the embroidered sleeves she'd seen in the vision, and felt the fine hairs on the back of her neck rise.

The Mori, her father's side of the family, whispered of spirits who, having escaped whatever confines existed in the spirit world, roamed the land of the living. Three years ago, she'd known of Khagan Nuray only academically, mostly from things Altan had said in passing. Now, it seemed that every time she turned around, the dead khagan was there. Was this what the Mori spoke of? Dashi knew—and she was grasping desperately for Altan's logic here—that her vision of Khagan Nuray in the Gateway hadn't been a dream. Nor was it attributable to the peculiarities of the taiga mist. She'd been wide awake one moment and, in the next, sucked into Khagan Nuray's...consciousness? Memories?

She almost expected the khagan to be watching her, but the statue's gaze was on the blocky pyramid at her feet. Her stone hand hovered close to its surface, fingers stretched longingly. Her exposed forearm was corded with tension. Khagan Nuray had been desperate in the vision too, Dashi thought suddenly. Those extravagant sandals had pounded the ground as she ran, trying to distance herself from her pursuers. Now that Dashi knew the vision was from Nuray's perspective, she realized how strange that was. Who would chase a powerful khagan? Where were her guards?

I'm acting like the vision is true, she realized with chagrin. *Proof. I have no proof.* She knelt swiftly, probing at the frozen soil with her knife blade, then sat back on her heels and stared. Stone roots, thin as thread and white as bone, stood out against the dark soil. No artist could have made this. Of that, she was certain. These were *real*. Or, they had been. Did it follow then, that the footprints in the garden—footprints she'd watched Khagan Nuray make in the vision—were real too? Dashi swore softly, suspicions beginning to coalesce in her mind. If the grass had once been alive, might the statue—?

The thought was nearly as bad as the idea of roaming spirits. Dashi rubbed a shaking hand across her jaw, wishing Sevlin or Idree were nearby so she could toss ideas at someone else. Edging closer, she studied the lines of motion in the strong arms and shoulders, the expression of fear and determination on the statue's harsh features. Unbidden, her hand stretched out to touch the stone. It was freezing cold, of course, matching the temperature of the air. Dashi felt it even through her fur-lined mittens.

She was so close that Khagan Nuray's upflung arm arched over her own head now. It seemed protective and frantic, an attempt to ward off a descending blow. Raised dots marked the inside of Nuray's wrist: blood droplets. The injury itself was partially hidden by the twist of her upraised hand, but Dashi recognized the jagged edges of the arrow wound she'd seen in the vision, now memorialized in stone. Slowly, Dashi shucked off her mitten and the gloves beneath and pressed her index finger to a petrified drop of blood. She drew in a shaky breath, her excitement fizzling as nothing happened

The feeling that washed over her was, surprisingly, embarrassment. She had believed in the vision, if not the veracity of its content, then at least in the fact that she'd experienced *something*. She could almost hear Altan's voice, chiding her for commingling the objective and subjective, for letting her awe at the otherworldly take the place of detached observation. Dutifully, she tried to recall what else she'd been doing in the stone garden at the moment she'd had the vision, but it was like picking at threads instead of holding whole cloth. She'd been following Nuray's footsteps. Could that be it? She'd also touched the blood splatter with her other hand, she realized, remembering the crimson slash of her own blood against the stone leaf. In a flash of inspiration, she drew her knife, opening up a line of fresh blood on the pad of one finger. She pressed it against the stone: fresh against old, alive against dead.

The effect was instantaneous, leaving her no time to wonder why her blood was the variable that worked. There was a sudden increase in the sounds and colors around her, too bright and too loud for a winter day. She had the sensation of plummeting. Her stomach gave a sickening lurch.

In the next breath, her senses merged with Nuray's, delivering a kaleidoscope of images:

The bright red bloom of Gossip's Tongue.

A long tunnel, earthy and dark, with a dim light at one end.

The harsh pant of Nuray's breath as the body of a priest flashed by on her right. Dashi recognized the golden, orb-like ornaments the man wore from Purek art she'd seen over the years.

A grid of what appeared to be giant, hexagonal beads. Nuray's hand spun the beads one by one, puzzling over the symbols painted on each facet.

The slap of freezing water, its brine sticking in her throat as she raised her head to draw a breath.

Then came a sight that Dashi knew intimately, one that made the smell of singed flesh haunt her nostrils: magic, raw and untamed.

This part of the vision remained, as her consciousness overlaid fully with Khagan Nuray's. Magic flashed in front of Nuray, not lazy and fluid, like the vein that Dashi had seen Idree access but charged with a barely leashed energy. It had that about-to-boil feeling that water gets just before it leaps in the pot. The color was different than the other veins Dashi had seen too, shifting restlessly from deep purple to magenta to indigo, the depth constantly changing. It wasn't so much a vein as it was a pool, or a snake coiled up on itself. Dashi wanted to take a step back.

Nuray, however, moved forward, either less fearful of magic than Dashi, or better practiced at mastering that fear. The magic coiled around her ankles, welcoming and sensuous. It was warm, without any of the white-hot pain that Dashi remembered so vividly from her stitching. This was what it felt like to touch magic as a seamstress: the embrace of family, walking into your own home. No wonder Idree didn't mind it.

Nuray seemed not to share Idree's attachment. "I don't want this. I never did. It has brought me nothing but *suffering*," Nuray said, as though the magic was sentient.

Her voice had the same rough quality that Dashi had heard before and, though she spoke in rapid Purek, somehow the meaning was clear.

"Even now, I must contend with manipulation and usurpers, with threats to my son's life. The same son who was forced into me when I was but the seamstress, and my life was not my own."

Knowledge flooded through Dashi, unspoken.

Nuray's fierce protectiveness for her son, despite his provenance.

The horror of finding that he'd been kidnapped: his empty bed, his forgotten toys.

The threats against him if Nuray did not give her stitching over to his abductors, if she did not make them an army of heralds subjugated to their will.

Filthy usurpers. Ancestors damned plotters. She had found him. She had freed him. Dashi saw an image of a boy lying on his back in a cave: bony in the way of a growing colt, his brown skin unnaturally pale, an arrow protruding below the jut of his collarbone.

He will live. His wounds had been cleaned and stitched—regular stitches, not magic ones. *He will live.* That's what Nuray told herself over and over. But it had been a near thing. She did not know if the arrow had been intentional or a stray, but it didn't matter. A little lower and she would have lost everything.

There was no choice but to hide him, she thought, with a mixture of pain and satisfaction. Far from her. Far from the tall trees that he loved so much. Far away, on the grim, treeless steppe. He was ten, old enough to gain knowledge and skill quickly but young enough to adapt, she assured herself. Doubtless, he would hate it at first—he would hate *her*—but she'd asked an old friend to take him in and she knew he would be safe there. Still, her heart ached. She wouldn't be able to see him for a long time, not until she was sure that it was safe for him to live openly as her son. And, if there was one thing Nuray knew, it was that the people close to the seamstress were never safe.

No more, Nuray thought in Dashi's head. It was a shout. *No more living as a tool. No more living as a target.* Power accrued to those who *took* it. Her true power had begun when she'd murdered her predecessor and usurped his place. It would continue only if she stopped being controlled by the magic. Dashi felt the tiniest splinter of doubt from Nuray. The other woman wasn't sure if this would work, though Dashi wasn't sure what *this* was. It made sense in theory, or as much sense as the magic ever did, but to Nuray's knowledge, it was unprecedented and she didn't know if—Nuray brutally squashed her own dissent. It would work because she *willed* it to work. That's what the magic responded to, after all: the will of the wielder. And Nuray had that in abundance.

Forcibly quelling her disquiet, Nuray waded deeper into the magic, taking Dashi with her. Something shimmered before her, there and gone again like a ghost. When Nuray was knee-deep, Dashi saw it again: an enormous tree, craggy and gnarled, with barren, twisting limbs. It was mist-white and translucent, not a real tree at all, but Dashi sensed that it was alive somehow. *Watching*. Its trunk was massive. Twenty people could have joined hands to encircle it. At its center, a jagged hole gaped, a deep, pitiless black that marred the beauty of the opalescent trunk. The magic pooled in it, or perhaps *from* it, pulsing in and out in a rhythmic tide—*a heartbeat*, Dashi thought—though the bright colors did nothing to lighten the dark hole.

The tree, the magic, even the shadowy echoing space around her, seemed to exist in a time and place untouched by human hands. As if it had always been and would always be. It was terrifying. Dashi felt her mind try to withdraw, to backpedal out of Nuray's consciousness and tiptoe back to the right time, the right body.

"I do not want this," Nuray said again. Though her voice rang loudly, this time there was an undercurrent of uncertainty. Dashi had the wild urge to look around—Where was she? More importantly, where were the exits?—but Nuray's eyes stayed focused on the ethereal tree. It quaked but not in the way a tree moves in the wind. It moved like the ground itself had rippled. If it'd had leaves, they would be dancing angrily along its limbs.

This will work, Nuray thought. *I will* make *it work. I will not be a slave to a trinket for the rest of my life.*

"I will take power for myself, not act as the conduit for something else," Nuray said. Plucking the golden needle from her pocket, she threw it at the tree's great maw.

For one long, shuddering moment, nothing happened. The magic continued its slow pulse in and out of the heart of the tree. Then sound boomed all around, so sudden and painfully loud that Nuray clapped her hands over her ears. The pool of magic trembled with the noise, shaking against Nuray's legs.

Nuray swayed, staring at the tree with her fists clenched. "I control it," she muttered. "No needle. No handlers." Her belief in her ability to control the magic was strong. But Dashi noticed with a spike of fear that the magic was changing, growing darker and darker until the purple verged on black. It surged higher, reaching Nuray's thighs, then her waist, then her chest, but Nuray did not notice. *Dashi* would have sprinted out of there, had she been in control of a pair of legs, but there was little she could do except watch the events unfold and wonder, with no small amount of panic, what would happen to *her* if Nuray died.

Nuray's mutterings continued. Her breath was deep and measured. It wasn't until the magic began to grow hot that she faltered. Dashi sensed her momentary confusion. The magic no longer felt comforting and familiar. It was alien now, a force completely separate from herself, and an angry one at that. *It isn't hurting me,* Nuray thought, seeking to assuage the doubts that were beginning to rise, serpents about to strike. In fact, the throb of the arrow wound in her hand was completely gone. Had the magic healed her? That would be a new, though welcome, development. Nuray glanced down, bringing her hand up to examine the wound as she did so. But as the filmy layers of magic parted, it was not her hand that appeared in front of her face but talons: four-toed and black. It changed before Nuray could react, becoming a wolf's paw with thick, dark fur. Then it was a fin, the spines rigid and stretched with wet, diaphanous membranes. Nuray's willpower slipped, no longer focused on bending the magic but riveted on what was happening to her body. Her hand changed again, becoming part fox, then mouse, then frog, switching so quickly that the outline began to blur.

Stop! Nuray made a single, mighty effort to reassert her control, but even with her eyes closed, she couldn't fully ignore her monstrous hand, couldn't behead all the doubts that writhed inside her. Her eyes popped open again. This time when she looked down, her hand was white and immobile, the arrow wound outlined clearly in frigid stone. Improbably, the golden needle was pinched between her frozen fingers, returned to her like the curse it was.

Stone.

The sight struck Nuray cold, her fear galloping out from under her without any semblance of control. With it came a paradoxical heat. The magic was burning. Nuray cried out, giving in to her urge to run, stumbling, from the pool. Dashi had a brief moment to assess where she was—some sort of cave—before Nuray's senses became so overloaded that hers were flooded in turn. The memories broke apart at the seams, becoming disjointed and separate, playing cards dealt in quick succession, one on top of the other.

Nuray, running hard, glanced over her shoulder at a black-blue wave. The magic was following her, curling over the island, spitting out tentacles in all directions, a monster unable to decide what it would eat first.

Nuray's feet pounded a shiny bridge, her stone hand clutched to her side, dead weight. Below the bridge, the teal water began to bubble and Dashi felt the other woman's panic grow. The land rose in a bowl around the lake. That made Nuray panic too. It had felt majestic before, as if the land had been formed and set aside, waiting to show off before its infrequent visitors. Now it was a trap, walls of soil and rock meant to prevent her escape. Would it be able to contain the magic? Could it protect her people? Her son?

Nuray cast a fearful glance over her shoulder. The magic cracked, cresting the bank like it was nothing. How far would it go? *Have to get to the waypoints,* she thought. *Have to close the Wellspring.* A blue tongue of magic followed close behind her, dogging the exact placement of her footsteps, turning the places she'd trod to stone.

Trees arched overhead, but the blue whip wove around them easily, darting in close to singe her before withdrawing again. Tasting. Toying. Her shoulder blade, her right elbow, her left calf and ankle were all stone. *Have to stop it now.* The pyramidal waypoint loomed in front of Nuray, but her body was weighted by all the stone. Each step felt like it would be her last. *The steppe...would the magic reach her son on the steppe?*

Nuray lurched up to the waypoint, legs stiffening until they were impossible to move. *Have to stem the flood. Have to keep him safe.* Through the tree trunks, she saw the blur of a priest moving away from her: one of her pursuers deciding to flee her instead. Nuray hailed him and saw him think about ignoring her. He turned around, the orb medallion around his neck swinging from the change in direction.

"Take this," Nuray gasped, using her working hand to pry the golden needle loose from her stone one. The needle seared her flesh like it no longer knew her, but she managed to hang on to it long enough to hurl it in the priest's direction. He looked at the glitter of gold on the ground, then back at her, confounded and wary. If she was wrong about the waypoint, if she couldn't fix what she'd done...

"Take it to the temple," she ordered. "Resanctify it. Find a new wielder. That will make it stop."

The magic loomed above her, flattening and lowering like the underside of a storm cloud. It was tired of waiting. Nuray stretched her good hand toward the waypoint—

Dashi broke out of Nuray's past and into the present day. The world wheeled around her, suddenly leached of its summer colors. She closed her eyes, sagging heavily against the statue for support, nauseous and panting. *Not a statue. Nuray's petrified body.*

"What are you doing?" Zayaa's voice came from over her shoulder.

"The cataclysm," Dashi whispered, so shaken by what she'd seen that she barely registered to whom she spoke. "*She* did it."

The knowledge sat heavily on her chest, preventing her from drawing a full breath. All those times she had spoken to Khagan Nuray...Dashi couldn't say she'd looked *forward* to their encounters, but there was some aspect of strength, of inner drive, to the dead khagan that she'd found admirable. But Nuray had caused the magical cataclysm. She'd single-handedly killed *millions*.

Dashi peeled her finger away from the cold stone of Nuray's wrist, staring at the single bloody fingerprint she'd left behind. "Listen to me, Zayaa. The Wellspring isn't going to give you access to the magic. It's going to kill us. Not just Sevlin or Idree or me but you too. And probably most of Karakal. I—I'm not sure of its reach, but I do know that taking Idree and the golden needle to the Wellspring risks another cataclysm and—"

Zayaa reached down to the stone pyramid and flipped the concealed trigger. A sleepy rumble echoed from the lake basin as she straightened.

"What makes you think," she asked, smiling, "that another cataclysm isn't *exactly* what I want?"

Chapter 36

"I thought you wanted power," Dashi said, staring at Zayaa. "To control the magic."

"No, *the khan* wanted to control the magic," Zayaa said. "And he thought it might cure the ravages of the poison someone's been dealing him. Neither is possible, as far as I know, although I didn't tell *him* that." Zayaa started back in the direction they'd come. When Dashi didn't immediately follow, Zayaa made an impatient gesture. "Come."

"But," Dashi stammered, her legs moving to catch up, "you'll end up destroying most of Karakal just to have revenge against one person."

"Karakal, the ally who abandoned my father?"

Dashi's mouth opened, then shut again. What kind of mad woman would doom an entire population for the transgressions of a few?

"Besides," Zayaa continued reasonably, "it's not just Karakal. If history is any guide, the magic will wash over most of Tyvalar too. Sevlin's country—and his family—will also pay the price."

If Dashi's feet had been under her own control, she would have stopped walking. "But you'd—all those people—this isn't....this isn't one of those strategy games you used to play with Altan. There aren't points to be scored, Zayaa, they're *human beings* and..." She cast about desperately. "What about Kurlar? Would your parents and brothers want you to murder the people they tried so hard to gain independence for?"

Zayaa's smile widened. "Do you remember the lechitite I showed you in New Osb?"

Dashi nodded.

"Do you know where lechitite is found? *Kurlar*," Zayaa said, not waiting for a response. "The hills are full of it. I've seen the old murals on my family's estate. I've read the records in the archives. Kurlar is the only place besides Yassar and the southern coast that survived the last cataclysm, and both of those only survived as a function of distance. *Kurlar* survived because it's protected by a natural fortress of lechitite. Everything closer to the Wellspring—everything that's measured in a journey of days and weeks instead of months—will be destroyed. Tyvalar will be destroyed for not granting Kurlaran independence. Karakal will be destroyed for not backing my family when they promised they would."

"You never struck me as the type for a suicide mission." It was the last objection Dashi could think of that might change Zayaa's mind. "Wouldn't your parents and brothers want you to live?"

"My parents and brothers were willing to die for Kurlaran independence," Zayaa said. "They would be proud of me for following them into martyrdom."

"They weren't *martyrs*," Dashi sputtered. "Your brothers tried to assassinate a queen! Your parents died by *accident* because Altan and Baris were too young and too stupid to check your house thoroughly."

Zayaa didn't answer; her attention moved to something else as they stepped from beneath the trees. She clapped her hands once, the sound jarring against Dashi's mood. The misty shroud that lay over the lake was moving, frothing like churned milk. Farther down the shore, a bridge was now visible, trembling just below the surface of the lake. Alarm washed over Dashi, tingling over her scalp and antennae.

"No speaking," Zayaa said, as she turned them back in the direction they'd come. "I don't want a last-minute revolt because a couple of soldiers are afraid to die."

Idree jumped to her feet when she saw them approaching. Her hand flew to her mouth, then dropped back to her side in a posture of elaborate casualness. Okhron, awake and propped against a tree trunk, touched her sleeve, surreptitiously soothing. Dashi could have laughed if the situation weren't so dire. Idree had always been as transparent as a pane of glass. It would've been clear to Dashi that her sister was plotting something even if they hadn't already talked about it. Instead, her dread felt almost too heavy to bear, a pestle, grinding her further into the ground with each second. Her eyes found Sevlin's and held. Did he know Zayaa's goal?

"Everything is ready," Zayaa announced, gesturing over her shoulder at the lake, where the fog was still tumbling ominously. "The heralds and the seamstress will accompany me over the bridge to the Wellspring. The rest of you will wait here. Except," Zayaa said, turning to Sevlin, "for you." She glanced at Dashi. "Kill him. No," she said when Dashi's hands reached for an arrow. "I want it to be personal. Use a knife."

Every one of Dashi's senses intensified as she crossed the space that separated her from Sevlin. She could see all their scents swirling together over the snow. She could see every ragged rise and fall of her sister's chest. The old scars on her back and along her side twinged, the twisted skin suddenly livid with heightened sensitivity until even the brush of her clothing bordered on pain. The outline of the knife pressed against her waist, its weight doubling with each step.

Sevlin watched her come, his expression clear and calm. They had tied him in a sitting position, his arms stretched back in an awkward embrace of the tree. When she stood before him, he had to twist his neck at an impossible angle to keep his eyes on her. Distantly, she was aware her hands were trembling. It took two tries to draw her knife.

"Lay your hand against my face, Dashi," Sevlin said quietly. "I want to feel your touch before I go."

Dashi stared at him, uncomprehending. The words were dramatic—romantic, even—and completely out of character for both Sevlin and the dynamic between them. The kisses they'd shared had been fierce, born of desperation and fear; their language had always been unadorned. Dashi licked her lips, torn between a desperate wish to do as Sevlin asked and a desire not to make the situation even harder. The corner of Sevlin's right eye crinkled ever so slightly, a not-quite wink that was decidedly incongruous with the circumstances.

He'd kept his voice low, but Zayaa overheard him anyway. "Ah, I did promise you a goodbye," she crowed, coldly amused. "Yes, cradle his face, Dashi—no, better yet, kiss him before you slit his throat." Her hand was playing with the wide amethyst pendant that Altan had given her, sliding it back and forth on its chain in a subtle grind of metal: the growl of a hungry stomach, Zayaa's revenge waiting to be sated.

Idree gave a muffled sob. Dashi's legs folded, dropping her to her knees so that she and Sevlin were level. Her eyes searched his, but any trace of levity was gone.

"Your skin," he said, breathing the word so quietly that, even from a hand's breadth away, she barely heard him.

Dashi closed her eyes, stunned by the pain in her chest. Pulling her hand free from its layers, she cupped her palm against his jaw and brought her lips to his. Sevlin's mouth moved against hers, murmuring something indiscernible. *Purek,* her mind supplied, he was saying words in ancient Purek. Her breath hitched, first from the hot contact of his mouth, then from something else: a violent sense of breaking in her sternum, a taut cord snapping under immense pressure. It was over almost immediately, leaving her gasping against Sevlin's mouth. Her hand slid along his jaw, holding them together, her fingertips brushing his short hair.

They were no longer kissing but leaning forehead to forehead, their breath mingling. Sevlin turned his head, sliding a line of kisses along her cheek, nuzzling against her hair.

"The seamripper isn't an artifact," he murmured, lips against her ear. "It's a person; it's me.""Enough," came Zayaa's voice. She sounded bored. "Kill him."

Chapter 37

Sevlin's words might have taken longer to sink in, had it not been for Zayaa's command, falling immediately afterward. Dashi's heart clenched with dread, but her hand never moved. It stayed pressed against the rough stubble of Sevlin's jaw, obeying *her* instead of Zayaa.

The seamripper isn't a thing. It's a person; it's me.

Dashi turned her head, finding Sevlin's lips again while she slowly raised the knife in her right hand, a slow deliberate gambit for the consumption of those watching. With her left hand, she palmed another, smaller knife. Still pressed against Sevlin, her left hand slid along his ribcage and then to his biceps, fumbling against the ropes. The next second stretched into a small eternity of physical sensations.

The back-and-forth saw of the knife against the coarse rope.

The jump of Sevlin's chest muscles, flush against her own, as her blade accidentally grazed him.

The sharp, collective intake of breath from those watching, as the knife in her right hand rose to Sevlin's throat, the flash of steel drawing their attention while the ropes on his arms sagged.

"*Now*, Dashi." Zayaa's voice shattered the quiet, not silky as it had been before but harsh. "Slit his throat." Dashi pulled back, her eyes opening slowly. The winter sun threw a bar of light across Sevlin's face, bleaching his eyes of color. He blinked once and, on that unspoken signal, they broke from the tree. A moment of astonished silence greeted them, but neither Sevlin nor Dashi hesitated. Dashi had relinquished both knives to Sevlin as she spun away from him. Now, he plunged toward the stag, holding one in each hand. Dashi drew her sword and thrust it into the nearest soldier as he raised his crossbow.

Zayaa found her voice in the next moment. "Kill them!"

From the corner of her eye, Dashi saw the stag swing his sword toward Sevlin's head. Sevlin barely ducked in time, leaning so far backward that he nearly lost his footing. He lashed out at the stag's delicate legs, but the stag made an astounding vertical leap, evading the move.

Two soldiers hurtled toward Dashi, pulling her attention away. She went low with her sword, slicing into the first soldier's knee, then swiping upward to parry the attack from the second. Zayaa screamed for the owl and the moth. Dashi registered their descent grimly—one hurtling toward the ground, the other floating—as she brought her sword up to block. She had one second, maybe two, before the heralds reached Idree.

A few soldiers pulled back, no longer willing to follow Zayaa's orders, but there were still far too many. Dashi blocked one attack, then rolled sideways to avoid another. She came back up swinging, her blade clashing in a rapid exchange. Steel bit into her side, just above her old scar, and she took another cut to her thigh. They were glancing blows only, partially deflected by her hardened skin.

The scream of metal on metal filled Dashi's ears, making it difficult to keep track of where Sevlin was. She stole a glance at the sky but couldn't see the owl and the moth. Where was Idree? The moment of inattention cost her: another wound, this time to her shoulder.

No matter how fast she maneuvered, there was always someone there. She jumped and swerved, relying on agility where her sword skills lacked, but her feet would barely touch down before she was matching swords with a new opponent. She took two more blows in quick succession, injuries that would have surely been worse if she were fully human.

Even so, the wounds wept freely. She could not continue this way much longer; a death by many cuts was still death.

From behind her came a curse and a bellow of pain. *Sevlin*. Half turning, she got a glimpse of him, feverishly ducking the stag's attacks. He'd managed to get ahold of a sword and was doubtless a more dangerous fighter because of it, but blood streamed from his left arm, spraying against the snow. He fought like she'd never seen him fight: crouched and defensive, *concerned*. He pivoted, struggling to follow the faster-than-human movements of the stag. The stag leaped like a marionette, his long, elegant legs transitioning seamlessly from one bound to the next.

Dashi lost sight of him as she moved again. She was solely on the defensive now. Block after block, keeping her feet moving even when her breath crashed against her ribs. She darted around a tree in a desperate bid to create some space between her opponents.

She had no idea where Idree was, but Sevlin moved back into her line of vision as she pivoted. He was swordless, on his back. The stag, also weaponless, knelt astride Sevlin, hands around his throat. The sight of Sevlin's lips moving soundlessly, begging for mercy that would not come—*could* not come, because of Zayaa's command—sent a bolt of agony through Dashi's chest. Her lips parted, but the sound that emerged sounded more animal than human.

Metal whistled through the air. Dashi staggered backward, pain searing her left shoulder where a soldier had finally struck her cleanly enough to split her tough skin wide open. Her right arm rose automatically, blocking the next blow even as she panted against the pain. An alien scent tugged at her senses. She ignored it, her attention trained on the four men about to deliver her to the ancestors. They fanned out, two in front and two on her injured left side. The tip of her sword rose slightly, defiant. She hoped Idree wasn't watching.

Suddenly, the soldier in front of Dashi faltered, his eyes going to something over her shoulder. A soldier to her left made a strange sound, more of a gurgle than a discernible word. He turned and ran. The remaining soldiers plunged into the trees after him.

Dashi had only a moment to wonder what would inspire such a retreat before the answer rushed past her: immense, copper-colored shapes, moving with stupifying speed. She turned to gape, finally placing the alien scent she'd been ignoring. An army of giant taiga ants was flowing down the slope.

Chapter 38

Dashi's hair stirred as an enormous taiga ant darted past. It caught a soldier up in its massive curved jaws and, with a sickening crunch, bit him in two. Dashi sucked in a breath, flinching away from it. The ant turned toward her, stepping delicately around the slop of human innards and blood at its feet. Both halves of the soldier's body lay next to his sword, still wet with Dashi's not-quite blood. The ant lowered its huge head, surveying her with indiscernible eyes. Its antennae swerved back and forth: an unknown code tapped against the air.

Then Dashi *felt* it: reassurance, seeping through her mind like a warm tide. The ant wasn't speaking, but she understood its message anyway. *You are one of us. You are not alone.* Slowly, Dashi lowered her sword. The ant turned away, darting after the fleeing soldiers.

Without a fight to distract her, the ants' scent was obvious, earthy and alive, and full of the acidic undertones she'd come to associate with aggression or anger. Beneath that, she caught...*Idree.* Panic dawned, quick and hot. Would the ants know not to harm her sister? Would they know not to harm Sevlin?

The remaining Karak soldiers ran in all directions, their erratic movements only drawing more ants. Dashi dove into the melee, surprised when the ants parted obligingly. She spotted Sevlin's tall figure. *Alive.* He was not running but stood with a sword in one hand and his back against a tree. His other arm was stretched across the stag's chest, holding him in place. It wasn't an aggressive posture; they were ignoring each other entirely. Their eyes darted over the ants instead. The stag was perfectly still, but Dashi could tell from his splay-legged stance that he wanted to run.

Sevlin's demeanor changed when he caught sight of her. Tension leached from the set of his shoulders and the right side of his mouth twitched upward, lightning quick.

"Idree?" she asked, skidding to a stop in front of him.

He shook his head. "I don't know."

"The consul took her," Tuya said, peering from the stag's other side.

Blood streamed from a set of parallel gashes on her face. They nearly matched the placement of Sevlin's scar, though on the opposite side. Okhron slumped on Tuya's other side. He was gray-faced with fatigue, but there was a sword across his lap. A few of his soldier friends stood on either side of him.

Dashi's gaze turned downhill. A misty dome still concealed most of the lake, but here and there, strips of teal water showed through. The dark mound of the island lurked at the center. *That's where Zayaa is headed.*

"They flew," Tuya said. She winced as she spoke, each word pulling at her fresh wounds. "The heralds carried them both. I tried to grab her but—" She shook her head once, gingerly.

Dashi swore. How long did they have before Zayaa got to the Well-spring? She hadn't seen much of Nuray's path to get there.

"I tried to stop her," Tuya said again.

Sevlin jerked his chin toward the ants. "Was that you?" His voice was low, wary of attracting the ants' attention. Or perhaps, she thought, of offending her.

Her shoulder twitched up. "I think my emotions sometimes...call them." "Good, then they won't attack with you here." He strode to the remnants of the camp, rummaging around for a few minutes before returning with a saddlebag. Dropping his sword, he began ripping strips of clean bandage using his right hand and his teeth. His left arm hung at his side.

Dashi, who was already vibrating to be after Idree, took a step toward the lake. Sevlin put a hand on her arm.

"Whatever is on that island, whatever you need to do to stop Zayaa, it will require your strength. Tend to the worst of your wounds, let me tend to mine, and then we will go together." He held out a strip of bandage.

Dashi exhaled slowly. She took the bandage. "One minute."

Sevlin turned his attention to his wounds, his fingers quick and sure. The skin along his cheekbone was abraded and raw. Livid fingerprints stood out on his neck. A smattering of cuts marred the rest of his face, though none were as serious as the deep cut into the muscle of his shoulder. Dashi peered at her own wound. Despite the toughness of her skin, the soldier's sword had carved out a deep wedge of flesh near her shoulder blade. She packed it with a folded square of cloth, not bothering with wound salve. She would heal it with her own methods later. *When Idree is safe.*

Dashi glanced at the stag. "You're free," she said softly.

He tilted his ponderous head, his dark, liquid eyes fixed on the landscape over her shoulder. "In some ways."

Sevlin glanced at him, then said to Dashi, "I saw my sword amongst the rubble. I'll grab it before we go."

"What about us?" Tuya asked, panic tingeing her voice. The taiga ants had mostly dispersed, but their copper bodies were still visible among the trees. "They'll come back and eat us."

Dashi glanced at what was left of the soldier she'd fought. The first time she'd seen the taiga ants, they'd been scavenging the bodies of dead racers.

"I could...try something," she offered, thinking of the way she'd felt—how *deeply* she'd felt—when Zayaa had ordered Sevlin's execution. Tentatively, she put one hand on Tuya's shoulder and, closing her eyes, tried to focus on happier emotions. She didn't think of Tuya—Dashi's history with the Yassaris was too mixed for that—but she thought of Idree and Sevlin, of friendship and loyalty and the bonds of family, both natural and created. Her antennae tingled, brushing against Tuya's dark curls. She touched the stag, then Okhron and his soldier friends.

Dashi opened her eyes. "I have no idea if that did anything." She could accept—theoretically, at least—that other ants could interpret her emotions through scent, but could a feeling of peace and protectiveness *stick* to Tuya and the others? "It might be a good idea to climb this tree, just in case."

She handed the remaining medical supplies to the stag. Sevlin hadn't landed nearly as many blows as he had received, but blood stained the stag's coat in several places. Tuya's face would need tending as well.

Sevlin strode up, a satisfied glint in his eye as he rested his palm on the hilt of his sword. He handed Dashi her bow, which he'd collected from her saddle.

"Let's go," Dashi said, turning.

"Wait!" Tuya flipped open a saddlebag at her feet and straightened, cradling a thick wool blanket. She unwrapped the fabric carefully, revealing one of the cases for the pyro-tipped arrows.

Dashi stared at her. "What...?"

"I grabbed one from the sledge just before it slid into the water," Tuya said. She flipped the clasps and opened the lid, revealing two intact pyro-tips nestled against the padding within. Tuya lifted one and offered it to Dashi. "I'll keep the other," she said, tipping her head toward the taiga ants, "just in case."

Dashi stared at her. "I was there when you caught up with us after the bridge. You weren't carrying anything."

"I hid it as I came up on the camp, then went back and got it later that night." The blood on Tuya's cheek was beginning to coagulate, but she still spoke carefully, each word considered and weighed against the pain it would cause.

"Why?"

Tuya shrugged one shoulder. "I...decided that I didn't want her to have them." The pyro-tip cut a line between them, balanced invitingly on Tuya's upturned palms.

"And you want *me,* a thief, to have them instead."

"Just one," Tuya said. "For Idree." She extended her arms, pushing the pyro-tip closer. "And for the belt."

Dashi slid her hands beneath the pyro-tip and lifted it. *Such a delicate weight for something so deadly.* She didn't say thank you as she wrapped it and placed it carefully in her quiver but nodded toward the ants instead.

"Good luck."

Chapter 39

They had barely started down the bank when Dashi felt a telltale pressure against her antennae.

"Sevlin," she cautioned, a hand on his arm.

The taiga ants overtook them, moving easily over the slick rocks. They fanned out in a semicircle, so close that Dashi could see the bristles on their legs. There were only six, a small contingent of the army that had come to her rescue, but the angry scent emanating from them was nearly overpowering. One of them flexed its jaws menacingly at Sevlin, who was still standing a step in front of Dashi.

They think they still need to save me.

The ant made a quick move to one side, intending to flank Sevlin. Dashi shoved herself in front, arms wide in what she hoped was a universally protective posture.

"*No.* He is a friend."

She tried to fill her mind with peaceful thoughts, with the kind of satisfaction she felt at working in tandem with Sevlin, with her utter confidence that he would not hurt her or Idree. Tranquility was nearly impossible, however, because of the tension emanating from Sevlin. His body was rigid behind her; she might have been leaning against a boulder.

"Relax," she hissed. "You're making this difficult."

Sevlin muttered something in Tyvalaran—a retort, by the tone—but he took a deep breath. His posture loosened. His hand went to the flare of her hip, as though he could keep the ants from prying them apart.

The ant dipped its head—a non-threatening gesture, Dashi was *fairly* certain—but continued to edge forward. The tips of its antennae brushed her face like two bristly fingers. The other ants crowded behind it.

"Deep breaths," she warned Sevlin when he began to tense.

Six pairs of rough antennae touched her own and meandered over her shoulders and down to her waist, feeling her wounds, past and present. Her old scars—the ones healed by the taiga ants after the khan's race—prickled with an uncomfortable, electric feeling. The ants rasped their antennae along Sevlin's hand and forearm where he touched her, then back to Dashi. Finally, they withdrew. Their antennae still twitched, but the sharp pulse of anger had disappeared from their scent.

Sevlin exhaled next to her ear. "What did you tell them?"

"I can't communicate with them like that," Dashi said, still watching the ants, "but strong emotions make...a flavor on top of the regular scent. When Zayaa ordered me to kill you...I think they caught that scent and came out of their tunnels to see who was in trouble. Just now, I was trying to project peaceful thoughts."

"So they don't tear me in half."

"So they let you ride on them."

He sputtered something else in Tyvalaran but released his grip when Dashi stepped toward the smallest ant.

"I've done it before," she said, with more confidence than she felt. *That* ant, who she'd nicknamed V, had been beholden to her; she'd helped it escape a taiga rat. What she didn't know was how *this* ant would react if she clambered aboard. She reached out a hand, gently touching the ant's side.

"I need your help," she said to it, using the same soothing tone she'd used when Spit was frightened. *Spit.* A well of grief yawned before her and she yanked her thoughts away, afraid she would rile the ants all over again. She pointed in the direction they needed to go and continued stroking the ant's side. The shifting fog had obscured the bridge and the island once again, but Dashi remembered how far away it had looked. She focused on her need, making her emotions beseeching. The ant turned its head, regarding her with gleaming eyes.

"We'll be quicker this way," she said, both to Sevlin and the ant. "Idree doesn't have much time."

She extended a hand behind her and, after a pause, Sevlin took it, stepping abreast of her. She pulled their mittens off, twining their calloused fingers and laying them against the ant.

"Are you sure about this?" Sevlin's face was a mask of doubt.

"Absolutely." She pulled herself onto the ant's thorax.

"Shouldn't I have my own ant?"

"I think it's best if you weren't alone on one."

"So when you said you were 'absolutely' sure, you meant 'not at all' sure," he grumbled, but he grabbed Dashi's proffered forearm and heaved himself up behind her. The ant started moving, a strange, lurching gait that was nonetheless much faster than a horse.

"I..." Sevlin trailed off, seemingly at a loss for words.

"This is the only way we're going to catch up with them, Sevlin."

He sighed. "Good enough."

She braced her arms against the tilt of the ant's thorax. Sevlin mimicked her posture, so that every time she shifted, she felt his arms bracketing her. They were careful to keep their legs clear of the ant's furiously marching limbs and, as one, they leaned to accommodate its efforts to balance on the icy slope. Even in such conditions, the animal's speed was astonishing.

Sevlin was quiet. When Dashi glanced back, his head was turned away, watching the five ants that trailed them. She felt suddenly uneasy at not being able to see his face. He was a featureless presence, a stranger. *The Seamripper*, she thought. He turned back and caught her watching.

"Where's Spit?" he asked. "I didn't see him with the other horses."

"Dead." She swallowed, plunging into a different subject before she could think about it too much. "Before we get there, there's something you should know." She gave a brief outline of the visions she'd had of Nuray's past. "Zayaa is trying to start a cataclysm like the one that wiped out the Pureks."

"And Zayaa's not...misinformed about the Wellspring? She knows what will happen?"

"She knows. Another cataclysm is her *goal*."

"Cursed ancestors," he swore. "Why do you think you saw the vision?"

"I've...seen Khagan Nuray before," she admitted. "In dreams. And sometimes when I'm in the taiga. She spoke of Idree protectively, like she wanted to help her. So maybe it's because I want to help her too."

In front of her, the bronze line of the bridge was just visible against the water. How much longer did they have? Where was Idree right now, and what was Zayaa doing to her?

"You had a vision when we were searching for the golden needle?" His voice was carefully neutral.

Dashi slid him a look. "You would have thought I was insane if I told you I was seeing a dead khagan so I'm not going to apologize for keeping that to myself."

"An apology from you is rare indeed." The undercurrent of humor in his voice made her smile.

"Speaking of apologies...The seamripper isn't an artifact, it's *you*, and you tell me at the same time you tell *Zayaa*?"

"I gave you a half-second lead."

The ant veered around a boulder and Dashi slid a little, pressing backward into Sevlin's chest.

"I have to be touching someone to alter the magic," he said. "I couldn't reach you in the Gateway. I couldn't tell you then either, not when there was a chance you'd report it to Zayaa."

Dashi shook her head, thinking of how close they'd been in the Gateway. What if Sevlin had broken her tether before this? She felt certain they wouldn't be *here*, chasing after Zayaa, trying to save not only Idree but most of the world—

A touch along her spine stopped Dashi's spiraling internal monologue.

"The ants," Sevlin said softly. "I think you're upsetting them."

Their mount had its antennae flicked back toward Dashi, absorbing her emotions. One of the ants behind them had stopped completely, and now stood uphill from them, its head turning slowly as it searched for threats.

"I was thinking about Idree and Zayaa," she whispered.

"No more of that," Sevlin said, his tone purposely light. "I'll talk. You can sit back and listen."

Dashi nodded.

"It took me an hour to get out of that cage in the Purek maze," Sevlin said. His voice was low and calm, obviously meant as a distraction. "Your knife broke against the second hinge, but I managed to use the broken pieces. The giant bats kept dropping from the rock wall to check on me—a little *too* invested in my progress, for my taste. When I opened the cage, however, they all took to the air."

Dashi could imagine the scene: the oppressive steam from the hot pools, the panicked flap of giant wings.

"The acid lake had begun to overflow," she guessed. She could feel herself relaxing as he spoke. The ants' antennae had returned to their lazy bobble.

"It looked like a silver tide. I was limping away from it as fast as I could when you dropped the box. Practically on top of my head."

Dashi watched the approaching bridge. *Almost there.* "I'd burned my legs half off, Sevlin. My aim wasn't what it normally is."

"The box splintered into a thousand pieces and the cup—" He slid one hand to her knee and squeezed. "The cup bounced into my hand, Dashi. Like someone had aimed and tossed it. The bottom had jarred open when it hit—

"I *knew* it had a false bottom!"

"There was nothing in the compartment, just an etched message. *'Balance and bravery in a sip. A taste of silver, a tyrant's power tips.'*"

A tyrant who was trying to use Idree to end the world. She glanced at the bridge again before her mind caught up to Sevlin's words. "Wait, a taste of *silver*?"

"I dipped the cup into the acid and drank."

Dashi peered back at him, her eyes wide. "The stuff that ate through my boots? And my feet? You *drank* it?"

His lips twitched.

"That verse could have meant something else entirely, Sevlin!"

He shrugged. "You said it would be cryptic but obvious at the same time. A cup fell from the sky and there was a flood of silver liquid at my feet. From where I was standing, it seemed like the two were related."

She could only shake her head.

"The cup vanished as soon as I pulled it back from my lips. Just—*gone.* Then my leg started to heal."

Dashi snorted, her mind going back to Idree. "I've been the recipient of magical healing. I bet you preferred the original wound."

"I did. When I woke up, the acid had retreated and a staircase had opened in the floor of the maze. It took me back to the mound where we'd started."

"Now can you free Idree from the magic?"

The old hope filled her. Without magic marking them as extraordinary, she and Idree could disappear. *Is that what you really want,* her mind asked in a sly voice. To go back to standing guard duty and leave your adventures in the past? To leave *Sevlin*?

Sevlin didn't answer. When she glanced over her shoulder, she saw that his expression had edged toward discomfort.

"I don't think it will work like that," he said, with obvious gentleness. "With the heralds, I can see every place Idree has stitched the magic. There are—it looks like threads made out of light. The tether is thicker, like a rope, but made of the same light."

Dashi nodded, picturing the shining lines in the aftermath of the khan's death.

"It's simple to break the tether because it's only in a single spot. The stitches, I imagine they would take longer, but at least I can see them clearly. With Idree—" He let out a breath. "She's *all* magic now, Dashi. No threads. No ropes. She's like a silhouette made of light. If I tried..." He trailed off uneasily.

He wouldn't want to experiment on Idree for fear of harming her. Neither would Dashi.

Dashi dug her fingernails into her palm, trying to focus on the fact that they'd nearly reached the bridge instead of her disappointment. *Stay calm for the ants,* she told herself. *The first priority is finding Zayaa.* Questions about what Sevlin could or couldn't do would wait.

Dashi slid from the ant and Sevlin followed, keeping one hand on his sword as he backed away.

Since Zayaa had activated the waypoint, the lake's water level had decreased. She could see the slick shadow of a waterline on the rocky bank, marking the spot where it usually lapped. Relief flooded her. *Idree. Idree. Idree.* The bridge, which was above the water now, appeared sturdy. The island was close. They were almost there.

Dashi studied the beaten bronze slats of the bridge. They weren't choked with algae or water weeds from their long submersion. Like so many other things of Purek provenance, they remained eerily preserved.

"What do you think about trying to take an ant over?" Dashi asked. "They're fast and I don't think the bridge will be weight-triggered—"

"Too late for that."

Dashi spun around to see the ants trooping silently up the hill. She swore.

"You were hoping to say goodbye?" Sevlin asked as they disappeared into the trees.

"I was hoping they'd be around to help us when we caught up to Zayaa."

"Maybe they had enough fighting for one day."

"No," Dashi said thoughtfully. "I felt relieved when we reached the bridge. Premature, I know, but we seemed so much closer to Idree. I wonder if they interpreted that as me no longer needing them."

"You could call them back if you worked your feelings up just right."

She was already turning away, shaking her head. "Too much time. Besides, I can't communicate anything detailed, so they'd probably think *you* were the threat. "

"Right," said Sevlin, his tone dry. "Let's carry on without them then. What kind of defenses do you think the bridge will have?"

"Not much," she said. "Zayaa said the Wellspring was only visited twice a year, for sacrificial rites. Any offerings would probably have been thrown directly into the Wellspring, which means the Pureks wouldn't have to worry about thieves."

Sevlin made a sound of protest as Dashi stepped onto the bridge. The air over the lake was damp and clingy. Standing on the land had felt warm by comparison. A dense cloud of mist wrapped overhead, making her antennae twitch. *I don't have time for visions*, she warned it.

"When we were searching for the golden needle, do you remember how the rooms near the temple entrance had spears and pressure plates everywhere?" Dashi asked. "But as we got closer to the needle, the obstacles became more finely tuned, like they wanted you to demonstrate some insider knowledge before you could pass?" She thought of Nuray, carrying a leather gauntlet so she could avoid the poisonous flowers in the Gateway Temple.

"Is *that* what the oven room wanted?" Sevlin asked mildly. Dashi started walking, then moved into a jog. *Idree. Idree. Idree.* The air was briny. When she licked her lips she tasted salt. The mist moved in an endless roiling dance, the upper layers sinking as warmer layers pushed upward, seeking the sky, only to eventually succumb themselves.

The bridge bounced as Sevlin fell into step behind her.

"If we'd been a Purek priest and priestess we would have known exactly what to do when the floor of the oven room started moving. It wouldn't have been difficult or even that dangerous," she called over her shoulder. "Here, we've already gotten through the Gateway Temple. Now we just need to prove we have the knowledge of the Purek priest class."

"We *don't* have the knowledge of the Purek priest class."

"We have these." Dashi tapped her antennae. "I'll be able to follow Zayaa. And, for what it's worth, I have Nuray's memories."

The wind rose without warning, levitating her hair and whipping it into her eyes. The mist slid across her face in chilly waves. Dashi shivered.

Dashiiiiiiii.

A gray figure, on her left, where only lake water should be.

Dashiiiiiiii.

She waited, breath dammed up behind her teeth, but the figure never came closer. When she blinked it was gone, lost in a swirl of pearly moisture.

The island manifested out of the fog, dreamlike and pale at first, but growing darker and more substantial with each passing second. It sloped upward, away from the lake, so that only the bottom of the slope was visible in the fog. Unlike the land that surrounded the lake, the island was bare of snow, covered instead by tufts of dark, coarse grass.

Her antennae sifted the air for traces of Idree or Zayaa, but there was nothing. Perhaps they'd landed in a different spot? She did notice another clue, however: a line of petrified grass running up the hill like a spine.

"We should follow it," Dashi said, pointing. "I think it memorializes Nuray's steps after the cataclysm." She thought back to the stone garden. "Maybe her steps before the cataclysm, too."

Dashi started up the rise, Sevlin's boots padding behind hers. Necklaces of moisture encircled each blade of grass, making Dashi's boots slide as she climbed. Halfway up, Sevlin touched her arm, pointing to the silhouette of someone lying in the grass: a man, ghostly pale, tipped over onto his back.

"A priest," she said, "petrified like Khagan Nuray."

The line of stone grass urged them onward. Dashi deviated only once. Her antennae arched, eager to read the information drifting toward her.

"Idree," she said, pointing to the spot. "They landed there."

"Anything else?"

Dashi hesitated. "She was scared," she said finally.

She turned, nearly running up the hill now. *Idree*. Zayaa's scent had been strong. Like Idree's, it held the tang of fear, though Zayaa's was tempered by the acidic taste that Dashi had come to associate with anger or aggression.

Through the pearly gray, she glimpsed something that brought her stumbling to a halt: dozens of motionless forms, straight-shouldered and forbidding, like sentinels standing a watch.

Chapter 40

Dashi's first, horrified impression was of dozens of bodies, petrified by the cataclysm. In the next moment, however, she saw that she'd let her imagination run amok. The figures were too blocky, too towering to have ever been human.

"Monuments?" Sevlin murmured.

"Or altars?"

She'd seen circular arrangements of altars before. It was supposed to represent the planet, the sun, or the life cycle, among other things. The desire to rush up the hill screaming her sister's name pulsed in her legs. It was a struggle to keep her voice low.

"Did you see any of this in the vision?" Sevlin asked.

"This part was jumbled." She spoke slowly, trying to remember. "I saw the bridge, but mostly I saw the Wellspring."

At the top of the hill, she forced herself to stop just outside the circle of sentinel stones, in case there was anything unpleasant waiting within. At close range, it was easy to see they were neither monuments nor altars but plain stones, tall and more or less rectangular, standing on end. Configurations of holes decorated the top edge of some stones, though if there was a meaning to the arrangement and number, Dashi couldn't see it. Khagan Nuray's petrified tracks crossed in and out of the stones, forming a white spiderweb in the tufted grass. Save for the low moan of the wind, the island was silent.

"Where is Zayaa?" Sevlin whispered, his eyes scanning the flat top of the island. The fog had thinned as they'd ascended, but it was still thick enough to make the other half of the circled stones appear vague and gauzy.

Dashi dropped to a crouch, bringing her antennae close to the ground. Considering how clear it had been on the side of the hill, Idree's scent was oddly degraded here, like the wind had conspired to wipe it away. Zayaa had been here too, of course, crisscrossing between the standing stones. Dashi followed slowly, her footsteps tracing the other woman's. She stopped in front of one of the stone behemoths, indistinguishable from the rest, at least to her eye. Zayaa had walked around it several times, so Dashi did the same, not touching it until she found the anomaly for which she'd been searching: a thin crevice near the bottom, not even wide enough for her finger.

"Look at those marks." Sevlin, who'd been silently trailing in her wake, pointed past her shoulder.

The ground at the corners of the standing stone was scuffed, the dark grass broken and uprooted. She could see her wariness reflected in his eyes. It could be a trap, but they were running out of options and time. Dashi slid her knife blade into the crack, using it to feel for a wire catch.

The stone began to swivel, slow and ponderous, an old man rising from a favorite chair. Rock ground against earth like the creak of stiff bones. The stone stopped. Dashi frowned, staring at the bare ground. She retraced Zayaa's footsteps, circling the stone until she stood by Sevlin once more.

"The scrape marks don't line up," she said, pointing. "When Zayaa triggered the stone, it must have moved over here, but now it's stopped just short of that."

"Could it be *when* the stones were triggered? Zayaa would have arrived right at noon. On the solstice. That might have been significant to the Pureks."

"I don't know. I thought there would be..."

"A hole underneath it?"

"Or hidden stairs? The Wellspring was underground in Nuray's memories."

"Maybe it's a decoy and another stone hides the real entrance."

Dashi nodded, eyes narrowed in thought. "That's a possibility."

Partway around the circle she found another stone that moved. The slit in the stone was located higher up, out of her reach but not out of Sevlin's. This stone scooted backward, leaving a trail of packed earth. They found a third stone and a fourth. Each shifted position, their movements not quite lining up with the marks left from when Zayaa had triggered them. All four stones marked a cardinal direction, Dashi noted. It was the kind of tidy, quintessentially Purek design that she normally delighted in, but today, without time on her side, she felt a tide of annoyance.

"I don't understand," she said, raising her voice to be heard. Sevlin had stopped following her at some point in favor of prowling around on his own. "Zayaa went to all four of these stones. I walked around the whole circle and none of the others show any sign of being moved."

"No, but I think you still found what we needed," Sevlin said, sounding distracted.

Dashi's gaze flicked up. She knew him well enough to recognize when he was chewing something over. A few beams of sunlight had found the gaps in the mist's armor, lancing across the top of the island to create a patchwork of darkness and surreal light. Sevlin stood in a dark patch at the center of the circle, a shadow as still and straight-shouldered as the stones around him.

Her feet slowed as she glimpsed the metal at his feet: hexagonal brass beads, strung on metal rods. The rods and beads were arranged in a square grid, with the ground below carved out to allow the beads to spin. One was spinning now, revealing a Purek word on each facet as it turned.

"Where was this?" Dashi asked. Zayaa had tracked back and forth over this piece of ground several times, which meant Dashi had too, but she'd seen nothing.

"There was a grass-covered *lid*. It slid underground when you triggered that last stone."

"I saw Khagan Nuray using this," Dashi said.

As they watched, the spinning bead slowed, finally stopping on a blank facet. A different bead began to turn, crawling at first, then transforming into a brass-colored whirr.

"When they started every bead had a symbol facing upward," Sevlin said. "Now they're changing to a blank facet, one by one."

Dashi studied the beads, reminded of the slow, methodic ticking of the clock above the fountain in Karak City's jade circle. "It's an association grid. Each bead has to be a word or idea that relates to the rest of its row. Since each bead belongs to both a vertical column and a horizontal row, it needs to make sense in both directions."

"Like a secondary or tertiary meaning?"

"Exactly. I saw one with Altan once, but it was smaller. Three beads on each side of the square instead of six. And I knew all of the symbols." She pointed to the top row, where two unfamiliar symbols stared back at her. "I've never seen those before. The top of that character refers to something about religious rites, but it must be something really specific."

"Zayaa must have recognized it though. The grid is mostly completed."

"I'm not surprised. She and Altan were always good at that type of thing."

"Once the beads have reset themselves to the blank facets, we're supposed to put them back in place?"

"Why wait 'til then?" Dashi grabbed the spinning bead with both hands, trying to stop its momentum. It whined against her, but its speed slackened. "If we start from here," she grunted, gripping it tighter, "we don't have to do the whole grid. We're only missing eight beads; Zayaa's already done the rest." Dashi jammed her boot against the bead, finally grinding it to a halt, then began rolling it backward until it stopped on the correct symbol.

"Hen," she said, pointing, before realizing she probably only needed to translate the more complex words for Sevlin. "That completes this row."

Sevlin pointed to two of the others with blank brass faces. "I remember which symbols these two started with. They started turning after I got here." He fixed them into the correct position. Dashi was pleased to see that no other beads had started spinning. Whatever mechanism unwound the grid, it appeared to have been disengaged.

She looked up sharply, searching the crepuscular maze of fog and sunbeams.

"What?" Sevlin's hand moved to his sword.

"I thought..." She paused, her antennae working. "I thought I caught the moth's scent."

"She would have landed here."

"On the breeze, not on the ground."

"If we can't see her, I doubt she can see us." He squinted at the splintered sunlight for another second before turning back to the grid. He pointed to one of the remaining blank beads. "The other beads in this row are numbers, right? Two, four, twelve, twenty-four." He glanced at Dashi, his lips twisting sardonically. "I only taught myself to thirty."

She laughed. "Like a Purek child. That's one hundred. What's on the blank bead?"

The bead was closest to Sevlin, so he leaned over to turn it.

"One thousand twenty." She translated the larger numbers as he turned. "Five hundred seventy-six. It's that one: one hundred forty-four. The number of Purek constellations in the winter sky. It's also twelve groups of twelve, so it's nice and balanced. Doubly sacred."

Sevlin gave her a swift look, settling the bead into place. "Zayaa isn't the only one with knowledge."

Dashi shrugged, brushing aside the warmth she felt at the compliment. It was honesty, not humility that prevented her from swelling with pride. The breadth and depth of Zayaa's knowledge far exceeded her own.

She pointed to another blank bead. "This vertical column is about the sky."

Sevlin turned it until Dashi stopped him on the Purek name for a winter constellation, a serpent that wound across the eastern sky. They moved through the rest, restoring one blank bead after another. Dashi couldn't help grinning wider with each success. More sunlight stabbed through the fog, lighting up the beads until they were almost painful to look at.

"Two left." Sevlin began turning both beads, pausing to let Dashi stare at each facet. Both were in the same row, the subject of which was esoteric religious rites. She shook her head at Sevlin over and over again, her heart sinking with each unfamiliar symbol.

We don't have the knowledge of the Purek priest class, Sevlin had said and he'd been right to worry. She wasn't as good as Zayaa. She'd identified the beads pertaining to legendary battles and Purek lore because those were the scrolls she'd always been in charge of translating. *These*, on the other hand...

Dashi dragged her teeth over her bottom lip before finally throwing up her hands. "I don't know any of them, Sevlin." *This close to the Wellspring and I'm held back by my vocabulary.*

A cool, invisible finger caressed the back of her neck as if a tendril of taiga mist had suddenly found her.

Dashiiiii.

Can't you see I'm trying, she wanted to shout back.

"We could guess," Sevlin was saying. "That's..." His voice trailed off as he calculated the possible outcomes.

"Too many," Dashi agreed. "And the Pureks tend to penalize guessers anyway."

Not being able to see what was beneath the grid made her nervous. They'd encountered nothing dangerous on the island so far, but any Purek priest or priestess who came here on the solstice would know immediately how to solve the grid. It wouldn't be surprising, then, if a wrong answer was designed to eliminate imposters.

Dashiiii.

This time the voice that called her name was gravelly and demanding. *Khagan Nuray.* Suddenly, Dashi saw the association grid on a different day, in a different century, as clear as if she was in a vision once more: Khagan Nuray's hand, precisely turning the beads along the top row.

Dashi reached out and spun one bead to the correct facet, then the other. A sudden, sharp wind stirred to life, pushing her hair into her eyes and dispelling the fog that lingered between the standing stones. A circle of blue winter sky showed above them.

"How—" Sevlin was looking at her like she'd sprouted a third arm.

"Look." Dashi pointed across the circle of stones, where a sunbeam was pouring through the holes along the tops of the stones. The sunlight, honed like a bright, sharp sword, bounded between each stone, glowing along the tops.

"There could be tiny mirrors embedded in the holes," Sevlin murmured uncertainly.

"You were right," Dashi said, gaping. "The stones shifted differently for me than they did for Zayaa because of *when* they were triggered. The sun was at a slightly different angle for her than it was for us. The stones *had* to shift differently or the light would never have lined up."

"But how did it know—"

The sound of ancient gears creaking to life cut off his question. Sevlin jogged out of the standing stones and into the drifting edge of the fog, stopping at the steep western edge of the hill to peer over.

"There's a length of chain being pulled into the rocks below," he called back to her. "It looks like...I think it's attached to a float of some kind, but I can't be sure in the fog."

Dashi stiffened, her response frozen on her lips as the breeze, still ruffling the mist, ran a scent along her antennae.

"*Sevlin!*"

He straightened, following Dashi's gaze to the figure approaching over the water. Through the blanket of fog, Dashi could see only the dark indentations of eyes and the suggestion of a mouth. A moment later, however, she made out the rhythmic sway of the fog just behind the shoulders, steady as wing beats. It was the moth, swathed in luminescent moisture. She darted a look at Dashi but headed straight for Sevlin, her sword raised.

Sevlin's sword cut an arc in front of Solongo, deflecting her approach without actually trying to hurt her. She flapped sideways, out of reach, her face pinched with a look Dashi knew all too well: the dread of carrying out an awful command.

Chapter 41

The fog conspired with Solongo, cloaking her movements one moment, then releasing her into a shaft of sunlight so that her wings flashed gold.

"I don't want to hurt her in order to save her," Sevlin muttered, watching as Solongo disappeared again.

"I think Solongo would take that chance. Zayaa is holding her child back in New Osb," Dashi said. "Leverage."

"All the more reason not to add to her misery if it can be helped."

Dashi scanned the fog, her antennae straining for Solongo's scent. She imagined the other herald waiting behind the misty shroud, ready to drop them to their deaths as Zayaa had commanded.

"I don't sense the owl," she said, though that didn't necessarily mean anything. Airborne scents depended a good deal upon the direction of the breeze. She'd had only the briefest hint of Solongo.

"Back to back," Sevlin said as Solongo made another pass. "Maybe Zayaa took her along."

Dashi stepped into position, feeling the warmth of his back against her own. "To a cave where she won't be able to fly?"

"She could be guarding the entrance."

Solongo flew another wide arc over them, unable to make the tight turns that the owl could have managed. Her sharp eyes searched for the opportunity to grab one of them, but the tactics that had worked well in the past were failing her. Solongo had easily dispatched the Tyvalaran soldiers on Sevlin's tower, but her quarry had been easy to pick off as they came through the hole in the roof. Here, they were caught in a stalemate: Solongo, unable to fly close enough to grab them; Dashi and Sevlin, unable to descend the hill while Solongo was poised above. Dashi thought briefly of retreating into the circle of stones—she would feel safer with Sevlin at her back and a towering rock guarding one side—but she didn't want to leave the edge of the hill. Right now, they had a good view of where the float would come in.

"I just need a second of contact with her," Sevlin murmured over the steady grind of the chain.

"Zayaa must have told her not to come close enough for you to break the tether." Dashi watched Solongo's dark outline flit beneath layers of gray.

The noise of the chain stopped abruptly.

"We have to end," Sevlin said. "Or we might miss our chance to the Wellspring."

Dashi sighed. "Fine. Get ready, Seamripper."

She dropped her bow and stepped away from Sevlin, deliberately leaving her back exposed and her arms at her sides. Her thrashing antennae betrayed her discomfort, however, swiveling like an extra pair of eyes in their search for scent.

Seconds ticked by. Dashi stared at Sevlin's face. She saw his readiness in the way his eyes darted over the sky. His jaw was rigid with focus. The tightness along the back of her neck died and the itch to take cover ebbed. She had only to wait for him.

His muscles bunched suddenly, the telltale coil of energy about to be released. He never took his eyes off the sky, but his lips formed her name, a silent signal. Dashi dove sideways, rolling beneath Solongo's outstretched arms and bouncing up to catch her ankle before she could fly away.

Wind buffeted Dashi's face as Solongo beat the air with her wings. Dashi's boots dragged over the ground, bumping against rocks before finally lifting off as Solongo began gaining altitude. Dashi's free hand slid to her sword, but she never had to draw it. Hurtling toward them, Sevlin leaped for Solongo's other leg, wrenching her to the ground. They landed in a heap of limbs and wings. Dashi rolled, grabbing Solongo to hold her still. Sevlin had one arm around Solongo's torso. He jerked her sleeve up, clamping his bare hand over her wrist.

It was over quickly. Sevlin closed his eyes, his lips moving, his face a picture of intense concentration. Solongo went limp, her wings flopping together.

"Be careful," she gasped. "It's—" Her eyelids fluttered shut. Her mouth went slack.

"She'll be fine." Sevlin let go of Solongo's wrist, laying her arm gently across her belly.

Dashi stepped back, trying to push off a sick feeling inside her. That had been *her* less than an hour ago: obeying someone else's commands. She'd come so close to cutting Sevlin's throat. The thought was staggering.

"It's harder when they fight it," Sevlin said, misinterpreting her anguish. "It didn't appear to affect you much at all, but you had no idea what was coming. The sable was strapped down, spitting and fighting, and when I broke the tether it knocked him—"

The wind shifted, bringing a scent that clanged in Dashi's mind. She whirled to see the owl slicing through the fog like a hot blade, barely stirring the white layers of moisture. She knew, in that fraction of a second before impact, that she would be too late. The owl was too fast. Sevlin's back, which Dashi had been guarding only minutes ago, was too exposed. He saw Dashi's expression and started to turn, reaching for his sword. Dashi raised her own sword and flung it, watching as it careened end over end, borne on a current of momentum and desperation.

All three—Sevlin, the owl, and Dashi's sword—collided at the same instant. Dashi's sword hit the owl as the herald banked sideways, the spikes on her boots flashing silver over Sevlin's side. He fell sideways, sprawling across Solongo. The owl fell next to him, one of her wings flapping in short, erratic bursts. Blood was everywhere: flooding the ground, beading off feathers, coating fabric. Dashi's sword lay in the spreading pool, studded with white down. The owl let out a terrible, inhuman scream. She writhed in the blood, holding her injured wing against her chest. Her boot spikes gouged the ground just as they had Sevlin's body. Despite her agony, Zayaa's command had the owl pushing herself upright, her eyes on Sevlin's prone form—

"No!" Dashi's boot connected with the herald's chest.

The owl screamed anew, but Dashi didn't look at her. *Sevlin*. She fell to her knees beside him. The expression on his face, a mixture of consternation and helplessness, made her heart catch. It was wrong, incompatible with what he was, like the sun suddenly refusing to rise or a bird forgetting its songs. Sevlin didn't look like that. He was capable and controlled, not frozen with surprise and blood loss. Her hands tripped over his blood-soaked side, patting at the contours of his wound. It stretched from his armpit to hip, deep enough that her fingers bumped into something soft, then hard. *Bone? Lung?* She was afraid to look. Blood spilled out and she felt that too, a slippery tide already coating her knees.

Too much blood. Too little movement. She'd seen enough game animals, felled by her own arrows, to know it was a fatal wound. That realization was followed by a moment of nothingness: no sounds, no thoughts, no motion, no feelings. This is what it would be like, she thought, to live in a world without Sevlin: an empty void, an open pit, a barren wasteland.

Somewhere deep in her brain, her ant instinct flared to life, taking over from her floundering human self. *Grass.* She ripped up a handful and stuffed it into her mouth, no longer self-conscious of this strange ability as long as it had the power to help Sevlin. This grass was different than the kind she'd used on her own wounds, tougher and harder to pulp, with a salty tang that grew stronger the more she chewed. Would it still work? She thought the healing properties lay with ants themselves, in some miraculous characteristic of their saliva or enzymes, rather than with the species of grass, but she didn't know for certain.

Logic told her she had to stem the blood loss; even healing poultices couldn't generate new blood. She spat the pulpy mass into her hand and pressed it against the deepest point of Sevlin's wound. He sucked in a harsh breath as the poultice touched raw flesh, his eyes screwing shut and his shoulders rising off the ground. Dashi frowned. It hadn't hurt when she'd tended her own wounds. Was it because of the saltiness of the grass or because his wounds were so severe? Or did it mean it wasn't working?

Sevlin turned his face toward her. His breath was shallow, his eyes slitted.

"You're hurt," she said. A needless statement, but she couldn't wrap her head around it. "I'm trying to help you." She wrestled another handful of coarse grass out of the ground and began chewing it, ignoring her multiplying doubts.

"The owl..." Sevlin started.

"Don't worry about the owl right now."

"Give me..." His hand fell onto her knee, showing her his bare skin.

Still chewing the grass, Dashi got to her feet, angry at herself for leaving his side, angry at Sevlin for not ducking in time, angry at the owl for those cursed spikes. She dragged the owl toward Sevlin, heedless of her shrieks, and pinned her to the ground. She knew she was being unfair. Cruel, even. It wasn't the owl's fault; it was Dashi's. She saw it clearly now. It had been Baris' right-hand/left-hand trick but played out on a grander scale. Zayaa hadn't told Solongo to go after them. She'd told Solongo to *distract* them so that the owl could take out the real target: the seamripper.

Sevlin's lips moved soundlessly as he touched the owl. As soon as the tether was broken, Dashi thrust her aside. By now, Solongo was sitting up, dazed, but Dashi ignored her too, pushing another grass poultice into Sevlin's wound. His reaction wasn't as visceral this time and Dashi didn't know if it was because this poultice hurt less, or if he was weaker than he'd been only a few minutes ago. She pressed her forehead against his. His skin was clammy.

Sevlin tried to speak, the words fading on his breath. Dashi watched the lopsided movement of his lips, mesmerized by the way the scar always asserted itself, even as the events that caused it grew more and more distant. It was foundational, the very soil from which the tree grew.

"—with me, Dashi—"

She swallowed. "I'm with you, Sevlin. I'm right here."

"Zayaa...float." The fast flow of expressions—regret, pain, sadness—moving unchecked over Sevlin's face was more frightening than the sight of his blood. Sevlin was *never* expressive.

"Don't worry about that." She pressed a third poultice onto his wound. He grunted in pain, his hand jerking up to stop her. "And stop being a baby."

That got a ghost of a smile.

"...goading me," he murmured. His shoulders relaxed a little as the burn of the poultice subsided.

"I'm only trying to keep you alive until these poultices work. This is how the ants saved me." Her tone was brisk and confident, a discordant clash with her thoughts. "I did it to my own wounds after my fight with Zayaa."

"Useful."

"Mmhmm." More grass, more chewing. She imagined her jaws like those of the ants, muscular and tireless. She watched Sevlin's chest, counting the seconds between each shallow breath. The blood flow had slowed, but his skin was cadaver gray. His eyes had closed again. She pressed the next poultice into place: a shallow section of the wound since she'd already covered the deeper parts. Sevlin didn't stir. Dashi shook his shoulder, gently at first, but turning rough when he didn't open his eyes right away.

When he squinted up at her, she sagged in relief, pressing her lips to his forehead. Another ghost of a smile from Sevlin.

"You have to stay awake." She knew that fatigue after blood loss was a normal occurrence, but she couldn't shake the feeling that, if he lost consciousness now, he might never regain it.

"Idree...catacl..." His eyes drifted shut again.

"Stay awake, Sevlin. *Sevlin.*"

His lips moved, but his voice was so hushed she had to put her ear to his mouth. "...Cataclysm...Go, Dashi."

Her throat tightened at his words, at the echo she heard, loud and clear. *I'm not asking you to stay, Dashi. I'm asking you to go.* He'd been injured then too, alone in a treacherous ruin, and she'd left him. He was always focused on the overall goal, not the game piece lost along the way, even if it was his own.

She grabbed another handful of grass. *One more poultice, one more chance to save him, then I'll go.* She forced herself to get to her feet and walk to the edge of the hill. There was no float, but the chain was still visible, sagging in the water. When she turned around, she noticed Solongo crouched over the owl, trying to bind her wound.

Dashi had already seen the pitiful threads of muscle straining to keep the nearly-severed wing in place. She was certain the owl would lose the limb. She didn't care. She walked back to Sevlin and applied the last poultice. He didn't move. She leaned over him, pressing her mouth to his scarred cheek, his lips, his neck. Her antennae drifted slowly after, touching him in all the same places. She was shaking with suppressed emotion, with the depth of her feelings. She could only hope that the message would be conveyed to the only healers with any chance of saving him.

"I need your help," Dashi said, picking up the small pack Sevlin had been carrying.

Solongo looked up.

"I need you to fly me to wherever you left Zayaa. I have to stop her from creating a magical cataclysm that kills us all."

"*That's* what she's after?" Solongo croaked.

"Revenge," Dashi said. "Against the whole world."

Solongo stood up. "Let's go then."

"There's one more thing," Dashi said, as Solongo lifted her. "After you drop me off, I need you to take Sevlin to the giant ants that just attacked the camp."

Chapter 42

I t hurt to leave Sevlin. It hurt more than it had when she'd left him in the Purek maze. Perhaps it was because Dashi's feelings had crystallized. Perhaps it was because, this time, only the thinnest of filaments kept him suspended above death.

Stop the cataclysm, she told herself, as Solongo's wings beat in her ear, *or he's dead anyway.* Damp swirls of fog slid by, numbing Dashi's face. Moisture beaded in her eyebrows and lashes.

"You're sure you know where?" Dashi asked. She couldn't see anything but fog.

"Would I ask you if you were sure about your aim with a bow?" Solongo's arms were looped around Dashi's waist; her voice came from just over Dashi's shoulder. "The consul said there was a raft to ride on but flying seems better to me."

"Especially in winter."

Solongo sawed up and down as she flew, a bobbing cork while the owl was an arrow. Dashi chafed at the delay.

"How long ago did you bring them?" she asked

"Thirty minutes? Maybe a bit less?"

Dashi grimaced. "How was Idree? Did she say anything?"

"No." A few more wingbeats passed before Solongo added, "She was unconscious."

Dashi sucked in a breath.

"She tried to escape while the consul was solving that bead puzzle," Solongo said. "I knew she was planning something—she was quiet and tense when I carried her to the island. She'd only taken three steps before the consul knocked her out cold."

"I'm going to kill her."

"Good." Solongo's tone was vicious.

They began to drop lower, the teal water peeking through the fog. Solongo angled lower still, until each downward beat of her wings cut scalloped impressions into the lake's surface. Ahead, Dashi glimpsed a hole in the lake, a dark stain against a swath of bright fabric. Water rushed in on all sides, but the center remained black and unfilled.

"That's it?" Dashi stared. There must be an underwater cave, with the lake draining through the roof.

"Yes."

"Where is the float?"

"Maybe the chain pulled it underwater." Solongo didn't sound particularly concerned.

"Is there...a ladder? How did they get inside? The owl can't hover and Idree was unconscious."

"There are rungs cut into the side of the rock," Solongo said. "I lowered the consul first. Idree was strapped into the owl's harness so, once my hands were free, I took her from the owl midair and lowered her down to the consul." The moth's voice took on a dark tone. "Then she ordered me back to the island as a distraction."

Dashi's jaw clenched, thinking of Sevlin's pallid face as his blood drained into the dirt. *The only thing to do is stop her*, she told herself. Her thumb rubbed the strap of his pack.

Solongo slowed her wingbeats and tilted her torso, maneuvering until they were just above the hole. Water poured over the edges, magnifying the rocks that formed the rim. It looked like a mouth, rounded to suck in everything around it. Dashi tensed as the logistics of what she had to do caught up with her. How deep would it be inside?

"Are you sure this isn't full of water?" she asked Solongo.

"No. Ready?"

Dashi huffed a laugh. Turning awkwardly, she threaded the rope end of Sevlin's grappling hook around Solongo's waist, knotting it securely. She let the hook end dangle into the hole, waiting for her. Then she began her descent, hand over hand, boots pressing against the rope. Solongo transferred her grip from Dashi to the rope, bracing against the knot. Her injured hand twinged each time she gripped the rope. It had only been a day since she'd hurt it in the Gateway temple, but already tender new skin was forming beneath the grass poultice. She hoped it worked the same magic for Sevlin's wounds. Would Solongo return in time? Would the ants know to help him?

The sound of falling water filled her ears as she got closer to the hole. She winced as the spray of cold water reached her. Now that it was at eye level, the water appeared to rush faster over the lip of the hole. The effect was vertiginous. Instead of Dashi moving downward, the hole was careening upward, rising to swallow her in one piece. There was no scent here to guide her. The water had carried away any traces of Idree's passage.

"I said I could hold you, but that wasn't an invitation to take as long as you possibly can." Solongo's voice sounded strained. "Not if you want me to also carry the Tyvalaran and then return here to see if you make it out."

With that thought to spur her, Dashi lowered herself into the blackness. As her eyes adjusted, she saw the walls were lined with shallow shelf-like protrusions, which caught the cascading water and redirected it in a hundred different ways.

Streams of water shot across Dashi's path, spinning her sideways and soaking her as she dropped between them. How had Khagan Nuray done this without a herald's help? The shelves would be dangerously slick. Even as she had the thought, however, the rope spun her around. Dashi found herself staring at a long overhang just beneath the hole, which directed the water to either side and left the wall below relatively dry. She transferred her grip from the rope to a sturdy handhold, then hauled the grappling hook up and wedged it in one of the rock niches.

She waved up at Solongo. The herald untied the rope at her waist and let it drop. It snapped to a stop, now hanging from the secured grappling hook.

Solongo hovered closer to the hole, her wings casting a shadow over Dashi. "May the ancestors guide your steps," she called down, before disappearing beyond the edge of the hole.

"Save him," Dashi whispered. *"Please."*

She descended in great bounds after that, her boots bouncing off the wall as she played the rope through her good hand. Solid ground jarred her unexpectedly, as did the rush of frigid water soaking her feet and calves. There was a lantern in Sevlin's pack, but she didn't want to light it yet, not without knowing where Zayaa was. Instead, she stood still for a moment, ignoring the water's pull on her legs while she tested the darkness with her antennae. Zayaa's scent came to her, faint and washed out. She stepped across the current, stumbling when the ground rose unexpectedly beneath her feet.

Her outstretched hand found a wall, damp and crusted with salt. She followed its bend, leaving the end of the rope trailing in the water behind her. If she and Idree made it back—*when* they made it back, she corrected herself firmly—they could use the rope to climb back to the surface. The water became shallower as she moved until, eventually, she stood on dry ground again. She paused, antennae twitching. Zayaa had been here not long ago. Her former friend's adrenaline still spiked the air, sharp and excited. Idree's scent was subtler by comparison, probably because she was being carried. *"She'd only taken three steps before the consul knocked her out cold."* Dashi's jaw clenched.

The wall bent again. Dashi followed, drawing back with a hiss when a line of purple appeared, crawling toward her. It was thin, a strand of gossamer compared to the vein she'd seen Idree use before, but the cave came alive by its light: glistening black rock studded with the white fossils of tiny organisms. The magic played over the wall, skipping here and there without warning but always staying in contact with the rock.

The vein thickened before it disappeared around the corner. Dashi followed it cautiously, moving quicker now that she could see where she was going. A second strand of magic appeared out of the rock, streaking in the same direction. Soon the air was suffused with a purple glow, which grew brighter the farther she went. She froze as a sound reached her. It was only one voice and only one word—a curse—but it was enough for Dashi to recognize the source. *Zayaa.*

Dashi untied her bow from the pack, stringing it with practiced ease as she walked. The cave was bright now, the biggest vein as thick as her arm. It danced over the wall, playing games with the shadows it cast, and with the other, smaller veins that had joined it since.

A cavern opened in front of her. Dashi's legs stopped moving, reacting to the terrifying magnificence of the sight before her. In her vision, Khagan Nuray had not been overawed by the Wellspring, either because she'd seen it before, or because her focus had been inward, on what she hoped to accomplish. Dashi's mind, however, stuttered at the sheer presence of the magic. A giant bone-white tree dominated the center of the cavern. The trunk was gnarled and deformed with several large burls. The branches were barren. It was exactly as it had been in the vision and, simultaneously, more: larger, bleaker, older, more powerful. The air crackled with energy, lifting the hairs on Dashi's arms and sliding along her scalp. Purple veins of magic snaked away from the tree, sometimes climbing the walls of the cavern, sometimes plunging straight into the stone, as they made their way out into the world.

In the vision, Dashi had only been able to see the tree and the magic pooled directly in front of it, so the size of the cavern came as a surprise. It was a great bowl of a room, with the tree at the bottom, while Dashi found herself standing atop one of the steep slopes that made up its walls. A path cut across the interior of the bowl. It wound lower and lower, circling like water being sucked into a vortex. It was there that her eyes drew next, pulled inexorably by movement.

Zayaa trudged along the path, struggling to carry an unconscious Idree, who was bent in half over her shoulder. Idree's bound hands hung toward the ground, bobbing with each step Zayaa took. Her hair was disheveled and loose, twining around the chain of Zayaa's necklace, which winked in the magic's light. The glare from the Wellspring painted Idree's skin purple, gleaming on a gash above her temple. Blood ran toward her hairline, disappearing into the black strands of hair.

Dashi blinked. She saw Altan's golden head, swaying to the rhythm of his horse's gait. She saw Baris, his once mighty shoulders now limp, his body so broad that it completely covered the saddle he'd been laid over. After all this time, after all that had happened, she was still in the same place.

Not again.

Dashi dropped into a crouch, an arrow already nocked. *Just out of range.* Her eyes traced the curvature of the path, anticipating how Idree's body would block most shots. At the bottom of the bowl, the path ended at a stone platform directly in front of the Wellspring. Zayaa would have to turn toward Dashi as she stepped onto it.

From this far away, Dashi couldn't see the rise and fall of Idree's chest. *She's the seamstress,* she assured herself. *Zayaa needs her alive.* But the sight of Idree's motionless body was almost more than she could bear. *Altan, Baris, Spit and maybe...*

No, she wouldn't let herself think of Idree or Sevlin. She wouldn't think of losing everyone she had left. There was only the silky grain of her bow and the uncomplicated satisfaction of her shot. *Aim and shoot,* she told herself. *Never focus on the fall.*

Dashi's hands were steady and her breathing smooth as she watched Zayaa make her way to the bottom of the cavern's basin. As she reached the stone platform that overlooked the Wellspring, Zayaa turned, her torso shifting so that it was perpendicular to Dashi for a single, beautiful moment.

I've been waiting for this moment for a long time, Dashi thought, and let her arrow fly.

Chapter 43

Certainty settled over Dashi as the arrow left her fingers. It was there in the smooth arc, a comet crossing the sky. It was in the speed, the way the white crane feathers blurred.

A true shot.

It hit Zayaa mid-step, punching her chest and sending her careening onto her back. Idree flopped partially on top of her. Zayaa's small pack broke apart, littering gear along the platform. A waterskin skidded across the stones and sank silently into the waiting pool of magic.

Dashi was already up and running. She reached the edge of the bowl and went right over, sliding straight down, heels skidding against rock. She hit the path at a right angle, jumped over it, and hurtled down the other side, a straight line toward the stone platform and the writhing pool of magic. She didn't take her eyes off Zayaa. Her mind plunged ahead to what she'd find when she arrived: blood pouring from someone she'd once considered a friend; the knowledge that, after all this time, she had avenged Baris and Altan.

Instead, Zayaa sat up. The amethyst pendant spilled out over her collar. Only a single fragment of the large purple gem remained. The rest cascaded over her chest in purple crumbs, as if someone had taken a hammer to the jewel. Or an arrow.

Dashi leaped the remaining distance to the stone platform, reaching for another arrow as she landed. Zayaa, however, was quicker. She pulled

Idree fully on top of her, pinning her limp body with one arm. Her other hand dove into the rubble of dropped gear, pushing aside a rope and a wallet of lock picks to grab a knife. This, she rested against Idree's belly.

"Stop where you are, Dashi."

"You need her alive," Dashi said, but her feet jammed to a halt.

"Barely alive will do fine. Drop your bow." Zayaa gave her pendant an amused flick. "It was a nice try, but it seems Altan's and Baris' generosity has intervened."

Dashi hesitated. The bow was her best chance at taking Zayaa out without accidentally harming Idree. Then she thought of Idree's fingers; she knew better than to underestimate Zayaa's ruthlessness by now. Her bow hit the stone with a dejected thud. The pool of magic looped and twirled behind Zayaa, watching the turn of events.

"*Barely alive?*" Dashi growled. "Are you sure she isn't already beyond that point?"

"Just a knock on the head." Zayaa sat up, Idree still held across her chest like a shield. From there, she awkwardly pushed herself to her feet. Idree's head flopped, one arm dragging lifelessly through Zayaa's dropped gear.

"You might have cracked her skull! Did that even cross your mind when you bludgeoned her?" She was yelling, furious that her shot had failed.

"Stay back," Zayaa said sharply. Her eyes flicked to Dashi's feet, which had edged forward mid-tirade.

"Idree has to be the one to throw the needle in. That seems unlikely in her current state."

Zayaa's eyes narrowed. "You don't know what you're talking about."

"She'll never do it. You can threaten her all you want—you could even threaten me—but Idree would *never* do something that would kill millions of people. You're the only one selfish enough for that."

"All that's mentioned is returning the needle to the Wellspring, not who puts it there."

"I watched it happen, Zayaa. I saw a vision—"

"Ha!" Zayaa's laughter cracked through the cavern. "And here I thought you might have actual information. All you have are fever dreams and feelings. I've done the *research*, Dashi. I have Khagan Nuray's writings." Zayaa patted her pack. "She never mentions any of that, just that the needle and the seamstress must both go to the pool."

A flicker of uncertainty wound through Dashi. She tried to recall the exact order of events in the vision, to remember if the magic had begun getting angry *before* Nuray threw the needle away, or if it was only after she'd shouted her rejection at the Wellspring that things had gotten out of control. What if Zayaa was right? What if immersing the seamstress and the needle in the Wellspring was enough to set off the cataclysm?

"Why not try to negotiate with the Tyvalarans?" Dashi asked, switching tacks.

"*Negotiate?*" Zayaa gave an incredulous laugh. "Sevlin led the palace guard in defeating my brothers. He ordered Altan and Baris after my parents. I won't come scraping and bowing to his table. I might as well spit on my family's grave. Sevlin won't get out of here alive, but even if he did, I would never beg a favor from him."

At the mention of Sevlin dying, Dashi flinched.

Zayaa's gaze slid to Dashi's hands, fisted at her sides. She smiled. "So my feint worked. I felt the moth and owl break free of their tethers and wondered."

A muscle beside Idree's eye twitched, as if, even unconscious, her sister sensed what they were talking about and was frightened. *Don't think of Sevlin,* Dashi ordered herself. *Think of a way to stop Zayaa that doesn't kill Idree.*

The bone-white tree towered behind Zayaa. A hungry tongue of magic panted in and out of the hole in its trunk.

What are your assets, Baris asked. *Think through all the outcomes*, Altan advised. Assets: she still had a sword and her knives, though Zayaa was too far away to use the former and too shielded by Idree's body to use the latter. She had Tuya's pyro-tipped arrow, but that might bring the entire cavern down on them. And outcomes? Those were even less certain. She didn't know if she was correct about what caused the cataclysm, or if Zayaa was. What she *did* know, however, was that Zayaa would not be talked out of this.

All those years of Zayaa's moods, of her wielding charm and warmth just as readily as a cutting observation: it wasn't mere fickleness, as a younger Dashi had assumed. Nor was it only about revenge. There was a coldness that went deeper in Zayaa. It was the desire and ability to do anything to get what she wanted. It was a trait found in Karak City's most hardened criminals and among the bands of raiders who roamed Thracedon, among the kind of people who killed and tortured indiscriminately, sowing fear to prop up their own power. It had just been more difficult for Dashi to spot in Zayaa because...*why, exactly? She's beautiful? Smart? Sophisticated? Because she fooled Altan and Baris?* Zayaa could be all of those things, Dashi knew, and still be the kind of cold-hearted crazy that people whispered about at night.

Dashi felt the weight of the knife in her boot. No matter how quickly she moved, it wouldn't be fast enough to prevent the downward stroke of Zayaa's blade. Her eyes shifted to the cavern's bowl sides. There was no grass to be had here, nothing she could use to heal Idree. She clenched her teeth, shoring up her will for what needed to be done.

Even if it means risking Idree.

With that uncanny ability to sense the turn of Dashi's thoughts, Zayaa stepped closer to the magic pool, dragging Idree with her. Her arm shook from the effort of holding Idree's limp body upright, but she was still smiling, still confident.

Now, before she steps over the edge, Dashi told herself. Her fingers clenched, balking at the idea of causing Idree harm.

Idree twitched once more, a subtle flex of her hand around something dark and metallic. Before Dashi could react, her sister bolted upright. Her hand flew up, punching backward over her shoulder into Zayaa's throat. Zayaa gurgled in surprise and stumbled backward, one heel sliding over the edge of the platform. A lockpick—one of Zayaa's own—protruded from her jugular like a tiny arrow. She teetered over the pool, blood flooding over her collarbones, pulsing from the small wound to the same rhythm as the magic. Her fingers curled, reaching toward Idree, but Idree jerked back, out of reach.

Dashi lunged as Zayaa began to fall. Somehow her fingers found the chains around Zayaa's neck, one silver and one gold. The necklaces pulled taut, momentarily holding Zayaa's weight. Zayaa's eyes went wide. She raised one hand, not to clutch at Dashi but to trail her fingers over her own throat, still surprised to find a lock pick there. Dashi gave a savage yank. The necklaces snapped. Zayaa collapsed backward into the pool of magic.

"Ancestors above," Idree murmured. "Is she...?" She scooted next to Dashi, peering over the edge.

Beneath the bright ribbons of magic, Zayaa's face contorted in pain. Her mouth opened, but the magic muffled the scream; no sound escaped. Dashi's eyes shifted downward: Zayaa's hand, clutched at her side, had become grayish and scaley, five fingers morphing into four. Idree gasped as diamond-faceted wings erupted from Zayaa's back and then collapsed into nothing. Zayaa's features writhed, trying on colors and textures before shucking them off again. Her nose grew, then shrank, then widened: a hawk, a lizard, a sow.

The magic thickened abruptly, obscuring Zayaa beneath layers of dark purple. Dashi glanced up in alarm, remembering the way the Wellspring had looked just before the cataclysm. Where it spilled from the tree, the magic was purple-black and completely opaque. Dashi thought of sprinting up the bowl of the cavern. She thought about telling Idree to run while she made some sort of stand, interposing herself between Idree and the threat. Both were equally fruitless impulses. She grabbed Idree's hand—a soft human palm against a tough herald one—and squeezed.

"I think...Is it getting lighter?" Idree asked after a minute of tense waiting.

A streak of magenta split the tumbling magic, followed quickly by a second.

Dashi let out the breath she'd been holding. "I think it is." She glanced at Idree, her eyes assessing her sister's head wound and then her expression. Idree would have hated hurting someone. "That was some move you pulled on Zayaa," she said, probing.

Idree grinned, unfazed and unrepentant. "Stealth. Not all of us are built for charging straight into battle."

When Dashi looked back, the pool had returned to bright translucence, revealing Zayaa's face once more. There was no glossy black hair now, no perfect ruby lips, no hectic flush to her sculpted cheekbones. There were no colors at all. Zayaa had been transformed into pale stone.

Dashi edged away from the pool, glancing down at the twined silver and gold in her hand. She extracted the silver necklace, holding it up. Zayaa's broken pendant glared at her like an empty, silver eye socket. *I should have told Altan and Baris to get it from the ruins themselves.* She threw it at Zayaa. It landed on her cold chest, splaying across the body it had once adorned.

Always tidy, Idree began gathering the items Zayaa had dropped. Dashi spotted a small scroll peeking from the detritus and bent to pick it up, unsurprised to find that it was Purek. It was dated at regular intervals. A series of journal entries, maybe. For a moment she wondered about the story behind its discovery. Had Altan and Baris known about it or had Zayaa found it after their deaths? Where had it been hidden, and what other belongings of Khagan Nuray's had been with it? Then Dashi shook her head at herself. "The past is only important so long as it informs the future," she'd told Tuya. She might hate the wanton destruction of Purek history, but no scroll was so important that it was worth leaving a trail to the Wellspring. Dashi rolled the scroll back up, not bothering to translate, and tore it into tiny pieces. They fluttered down into the magic.

Inside the statuette, the needle whirred anxiously. Dashi stuffed the artifact into her pocket and turned to follow Idree up the path.

"Through there?" Idree asked as they crested the top of the cavern's bowl sides. She nodded to the shadowy tunnel, panting slightly from the steep climb.

"Yes." Dashi started toward it. "You were really unconscious the whole time Zayaa was carrying you then?"

Idree nodded. "I was only faking it after she fell. That jarred me awake. Before that, the last thing I remember is running away from her on the island."

"We're below the lake right now," Dashi explained. The sound of falling water filled the tunnel. They'd nearly reached the end already; she could move much faster when she didn't have to worry about sneaking up on Zayaa. "At the end of this, there's a cave with a hole in the roof. A thin stream of lake water falls over the sides, but there are shelves below the lip that divert the flow so that you can climb up. The Pureks had set up a chain pulling a float to get the high priests and priestesses across the lake to the Wellspring, but I missed it. Solongo flew me out here and lowered me through the opening."

They reached the end of the tunnel and splashed into the cave.

"So we climb out of the cave and then what?" Idree asked. "Will the float take us back?"

"Then *I* come to the rescue," Solongo called down, her voice echoing like the water. "But if you two take much longer, I might leave without you."

Dashi pointed out the rope she'd left, squinting up at the cave opening while her sister climbed. She opened her mouth, intending to ask Solongo how Sevlin was, but she caught sight of the herald's face and stopped. Solongo's features were drawn, her expression sorrowful. *What if...?* Dashi's heart twisted in her chest. *I'm a coward,* she thought and shut her mouth.

Idree pulled herself onto the highest shelf and grabbed Solongo's hands. Despite Solongo's obvious fatigue, she'd donned the owl's flying sling, clearly intending to carry them both in one trip. Dashi started up the wall, moving surely with the help of the rope.

The needle buzzed in its home, rattling against Dashi's chest as it demanded an answer she hadn't yet formulated. She grabbed another handhold, climbing automatically. She could leave the needle here, not in the Wellspring itself but in the cave. It could take centuries before someone found this place again. Wasn't that the mistake she'd made before, not leaving the needle behind in the taiga? She reached the top, balancing on the shelf while she retrieved the grappling hook and slung the rope over her shoulder. Solongo lowered fractionally, dangling the sling into the hole. Dashi paused with her hand on the straps, her mind still prevaricating.

"Any day now," Solongo said.

Dashi could feel Idree's eyes on her. She could hear Idree's voice, earnest and soft. *"That's what I like about being the seamstress: I have the chance to save people."*

Sighing, Dashi pulled the statuette's chain from around her neck. "Here," she said, holding it up to Idree. "You should be the one to decide whether we bring this along or leave it here."

The tense look on Idree's face melted as Dashi held out her hand. Idree slipped the statuette around her neck. The needle's buzzing quieted.

Dashi climbed into the sling, buckling a strap around her waist and another around each thigh. Solongo took off before she'd finished, not toward the island but toward the lakeshore, aiming for a point west of the bridge.

"Hold here," Dashi called when they were partway across. *A safe distance,* she thought. Solongo pulled up short, the sling swaying from the abrupt cessation of forward momentum. "I'm tired," she warned Dashi.

"I only need a minute." Dashi pulled out the pyro-tip Tuya had given her. She took in a deep breath, attuning to the slight up-down bounce of Solongo's wings as they hovered. She focused on the opening in the middle of the lake, the dark mouth sucking the water into itself. The bow thrummed approvingly as she released her shot, but Dashi felt no satisfaction. She followed the shot with her eyes, watching as a wall of water erupted from the center of the lake. The mouth of the cave widened—too much, too fast—then the lake rushed in on all sides, shoving through the collapsing ceiling. Idree and Solongo cheered as the water smoothed over.

Idree peered down, the teal surface of the lake reflected in her dark eyes. "Smile, Dashi. You saved the world. No one can find the entrance to the Wellspring ever again."

Dashi watched the rings of ever-widening wavelets—the only evidence that something else had once been there—and was silent.

Chapter 44

Dashi had done her best to make the chamber comfortable. It was dark and cool. Two bedrolls lay on the packed earth, one right next to the other. A full waterskin and a saddle bag lay beside that. From her spot on the bedroll, Dashi poked the saddlebag with the toe of her boot, noting its slack sides. She'd have to restock soon. Despite being stranded in the taiga during winter, supplies were relatively plentiful; the ants had inflicted a large number of casualties when they'd come to Dashi's rescue, making the ratio of people to food favorable.

The sound of deep, even breathing filled the chamber. She was thankful for that as her mind drifted toward sleep. Sevlin's breath had been patchy and shallow when she'd first arrived. She'd shoved through the crowd of giant ant bodies to find him, pale and motionless, at the center. Sending Solongo here with him had been a gamble. Dashi felt confident that Sevlin, who'd been facing death either way, would have accepted the risk, but the stakes had been different for Solongo. There'd been no way of knowing how the ants would react to *her*. Solongo had done it anyway, following the ants until she found the entrance to their lair, then plopping herself in front of it with a nearly-dead Sevlin held before her like an offering. "I didn't do it for you," Solongo said when Dashi thanked her later.

Of the survivors, Dashi was the only one who didn't mind being inside the ants' lair. Idree swore she went outside every day only because she needed to stay with Okhron while he tottered about, strengthening his legs, but Dashi had seen the way her sister flinched when the ants' antennae whispered over her. Idree pretended to like the ants and their accommodations out of loyalty for Dashi, nothing more.

"I'd rather freeze to death than stay in that hole longer than I have to," was how Solongo put it. She and the stag logged long hours looking for fresh game to supplement their stores. Tuya spent the days searching for edible roots and fungi, which she'd read about before leaving Yassar. The owl preferred her own company. She'd lost the wing and could most often be found standing beneath the trees with her good wing wrapped around her middle. Only five of the Karak soldiers had survived besides Okhron. At first, they'd clumped together like scared lambs, but Okhron's repeated overtures had eventually won them over and now they didn't think twice about sharing a meal with someone who was part animal.

Sevlin's breathing shifted, but Dashi didn't turn over. This had happened so many times already. She would spring to his side, hands shaking, only to find his eyes closed. *Maybe he lost too much blood. Maybe—*

Something brushed the small of her back. She turned her head slowly, cautious with the hope that was rising in her.

Sevlin's eyes were open, gleaming with reflected lantern light. His lips parted silently. Dashi grabbed the waterskin and, as she had done countless times over the past days, slid her hand beneath his head to lift it. His throat bobbed as he drank. His eyes stayed on her the whole time.

"Not too much," she said softly, pulling the waterskin from his lips. She rummaged in the pack and tore off a piece of dried meat. "Here."

He chewed slowly, as though he'd forgotten how, or perhaps lacked the energy for it, then drank some more. Dashi blinked quickly, afraid he would fall back into unconsciousness if she took her eyes off of him.

"How long?" he asked in a hoarse whisper.

"Just shy of a week."

He glanced around the chamber. "Idree?"

"She's fine. Outside with everyone else," Dashi said, rattling off the names of the other survivors. "Zayaa is dead." She summarized everything that happened while he'd been unconscious. He closed his eyes as she spoke, but the periodic twist of his lips told her that he was still awake.

"Did the ants do this, or did you?" Sevlin's hand drifted to his chest, gingerly touching the edges of the dried green poultice.

"Both."

He slit open an eye, suddenly concerned. "Where are they now?"

"Mostly back to sleep." The taiga ants appeared to prefer dormancy for the cold winter months, though Dashi had seen a few of them moseying around, tending to the tunnels. Sometimes a few of them would descend into the deeper chambers that she knew, through some instinctive reasoning she didn't quite understand, contained eggs.

Sevlin's eye shifted to her bedroll, stretched beside his. "I wouldn't think you'd like being closed in down here."

Dashi shrugged. "It's warm."

She didn't voice the real reason she'd stayed inside all day, every day, which was that she didn't want him to wake up alone. Sevlin's mouth rose in a half smile anyway.

"Appreciated," he said, his eye drifting shut again. He shifted his arm off of his chest, opening it wide in invitation.

Dashi curled against his side and slept.

Sevlin had never had much fat to spare, but a week without eating had left him practically gaunt. His strength had also eroded, so much so that the next day he only managed to walk across the chamber once, leaning heavily on Dashi before collapsing to his knees.

"Ancestors, that hurts," he sputtered, chest heaving. Sweat slicked his forehead and dripped onto the sharpened angles of his cheekbones.

Dashi chewed her bottom lip, looking down at him.

"I want to see the wound," he said.

"Not yet." Dashi had checked it before he'd woken and the poultice still had some life in it. The skin had closed already; it would be a wicked scar, wide and carved out. "When it's healed, it might warn you when a taiga ant is nearby."

He raised an eyebrow, momentarily distracted.

"My scars from the khan's race twinge whenever one comes close. When we searched for the seamripper, they felt strange the whole time we were beside the river. It turned out an ant was following us, remember? And I felt it again just before these ones attacked the soldiers."

"And now?"

"It's constant." Dashi shrugged. "I've gotten used to it."

Sevlin considered this. "It's not a bad thing to be able to tell if a taiga ant is nearby."

"I don't think so."

His eyes slid to her antennae. "Do you think my scar will do that when you're near?"

"I don't know. You'll have to tell me once it heals up."

The side of Sevlin's mouth curved upward. He reached out and took her hand. "Tomorrow, I want to go outside."

"Day after tomorrow, and only if you can cross this chamber ten times without needing to rest."

Sevlin did ten laps across the chamber the next day but was so exhausted by it that he slept through the afternoon and into the night. The following day, he made it outside, staggering into the bleak winter morning. His head turned, taking in their surroundings, one arm sprawled across her shoulders to steady himself.

"You're a good patient," Dashi said, monitoring the rate at which his chest was heaving. Snow sprinkled from the sky, dusting their shoulders. "Much more tolerant than I am when I'm hurt."

"I have no trouble believing that," Sevlin said. "You're prickly in perfect health."

When Sevlin's breathing normalized, they started again, heading slowly toward a stand of trees.

"Did you tell the other heralds that I can reverse stitching completely?" he asked.

Dashi shot him a sideways glance. "Should I not have?"

Sevlin shrugged. "I would have talked to them anyway. Now they've had a chance to mull it over."

"The owl wants to be made human again. Solongo and the stag are still deciding."

"At least they have a choice now." He gave her a sideways look. "I expect Idree was glad to be the one to decide about the needle."

"She says she wants to try to save people. Okhron healed really fast and really well. Idree has some theories on why and she wants to try to replicate it so that fewer patients die." It would mean stitching patients close to the taiga mist, since that figured prominently in all of Idree's theories, but Dashi didn't want to think about the logistics of that.

"What about you?"

Dashi's eyes followed the twisting tendrils of Idree's scent, smudging the ground in front of them. "Sometimes I think I'd prefer the life we had. Idree says I would've gotten tired of it and that I should be happy about her being the seamstress, because," she paused to imitate Idree's voice, "*this way I won't die of boredom.*"

Sevlin gave her an amused glance. "I wasn't asking how you felt about Idree deciding to remain the seamstress. I was asking whether you'd decided to remain a herald."

"Oh."

He was quiet, choosing his words and his steps with equal care. "Toughened skin and the ability to track scents seem like traits you would find very appealing."

"As is the ability to heal myself."

He grabbed hold of a fallen log, lowering himself slowly. He leaned against an adjacent tree and he shut his eyes. "You're not the only one grateful for that."

She studied the lines of fatigue etched into his face. "Maybe this walk was too much."

He snorted, eyes still closed as he slouched against the tree trunk. "Are you hovering?"

"Being practical. You walked more today than you have in a week."

"All that bluster and you're a mother hen beneath."

"Well, I have to be," she said sweetly. "You were quite beat up. The stag got several good hits in before the owl ambushed you. Bet that hasn't happened in a while."

Sevlin cracked one eye. "At least my wounds were dealt by someone with supernatural speed. That shoulder of yours was cut open by a regular soldier."

Dashi grinned. *I knew you couldn't ignore that one.*

She glanced at the sleeve of her winter furs, thinking about the hardened skin beneath. "If you were to change me back, reversing all the physical changes would be..."

"Painful," Sevlin agreed, all traces of humor gone. "Sable declined, however, so it is still an untested hypothesis."

Sable. Dashi had nearly forgotten about the other herald. "*That's* why your soldiers were trying to capture us alive in Rucharla. So you could free him?"

"I wanted to free *you*," Sevlin said.

"But we fought. Face to face." Dawning incredulity filled her voice. "You could have reached out and touched me at any time."

"I had never done it before, Dashi. I didn't know if breaking the tether would hurt you."

"I would have borne any pain to be free of Zayaa," she said fiercely. All she could think of was Idree's finger, falling beneath her blade.

He opened his eyes but didn't look at her, instead staring at the falling snow. "I didn't know what the consequences would be if I did it badly," he said in a quiet voice. "The Pureks didn't exactly provide a wealth of information on the subject. I wondered if it might be like the stitching itself, if there was a chance that you might die. I knew it wasn't fair to test it on Sable, but," he blinked once, exhaling, "I could not *live* with testing it on you."

She could hear the vulnerability in his voice, could feel the fear of loss thudding in his chest, because it was thudding in hers also. *He almost died. I almost lost him.* Dashi took a step forward, stopping when she stood between his knees. Sevlin sat up, his expression still and alert. His head tilted back, studying her as she moved further into the vee of his legs.

Her mind, as was typical, did not supply her with the vocabulary necessary to wade through sensitive, emotional subjects, but she felt her body draw closer to Sevlin with a language of its own: her legs brushing against the inside of his, her head canting forward. Her hand floated to his shoulder, then his jaw, before sliding to the back of his neck. He grasped her hips in both hands, rocking her forward so that she was flush against him. Even sitting, his face was level with hers. The first brush of his lips was light, not tentative but savoring. It was the first time they'd kissed, Dashi realized, when they weren't under duress. It wasn't done as a distraction, or because one of them might die, but because they just *wanted* to. Her mouth parted against his, their tongues dancing, breath mingling.

Dashi pulled back slightly. "It's—I wasn't blaming you, Sevlin," she said hoarsely. "The only people to blame are Zayaa and the khan and, if our positions had been reversed, I would have done the same thing."

He pulled her back to him, kissing her for longer this time, until Dashi's fingers were knitted in his hair, and Sevlin's breath again became labored.

Voices filtered through the trees, startling them into coming up for air.

"I'm not sure if sitting here was a good idea," Dashi said, eyeing the rapid rise and fall of his chest. "You haven't caught your breath."

Sevlin's mouth turned up at one corner. "I've recuperated from wounds before. This way is a vast improvement, I assure you." Wrapping an arm around her shoulders, he tugged her down onto the log and against his side.

The voices in the trees grew louder. Dashi could pick out Idree's laugh among the rumble of male voices.

"Tell me why you are undecided," Sevlin said.

"I've grown accustomed to being part ant," Dashi said slowly. "I hated it at first, but now I can see its usefulness. I guess I think of it," she gestured toward her antennae, "as someone else's—the khan's or Zayaa's—not mine."

"Was it someone else who called to the ants for help? Or made a poultice to save my life?"

Dashi didn't answer aloud, knowing he didn't expect one.

"You don't have to decide today," Sevlin said. "Or even soon. I'll be around, even after we leave the taiga."

"Is that so?"

"Queen Lyazzat will want me to stay in New Osb to keep an eye on the new regime." He nodded to where Idree had emerged from the trees, talking to Okhron and the stag.

Dashi shook her head. "Okhron's family is powerful, but he's only a younger son. His family would be more likely to support one of his brothers in the claim."

"I meant Idree."

"*Idree?*"

"When there are no clear heirs, the advantage goes to whoever moves first. Currently, only a handful of people know that the khan and his consul are both dead. By the time the news gets out, Idree will already be back in the khan's suite in New Osb. She'll have you and Okhron with her, probably Solongo and the stag too. The heralds are a potent symbol of power, and you are all very loyal to Idree."

In front of them, Idree gestured toward the hill and then back over her shoulder. Okhron and the stag dutifully split up, each going in opposite directions.

"She's so young," Dashi murmured.

"She's around the same as Lyazzat was. And, like Lyazzat, Idree has a sibling who will do anything for her. If the Tyvalaran crown were to quickly offer recognition, Idree would have a lot of momentum on her side."

Dashi blinked, watching her sister through new eyes. "And will it?"

"I think she'd make a good leader and Tyvalar would prefer a friendly regime on its borders. If she's determined to keep the needle, then it's certainly preferable to having someone else in power over her."

"It would have to be Idree's decision."

Sevlin nodded.

"What about when there are complications between Tyvalar and Karakal?" Dashi asked. "We'd disagree on something eventually."

"People do that."

"My first loyalty would be to Idree."

He leaned his head toward her, his nose brushing her temple. "I know."

"Sevlin!" Idree called, her face lighting in a smile. "You're up!" She rushed up the slope, breath puffing in the cold air. Dashi thought her sister might bowl Sevlin over in her eagerness, but at the last minute, Idree slowed and, very gently, wrapped her arms around Sevlin's waist. Sevlin returned her hug with his free arm, keeping the other draped over Dashi's shoulders.

"I was very worried about you," Idree said, her voice muffled. "You lost so much blood. Dashi was beside herself."

Over Idree's head, Sevlin's eyes shifted to Dashi.

I was not, Dashi mouthed.

"I suspected as much," he said to Idree. "She cried when I woke up."

Startled, Idree pulled back. "Really?"

"Yes," Sevlin said.

"No," said Dashi.

Idree's eyes narrowed as she tried to decide which one of them was lying. "Are you going to be out here much longer?" she asked, changing course. "Solongo would like to talk to you."

"She went up the hill to collect wood," Tuya said, coming up behind them. She set down the armload of kindling she carried before straightening to face Dashi.

Sevlin glanced between them. He held his arm out to Idree. "Idree, I'd like to walk a little more before Dashi banishes me underground again. Would you be my crutch?"

Casting a wary glance between Tuya and Dashi, Idree joined him.

"I wanted to let you know that I've come to a decision," Tuya said when they were alone.

It was the first time they'd spoken alone since Dashi had returned from the Wellspring.

Dashi raised an eyebrow. "A decision about what?"

Tuya shifted on her feet, making her curly hair sway, but her face remained immobile. "I won't be going back to New Osb."

"The mercenary-tyrant relationship does appear to have reached an end," Dashi agreed dryly.

"Your sister has agreed to send a message to Yassar telling them that I went into the river along with my countrymen and our sledge."

Dashi blinked.

"I broke neutrality when I gave you the arrow. If I admit what I've done, I'll be executed."

"Were you supposed to step aside while Zayaa destroyed the continent?" Dashi held up a hand, exasperated. "Don't answer that. Why tell your people anything? No one will know what happened out here."

"*I* know," Tuya said, not quite meeting Dashi's eyes. "I cannot pretend to carry on under a vow that I've already broken. I understand the reasoning behind the neutrality. I know what the war cost us, but putting one's own interests above all else is not always a tenable policy."

"No," Dashi said. "It's not."

Tuya picked up the armload of kindling and stepped past Dashi.

"Wait, why are you telling me this?"

"Because Idree only offered to report my death if I agreed never to identify you as a thief," Tuya said without turning around. "The thiefmark can no longer recognize your scent now that you're a herald. Every other Yassari who knew you is dead. You can return to New Osb without worrying about Yassari justice tracking you down. But I wanted you to know," she said, "that, even without Idree's deal, I wouldn't have revealed you."

"I did steal those boots," Dashi pointed out, unable to help herself.

"You also saved me from being eaten by a giant worm. It turns out some things matter more than property rights."

That evening, Dashi shot a pair of hares, retrieving and wiping her arrows after each kill. They didn't strictly need the meat—yet—but she was tired of the tough, salty stuff from the saddlebags. Better to save that for travel since it wouldn't go bad. She huddled partway under the sheltering arms of a fir tree, skinning her kills and making a neat pile of the entrails for some scavenger to feast on. The snow was falling heavily, melting where it touched the still-warm flesh of the hares. Spit had always hated an impending storm. *He would have shoved himself right under this tree next to me.* The thought brought a sad smile to her lips. She straightened, then took a quick step backward at what she saw. The taiga mist had ambushed her.

It slid down the tree trunks to puddle on the ground, collecting deeper and deeper until she could no longer see the way back to the others. She heard it as it closed the distance to her: a multitude of voices, rising and falling and twisting over one another, whispering without saying words. The snow stopped falling. The air held still as a gray figure solidified along the edge of the mist. She was out of focus, the details never forming on the face or the clothing, but when she spoke, Khagan Nuray's voice sounded close.

"You have done well, Little One."

"Thank you," Dashi said, after a beat. She couldn't recall Khagan Nuray ever complimenting her before. Silence stretched for several long seconds. She could feel Nuray regarding her, even though the dead khagan's face had no discernible eyes. "Uh...is there anything else?"

"Assess your strengths. A well-honed blade is always of use."

"What does that even..." Dashi trailed off, her fingers straying to the top of her head. "My antennae? Is that what you're talking about? That I should stay a herald because it could be an asset?"

"Choose wisely, Little One," was all Nuray said. "As long as she's the seamstress, she will need you."

Dashi nodded, absurdly pleased that she'd understood. Maybe she was finally getting better at the spirit world's penchant for metaphor and double-speak.

"Goodbye, Little One."

Khagan Nuray began to fade, her edges twirling away into the mist, a ball of string unraveling into nothing.

"Wait!"

The strings of mist paused.

"What happened to your son?'

"My son survived the cataclysm," Nuray's voice floated to her, eerie and echoing now, "but he never came back to the forest of his birth. He fell in love with the land of the wide sky. It became the mother he had lost. His people still ride there today, but occasionally"—a smile in Nuray's voice—"they venture back into the trees."

"Idree and me?" Dashi asked. "Is that why we're the only ones who remember these visits? Is that why my blood opened up your memories?"

"Day and night always brush up against one another, but only those with magic in their blood remember the twilight."

The mist dissipated quickly, rippling back up into the trees. The snowfall resumed. When she was sure she was alone, Dashi picked up the brace of hares and headed back to Idree and Sevlin.

EPILOGUE

EIGHT DAYS EARLIER

I n the dream, Jochi was aggrieved. "I've always wanted you, since the moment I met you but—Ancestors above, Ese, how could you do something so imbecilic?"

Even when he was trying to be insulting, Jochi sounded warm and cultured. He wore a light summer deel and, as his hands rose in a gesture of exasperation, Ese noted with envy that they were bare. The advantages of going to the spirit realm grew by the second: it had Jochi and it was warm.

"I wouldn't call it imbecilic," Ese said. Courageous or desperate, he would accept. Above all, however, it had been *successful*.

"No? You're bleeding, your clothes are literally frozen to your balls and you're about to be eaten."

"I did it though. I finally killed Temur. I'm sorry I haven't been able—"

"I don't care about my bones being in that cursed cage and I don't care about Temur. I care about *you*, you wood-headed clunk, and if you don't grab hold of yourself right now, you'll be joining me sooner than you should."

Ese was taken aback. "You say that like it's a bad thing."

"It *is*." Jochi blinked rapidly, his voice cracking. "I want you to have a long life, Ese. I want you to have adventures and fall in love again and learn new things. I want you to be *happy*."

The sensation of movement woke him. Of being dragged, specifically. Ese tried to blink but found that his eyelids had frozen shut. Something jerked at his boot, pulling him away from the roar of the river. He finally managed to crack his eyes and lift his head enough to see the dark, shaggy shape that had ahold of his leg. Whatever it was, it was huge. His eyelids closed wearily; even that small movement felt like too much effort. He tried to go back to Jochi, to that blissful floating feeling that was completely separate from his body. Something held him to consciousness, however. *Jochi, ancestors damn him. "I want you to have a long life, Ese."*

His numb fingers moved uncertainly over the knife at his waist. It was long enough to do real damage, even to an animal that size, but he barely had the strength to grip it. The animal dragged him over a rock. His arm smacked the ground, nearly jarring the knife from his grasp. Where was the beast taking him?

The animal halted suddenly, turning so that Ese could see more than just a set of patchy hindquarters. It was a taiga rat, though a miserable specimen of one. Its right foreleg dangled uselessly from an old wound that hadn't healed well. Its tail had been reduced to a nub. It stepped closer, eying Ese's unprotected abdomen, either unaware or uncaring that he was now conscious. Ese tried to tighten his grip on the knife. He couldn't tell if his hand had obeyed; like most of his body, it was numb. His heart, on the other hand, he could feel just fine. It pounded against his ribs, frantically trying to escape.

Snow shifted softly as the rat took another step, one of its legs now on either side of Ese's waist. This close, he could see the thin scars lashing its face in lines of white. He watched, mesmerized, as its lips pulled back to reveal rectangular incisors, glistening with saliva. His arm hammered sideways, thrusting the knife into the rat's neck; Ese was nearly as surprised at his success as the animal was. Blood sprayed over the snow, startlingly bright in a world of white and gray. The animal lunged at his face. Ese managed to bring the knife up again, blocking the attack with a scrape of metal on bone. Staggering sideways, the rat caught itself and crouched, muscles taut for another attempt, before silently toppling into a pool of its own blood.

Ese let his head fall back against a pillow of snow, his breathing ragged. Hitting the artery had been more luck than skill. It had certainly taken all of his strength. Blood puddled next to him, melting the snow and soaking through a rip in his furs. Ese sighed as it touched his skin. So blissfully warm. It was the only warm thing out here, blood. Maybe that's why this cursed forest seemed to demand it from everyone. He knew killing the rat would make no difference. He would freeze to death. The taiga would have his blood in the end. His eyes drifted closed.

"When I was little, my father told me a story about a Mori man who ventured too close to the taiga's doorstep and was caught by a winter storm. He killed a bear and climbed into the still-warm carcass to keep from freezing to death. The wolves came and ate the bear's body and the man's too."

Ese's eyes cracked open again, staring up at the leaden sky. The words felt like a lifetime ago, but somehow his cold-dulled mind directed his body to apply the lesson. Where he found the strength, he couldn't say, only that he found himself on all fours with Jochi's words running through his mind. *"I want you to have a long life, Ese."*

Ese slit the rat from neck to groin, managing to only drop the knife twice. He plunged his hands into the slick, hot innards, groaning as the sensation began to burn his fingers. He wanted to rest there all day, basking in the heat, but he forced himself to keep working. The temperature of the opened carcass fell with every passing second. He pawed and sliced at the contents as best he could, carving out enough room for his body. Then he curled up in the red well, pulled the carcass closed over himself, and fell asleep.

He wasn't sure how long he dozed, pleasantly groggy while the smell of iron filled his nostrils, but eventually the temperature of the rat's body dropped enough that he began to shiver again. Something thumped nearby, and he started, his mind immediately going to wolves. Cautiously, he parted the carcass enough to peek out.

Ese stared. Wiping at his eyes with the back of a bloodied wrist, he looked again. It was still there: a sledge, listing to one side as it bumped along the river bank, a ship seeking a harbor. Ese fell out of the rat's carcass, leaving a trail of crimson as he floundered through the snow. The sledge *looked* full, plump beneath its oilskin cover. His fingers hesitated just before making contact, afraid to find he was dreaming. The broken harness strap felt real enough, however. Ese pulled on it, slipping in the blood and snow, hauling the floating sledge toward him until its runners hit the bank and he could pull it no further.

The sledge bobbed unsteadily, still half in the water. Ese braced his knee against the side and sliced through the oilcloth, desperate to see—

Blessed ancestors, it's full of supplies.

He mauled the dried meat and left red streaks over the extra weapons. When he found someone's spare set of winter clothing, he nearly wept. He ripped off his own clothes, which were soaked with blood and in the process of freezing to him a second time, and put on the dry ones. He stopped shaking almost immediately.

Ese made a pile of items necessary for his immediate survival and repacked the rest. Towing the sledge along the shore, he found a place where a tree had fallen. He tied the broken harness straps around the trunk. Whatever had transpired to send one of the khan's sledges into the river, he didn't know, but he doubted anyone would take the time to come looking for it. *Animal* scavengers would be interested, however, and he needed to keep the supplies safe until he got back.

He would need to get the oilskin cover off the sledge eventually, he decided. It could be used as a tent, or perhaps as a roof if he could find a configuration of boulders to stand in for walls. He might even stumble upon a shallow cave. The topography looked promising for caves—rocky and steep—and he was suddenly feeling lucky. Hefting his spoils, Ese started along the bank, sharp eyes bouncing from boulder to boulder, searching for a place to hold his vigil for spring.

* * *

TO MY READERS...

After many long days (read: years) of writing, it's exciting to finally share
the conclusion of Dashi's adventures with you...so thank you for being
here! Reviews really help drive sales for indie authors like me. If you
enjoyed *The Wellspring*, please consider leaving a review so other readers
can connect with my work.

Acknowledgements

In my (admittedly short) experience, creating a book has been an exercise in hope; creating a series has been an exercise in madness. Brad, thank you for helping me manage the insanity and untangle the mess of plot threads. You are a rock-solid source of optimism and encouragement. To C, G and R: sharing my writing journey with you and seeing your excitement has been one of the most gratifying experiences of my life. Dashi's story is for you, just as much as it is for me.

To Mom, Dad, Dan, Clay, Ty and Ross, I cannot express how much you mean to me. Thank you for everything.

Clare, you have stuck with me through so many drafts. Without a doubt, your critiques have honed my writing and improved this series. Thank you for recommending books when I need a diversion and for being a sounding board when I need to vent.

To Peggy and Susan, I am beyond grateful for your grammatical knowledge and typo-catching skills. Just when I think I've corrected all of my most horrifying mistakes, you deliver a list of dozens more and save me from public, face-palming mortification. A million times, thank you.

Piper, you have gone above and beyond for this series. Thank you for proofreading, for your full-throated endorsement, and for all the book recommendations since then.

One of the best parts of writing has been the response from my friends and extended family. Kirsten, thank you for the promotion and for your endless encouragement. Your support lifts me when I am fatigued. Trisha, Shari, Karen, Liz, Don, Sara, Ronnie, Emily, Katie & Sarah: you not only enthusiastically read, but then enthusiastically discussed, reviewed and recommended my books to other people. I am both humbled and honored to have that level of support. Matt, thank you for helping me parse the confusing world of publishing. Arial, I am grateful for your beta-reading skills—your insights have been invaluable. Nick, your willingness to share both your writing and "blurb" expertise means the world—thank you!

You all are the best!

About the Author

T.J. Carroll has lived all over but now calls Earth home. When she's not writing, she enjoys hiking, saying she's going to establish a family game night, and lurking in bookstores. The books of The Taiga series are her first published works. She avoids social media, but you can find updates about her upcoming releases on BookBub and Amazon's Author Central.